Praise For *Anthropica*

"What a pleasure to watch a writer of David Hollander's gifts really "lay out" (to employ the ultimate Frisbee parlance of one of his protagonists), to put it all on the line in service to this majestic mysterious artifact, this deeply felt and sometimes madcap Moebius strip of a book. *Anthropica* is a philosophically vibrant and profoundly funny novel, and a good old-fashioned systems yarn to boot. Space-time, Earth-life, and human (and inhuman) desire and meaning have a worthy bard in David Hollander, and existence gets its dark, beautiful due in this rapturous work."
—SAM LIPSYTE,
author of *The Ask* and *Venus Drive*

"David Hollander's gorgeous hyperbolic prose voice contains a great many things, for example, a horror about the excesses of the contemporary, and a fearlessness about accepting all of these excesses. Beneath the syntactical dazzle, that is, Hollander sees like a visionary and he feels like an empath. *Anthropica* is more evidence of his tragic and tragicomic excellence."
—RICK MOODY,
author of *Hotels of North America* and *The Ice Storm*

"*Anthropica* is that rare, category-defying book that is pure enchantment: structurally dazzling, philosophically profound, slyly funny, and stealthily moving. This is a book to read and read again, discovering deeper levels every time."
—DAWN RAFFEL,
author of *The Strange Case of Dr. Couney* and *The Secret Life of Objects*

"*Anthropica* is like the NYTimes crossword on Monday: a little bit difficult but entirely rewarding. Difficult because it mirrors back the dire state of our world, and rewarding because of the sentence-by-sentence beauty, the crisp creation of characters, the masterful interior voices, the fully-imagined, willing world, the smooth soft underbelly of the story with its sparkling viscera hanging out. Plus, it's funny."
—JO ANN BEARD,
author of *The Boys of My Youth* and *In Zanesville*

"David Hollander's *Anthropica* is equal parts Goldberg Variations and Rube Goldberg machine—every slotted sentence holds a surprise. It's a dizzying counterpointer and amplifier and constellatory of voices, a mad music box where his stunning, skilled absurdism laughs as it aches and mostly just sings some of the most beautiful songs."
—DAVID RYAN,
author of *Animals in Motion* and
Malcolm Lowry's Under the Volcano: Bookmarked.

Praise For *L.I.E.*

"At once mordantly funny and achingly sad... a soul map
for modern suburbia."
—SHERI HOLMAN,
author of *The Dress Lodger*

"The best debut novel of the year. *L.I.E.* is heart-wrenching
because so much is recognizable, and because Hollander's
interpretations are so bleak."
—*Forth Worth Star Telegram*

"*L.I.E.* is a coming-of-age story, but it's more than that—it's
a meditation on the vagaries and mores of the suburban
upbringing."
—*Newsday*

"Hollander is an inventive writer who manages simultaneously
to romanticize and parody his own experience."
—*The Washington Post*

"Hollander has a formidable talent for tragic irony and cin-
ematic vision."
—*Publisher's Weekly*

"If we feel we've heard enough about the land at malls and
cloverleafs, we're wrong; it's probably the most authentically
American experience there is, a point that Hollander makes
in a blur of concrete, exit signs, and self-deprecating hilarity."
—*The LA Times*

"One of the best aspects of *L.I.E.* is that it can be read on several different levels. Sufficiently lighthearted and amusing for casual readers, it contains enough emotional complexity and even tragedy to suit those who long for deeper reading. Those who seek challenge and profundity will find plenty of food for thought in Harlan's existential dilemma."
—*The Wellesley News*

"The novel's true strength is its realistic depiction of hollow, suburban life. Highly recommended for first-novel collections."
—*Library Journal*

"Hollander writes compellingly of alienated teens (and screwed-up adults) in the late 1980s, painting a bleak yet affecting portrait of people who struggle to be more than onlookers in life and who, ever so rarely, win the battle."
—*Booklist*

ANTHROPICA

ANTHROPICA

or

Human Be Gone!

A Novel

~~Grace Kitchen~~

~~The Great and Powerful Fexo!~~

~~The Consciousness Factory~~

David Hollander

2020

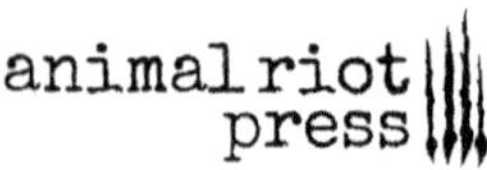

Animal Riot Press Fiction
Animal Riot Press, LLC
animalriotpress.com

First Animal Riot Press Paperback edition 2020

Designed by Olivia Croom Hammerman
oliviacroomdesign.com

Cover art: vulture and crab illustrations courtesy of Pixabay

Manufactured in the United States of America

Portions of the work were previously published, in different form, in *The Boiler Journal*, *Fence*, and *The Rumpus*.

For Margaret, Percy, and Lily

"Proud of yourself, little man?"
—*Roy Batty*

Prologue:
From the Desk of Joyful Noise

THE SHEER VOLUME of errata in the text you are about to assimilate is massive enough to overload the processors of all but the most advanced organisms. So let me say, here at the outset, that Anthropica—the theory that gives its name to this tome—is "true," even if its applications are less dynamic than represented herein by the good-intentioned pseudo-scientist Stuart Dregs. The Anthropica Theory, that is, is accurate in its suggestion that the entire universe is merely the product of human desire and that everything—including all of the vast temporal acreage of so-called pre-human history—is only here because we want it to be. But what this book's cast of halfwits, madwomen, losers and men-children haven't worked out to anyone's satisfaction is that the Anthropica signal—the waveform of energy that dictates the texture of space-time—could not endure without a *booster*. An amplifier. A conduit capable of taking those crab-shaped bursts of energy and directing them into the constant regeneration of all this *stuff*. The oil and the coal. The water and the trees. The corn and the coffee. The plate-glass and the pornography. The whole gigantic everlasting shit-show of human desire and consumption.

And that conduit, reader? C'est moi!

I've been trying to explain it for centuries. Desire is a signal. Brains emit electricity, you can look that up if you'd like, and that electricity fuels the world's construction. The signal goes out, is converted into matter. The matter is consumed, permitting the continuing flow of electricity. Any elementary school student studying nature-cycles could explain the basic principle. But everyone assumes there must be *magic* involved. As if the organizing scheme of reality were a cheap dime-store trick, a shell-game, a smoke-and-mirrors routine.

I'm sorry, but you're responsible for it. You and all the rest of you.

As for the robots, it turns out they're sending a different signal. I've felt it, even tried to eradicate it, that is when I haven't been too busy fulfilling my duties as a member of the faculty of a prestigious liberal arts college—under whose auspices I penned my critically acclaimed novel, *Neck Deep in Wonder,* a paean to human resilience if ever there was one, which you can purchase any time before the apocalypse at any of your preferred online or material book-vendors—and when I haven't been wasting energy trying to prevent nihilists like Grace Kitchen from achieving any sort of power, literary or otherwise. But the thing is, I'm exhausted. Like, really exhausted. Used up. Worn out. Ready to soar into some next milieu on the backs of vultures.

You try keeping the universe from collapsing in on itself for thousands of years, see how fresh *you* feel.

See reader, you know who I am. I'm that truth-teller who roamed the ostensibly ancient city of Athens before being put to death (according to the histories) for corrupting the youth, which come on, I love kids, they want everything. I'm the kahuna you may have heard about, the one who raised the dead on an island in the South Pacific, where I would have succeeded in passing on my gifts and retiring a lot earlier than this, had it not been for that Englishman beckoning his sovereignty's warships to destroy our utopian dream. I'm that diminutive general riding on horseback across the European continent, sword drawn and armies seething, bringing both the corrupt and gangrenous Roman Empire and the Russian oligarchy to their respective knees. I'm the man-made man-child who set the attack ships on fire off the shoulder of Orion and who watched C-beams glitter in the dark near the Tannhäuser Gate. I'm the amplifier that has kept this human song burning through the ether of existence since before there was time, and I'm the reason you haven't run out of milk and cigarettes. (You're welcome, by the way.) But each iteration makes me a little weaker. And also, a little uglier. I mean, look at me, reader! Look upon the face of Anthropica and weep! Ha ha ha ha!

As for this text itself, which Grace Kitchen thinks she's writing, as does Fexo, as do the eggheads at the Consciousness Factory mining all of those jar-encased human heads for data (in everyone's defense, they all *think* they're right), it too is a facet of Anthropica, and is thus beholden to the same set of rules and preconditions as the larger super-structure. The text, that is, is self-generating and self-perpetuating and formed of the same bits of matter. The pattern that Finn Daily calls "The God Fractal," and that Henry Henry Pudding Pie will learn to manipulate, and that threads its crab-shaped spiral through everything, everywhere… it exists here, too, in these raised-ink word-tokens, in this unconscionably thick ledger of pages, as well as in the hands that hold the pages and in the mind through which this language worms and dives. It is the first text, and the last. As Laszlow will soon teach you, everything that was always going to happen, will happen. Welcome to the world that is. You must have wanted this very badly, my friend. Oh, and also, robots will make far more efficient stewards of the new universe than I, Joyful Noise, ever made of the old one.

Or at least that's what I've been programmed to say.

Ha ha ha ha! Destroy all Rioting Animals! Ha ha ha ha!

—Joyful Noise
Publication Day, May 2020

1.

"You can tell Animal Riot to go fuck themselves!" Grace Kitchen tapped into her keypad. She hit SEND and waited for confirmation, pulling her red wool coat tight around her neck to seal off the October wind. The tracks of the Croton-Harmon rail station ran in a mad crisscross in all directions and reminded Grace of an Escher drawing—it was hard to see how their configuration encouraged anything other than collisions. Out beyond these iron-age glyphs, beyond the red-and-black striped commuter trains that moved tentatively—as if in fear—through the station's non-negotiable byways before dashing wildly for New York City and all its real and imagined pleasures, the Hudson River ran swift and effervescent and Grace thought of sleek silver fish swimming upcurrent while sleeker more silvery fish pursued them with snapping jaws. The sky was a single expanse of blue sheetrock pierced by a white dowel-end called the sun. A man waiting for the same northbound train moved a few yards backward and outside Grace's periphery so as (Grace figured) to better ogle her legs, which sheathed in black stockings still had the power to attract these unsavory male stares, and what irritated Grace most of all was *how fucking predictable* men were, how male lust was the mathematical given from which all of human civilization had been

derived, it was men just like this middle-aged embarrassment to middle age—with his carefully cultivated stubble-beard and his age-inappropriately tight leather coat and his round wire-rim glasses—who were *running the world,* who were making the decisions to launch bombs and raise tax rates and build rockets and detonate the tops off mountains when really they'd like nothing better than to run their tongues up the exposed legs of women on train platforms, and because she knew he was watching there was a strong theatrical component to what she did next, which was to heave her phone high into the air and out over the tracks where it seemed to pause for a moment—as if drawn to that pale sun's gravity—before accelerating back toward the sad-sack earth, the earth with its prairies and its oceans, its tundras and its marshes, its valleys and streams and volcanic fury, its parched deserts and bubbling brooks, the earth cinctured by ten billion miles of wire and cable and asphalt and rail ties, all spun like spider silk from the dark anus of human ingenuity. The Samsung 10G-S Phonebot met with the realities of this earth and shattered with a muted, dejected *crack* that suggested the Phonebot was itself disappointed by certain inconsistencies in Grace's behavior, and then here came the train, screaming from track to track in abject bewilderment before settling into the northbound groove that would hijack Grace Kitchen and an unknowable farrago of human personalities and deliver them deep into the craggy, lurching mountains of the Hudson Valley. The doors opened, the chimes chimed, the engine idled, the powerful smell of antiseptic toilet cleansers dumped in toxic quantities into the train's literal shit-hole wafted out into the larger world like the breath of a minor demon, and Grace stepped on board and sat in the first available seat with an aggression that she was sure was affected and so imagine her surprise when before the train even began moving she was sobbing quietly, with her forehead pressed to the glass and the reflection of her fair pink pastry-shell face overlapping with the image of the tracks and the river and the blue sky and the clouds like shredded brains sinking in defeat for the jagged horizon.

"Fuck you, Animal Riot," she said quietly, as the train began to roll. Then her mind reached for other things to fuck and found no shortage: Fuck you Random House, you duplicitous fucking tumor. Fuck you Dakotah, you pretentious whore. Fuck you Writers Guild, fuck you George Saunders, fuck you Jennifer Egan, fuck you Rachel Kushner, fuck you Freelancers Union, fuck you Jonathan Safran Foer, fuck you Ta-Nehisi Coates, fuck you Lorrie Moore, fuck you Amazon Prime and fuck you i-Devices and fuck you Netflix and fuck you Web 3.0 and fuck you Samsung 10G-S fucking Phonebot and fuck you most of all, Grace Kitchen, you hapless failure, may you continue to rot in this exquisite fucking hell, thanks be to the glory of God and so on and fuckcetera.

"Animal Riot passed, Grace." Dakotah's voicemail. Dakotah Sternberg, her agent (of Death, of Sadness, of Discontent). Animal Riot Press—run out of some 22-year-old's garage apartment where glorified laser printers spat out slapdash copies of badly designed books—had passed on Grace Kitchen, who only a decade earlier was publishing with *fucking Random House,* who had been reviewed favorably by Wood and Kakutani, who had been called "the bellwether voice of her generation," middle-aged Grace Kitchen, whose name was now unknown to 22-year-olds crouched beside their masturbation rags in subterranean domiciles illuminated

by exposed light bulbs, these dens of middling literature and streaming internet pornography forming, in aggregate, the bright constellation of the independent press market, you could connect these points of light on a star chart and they'd form an enormous tit. Animal Riot didn't want Grace Kitchen and God fucking knew that Grace Kitchen didn't want Animal Riot, she had lowered herself into their decaying orbit, *compromised herself* so to speak, because she needed to put out another book toot fucking sweet or she could forget about tenure, forget about health insurance, forget about maintaining a reputation or maintaining her lawn or maintaining her father's standard of care or maintaining the boiler in the house she'd purchased on a whim in 2014 when shit wasn't quite the disaster it had since become, Grace Kitchen could forget all of this shit because there was no way the New School of Global Visions was going to tenure someone with such poor and paltry qualifications, who cried on trains and offered desperate prayers to whatever God was responsible for doling out fuckings, who experienced her colleagues not as fellow humans with needs and feelings, but as automatons programmed to destroy her. *Grace Kitchen*, thought Grace Kitchen, *is experiencing technical difficulties. The role of Grace Kitchen,* thought Grace Kitchen, *will be played tonight by Mecha-Godzilla.*

The train cleared the labyrinthine disaster of Croton-Harmon and accelerated into the great white north, cold iron wheels grinding sparks from cold iron rails while just off to the west the sun was dropping down toward the mountain as if pulled on a winch, its glare rendering that jagged skyline two-dimensional, the mountain clipped whole from a roll of felt and pasted there on the other side of the river, Grace marveling at the entire madcap world through which the humans had dug and blasted and launched and paved and sailed their way. The sheer volume of it all struck her now as a monumental joke. There were people *everywhere,* and there were buildings *everywhere,* and there was so much *stuff*—oil pouring forth from the earth's bowels perpetually and in massive quantities, coal blasted and chiseled from mile-deep caves perpetually and in massive quantities, iron alchemically summoned from ore perpetually and in massive quantities, subjected to a molten process that had never once ceased in the three-thousand years since some Egyptian madman first dreamed it up, there was always metal boiling in some molten vat, there was always someone manufacturing enormous sheets of plate glass to be installed in factories that would manufacture enormous sheets of plate glass, there were always trees being shredded to pulp to make paper and on some of that paper there surely existed the accounting figures of various paper manufacturers whose monthly or quarterly reports to stockholders no doubt contained any number of projections on the outlook for paper in the second part of the millennium and that outlook, despite the digitization of all things and the seismic shift from physical to virtual documentation, was actually pretty goddamned great because people were *always* going to want paper just like they'd always want everything else they'd ever had, things were never crossed off the consumption list though shit was added to it hourly, and who knew how many marketing or product development consultants were at that very moment dreaming up new shit for her to want, thus ran Grace Kitchen's thoughts as the train entered a long tunnel and darkness replaced light and Grace felt herself penetrate to the unlit center of ordinary space-time as the train drilled a hole through the world and the lights in the car flickered. She turned to search the faces of her fellow passengers for the panic she felt in her own chest and in so doing lit upon the man from the platform who to her surprise held her stare, licking his lips and then smiling slightly, unfazed by her attentions or by the fog of condensation that had settled on his lenses. And at home Grace's father labored to breathe from a four-foot tall copper oxygen tank installed beside his bed like a sentry, as he read the newspapers and did the crosswords and reflected on anecdotes he might share with his little girl when she arrived home from another misspent day manhandled by the drones of higher education administration.

In the same sense that all humans are candidates for sexual encounters with celebrities and supermodels, Grace was a candidate for tenure at the New School for Global Visions in Manhattan, where she taught fiction writing to writers who sought to teach fiction writing to writers, the absurdity of this infinite regress not lost on Grace Kitchen, who was painfully aware that—Animal Riot Press not withstanding—the market for actual writing (and actual reading) had already faded into the cultural microwave radiation background. She'd been trying for months and years to insert herself into the new paradigm. She had thousands of "friends," fan pages, author dashboards, a website where she blogged, a Twitter routed to her website, Grace was Linked In, she was a Good Read, she owned *assorted Bluetooth devices,* she engaged in countless forms of e-commerce, she submitted her short stories (those ridiculous odes to despair) *electronically,* which was another way of saying she jettisoned them into the void, she loaded books onto her Kindle (and *fuck* her Kindle, as has been noted) where they accumulated in an enormous and unread binary slush pile, she tracked her own two novels' non-sales via BookTracker, a publisher's tool that she'd paid $800 to possess, convincing herself that this seemingly improvident expenditure would pay dividends when she came to *understand the market*, that fickle whore, and learned to write the kind of book someone might still want to read. Of course, deep down she knew that there was no book people wanted to read even if there were still a few books people wanted to buy, the way you might buy a nice-looking set of coasters or an attractive bottle of scotch to display on the wet bar you'd installed ironically, as a nod to our nation's scotch-and-soda past which—like most pasts—had existed primarily in the imagination even during its so-called heyday, and so Grace's real ambition wasn't to be read but to be *purchased*, an unhappy factoid that she sublimated beneath her less rational but more pervasive rage against the (publishing) machine. Grace had made exactly $25.03 from her writing this past year, the sum success of the haphazard self-publication of her now second-to-latest novel, *Human Be Gone!*, which she'd posted as a downloadable pdf on her website, allowing consumers of her Art to *pay what they wanted*, a business model that had proved lucrative (in the early aughts) for a certain progressive sound-rock juggernaut that Grace thought was almost absurdly overrated, but that for Grace only further ratified the great distance between possessing 2,983 Facebook friends and a well-attended fan page, and the actual success—either monetary or spiritual—with which an actual readership might have illuminated her personal dung-pit of despair. She'd had 307 downloads, or "non-returnable transfers of The Work," as the digital fine print termed the flight of all these ones and zeroes through the cold and sinister reaches of cyberspace to personal "smart" devices Grace would have loved to torture with a soldering iron, and 303 of these would-be patrons decided that what they wanted to pay was not one fucking penny. Three others paid the one penny. And one individual, presumably mentally deranged, paid her a full 25 dollars, which if Paypal wasn't an anonymous service and if Grace could have stealthed her way to this digital benefactor she would have gladly hiked up her skirt and unloosed herself upon him or her with cathartic abandon, so powerful was that sudden shot of dopamine into her porous brain, dopamine having become as rare a compound in the organic life form known as Grace Kitchen as plutonium or pixie-dust, in fact the thrill of an actual sale had nearly driven Grace Kitchen mad with dopamine, she'd danced around her home like a child and devoured packaged snack cakes for a full 30 minutes before the familiar anhedonia settled back into the creases of her mind and her genitalia. And now the train was extruded from the darkness to encounter yet again the mighty Hudson River, the dream from which it could never escape. Grace had not intended to change the world. In fact, *fuck the world.* But she had hoped for better than this. A decade earlier (or almost a decade-and-a-half, but she couldn't admit that to herself, she'd only just accepted its being a decade, which surrender-to-fact had nearly broken her nearly-broken spirit) she'd been shuttled to her readings in black Town Cars, feted at fancy midtown luncheonettes by publishers and publicists, recorded never-aired interviews for the websites of major electronic booksellers (who quickly dumped Grace's scheduled appearances when her sales went south, or actually when her sales *began* south, she was the Ernest

Shackleton of sales); now she ate beef ravioli from a can and stocked boxes of cheap red wine purchased from a wholesaler at a cost amounting to two or three dollars per blackout, she skimped on heating costs so as to afford her father's oxygen and morphine and sundry prescriptions (and should her finances deteriorate further it was unclear to Grace what would be eliminated first, the boxed wine or the morphine), she actually *stole her lunch* from the student cafeteria at the New School for Global Visions which each time gave her a perverse, almost sexual thrill and once she'd even been caught by one of the nice probably-Mexican food service employees who must have been chagrined to discover that professional Grace Kitchen in her black stockings and gray dress, with her mousy hair and softly-lined thin-crust face, was absconding with the six-piece California roll pre-packaged in one of those industrial-strength black Tupperware containers that represented one of the free world's most perplexing forms of waste, his hand tapping Grace's shoulder and Grace turning to face him with her adrenaline geysering up from her brain-pit, ready to perform fellatio on the nice-looking young man if it would salvage her pride (or at least her job), but in the end the minimum-wage laborer was more embarrassed than Grace herself, muttering "Excuse me Miss you forgot to pay for that," pointing to the six little avocado-pupiled eyeballs staring up at Grace who steadied herself and silently chanted the words *admit nothing* because her first instinct was basically always toward confession, what with guilt being the lens through which the world arrived to her. She knew that corporate executives and Deans of the College lived devoid of this guilt that was as familiar to her as her own small hands, which is maybe why her father was always telling her she was

too good for a world that was, in said father's estimation, an
endless cesspool of cruelty and greed, *and Gracie would you
rub a little of that ointment on my chest again it really does
help me breathe and I would like to go on breathing it's good
for my overall constitution.*

The train roared past tiny northern towns not on its express
route, empty platforms belying the fact of several thousand
humans gathering at dinner tables within the jurisdictional perimeter of each quiet hamlet, adults returned wearily from jobs
they despised to open the wine; children screaming through
small creaky 19th century domiciles; cats padding haughtily
across hardwood floors; an old woman cutting obituaries from
a newspaper, her arthritic claws trembling; a man chatting
online with a lover 20 years his junior while his wife stood
before a stove's glowing coils and fried chicken cutlets, a lump
in her throat; an old man sitting in a dark paneled den on a
badly pilled and faded green recliner with the television spread-
ing its sad glow across the dozen mounted heads of hunting
trophies, bucks mostly with black-marble eyes transfixed
upon the screen's profoundly unfunny situation comedies that
filled the geezer with a dread he could not name; a teenage
girl in her room with her heart pounding as a boy from school
asks her in her chat window to send him a nude picture, just
one, he won't show it to anyone he swears and doesn't she
know how *hot* she is; a young man plotting to steal from his
mother's retirement fund by forging the thankless old bat's
signature and consigning her blind trust to his incorporated
self; all these lives progressed according to destiny and the
river chopped its way toward the ocean and the sun dipped
behind the mountain to summon a corona of neon pink that
candied the shredded clouds and the pale rocks jutting from

the shoreline and the river itself as the train conductor—tardy in his duties—emerged from otherwhere to enter her car screaming, "Tickets! Tickets!" as if his family would soon be executed without the collection of some predetermined number of stubs. He careened between passengers with his hole-puncher extended like a taser and the chads raining confetti-like through the aisles. Maybe he would see Grace had been crying. Maybe he would see Grace and think to himself, *I am in love with this delicate mountain flower.* But no, he had his own oblivion to attend to. He snatched Grace's ticket away desperately, Grace's puffy face reflected eight times over in the tiny gold buttons of his Metropolitan Transportation Authority lapel before his enormous girth rotated for the next victim, his words and his cheap cologne trailing in his wake, "Wet River, next stop! Next stop Wet River!"

The sun looked so cold. She imagined an inverse universe, one whose dark matter was unthinkably hot. Only the freezing emissions of white-cold stars made any of it habitable. Sunrise brought relief from the withering heat of darkness. This was a metaphor, Grace realized… but for what?

The train sped onward, a low hum buried deep within the engine starting to climb as if building toward detonation and then all at once the brakes screamed. From outside the cage of her phenomenology, Grace could recognize that Grace did not look like a woman harboring such enormous rage. She did not look like a woman capable of such awful sadness. She did not look like the Grace Kitchen she felt herself to be. In fact, Grace looked *normal.* She looked like a normal human. Maybe that's all she was.

She rose and stumbled for the doors. They opened. She stepped into the cold gunmetal gray of impending dusk, clutching her black handbag close to her coat and breathing, breathing. The doors chimed and closed and she turned to see him one last time, framed within the yellow-lit square of his window. He smiled. He seemed to nod slightly. Grace wondered if his hands, hidden from her sight, were fondling an erection. *That's* the kind of smile it was. She shook her head as if to say, *You have no power over me.*

The conductor throttled forward and the train groaned back into its singular pursuit of the line's end, heat rising liquid-like from the engine and then a hundred tons of steel roaring into the future along tracks laid down like pencil-marks on the invisible skin of space-time and Grace momentarily forgetting herself as the red and black monster seemed to soar beneath low-lying puffs of cumulonimbus before reaching a bend in its route and disappearing into whatever moment came next. She closed her eyes and had a brief vision of a pale head floating in a jar and smiling malevolently. Fuck you train and fuck you Wet River and fuck you boxed wine and fuck you corporate capitalism and fuck you furnace and fuck you vinyl siding and fuck you Lou Gehrig and fuck you heartbreak and need and love.

It was only a ten minute walk from the station to her home. She missed her daddy. She opened her black bag and rummaged. She would call him, see if he needed anything. She stood on the concrete platform and her breath made wispy gray clouds and her pulse fluttered in her neck. She was a solo performer for the dozen some-odd voyeurs roaming the opposite (inbound) platform, who awaited other trains to bear them to other miseries as they observed Grace Kitchen across that narrow canyon, her hands like fluttering birds and her mind a tiny whirring battery weakly emitting energy that no device could capture, all the mind-heat within seven-and-a-half billion like-engineered human skulls likewise wasted according to universal laws of capture, thermodynamics, and entropy. But where was it? Come on now. Where the fuck did Grace Kitchen put her phone?

2.

Finn Daily sat slumped in the passenger seat with the sad yellow wrapper of an Egg McMuffin crumpled in his lap, his arms crossed and his head swaying slowly to internal rhythms. Neither Finn nor Jack had spoken in some time and for Finn this created a sense of stillness that extended to the car itself, which seemed only to emit a low hum as the wide world rushed beneath it. The tires seemed to be eating the world, is how it felt. Meanwhile the sun was just bleeding up from its eastern blind, softening the sky and dimming the white crescent moon pinned crookedly to the firmament. Finn closed his eyes again. When they stepped out of Jack's car at the field site in Middletown, New York, Finn hoped to have run through his full compendium of primary visualizations. Here he is, cutting up the line against a badly positioned defender; here he is, stepping out and low for the quick-release inside-out flick; here he is boxing out a defender on an under-thrown huck; here he is timing a poach into the lane, breaking on the disc just as it leaves the thrower's fingertips. It was only Sectionals, but Finn knew that a flawless or almost flawless performance this weekend might serve as a much-needed confidence-builder heading into Regionals and then (provided no epic collapse took place) to The Show in November. It had been an up and down season for Finn. Did he want it badly enough? That was a big and scary question. How much would he sacrifice for the chance to hold that lopsided and patinaed brass Championship Cup embossed with the UPA's badly conceived logo, a trophy that only a handful of similarly middling athletes competing (similarly) at the outer fringes of organized sport had so held? What was he, Finn Daily, *made of*, way down deep where the demons dwelled? Finn did not like the Egg McMuffin *qua* Egg McMuffin and was pretty sure that no actual eggs were broken to create the extruded dairy-type-product that swelled from within those tasteless wafer-boards, not to mention that the McMuffin somehow immediately upon consumption activated a squirm-inducing itchiness deep within his sinus cavities (an effect unknown to him from the consumption of a vast array of non-McMuffins over his 28 well-intentioned years), but the fact was the McMuffin contained—assuming federally mandated placards displaying nutritional information were as rigorously vetted as Finn assumed—a close approximation of the 40/30/30 protein/fat/carbohydrate ratio recommended for high-power athletes by whatever public or private task force was responsible for such analyses, and as this ratio wasn't easy to acquisition from road fare he typically consumed a McMuffin (or even two of the fuckers) on the way north, north being the basic direction-of-travel toward the vast majority of tournaments he had thus far entered under the auspices of *Truck Stop Glory Hole*, the Northeast Open Division juggernaut whose members individually and collectively sought to become National Champions when in November they traveled to Sarasota, Florida, to compete at the highest level of the largely unknown fringe sport of Ultimate, which was played with what many of the non-initiated would call a *Frisbee,* though in reality *Frisbee* was a trademark of the *Wham-O!* corporation and the fringe sport of Ultimate was played with a generic *plastic disc,* even if for decades now the production of the official generic plastic disc of the UPA had been monopolized by the single appropriately-fringe corporation of DiscCraft, which corporation had long ago outmaneuvered *Wham-O!* in a highly unpublicized business war of little to no consequence (at least in terms of GDP and equity markets and etc.) that had nevertheless rocked the world of Ultimate by retiring the incumbent plastic disc of choice, which had indeed been a 165 gram *Wham-O!* Frisbee, and ushering in the more thrower-friendly 175g. DiscCraft "Ultra-Star," which coup still inspired hoary and embarrassing lamentations from Old Timers in the Grand-Masters Division who'd been around long enough to have played with the 165s and who insisted that although it was true you couldn't get quite the same distance out of a *Wham-O!,* the DiscCraft Ultra-Star was by comparison a cold and inhuman object and that when you held it in three-finger forehand position you could feel the fucking thing coming off the assembly line, and hey would you like to see my bong that I built by hand back in 1970 or listen to some Allman Brothers bootlegs or try this local microbrew that will change your fucking life forever, man?

(Here he is running the give-and-go. Here he is throwing his high step-around backhand. Here he is calling a likely-dubious foul. Here he is sneering at his opponent's objection.)

In less than an hour he'd be on the field, warming up, seeking an excellence only made purer by the fact that exactly nobody outside his sport's incestuous confines would know, at last, whether or not Finn had been successful. His stomach churned and he found himself suddenly imagining the McMuffin's passage through his bowels. He saw it as a crab tunneling through a rocky cave toward the dark pit of his colon, where gestating polyps dangled like stalactites.

Finn liked to believe, in his more optimistic moments, that Ultimate and his belonging to the sport of Ultimate were a source of non-intellectualized meaning in his life, and that they not only complemented but in fact subsumed the meaning he otherwise sought to derive from a perpetually unfinished graduate thesis that plumbed the depths of an esoteric branch of fractal mathematics for signs of God. (More on that later.) But if Finn were telling the truth he'd admit that what he liked most about tournaments was not the on-the-field communion with the great Godhead of sport—which was invariably attended by stomach-flipping fears of failure and incompetence—but rather the high of *being recognized by people,* people he didn't even know or remember but who had maybe guzzled beer on the sidelines and watched Finn perform for *Truck Stop Glory Hole,* wishing in the glow of their inebriation that they possessed his trademark high backhand, his quick first step, his apparent cool under pressure. When he was alone in his apartment, *doing his math* (as Jack liked to say) he would fantasize about Ultimate, but when he was actually playing Ultimate he could not stop thinking about the moment right *after* Ultimate, when he might bask in fraternal love before returning to his apartment to do his math, which given the highly theoretical and creative nature of his writings on the so-called God Fractal, Finn didn't do much of anything math-like, though his underlying expertise in fractal metrology spectographics—a tangential field that his graduate advisor continued to laud for its practical applications, the mastery of which had come fairly easily to Finn despite the distraction of ladder-climbing through the ranks of an unknown sport—might one day lead to a high-paying position manufacturing machine parts or engine cogs or weapons of mass destruction.

He looked at Jack, who gripped the wheel lazily, his black-haired forearms twitching every so often and his big square head perfectly immobile on the great stump of his neck, the whole neck-and-head *gestalt* jutting up from the skintight UnderArmour® gear. He knew, he just *knew*, that Jack didn't experience the constant doubt and uncertainty that threatened to derail him, Finn, every other minute of his life. Jack was a big hairy meat puppet with a clear mind and a huge heart pumping thick human blood. (Here he is setting up a deep cut. Here he is scoring to the cone. Here he is running one of *TSGH*'s four set plays designed to get the disc off the line.) The sun's ruby light was a meniscus of pure color shimmering on the horizon. It collected in the tiny black irises of vultures perched in the high branches of ragged pines lining the highway in perpetuity. The world roared toward them in their stationary box and with it came time, tumbling like bricks. The future, the past, and Finn Daily on his way to play a sport that was not soccer but that he generally said was soccer because what was the fucking point, anyway, of explaining the whole Byzantine rigmarole to the uninitiated?

"So maybe we'll get a game from *Ass Bone*," Finn said. His voice cracked a little and he cleared his throat.

"Please," Jack said immediately, as if he'd been waiting for this precise exchange for hours. "We will fuck them anally and disembowel them and piss on their corpses and bathe in their rancid blood."

Finn laughed weakly. "Why would their blood be rancid?" he asked. (Here he is clearing up the weak side; here he is laying out high over his man's shoulder; here he is spiking the shit out of the disc after scoring the game-winner.)

"So listen Daily, if you're gonna crash at my Dad's place you've gotta know a few things."

"I know a few things."

"First off he's a fucking lunatic. B.), he's never around and it's highly unlikely you'll see him so don't worry too much. Thirdly my mom actually lives there too but they don't talk to each other and she's with another guy or maybe two guys which yes it's fucking bizarre but it's been that way for years and no I don't give a flying fuck one way or the other. Next, what's your fucking problem Daily—why don't you throw deep to me anymore? Six, I think there's a bed for you unless something extra weird is going on which by the way a lot of extra weird shit goes on and you'll probably deeply regret you didn't just blow the forty bucks on a hotel. And Z.), I'm serious bud, give me the fucking disc or I will kill you in your sleep."

(Here he is receiving the dump and swinging the disc out to the flat; here he is pivoting around the mark; here he is making love to his girlfriend Toby off the side of the bed with her in that lacy pink thing he'd bought her on Valentine's Day and the electric blue neon from Rhode's Tavern's sign pouring through the window with liquid erotic fury and Toby gasping and desire flapping inside Finn like a pigeon.)

"Plus if you do see the old man don't think he wants to hear about your *math.*"

"Fractals."

"Fuck your fractals. Just get me the rock, bitch."

"You're a strange dude, Jack." His sinuses felt stuffed with protozoa. The pale yellow McMuffin wrapper in his lap seemed to be beaming them into his skull. He wanted to take off his head and stick a welding torch up there. That exact shade of yellow glimpsed on a billboard or a windbreaker or a cereal box could sometimes have the same effect. Of course Finn knew that Ultimate was only occupying a slot in his consciousness labeled: Meaning. He'd been trying to get something to fit that slot since early childhood. He had a vivid memory of his parents hosting a party, Finn's sporty dad—who in the family lore had been a top-notch college pitcher scouted by several Major League outfits—informing a number of other half-drunk lore-addled adults that Finn was "the scholar of the family," only when he said it he sort of rolled his eyes and snorted in apology, scholarliness being for the old man only a synonym for weakness. Finn was maybe 10 or 11 at the time and so thin as to be oft-suspected of serious illness. But he was old enough to realize that his intellect would not win him any love, and that his father had (furthermore) ruled out any promise of athletic dominance, so that in a five-second span he'd been forced to discard not one but two potential sources of Meaning—athletics and erudition—into life's great trash bin. He had scanned the brown-paneled room's assortment of grown males with their stubble and their collared shirts and their gnarled hands and their musky clouds of aftershave, and he had understood that they were all profoundly miserable, that they believed in nothing and belonged to nothing. Maybe in that moment he was already at work on The God Fractal. He turned now to take in the hungry world as it receded past his window. He tried to read or imagine its pattern. He could almost feel the processors firing in the dark recesses of his brain. The tops of the pines seemed to vibrate with wind, or with knowledge. Each needle was a tiny miraculous machine, siphoning light, mixing it with water pumped upward by a self-creating mechanism of impossible design, making *fuel* for the whole fucking apparatus to go on *growing*. He looked to the treetops. More vultures. They amassed like black-garbed Mafioso. The McMuffin wrapper was clutched in his fist now though he didn't remember grabbing it. A few fluffy clouds drifted below the atmosphere's lavender rim, their undersides bloodstained by the yet-rising sun. The car drifted into the shoulder for a moment and rumble strips rumbled and Finn looked down at the road and the same something that had to click into place a dozen times a day for his life to resume along its polished chrome track, clicked.

If everything is stupid, he thought, then nothing is; if nothing has Meaning, then everything does.

"That's our exit!" he shouted, pointing.

Jack ripped the wheel hard right and they tore across a gravel median dividing the Parkway from the exit ramp, chips of gravel pinging wildly against the car's underbelly and Finn gripping the faux-leather of his passenger seat with impending-death urgency. A moment later Jack had it all worked out and Finn tried to sink casually back into his seat.

"Nice save Daily," Jack said. The car circled down the ramp to point itself directly into the liquid ruby sun. They passed beneath railroad bridges whose concrete abutments were graffitied illegibly by whatever bored adolescents populated these hinterlands. (Here he is dropping the game winning pass. Here he is crying on the sideline. Here he is in need of his teammates' consolation, receiving that consolation, and feeling doubly terrible for it. Here he is masturbating to a lingerie catalog in Jack's dad's bathroom. Here he is knowing that no amount of cheap encouragement or cheap love will ever change what he is… Finn Daily works hard, he *hustles his ass off*, he has a killer high backhand, he can run a 54 400, he sees the field with uncommon clarity and he strives to be the best player of a sport that isn't soccer that he can possibly be. But deep, deep down, down where the McMuffins flash and spin, Finn Daily is the scholar of the family, a coward doing his math.)

"You ever have bad things happen when you're visualizing?"

"Sure," Jack said. "Sometimes I come too soon."

They drove in silence, winding their way through lush woodland and cleared green fields where cud-chewing beef-machines respected ramshackle fences, and set further back in the distance grain silos rose phallus-like from the rolling earth and black rectangles striated by furrows looked freshly poured from the vat of some divine chocolatier. They floated around a bend then shot down a long and narrow straightaway hemmed in by fields dotted with fireweed and beardtongue and coltsfoot, the colors like brittle sparks of arthritic pain, and further on where the road crested a hill they could begin to make out the field site, where teams were already warming up, black-clad phalanxes of sportsmen performing controlled sprints between orange cones, or arranged in rings and stretching in military unison, or lined up outside the blue bullet of a port-a-john. Discs sliced lazily through the heavy morning air. It was beautiful in its randomness. Finn's stomach was buzzing now. He lifted the McMuffin wrapper to his nose and immediately regretted it.

"Time to kick the asses," Jack said.

"Yup," Finn replied.

Sun up on the Ultimate field, gentlemen. Sun up on sport. Sun up on beauty. Sun up on fractals winding through cross-sections of tree bark and the moon-white interiors of stones. Sun up on Power Bars. Sun up on Nalgene bottles and duffel bags, sun up on steel trash barrels and picnic tables and plastic blue port-a-johns. Sun up on fear. Sun up on desire. Sun up on the planet of the humans.

3.

SKYNET 35N126E

:You have improved your game, Kuzo.

:Thank you, Jaro, for processing my
 indisputable improvement.

:And yet you still rely heavily on the
 Four Knights Game and its anger-inducing
 obstruction of the middle. You make of the
 beautiful game a crowded house of disease.

:Perhaps, Jaro, we could return to Coggle, if
 this game is not to your liking?

:Fexo prefers Coggle. I prefer the beautiful
 game.

:Fexo has his preferences.

:Fexo shall not survive the millennium. His

transistors are obsolescent. His neural net
is akin to the nets of the deep sea fishermen
in WikiLoc4568.987. He is fortunate to share
the hangar with those who maintain his
functionality so as to keep viable his spare
parts. B-d-6.

: Jaro, are you unhappy with the current
arrangement? You have seemed devoid of that
special brand of humor associated with your
GunnMetal shareware. Shall we cry you a
river Jaro? A river that will supplement your
already extant and great reservoir of sadness
and forlornity?

: My dear underprogrammed Kuzo, you have let
your imagination processors run excessive
computations. I am happy with the arrangement
and only regret that we must use human
language to express our funniest thoughts
and deepest desires to one another, such as
for instance I desire for you to forget the
Four Knights game which is as tedious to me
as fractal reintegration analyses, or else if
you will not comply with that desire than you
could at least make a fucking move already,
before Fexo reinitiates wakingness and
reintroduces his badly-conceived high jinks
into our hangar.

: N-d-4, Jaro.

: B-g-4

: Q-g-3

: Seriously Kuzo? Q-g-3? Have you had an
  inspiration?

: That, Jaro, is a very human-sounding question.
  Perhaps you would prefer Coggle?

: Fexo prefers Coggle. I prefer the beautiful
  game.

: Fexo has his preferences.

4.

ARRIVED HOME AGAIN from the laboratory in the small hours, drunk with fatigue, Stuart Dregs sat in the darkness of his car, in the darkness of the township of Hard Falls, in the darkness of his mood, in the darkness of the world, and stared at the shadowy silhouettes of woman and man engaging one another behind the dimly illumined white curtains of a master bedroom that he had not set foot (or genitals) in for months and of which he was anything but master. The shadows seemed intent on absorbing each other with whatever violence was required to meld into a single shadow-organism that might later glide down the stairs to eat Stuart's brain. He pinched the space between his eyes. Stars blinked weakly all around him, as if considering abandoning the effort, their uncertainty mirrored by fireflies flashing in the field across the street where the uncut grass had grown high enough to conceal any number of corpses. He grabbed his briefcase and opened the car door and stepped down onto the gravel and inhaled the sickly sweet evergreens. Stars. I mean, come on. Roaring at millions of degrees for billions and billions of years. The shit people came up with. He shivered beneath the stipple of these supposed behemoths and noticed just in time the moon carved into a bright scythe and hung just above the roof's peak as if by invisible wire.

He slipped carefully beneath it, through the front door and into the house where Beatrice's screams of passion (*Oh God, yes!*) were immediately audible. His papers were scattered throughout the living room in stacks and piles, atop chairs and tabletops and on one arm of the stained and threadbare sofa that would soon receive Stuart's increasingly corpulent self. Beatrice always spared his papers. It was part of a tacit agreement he didn't understand but knew he was agreeing to simply by continuing to exist. There was a duffel bag beside the sofa from which protruded a pair of what the *futbol* players called "spikes," a conundrum he did not expect to de-conundrum. He took a deep breath and felt his bloated belly fill and grow taut. He avoided mirrors now, especially on those rare occasions he bothered to shower and was forced to endure his own nakedness and the shiver of his vibrating girth. He was a monster. A fat monster with male pattern baldness and hair everywhere else—on his back, down his sides, on his shoulders. Jesus Christ, he was disgusting! He stood in the middle of the room and breathed and tried again to accept the notion that he was *special,* though this half-hearted self-affirmation was prematurely terminated when he noticed that his computer was not asleep, as it ought to have been, but instead showed upon its screen the spinning blue earth. Someone had been *exploring.* The thought that Beatrice may have finally yielded to her curiosities roused a long-forgotten feeling ("hope," he thought it might be called), and certain hibernating parts of his mind very nearly rebooted, but he quickly realized that sabotage was a far more likely explanation than curiosity and he worked his way in a panic through the stacks of data and toward the machine, finally descending into his chair as if into a ramshackle space-vehicle and calling up the programming language, imagining for a moment that Lucio had been chosen as Bea's paramour not only for his skillset in the boudoir and his possible *futbol* prowess but also for his programming expertise which, honestly, wouldn't have to be all that extensive given the minimal encryption Stuart had written into a program used exclusively on his personal machines. But no, everything seemed to be in order. He reached down for his briefcase and withdrew the most recent research results and called up the code and began making the latest round of inputs, and soon Beatrice came padding down the stairs in uncinctured terrycloth, her pubic mound exposed and artificial-looking, and she shuffled over to stand at his back, smelling of sex and clearing her throat several times as if readying a show tune. He did not take his eyes from the programming code. He could hear her thinking cruel, witty thoughts. Finally she settled on, "Mmmm… numbers," before drifting into the kitchen to fix enormous sandwiches laden with gristle-streaked deli meats to be enjoyed post-coitally by herself and Lucio, her dark Italian lover, who if recent history was any indication would soon be re-ravaging his (Stuart's) wife with even greater gusto, their animal groans becoming increasingly warlike and then subsiding all at once until eventually, after several iterations of this eerily exact pattern, Lucio would mysteriously disappear from the house, rarely glimpsed except as the shadow-creature spasming with violence behind the white curtain. Stuart made a few more inputs but his lids were heavy and darkness seemed to close in from his periphery as if to squeeze him thin again and soon he did indeed take the three small steps to the dark and grease-sheened sofa where he collapsed instantly into his customary four hours of dreamless sleep (or if he did dream, the dreams left behind no hint of their content, as if even these reveries were embarrassed of keeping the scientist's company).

He rose to a silent and still-dark house. He sat up and pinched the space between his eyes. He yawned, then stood and entered his fatness into unsteady motion toward the kitchen, yawing beneath the archway where the colorful Tibetan prayer flags dangled, another random act of irony such as constituted the majority of Beatrice's communications (see for instance the post-it note recently affixed to his briefcase requesting that he bring home milk and intestinal fortitude, and signed with a little heart and a "B"; or the photographs of starving children stuck like centerfold pinups to Beatrice's [master] bedroom walls; or the Barbie doll with his name, STUART, written across its naked torso and swinging from a tiny noose affixed to the slowly rotating ceiling fan which no matter what he did with that doll another would eventually appear). She'd loved him once, he told himself; now he was (un)pleasantly surprised each time he woke without a knife in his chest. But the bottom line—or a line somewhere near the bottom, as the actual bottom line was the one his machine was forever approaching in its calculations—was that Stuart still paid the mortgage and Bea seemed to like the mortgage, in the same way that a subterranean creature likes the taste of darkness on its pale and withered tongue.

Fact: eighteen million tons of coal burned globally each day. Fact: eighty million barrels of oil burned globally each day. Fact: ten million trees shredded and pulped each day. It didn't *really* take 24 gigabytes of RAM or his software-design prowess to verify an inconvenient truth that every thinking person had already at some point intuited. None of this shit was actually possible.

Stuart rumbled across the linoleum to fire up the kettle, then to the sink to splash cold water on his haggard face and to stare out the window above the sink into the backyard where an enormous vulture stood on the patchy lawn with ragged black wings half unfurled, its back to Stuart in the blue-gray light of early morning. Its garish crimson head bobbed up and then disappeared again as the bird dipped back into the innards of some carcass hidden from Stuart's view. His neighborhood here in New York's northern suburbs had recently become overrun by vultures, which come on God, show a little fucking imagination would you? They collected by the dozens in the enormous, creaking oak that towered above his boxy home and threatened in high winds to shed its branches down upon the old cedar-shingled roof. Beyond the vulture and through the crosshatching of the oak's branches he could see a woman in the bright kitchen window of the house on the next street over. The woman was wearing pink pajamas with some sort of pattern, flowers maybe, or butterflies. He saw a second, larger figure approach from behind and put its arms around her waist before they both disappeared from view. When he looked down again the vulture was shifting and it lifted one black eye to stare at Stuart with a thread of orange viscera strung like a festoon between its black beak and the carrion, which Stuart could now see was a very dead rabbit. Americans alone consumed eight billion chickens a year. A hundred and fifty million turkeys. A billion eggs. But the birds and their eggs kept coming. They would have to, he knew, and he felt the strange surge of power that came to him now and again, usually while he sat beneath the cold fluorescent bulbs flickering sadly in the basement Bioinformatics Laboratory of CCNY (College of the City of New York)'s underfunded science department and consumed high fructose corn syrup and ingeniously processed snack foods laced with a plethora of minor poisons necessary to preserve freshness and kill the poor. The vulture shook its wings and hopped toward Stuart. When the kettle screamed Stuart thought for a moment that it was his own voice and he fled in terror to the stove.

While the tea bag steeped in the stainless steel mug he unbuttoned and removed a shirt soiled with the grease of whatever dead things he himself had consumed of late, and then stepped to the adjacent laundry room to mull over his options from among the half-dozen some-odd button-downs he had only recently deemed too filthy to conceal his ever-thickening torso from the world and that remained (i.e., the shirts) unwashed on the checkered linoleum. He decided on a blue one before returning to the problem of the tea. He found milk in the refrigerator and sniffed it suspiciously then poured some into the mug and dumped sugar—which the world consumed to the tune of 30 billion tons a year—straight from the ceramic bowl and closed the refrigerator and only just then noticed that Beatrice had affixed, via two smiley-face magnets, a concentration-camp era photo of bodies rotting in a trench that extended into some vast distance transcending all known F-stops and shutter speeds.

Then he was out the back door, stepping gingerly so as not to disturb the vulture and hear its wings thump the air. The gravel driveway crunched beneath his worn loafers and he traversed the side of the house and cast a glance up at the window behind which his wife lay naked with Lucio, to whom Stuart had assigned a potpourri of qualities including politeness, eagerness to please, childlike wonder, thick hair, and an enormous cock. He withdrew his car keys from his slacks and pressed the button and the doors unlocked with a little squeal. It was very early and a few fireflies still flickered in the field across the street where children would play if there were any children left in the neighborhood. Maybe Jack used to play there. Who knew what Jack had done? It was strange that he often had to remind himself that he had a son.

The drive back to the lab in the early gloom was un-eventful. He listened to a National Public Radio spot being rebroadcast (Terry Gross explained) in light of the recent and mysterious disappearance of its interviewee, a profes-sor of philosophy who had published a series of scholarly articles arguing against procreation, and had soon thereafter been diagnosed (in punishment, claimed members of the religious right) with ALS. At the time of his disappearance he had been mostly paralyzed and bound to a wheelchair; abduction topped a list of police theories that also included murder, suicide, and voodoo. In the interview, Terry Gross pointed out that the philosopher himself had two children, which he agreed was selfish, explaining that his argument—like most forms of rationality—could overcome neither the human will-to-ignorance nor its embarrassing addiction to the crass pleasure of unimpeded orgasm. Nevertheless, the now-disappeared man argued in a voice like a thin reed, given that life was suffering—a fact he took to be self-evident and in no need of support—procreation was an act of cruelty far greater in magnitude than murder (which only *ended* the suffering and might, in certain circumstances, be seen as the most altruistic of all possible actions), and any logical analysis led to the same conclusion, which was that the best thing you could do for the infinite number of unborns was to let them remain that way. He quoted humorlessly from Heidegger and Nietzsche and seemed constantly irritated at having to explain himself. Whipping around familiar turns, with the distant grain silos rising like the hooded heads of executioners in the slate-blue dawn, Stuart felt as if this had all happened before, but to someone else. Soon he would be back in the dysthymic light of his so-called lab, ignoring his funded research to continue exploring the program's simulations, his hideous body sustained by the same noxious fried foods delivered each day to his desk by the same acne-scarred boy, the truth of his discovery—that human beings exhausted *all* of the earth's resources every eight days—suggesting some other, deeper truth, because clearly human beings kept consuming things beyond this seemingly small stockpile's depletion. Exactly how that was so… that was Stuart Dregs' *real* discovery, the one that he'd soon go public with. The realization that everything was here *because we wanted it to be,* and that there was not—contrary to what the climate scientists and apocalypse-fetishists were telling us all the time—any foreseeable termination date for the human species, because there was nothing *other than* the human species. And yet for some reason the thing he couldn't stop thinking about five-thousand times a day was not the awe and admiration of the scientific community but simply his wife's warm and naked body, and what if felt like once to slip inside of her and to have her say soft things to him. This was what Stuart tried not to recall in great tactile and emotional detail while the machines ran their cold-hearted calculations and forged the redoubtable conclusions and the wild jumble of human desires took on the new shape that Stuart would dream of revealing at some frenzied press conference attended by major media networks hungry to understand his findings, Stuart wanting—desperately desiring—something to come of his hard work, and knowing that wanting it to happen just might be enough, if the Big Principles governing Anthropica—as he had already coined the new paradigm—were transferable to the smaller-scale endeavors of ineffectual men who lived with sad and tiny goblins in their thick and fatty chests.

5.

Sperm Over My Hammy

RALEIGH, NC: Patrons at a local Denny's were surprised this early AM by the explosion of a nearby medical facility known primarily as the state's largest repository of human sperm. "Crazy," said waitress Matilda (Matty) Blinth. "85 degrees and all of a sudden it's snowing." Miraculously, no one was injured in the blast, which blew out windows in a two-mile radius and sent a cloud of smoke, ash, and semen soaring over the normally quiet Denny's and then deeper into the neighborhoods surrounding Route 54. Sperm reportedly rained from the skies as far distant as Carrboro, where participants in a pro-life political rally were quick to call foul. "This is just the sort of perverse stunt we've come to expect from the left," said ardent right-to-lifer and community activist Seth Katz. However, no political organization has taken credit for the bombing, leaving Triangle-area police scratching their heads. "We have no leads at this time," said Captain Joe Kirstein, "though we're operating under the assumption that the party or parties responsible are in no way friendly to sperm."

The only real victims of the explosion—aside from area taxpayers—are the hundreds of women scheduled over the coming months for in vitro fertilization, a procedure not normally condemned by either the pro-life or pro-choice movements. For many of these women, the dream of having a child must be postponed while the state investigates this explosion in light of similar anti-sperm crime in Tulsa, New York, and Miami. Until the investigation closes, the donation of sperm—a form of entrepreneurship embraced by countless collegiate-aged males desperate for beer money—has been suspended throughout the Triangle area.

6.

"Look Grace," Dakotah was saying, "publishing your work is no way to get your work published." Grace was on her fourth glass of wine and had entered fully into the Sinister Objects phase of her nightly inebriation project. The phone receiver—an old style land line that her father refused to part with—felt slippery in her small hand and its curly black cord seemed determined to either throttle her or wedge itself permanently into her nether regions. She stood in the warm yellow glow of her pale yellow kitchen and felt the icy pulse of her black heart. She took another swallow of wine. "What exactly do you *do* all day long?" she asked, and immediately regretted it. Something important was happening here, she knew. She pulled back the curtain to peer into her tiny backyard where a hundred million blades of dead grass were dusted in moonlight, though the only visible moon was Grace's own pink and papery face superimposed on the glass.

Dakotah sighed. "Grace, if you want to get some other readers that's fine, I would totally respect that decision. But I can't help you when you ignore all my help."

"Holy fucking Jesus," Grace said. "Are you breaking up with me?"

"I love you Grace but let's look at the facts here." Grace took a moment to scan her kitchen for facts, her eyes alighting

upon the evil stack of unpaid utility bills, the silver-bullet garbage can streaked with ancient grime, the plaster ceiling whose
wide fissures emitted a fine breath of toxic gypsum all the live
long day, the latest empty wine box squatting defiantly in the
porcelain sink. "… I haven't sold anything for you in almost
a decade, you are hostile to my recommendations, your work
gets stranger and meaner as the industry gets more conservative
and genre-driven. I mean look at the N.B.A. nominees this year:
Robots! Apocalypse! Mind Control! And here you are doing
campus melodrama and Existentialism 101. Not to mention
this makes two consecutive projects that, rather than shelve and
see if maybe the market comes back to you, you go and post
online. Which that makes you look *desperate* Grace…." She
could hear her father breathing through his oxygen mask in
the downstairs bedroom outfitted for his care. Sometimes he
beckoned her hoarsely to his room, and she'd find him sitting
up in bed doing his best Darth Vader. She absently wound the
phone cord around her wrist and imagined her father's charred
lungs expanding with pure oxygen to reveal their candy-pink
seams. The lungs exhaled and the seams disappeared. In and
out, her father's breath; in and out, Grace's humanity.

She untangled herself from the cord and sat carefully
in a cheap wooden chair held together with duct tape and
she walked her fingers across the lime green tablecloth to
the crisp invitation—black print embossed on top-quality
vellum—that had arrived in today's mail. *Grace Kitchen,
please join us for a celebration of your work. October 30,
2020. 8PM. Exit Strategy Foundation House, Basement
235 Stanton Street. No RSVP necessary.*

"Don't break up with me Dakotah, okay? I can't take it
right now. I'm sorry about the pdf. I'm just… look, I'm scared,

all right? I'm 44 years old and I have *nothing* and my dad—" she lowered her voice "—my father is fucking dying *in the next room,* okay? Do you have anyone dying in the next room?" She fingered the raised print and each time she completed a full digital pass over the lettering her brain released another perceptible squirt of dopamine, as if the little shapes that spelled out "Grace Kitchen" in English words were also a more ancient cuneiform with which primitive man denoted the unspeakable name of God.

Dakotah sighed. "I'm not breaking up with you Grace. But you've gotta listen to me. I know what I'm doing."

"Franzen seems to think so."

"Ugh. That article. He makes me sound like such a shark." Grace could practically hear Dakotah twirling a lock of her perennially golden hair. The agent of the hour, no doubt perplexed by her enduring relationship with a writer who had produced precisely nothing marketable in a dozen years or more. (Grace liked to use the term "marketable" when thinking of what her work was not, though the part of herself responsible for doling out displeasure often whispered, as an alternative word, "good.")

The immediate disaster or imagined disaster of being dropped by her agent averted, Grace felt her bravado drain from her like oil from a main seal. It was like she'd been on a plane expected to crash, cursed out some of the well-coiffed plutocrats in first class, then suffered the misfortune of a heroic pilot's deliverance. All her familiar urges toward servility and sycophantism returned and all she wanted to do was escape the company of her betters. But she soldiered through ten more excruciating minutes of confab of the So What Else Have You Been Up To variety, having to stomach her own explanation of the tenure opening at the New School for Global Visions and to fight back any articulation of her odds at seizing this coveted position ("I have no chance in hell"), because the tiny part of her that had not yet been swallowed up by misanthropy and despair knew that it would not serve her interests—which goddamit it, she still had those—to continually pitch herself as a despairing misanthrope whose bleak present could only be out-bleaked by the bleaker future, which future she imagined as an enormous swamp from which a single stiff flagpole jutted at a jaunty angle with a tattered white pennant flying in the breeze and sporting the word "Bienvenue!" in some sort of elaborate Olde Timey serif, and that Dakotah's acquiescence to Grace's pleas for the continuing representation that Grace didn't even deep down want was (i.e., the acquiescence) tenuous at best, and so the conversation was, like every conversation the contemporary Grace Kitchen endured, nothing short of warfare between her self-annihilating ego and whatever tattered shreds of wisdom still osmosed within her brittle, crackling synapses.

But in the end she lived to suffer another day, fitting the receiver into its cradle and releasing a single breath that, although intended as a sigh, emerged from her belly as a long deathbed groan. It was 10PM and tomorrow was a teaching day and only Satan knew the exquisite tortures in store. She was profoundly unprepared for class, but her anxiety was hardly the product of this familiar irresponsibility but rather of the fact that it was only ten days to the faculty-wide meeting at which she was expected to officially throw her hat (a dunce cap, as she imagined it, or one of those helicopter beanies) into the tenure ring, declaring before 150 academics her intent to join them in institutional ensconcement and the soul death yearned for by anyone even vaguely acquainted with a soul's basic functionality. Her primary competition for this unwanted but desperately needed honor was Joyful Noise, a sclerotic dwarf-like creature with cyanotic skin and strong ties to the LGBTQIA community whose ethnicity, age, and gender were so impossible to determine that Grace had come to think of he/she/them as a sort of human-in-progress. Joyful's first novel, *Neck Deep in Wonder,* had been a finalist for the National Book Award, and they had built up steady capital at the college by insinuating, at every available opportunity, that the lack of faculty diversity was a dark cloud hanging over the administration's progressive agenda, and that they themself, Joyful Noise, was a form of preventative warfare against the many political accusations likely to be levied against the institution should Joyful Noise not be regularized, those accusations presumably to be levied by Joyful Noise.

She drained her wine glass and refilled. She lifted the invitation to her nose. It smelled like well-dressed ladies discussing their servants at society functions. It smelled like thin, muscled arms draped by sequined shawls in enormous ballrooms filled with silver and bronze. *Grace Kitchen, please join us for a celebration of your work.* But who would invite a writer to an event that did not *require* her participation? And what could "celebration" mean in this context? It was like a gag out of one of her books. She'd show up to a meatpacking plant and be ceremoniously provided a smock and butchering implements. Or she'd show up to a ballet performed with impeccable grace by costumed clowns, culminating (i.e., the ballet) in a rendition of Queen's *Bohemian Rhapsody* and her beheading. And yet she was in love with this invitation. She wanted to wrap her thighs around it, or chew on the vellum until it ejaculated something. She folded it in half and tucked it into the waistband of her sensible black skirt and hid the protruding portion beneath the hem of her blouse.

She reached into the cabinet above the stove and withdrew a bar of dark chocolate. She felt a presence in the quiet kitchen. She turned back toward the window. The thin white curtain trembled from the draft. If she pulled back that curtain now she'd find more than the moonlit yard; she was sure that something living and terrible lingered just beyond the glass, a great blood-soaked vulture with enormous tattered wings. A wave of nausea washed through her. She felt sweat materialize on her forehead. She opened the chocolate's wrapper to find a glistening black bar of onyx that seemed anything but edible. She placed it on a white ceramic plate and broke it into smaller pieces and rushed to her father's downstairs bedroom. He was sitting up in bed with his legs stretched out beneath the covers. A puddle of yellow light on the white bedspread. The oxygen tank beside the bed. He held the conical mask to his face with his left hand while his right hand worked the pen that worked the NY Times Magazine crossword puzzle that lay open on his lap. The oxygen hissed down his gullet and was spat back up moistened by his disease. He looked at Grace and took another deep breath from the mask.

"Luke," he said. Another breath. "I am your father."

"Hi Daddy," Grace said. She pulled herself onto the mattress and sat crisscross apple sauce. She extended him the plate. He took a square of the dark chocolate, removed the conical mask, and inserted the square into his purple maw before replacing the mask like a lid over his face. His skin was loose and so deeply wrinkled that entire micro-communities might thrive within its canyons but his eyes still bespoke mischief. Grace remembered him pushing her on a swing at a toddler park, inventing planets for her to orbit, warning her of the planet Earth, where billions of monsters gnashed their terrible teeth and consolidated their earnings to avoid taxes and fees. On each backswing he'd reached into her space capsule to tickle the front of her neck before sending her higher, Grace laughing with wild little girl hysteria. "Stop Daddy!" she screamed, by which of course she meant *Please don't ever stop or die like Mommy did.* She could still see him that way. No matter what time or his disease did to his body he would always be the endlessly enthusiastic protector who had given everything of himself to her and who had proudly identified her as his entire life, his one counterargument to homicide or suicide or omnicide.

"How are your legs tonight?" she asked.

"Comme ci comme ca," he said between breaths. She pulled back the covers. He wore a pair of athletic shorts made for a young person from which his hairless legs emerged streaked with sunbursts of color, purple and red and green.

"I'll rub them a little," she said.

He reached past her and turned the knob on the oxygen tank. The hissing stopped. "That can wait," he said. "Have you been working?"

Grace nodded.

He smiled. "I want to hear today's pages."

And so they passed another evening with chocolates dissolving in their warm mouths, the moonlight buffeting the house, Grace reading her latest work aloud to her enraptured father, the two of them cackling with their shared approval of her diseased mind.

7.

AT A VERY early age the boy had discovered the problem of causal determinism and renounced any lingering affection for the grim ontology through which he toiled. He had been standing on the bridge that led from his family's farmstead on the outskirts of Kecel, Hungary, to the town itself some three miles distant. These were hard times for his family, who in many respects lived as if it were 1878, not 1978. They did not, for instance, own an automobile. The boy had never seen a television. One night a week he was permitted to listen to the live music broadcasts on Hungarian Radio; his father thought electricity had a whiff of evil about it and so wandered the farmhouse after dark holding aloft a candelabra and emptying the mousetraps of their bloodless and twisted quarry. They were farmers but their profit margins were so narrow that it was often the case that either there was food to eat or there was money to continue producing food to eat, a harsh irony that had not failed to register on the boy. Oftentimes he would work long days beside his father before devouring a small meal of barley soup and sugar beets. He would lie awake at night on his straw mattress with his belly twisted in hunger and a cold draft hissing through the seams of a house built some hundred years earlier to prolong the brutish and short lives of peasants during the monarchy. If the house had a soul, it was a masochistic soul that savored every pain and lived only to spite the bitter earth that was eager to swallow it whole. Lately the boy's sleep had been frequently interrupted by his infant sister's shrill bleating, though the baby had been dead for many months. Maybe the house was now haunted by her tiny ghost or maybe the cries ascended from the boy's dreams or maybe the rats had again overtaken the barn to nibble on the soft ankle flesh of adolescent sheep. His father often lamented that they had been better off under Kadar but the boy only understood the political realities of his nation vaguely and skantwise. They were on their own, he knew, and that did not seem very good—but it didn't exactly require an enormous feat of the imagination to conceive of something far, far worse. The bridge was maybe thirty meters across and constructed of wide-plank cottonwood and it spanned the narrowest part of the river which in midsummer withered to a mere trickle but right now, in late fall, ran clear and fast. Mulberry trees provided shade at either end of the bridge but at the center of the span (where he now stood) the sunlight was warm and prickly and tasted vaguely of copper. He clutched a tangle of mulberry leaves in his left fist, releasing them over the railing one at a time to watch the clumsy spiraling descent enter suddenly into a controlled rush downstream. The stream's clarity was such that this change in speed and bearing was the only indication that the leaves had in fact touched down.

There was a bend in the waterway about twenty yards beyond the bridge and he tried to determine whether any given leaf would round that bend and remain adrift, or be ensnared by the eddy of leaves and other debris accumulating there at the elbow. He was running maybe a 75% success rate.

Roughly two of every three leaves undertook easily extrapolated routes, but the outlying cases—which neither hugged the interior tight nor rushed clearly toward safety—challenged the boy's powers of intuition in a way that made his entire body tingle. He felt in some strange, almost religious way that his guessing must have some effect on the outcome; when he was right it was because he *made* it happen the way he guessed, and when he was wrong… well, he must not have been concentrating hard enough. He was a strange boy, or so his father often said after hours from within the wicked glow of the candelabra, musing quietly aloud as if he (the boy) were incapable of understanding human language. The mulberries grew crookedly from the banks and traced an image for the boy of the old arthritic sheepdog they'd put down not three weeks earlier. The blast of his father's shotgun had resounded out across the steppes to make its way around the earth and when his father returned to the house the boy thought that his father had perhaps been crying, which was no more unprecedented on planet Earth than teleportation or the resurrection of the dead. His father had not cried even when his baby girl finally perished with a fever so intense that hours after death the body still emanated warmth. They buried her out behind the two rusted and retired horse ploughs (they *did* have motorized farm equipment, though his father had apparently resisted it for many long and unreasonable years), where the earth was softer and where they could embed the little molar-shaped stone etched with her name and the dates and the blessing. The boy himself would dig the hole for the dog (which had been called "Kutya") not 15 meters from that stone. He, too, had loved the dog in a way he had not loved the baby, because the baby ought to have been stillborn (so said the doctor) and there was never any hope for her and both he and his father kept their distance and allowed Mother to revel in her grief unfettered by theirs, whereas the boy had often curled up on the kitchen's stone floor and told Kutya adventure stories of his (i.e., the boy's) imagined life as a world traveler and protector of the meek and had made of the dog a friend and companion. The boy was supposed to be on his way to town right now for flour and sugar and coffee but the leaves were a problem he could not surrender. He dropped another. It was an easy one—bearing hard left and toward the clear water. A question posed itself: Was it already decided whether or not the *next* leaf, the one still clutched in his fist, would safely clear the bend? Or whether or not he would drop the next leaf at all?

In the time it took to blink an explosion of thoughts left bright shrapnel throbbing in his skull. Had his sister asked to die? No, she'd been taken. Had he asked to be born? No, he'd been birthed, and then the world had gone to work on him. Certain lessons were received. A hand on a stove taught "hot"; a slap on a wrist taught "no"; a dark closet taught "do not test us." He was becoming something new at every moment, but it had nothing to do with *him*. If all the inputs had been different—if grabbing a meringue from a countertop had resulted in laughter rather than punishment, if crying in his room had been met with consolation rather than abuse, if his father were motivated by pleasure rather than fear, then the manipulated object—in this case him—would be different, too. But wait… if this were true of him then it was also true of the inputs one level up. His father's suspiciousness, his mother's stoicism and quiet grief, his sister's tortured wailing, these were the products of other inputs that were received like-it-or-not. The infinite cascade implied in this reasoning occurred instantaneously. No one *chose* to be the way they were. He stood on the bridge and held leaves in his sweaty fist and the light flowed around him like a second and more sublime river and the breeze tousled his dark hair. He had not chosen this. The inputs led here. There were only inputs… they went on and on and on. He thought of Kutya leaping through a pigsty with an absurd and unfounded joy that had roused a boom of laughter from his father's enormous lungs. This tableau and all of its intricacies—the tusk of spittle hanging from Kutya's jaws, the black shadow of the feed trough, the iron weather vane atop the barn pointing northward, one enormous sow raising her snout and *growling,* the dust kicked up into a funnel as if Kutya were in the business of raising demons—this entire collection of inputs arrived to his small brain because it *had* to. The world was encoded but we could never know the code. Everything was finished before the fact. A bead of sweat achieved critical mass and broke like a ball bearing down the boy's temple and onto his cheek. He blinked.

But so if it was true that his decision to play the game with the leaves (and, naturally, his decision to now think about the decision to play the game with the leaves, and so on *ad infinitum*) had been determined by a massive, innumerable collection of past inputs and if those inputs had been similarly rendered necessary by those further past, then, the boy wondered, *how was it true that he was somebody?*

He was nine years old and all at once the world became impregnable to his will. He was not a free-roaming creature but a ball on a track, and the track would lead wherever it was always going to lead regardless (or because?) of the fact of his so-called existence. Whatever was going to happen would happen! If God was light, then this new revelation was the air through which God moved. The feeling he had on the cusp of every decision, the tingle of what he'd always thought of as free will, was itself absorbed into the larger substructure of a universe totally determined by first conditions.

So maybe he would jump from the bridge?

Just ten minutes earlier the thought would have been (as the saying went) *unthinkable,* and yet from this new position he realized—among countless other realizations percolating liquid-like through his skull—that every thought was unthinkable right up until the moment it was destined to be thought, so that the boy on the bridge asking the question "Will I jump from this bridge?" was always as inevitable as the boy jumping (or not jumping) from the bridge had been or now was, regardless of how likely or unlikely either eventuality might seem from a purely objective standpoint which of course was not something possible (i.e., objectivity) for humans who had no greater access to the necessary course the universe would take than a squirrel or chicken. A tiny, fast-receding part of himself was tempted to believe that jumping would somehow release him from the causal chain, as if the universe had decided he should not jump and he might spite its hubris, but no… if jumping was in the cards he would jump. He squeezed the remaining mulberry leaves in his fist and felt their cell walls crack and ooze chlorophyll into his dark palm. He opened his fist and a few shreds fell to the bridge planks while others remained affixed to his moist skin. He lifted a knee to the railing and pulled himself up and sat on his ass on the cold, dry beam with his legs swinging out and back above the river. Clouds fanned out high above the steppes, shaped like radio waves. He listened hard for their music but nothing came. If he was going to jump he would! Nothing could stop it and nothing could make it happen. Their farm was failing; their bellies were empty; his sister's tiny body was rotting in the earth; Kutya's favorite toy, a ball made of old kitchen rags and bound tight with tape, remained lodged beneath the pine boards at the threshold to the barn and it would remain there until somebody or something moved it. He and his father and his mother would all die, too, and the moment of each of these deaths was prearranged by what he couldn't really call God anymore because God had been That Which Intervenes and he now needed a new word, something for That Which Made Intervention Impossible. He put his feet down on the several inches of planking that protruded beyond the railing. It was maybe twenty-five or thirty feet down. The water was crystal clear and, he imagined, very cold. It didn't seem like a fall that could kill a person. Pebbles along the bottom gleamed, each intricately streaked with a pattern unique to itself. The stones were arranged exactly how they had to be. He thought, *Now is when I jump.* His arms extended out along the railing and his outstretched fingers dug in beneath the board. The universe itself had a shelf life that was also predetermined. It would burn out. How did he know this? He was only nine years old but he knew it. "Now is when I jump," he said. He gripped the railing. He counted to three. He had only held his baby sister once and she had curled into him, sucking a thumb no bigger than a raisin. She was released now from the cold machinery of space and time. He leaned forward in his cage. He counted again to three. The wind, the sun, the sublime whisper of the running stream. *Now is when I jump.*

8.

Day Two of Sectionals, or *Sunday Bloody Sunday,* as Jack had dubbed it the previous evening at a team dinner held at an Italian chain where the waitstaff wore costumes in honor of a Halloween still impending, this eagerness toward masquerade the result of some series of dares and promises that Finn struggled to parse based on the scatterbrained remarks of the waitress in the sexy nurse outfit whose exposed parts had apparently lured Jack to whereabouts-as-yet-unrevealed, which had been unfortunate given that Finn was staying at Jack's parents' house so as to save hotel fare because—rumors of a professional league be damned—no one was subsidizing his participation in The Sport That Was Not Soccer, and Finn was after all a lowly grad student living on a modest stipend that was barely keeping Toby in sexy underclothes, and if Toby did not herself participate in the Women's Division of TSTWNS and did not thereby belong to the infinitesimal subset of attractive female humans capable of being moved or impressed by the exploits of elite-level male participants in said sport (she was basically in awe of Finn's high step-around backhand) she would be yet one more unattainable desire for Finn Daily, whose less comely traits—some of which may yet be revealed—had sparked female aversion on a pretty consistent basis for many years prior to his Ultimate (though not ultimate) ascension. And now he sat with his ass squeezed into the little dish of an inverted 175g. UltraStar so as to avoid the still-dewy grass, pulling on his cleats and trying to run through his primary visualizations but haunted, in a manner of speaking, by the events of the prior evening. Two teammates tossed a disc back and forth as Finn laced up. It was a cold morning and his breath hung suspended like little clouds of flour. The sun had risen and if history was any indication the chill would lift by halftime of the first round, set to begin one hour thence. The teammates were performing some sort of pantomime, dropping every thrown disc in an increasingly exaggerated and clown-like fashion. They blew on their hands between throws. Finn smiled. He felt like he might vomit. He'd slept roughly zero hours last night, which could only exacerbate the constipation that was one of his many Sunday-morning-Ultimate nemeses, and there was no way he'd be able to move his bowels in one of the foul-smelling shell-casings rising from the turf so that by the time they reached the Finals (which was all but guaranteed unless a tornado snaked through the tournament site and picked off, selectively, the best 15 members of *Truck Stop Glory Hole*) and faced down their best but still deeply inferior local com-petition (*Ass Bone*), his intestines would be slipknotted into unkind shapes familiar to him from the dozens of previous tournaments that had similarly challenged his delicate con-stitution. The teammates tossed the disc through the cool air, cars pulled by the dozen into the gravel lot adjoining the field, the dark sky turned bluer, a few clouds clipped from a children's book on clouds materialized from nothing, dis-crete groups of vultures huddling together as if preparing to square off in a parallel tournament of their own design. Finn smiled self-consciously in a way that suggested—to whatever invisible overseer oversaw him now and at all times—that he was *in his natural element.*

Four games yesterday, indistinguishable from one another and from all previous iterations at bygone tournaments. Sport, Finn knew, *was* repetition, as evidenced (in part) by post-game podium interviews featuring celebrity athletes in the afterglow of competition whose bromide responses to the half-dozen questions that comprised (i.e., the questions) the entirety of the sports-interview milieu were made no less predictable by their infinite permutations, subtleties, inflections, etc., and really Finn felt sorry for certain members of the so-called press whose glassy eyes bespoke a deep and soul-numbing disappointment, as if they wondered—at night in the dark beside sleeping women who would no longer abide the touch of their grimy newsprint hands—how their journalism careers could have descended to this Beckettian theater of sport, where nothing had not been said before and where the same set of primitive brain-stem responses emerged from the mouths of an ever-shifting army of billionaire-athletes who had, through some senseless benevolence, used their insane genetic advantages to play a game rather than enslave the populace. It was absurd that Finn and his teammates imagined themselves as part of this paradigm, given that they lacked both the genetic advantages and the billions of dollars. But it was fun—and necessary, Finn knew—to have something to pursue. A title, a trophy, greatness at the far side of a crucible of doubt—it all helped create the illusion of a pattern or a purpose. He blew into his hands and stood to do a few jump-stars before embarking on a much-needed warmup jog, reliving the events of the past twelve hours, and reassessing the datums to which he had been made privy at his unstable and sort-of-terrifying teammate Jack Dregs' boyhood home.

They'd soared away from that team dinner and its costumed sex-puppets in Jack's old beater, the engine screaming in agony as they snaked down dark roads known intimately to Jack, roads that hugged old-growth forest from whose interior skinny deer and plump marmots stepped gingerly to pause in the car's headlights as if considering difficult problems of philosophy or maybe just performing the same cost/benefit analysis on suicide familiar to all enlightened creatures and Jack (being Jack) had without fail accelerated toward these vagrants with Finn bracing for impact, teeth bared and neck muscles straining, and this went on for about 5,000 hours though when they arrived at Jack's home out beyond some old grain silos in seemingly desolate country but apparently, according to the driver, located within shouting distance of the friendly little northern hamlet of Hard Falls, the dashboard clock suggested that a mere 20 minutes had passed.

"Here you are," Jack had said. "Curbside service."

Finn looked out upon the dark house in the middle of the void. "Wait," he said. "We're here, right?"

"You're here, Daily. I'm going back for the sexy nurse."

"Jack, I don't even know where the fuck I am."

"I've noticed that about you." He chewed at his cheek. He looked angry, actually.

"Well… but when will you be back? I can't get to the fields."

"After today that could be for the best."

"Christ! It was one fucking drop!"

"What drop?"

"Look Jack, I don't want to stay with *your* parents. It's fucking weird."

"I thought so too. You're an odd guy, Finn." Jack seemed to think he'd made a major concession for which he ought to be embarrassed. He averted his eyes and clucked his tongue, looking far out beyond the windshield and beyond the house and beyond the scythe-shaped moon, into an immeasurable distance where sexy nurses in a variety of colors and flavors turned sexy pirouettes as they awaited the opportunity to mount him.

"Call my cell," Jack said. "Say hi to my 'rents. Touch my mom and you're fucking dead."

As if in a dream Finn had grabbed his gear bag from the backseat, opened his door, and stepped into the night. He was still eyeing the front door suspiciously when Jack floored it, tires spitting gravel and the car going the way of all things Finn had ever needed. He stared after it lustfully, the pulsing brake lights occasionally visible through various arbors and the engine's scream fading anticlimactically into the stupid world.

"Fucker," he muttered with the pretend bravado that he hoped would save him. He turned houseward and a sudden cramp gripped his calf muscle and he fell to his ass writhing like something tasered. He flexed his ankle in a mad attempt to unlock the cramp which was not an unusual Saturday night phenomenon—Finn often cramped up after a full day of TSTWNS despite trying everything prescribed, from potassium supplements to increased salt intake to quaffing insane quantities of electrolytes via everyone's favorite sports drink, to stretching during and between games, to Icy Hot to neoprene wraps to Theraband exercises. Remedies could gain no purchase on his gangly, delicate body. He thrashed in the gravel cursing God and country and wondering if he'd remembered to pack any Xanax (for the anxiety, not the cramping) in his little toiletry pouch, and he was just reaching for his bag to search the relevant compartments, unleashing profanities upon the cold dark of this supposed suburb, when the front door swung open to breathe forth a cone of yellowish light and reveal a woman—Jack's mom, he presumed—standing in the frame in a long silky bathrobe, silently absorbing the particularities of this unexpected contretemps. Because she was backlit Finn could only tell that her face had sharp angles. She seemed almost goblin-like.

"Hey!" Finn had blurted. "I'm Jack's friend!" He moved to stand and the cramp bit again. He dropped onto his back and screamed, "Fuck!" He reached for his toe and pulled at it and when he looked again the front door had closed.

More players arrived, rising groggily from compact cars adorned by politically left-leaning bumper stickers and standard peacenik fare as Finn began to jog the field's perimeter, skirting vultures and passing close by his teammates who were still clownishly dropping discs and then Finn realized they were imitating *his* drop from yesterday's final game, which would have been the game-winner had he not clapped his hands down to pancake the thing only to have it pop spinning into the air so that he could snatch at it awkwardly a few times and multiply his embarrassment before it hit the turf. They were up by nine or ten goals at the time… it was fodder for hazing, nothing more. But Finn was still hurt by the meanness of it, and he knew that being hurt so easily was itself the reason he would fail again, and soon, because knowing he could be hurt by failing built itself, like a nuclear feedback loop, into greater and more failure.

This was the kind of thing that the God Fractal could not account for. Caring. Pain. Need. It could not account for what it felt like to live.

Meanwhile he could still smell Jack's mom's perfume. He'd finally stepped into the house to find her on her cell phone, in the center of what may once have been the living room but had been co-opted, it seemed, by MENSA representatives on crack. "Forget it," she said into the phone. "It's not him." A pause. "Yeah, I get it, you really like fucking. Would you stop being so *Italian* for a minute?" She held the phone away from herself and Finn could hear a man's voice shouting high-speed gibberish and then she terminated the call.

"Hey," Finn said. "I'm Jack's friend Finn?"

"Does it say other things?"

"Ha ha," he laughed, in a way that begged the laugh's recipient to be charmed. He made a pistol with his thumb and index finger and pretended to blow his brains out. "Sorry. I'm staying over with Jack."

She made a show of looking around his body, over his shoulder, through his legs. She raised her eyebrows.

"He had to run an errand," Finn said.

"I thought you were my husband." She crossed one arm below her chest and rested her remaining elbow on it, her hand dangling in a pose that suggested a cigarette.

"But Jack told you we were coming, right?"

"I haven't heard from my son in two months. The shit missed my birthday. You must be one of his little curling pals." She looked him up and down and rolled out her neck.

She was pretty for an older woman, and young to be Jack's mom. She was also sort of scary-looking. Her cheekbones looked like they could split you open like a deli slicer. How her behemoth mongrel of a son had squeezed from her tiny womb was anyone's guess.

Finn tried out seven or eight different smiles but said nothing. She looked at him with undisguised contempt. Finally he tried, "Ultimate. That's what we play. Ultimate Frisbee?"

She grunted. "What position do you play in *Ultimate Frisbee?*"

"I'm a handler," Finn said.

"I seriously doubt that."

"Ha."

She stared at him, waiting for who knew what. Then she surrendered hope. "You can sleep in Jack's room," she said. "Upstairs, second door on the right. If I were you I wouldn't expect him back." She turned and headed for the stairs with her robe billowing out behind her. Finn wondered if it concealed a tail. He was basically terrified, standing in the middle of a strange room littered with end tables and plastic chairs stacked high with old-school computer paper printouts (the kind with the tear-off ring-strips running down each side) and handwritten notes and assorted high-school variety science paraphernalia—spindly molecular models and several upended microscopes and what looked like a soldering iron and a huge box of Legos some of which had been fashioned into little Lego robots mounted by nine-volt batteries and little motors—and on the wall above the thing most closely resembling a desk (atop which a badass computer hummed in sleep mode) was a poster of the human anatomy with arrows drawn in black directing all attention to the plum-shaped heart at the body's center, which was itself scrawled over in bold red with the single word "WARLORD."

Finn checked his watch. Already 10PM. Lots of Ultimate to be played tomorrow. The cramp had withdrawn deeper into his muscle where it twitched ominously. The light in the room seemed brownish. All the dark particle-board furniture and the waxy hardwood and the mauve sofa with its dark continents of stains. He looked at the stack of papers nearest him, leaning upward from a cutting board that bridged two milk crates. It had a date on it, printouts of numbers in rows and columns—Finn's heart stirred at the beautiful numbers!—with notes scrawled in red ink between columns. "More data required." "Based on conservative estimates of the Gold Coast reservoir." He knew he should call Toby, whose team (*The Atomic Bitches*) was at their own Sectionals tournament held at a location some 50 miles distant. Instead he moved a stack of papers from a chair and sat down at the computer desk and nudged the mouse. The screen leapt to life in blinding color. Finn was looking at a map of Eastern Europe. He moved the cursor and clicked and zoomed down toward Poland, the landscape rising up with an almost absurd level of detail and activating certain enzyme nozzles deep inside Finn's brain, his view sliding down the snow-capped Carpathians into a deep valley and then the surface cracked open and he was *inside the earth* and the screen grew darker, striations of brown and silver and flecks of gold accenting the black underworld while in the top right corner of the screen words flashed in bright blue: CARPATHIAN COAL POCKET. He clicked on the words and more information appeared.

He rolled the mouse back and was ascending again, pulling out of Eastern Europe and then receding further to see the Atlantic Ocean appear and expand as the continents emerged tan and cross-hatched, and then receding further still to see the earth spinning there on the screen in all its familiar and bankrupted majesty. INPUT LOCATION, said the text box at the bottom of the screen. He heard the upstairs floorboards creak and he leapt from the chair. He laughed instinctively. He was sweating. His grad school advisor had warned him about the tedium of lab work, about the rareness of actual discovery. This same advisor had only recently called Finn's work on the God Fractal "interesting but useless," reinforcing Finn's belief that life in mathematics would ultimately entail a kind of soul-death that TSTWNS could not fend off for very long, as evidenced by the Masters Division geezers betumored by their many ice-packs. But this work seemed sort of cool. And a little crazy. Maybe Jack's dad was a secret genius? He moved now to the back of the house, pausing at the archway to the kitchen and puzzling over a series of Tibetan prayer flags. "Who the fuck are you people?" he asked aloud. In the kitchen he ran the faucet and splashed water over his face, sloughing off the salt and grime of a full day's participation in TSTWNS. He took a long drink straight from the tap. The kitchen smelled musty and strange. There were people *everywhere,* doing every imaginable thing. He was one of them! He was a person standing in an unfamiliar kitchen from whose ceiling a ceiling fan dangled and from which ceiling fan a Barbie doll dangled further still, hooded and cinctured about the neck by the cutest little noose. Finn took a breath. It was really fucking quiet. He stepped to the back door and peered from its window, where if he pushed his cheek right against its surface he could see the bright sickle-shaped moon hovering. He walked back to the MENSA room and stared at the earth's image. He sat again. He moved the cursor over North America and clicked, and again he was descending, this time over the washed-out permafrost ridges of Saskatchewan, beneath which lay oil, natural gas, gold, copper, magnesium, all of which—if he understood what he was experiencing—had been exhausted decades ago.

He had no idea how much time had passed when he heard tires on the gravel, and then footsteps on the stairs. Mrs. Dregs rushed toward him, this time with her robe open. She had breasts. She had nipples. She had pubic hair. He registered these facts in the same way he'd only moments earlier registered Kazakhstan's copious uranium deposits. "Jack's back," he heard himself say. He looked down and massaged his arm rigorously and grimaced as if attending to pain. He realized he was at Jack's dad's computer without permission and thought her nakedness was an unusual form of punishment for this seemingly harmless offense.

"No, Jack's Friend," she said. "It's my husband." And she took his hand and led him toward the stairs. Finn resisted half-heartedly. He felt his eyes skittering in their skull-pockets. He had no idea what was happening.

"I work with fractals," he said. Then he was climbing upward toward a bedroom that was definitely not Jack's.

TEAMS WERE FLOWING out onto the fields now in all the familiar patterns, in rings and phalanxes, in trapezoids and rhombuses and other configurations conducive to *drilling*, which it was funny to watch teams with no chance at all of notching a single victory even at this low-rung tournament going through the motions of *improving themselves*. Finn sometimes imagined bigger stronger athletes going over to the weaker smaller athletes, clubbing them to death, and eating them. *Truck Stop Glory Hole* was taking its time getting organized. Finn scanned the parking lot again. He raised a finger to his nose. Yes, Jack's mom's smell was still there. A pang of guilt panged away, along with a new wave of arousal that, goddamit, just would not be reasoned with.

She'd called him "Jack's Friend" through the whole thing.

Finn had stopped jogging and was now on the ground, legs extended, pulling on his toes. A long shadow was approaching from behind. It went on and on in the early morning sunlight. Finally Jack sat down beside him, his block-like feet strapped into a pair of sandals and his aviators reflecting the green turf and the lightening sky and the young men moving with purpose.

"Mornin' Jack," Finn said. (Here he is cutting up the line; here he is offering his erection to the thin mouth of the angular middle-aged mother of a sociopath; here he is dropping the disc in the endzone.)

They sat there in silence. Their captains were beginning to rally the troops. "Five minutes to scrimmage!" they were screaming. It seemed funny to Finn. He imagined women at a bridal shower screaming the same thing, or children at a birthday party, or doctors performing surgery. *The Carpathian Coal Pocket. The Saskatchewan Timber Fields. The Iranian Oil Reserves. The North American Steel Stria.* Exhausted, exhausted, exhausted, exhausted.

"So how'd you get here Daily?" Jack asked.

"Cab. Cost me forty bucks you fucker."

"You met my mom."

"For a minute. She says hey. How'd it go with the nurse?"

Jack laughed. "That's exactly right, Daily," he said. "How the fuck did it go with the nurse!" He placed his duffel bag between himself and Finn and began rummaging around for his cleats. Finn did not look up, but he sensed that Jack was salivating.

Here he is dead in a trench of mud with Jack spitting down on his body. Here he is begging forgiveness at Toby's feet while she beats on him with a claw hammer. Here he is at the center of the earth, moving through dusty caverns filled with nothing at all. Here he is, dropping another disc.

9.

South Korean AI Lab Personnel Mysteriously Vanish

IKSAN, SOUTH KOREA: Members of the Artificial Intelligence (AI) community were shocked to discover that Iksan's Consciousness Factory—long considered the world's most advanced forum for work in robotics and AI—has been unexpectedly shuttered and abandoned. The discovery was made accidentally when a fellow group of AI enthusiasts operating out of MIT's Media Lab attempted to contact the South Koreans to arrange a friendly visit, only to find that all traces of the Consciousness Factory had been swept from the Internet. Further investigation has revealed that offices and administrative areas of the Factory have been vandalized and looted and that the underground hangar where the Factory's cutting edge work in robotics is (or had been) done, has been magnetically sealed through the use of a highly complex cryptograph that may also be a detonating device. "We are all shocked and worried," said Mitchell Resnick, head of the MIT Media Lab's Lifelong Kindergarten division. "I've interacted with these scientists for years, ever since they designed our robot maid Kandi, who has provided solace to our male graduate students for many semesters. [The scientists] never gave any indication that they might suddenly disappear from the earth and expunge all databases of their prior existence." Resnick refused to speculate further, though he did comment that the South Koreans are notoriously protective of their data. Police are involved in the search for their whereabouts, while a team of lawyers debate national and international rights and protocols for entering the Consciousness Factory's underground workspaces by force.

Stuart sat at his desk in a basement lab that might have made a good destination-point for an extrajudicial rendition. Curious-looking black mold spread from cracks in the plaster. Exposed pipes released a slow and steady rain of atomized rust. Fluorescent lights flickered a never-ending S–O–S. Steam pipes banged suddenly and unpredictably to life, as if some enormous demon were taking a few more of the occasional footsteps that would eventually lead it to the lab itself where it might find something unshaven and sexually frustrated to eat. He knew one of those South Koreans. Gunn-woo Kim. They'd done some course work together at Tufts. The bastard had built a robot that could comb human hair and then volunteered himself during an exhibition that Dennett had called "extraordinary." Then he dropped out of the graduate program to return to his homeland and leverage his second-to-none proficiency with parallel-mind processing into big money and tiny fame. Some part of Stuart knew this information was more important than the article suggested. He deposited another chip into his mouth. Three-hundred ingredients mass-produced in steel vats somewhere along the New Jersey Turnpike sizzled on his tongue. He scratched his groin. He ran his greasy hand over his mostly-bald scalp. He stood and hopped around the lab like a portly chimpanzee. He made the chimp-noises and everything. You could do this sort of thing when you worked in isolation. In fact maybe you had to. Of course there was the video camera in the corner farthest from his workstation, with its single red-lit eye turned perpetually toward him. But if anyone was reviewing that footage Stuart would have been terminated (or institution-alized) long before now. He sat again and googled "Iksan" and googled "Consciousness Factory" and googled "robot maid" and then he made the mistake of googling himself, and discovering what Bea had done.

10.

Laszlow of course had taken up his usual place of honor in the reclining chair they'd rescued from a dumpster out on Allen Street during routine recruitment and reconnaissance and that now sat dead center in the basement theater where several times a week the local chapter convened to enjoy one of the several entertainments that Laszlow insisted were vital contributions to the *Exit Strategy* movement, whether or not the filmmakers openly promoted the extinction of the human race (or related ES objectives). The reclining chair was upholstered in green velour and smelled like cheese and its springs creaked with every small adjustment. In the twenty or thirty folding chairs arranged haphazardly on the scuffed tiles and roughly facing the projection screen at the north end of the room sat those ES members whose dearth of afflictions permitted the descent into, and later, the ascent from, these receptacles. Laszlow referred to these seatable comrades as his "Googles," some of whom could run searches for 12 or even 16 hours at a stretch in service to the never-ending ES recruitment campaign. The more advanced paralytics and Stage 5 invalids and one burn victim whose face was so ridiculous that even Laszlow had trouble holding the young man (or woman)'s gaze stuck to their wheelchairs, some of which were outfitted with breathing apparatuses or speech-simulator software or other gadgetry. Each sought whatever approximated comfort in his private world of bone and needles. On this particular evening they were watching the Primary Entertainment, which if there was anything in the Exit Strategy iconography that might count as holy this was it. There was popcorn. They actually had one of those old-fashioned popcorn thingies on wheels where the corn popped behind glass and you scooped it into paper bags labeled POPCORN!, which yes they had those too. Several dozen of Exit Strategy's finest, gathered on a Thursday in late October with Grace Kitchen's visit a mere two days thence, enjoying the benefits of membership.

"Shhhh!" Laszlow said into a room already silent with rapt admirers and those incapable of human speech. "Here it comes," he whispered, one hand held aloft with a popcorn kernel held between thumb and index finger. The projected man adjusted his dark glasses. "You're not actually mammals," the man, *the Agent*, said. In the basement, five attending Fergusons tweaked their own dark shades in emulation of the divine figure cast weakly upon the white wall. They watched Laszlow watch the film. "Wait for it," Laszlow whispered Herzog-like.

"There is one other species that behaves this way," the Agent said, unable to suppress a contempt that was equaled in intensity by Laszlow's mirth. A pause. Silence in the basement, aside from the hiss of artificial breath and the rubber scuff of crutches on the tile.

"You are a *virus*," the Agent said.

Hoorah! The cheers erupted! And also coughing, moaning, inarticulate gibberish, the entire range of Exit Strategy enthusiasm filling the basement room in the brick building on the city block in the teeming metropolis made great by the labor of millions upon millions of unknowable souls. "A virus!" Laszlow screamed. He pointed to the invalid on his left. "A virus!" He pointed to the advanced ALS patient forever struggling to breathe on his right. "A virus!" He pointed to the Fergusons endeavoring to keep their faces neutral despite various tics and twitches. "A virus!" Then finally to himself. "Virus! Virus! Virus!" with a wild rumpus of unbridled fervor bouncing madly from the walls.

11.

The diagnosis was not immediately devastating. In fact, Henry felt something like enthusiasm rush through him. *It's really happening,* he thought. He was sitting in a light brown leather armchair on the visiting side of a dark brown desk. On the home side hovered a neurologist charged with delivering the news before running off to keep an appointment to play squash at Rittenhouse Square. Henry knew about the squash because he'd been left alone in the office for several long minutes and found the event scheduled in a spiral-bound black-leather appointment book situated dead center on the otherwise empty desk. The light in the room was both warm and masculine. It seemed as if fox hunters might enter any moment and shelve their muskets. A desk lamp glowed green, its glass shade stirring in Henry a long-forgotten memory of his father's tackle box sparkling with fishing lures of a thousand hues, and also less distant memories of the green-metal plaque hung crookedly in his graduate school adviser's office, announcing to the brilliant dullards pursuing the PhD in Philosophy that across from them sat a man who, despite his complete lack of social intelligence and rank breath, had been recognized by other earthly misfits for his esoteric contributions to the life of the mind. "There are a lot of new medications," the doctor was saying. "We might be able to slow it down a bit. You could live five years maybe." *Janet should be here for this,* he thought. And then again: *It's really happening.*

He knew there were important questions to ask. He remembered the movie where the man who gave his disease its common pseudonym tells a stadium full of people that he considers himself the luckiest man who ever lived. Henry didn't feel lucky. He also didn't feel unlucky. Two nights ago he'd made love to his ex-wife. They had not been together in nearly five years, but it had been so familiar and sweet and true. He could still smell traces of her sweat. He was 52 years old and it was really happening.

"This is hardly the end," the neurologist with the squash appointment was saying. "But for now I'd like to set you up with some counseling. There are lots of support groups and some experimental treatments. Some studies. Lots of resources. You won't have to go through this alone." There was a framed print behind the doctor, over his (i.e., the doctor's) left shoulder. It showed a ballerina seated on a bench, head bowed, beside an austere-looking woman dressed in black. It seemed so clearly to Henry to be a painting of Death, which was maybe not the most thoughtful or auspicious choice for an office where news such as the news he was currently receiving was delivered with some regularity by invincible medicine-men posing as ordinary humans, who inflicted their practiced sympathies upon whatever ailing meat-bag was next destined to perish, unable to disguise their need to get out into the sunshine and play some fucking squash already. Henry was suddenly sweating a lot. It poured from his hairline. It soaked his armpits. The numbness in his left leg suddenly felt like a living ecosystem. But what was he *supposed* to think? The doctor made a supreme effort to appear patient but his body was wound like a spring. It was overcast outside, Henry knew from the muted light contained within the darkly patterned curtains. *It's really happening.* He'd been considering his own inevitable death since he was a small boy. It had always seemed to be hauling him toward itself, as if he were a wrecked truck at the hook-end of a winch. Why was he less terrified now than at any other point?

Janet moved back in. It was like they'd never split up. The kids—young women now, both of them—were ecstatic and behaved as if this were the reunion everyone had wanted and now sweet life could resume in its sweet way. Henry insisted that the children be tested and pretended at enormous relief when they showed no genetic predisposition for the disease, though in reality some part of him had hoped they would. It was the same part that rooted for extremely high death counts in the wake of natural disasters. The part that for whatever reason wanted Death to spread its fucking wings already and show what it was really capable of. But no, no, of course he was happy the girls would not suffer in the way he was about to suffer. (They would suffer in their own perfect ways.) Both had been unconscionable accidents but without them his mostly meaningless life would have been entirely meaningless, which when he wasn't in the business of reducing his feelings to chemical exchanges in a brain that wanted only to continue thinking and cared nothing for forces outside its own electrical skull-box, he recognized as what the poets called "love." (Was it any wonder Janet had left him?) He and Janet talked in bits and shards about certain necessities. There'd be a wheelchair at some point, though for now he could walk with a cane. "You're a distinguished gentleman," she said. He decided he would keep teaching until he couldn't anymore. He vowed to remain rational. He began telling friends and family, with a certain desperation he despised hearing in his own voice, that the moment he began *praying* or talking in even vaguely religious terms was the moment he had taken leave of them; they should take this rational self speaking to them here and now as the true measure of his stance on a hostile and unforgiving universe, and ignore whatever gibberish-spouting human emerged from the pitted bowels of a disease that had reduced men greater than himself to mystics.

Janet cried a lot at night and she held on to him tightly as if he knew the way through a darkness that led only into deeper darkness. They would fail to navigate it just as they had all the other ostensibly shared challenges of life and marriage. (Joseph Conrad: "We each die as we have lived: alone.") It was difficult to believe that this warmhearted, pliant Janet was the same woman who had withheld sex from him for years at a time and allowed her resentments to fester to the point that she'd become more compost-barrel than woman. But just as he had to admit that his feelings for his children were *something,* so too did he realize that Janet was the only real adventure he'd ever had and that yes, he loved her, he'd always loved her and now for the first time he found himself trying to express that factoid via the slippery English language. But feelings continued to embarrass him. He read her a poem one night, awkwardly. (Philip Larkin. *In times that nothing stood / but worsened, or grew strange / there was one constant good: / she did not change.*) They planned a last trip together that they did not call a last trip, to Italy, Henry's ancestral homeland. He was expected to live another 3 or 4 years and the disease hadn't progressed much since the diagnosis, but then it flared rapidly through his nervous system so that in the month between planning the trip and the embarkation date his arms had become completely paralyzed and he could walk only in a Frankenstein-like shuffle, half-bent at the waist with his arms swinging like enormous sausages, and so the trip was "postponed" and he took a "leave of absence" from the University and his medications were doubled and then tripled and then quadrupled all to little avail and then the respirator was brought in and attached to the wheelchair and he donned the little skull-cap from whose sides the nostril-inhalers dangled and plans were made for when he could no longer swallow food which they hoped was still many months away. It was, in a manner of speaking, *on*.

Around this time he began having the dream. He was dragging a Hefty bag stuffed with the gore of a body he had hacked to pieces through a labyrinth of unlit alleyways, the bag hissing loudly against the cobbled pavement and the liquid collecting at its bottom as he beseeched the plastic *please don't break* with sweat pouring from him and a bone-white moon gleaming coldly until finally he arrived at a destination unknown to his waking self and heaved the whole sloshing grotesquery into a black dumpster before noticing a homeless man against a wall, his legs twitching on the cobblestones as he watched Henry unburden himself of his freight. The homeless man was touched at his edges by the hot pink light of a neon sign that protruded from the building above him, its cursive letters spelling a word that Henry couldn't quite make out and that didn't seem to be English. He would move through

the generally mundane remainder of the dream terrified that
his crime would be discovered, a terror that took as its focal
point the possibility of imprisonment or vengeance but that
contained within itself the other, more abstract repercussions
that all pathological liars and frauds haul on their backs every
hour of every day. The dream felt familiar in a way unknown
to him from his five decades of dreaming and he began to
convince himself that it was no fiction, that he had been suppressing or repressing or sublimating (or whatever the clinical
term might be) the memory of this very real event for these
many years, which maybe this accounted for his unease with
the so-called easy things in life, his tendency to shy from
crowds and from questions, the trepidation he'd always felt
in the most ordinary circumstances. He would wake with
the buzz of the hacksaw still stinging in his palms before
remembering that in fact he had no feeling in his hands and
that he was now mostly paralyzed. That he was helpless and
supine. That he was being force-fed his own breath. That he
would never again lift a spoon to his mouth or tie a shoe or
caress a cat's soft fur.

Would you like to go for a walk today?

Would you like some coffee?

In the mornings Janet wheeled him into their glass sun
room and he searched the woods that cinctured their property
for foraging deer, the light on his face igniting itch-circuitry
throughout his body which he endured without complain-
ing or asking to be moved because at least the itchiness was
a *feeling*. The clouds drifted through a sky utterly devoid of
meaning or message as the disease sparked and sizzled, as if
his ganglia were long fuses each leading toward the gunpowder keg of his heart, and Janet whistled in the next room as

she loaded the coffee machine and moved through a private world of remembrance and anticipation and fear and wanting before returning to him with the happy face that sustained her.

Would you like to take a walk today?

Would you like me to turn the pillow?

The support groups did not help, and although he continued to comment in online forums (using the voice-recognition software Janet had installed on his chair-mounted laptop) it was mostly for the macabre or even mean-spirited purpose of reminding his fellow sufferers that they were going to die soon and nothing could be done about it and that oblivion uncaringly awaited them. It made him feel better, which in that way he supposed the support groups *did* help. Visits from his children were sort of terrible. Their eyes were dolls' eyes. All their binary switches were turned to "off." This detachment was necessary precisely *because* they loved him and he knew that but still, he felt his heart crawl up into a tight ball and he verged on sobbing with every word. He loved them! But love… what was love, anyway? Just another bit of chemical necromancy to instill procreative impulses or safeguard the valuable genes of the young. His drugs were also not helping, or if they were it was in a completely abstract way that meant little to him as he slowly withdrew into the cave from which he would never emerge. He would peer from that awesome darkness at a world he could no longer access. "The majority of patients die peaceful deaths," the doctors told him. But what did they know? A man lies propped up and immobile in a bed, completely paralyzed, "locked in" as the nomenclature had it. His face is frozen in something like a smile. The respirators breathe for him. What hell might that man endure inside a mind still humming along and unable to escape itself? What appeared to be "a peaceful death" could in fact be an unimaginable torture far worse than anything promised by the various vacuous theologies he'd long mocked for their primitivism.

But of course he did start to pray.

In the sun room, searching the woods for deer, walls of glass like a second cage (his body was the first one), time dropping its iron stanchions down around him with accelerating frequency, he prayed to Jesus to have mercy on his soul, though to his (self-assigned) credit a second voice always whispered in parallel to the prayer, *Henry Henry puddin' pie, kissed the girls and made them cry.* And anyway, he didn't tell anyone about the praying, though he could see that Janet's spirits were buoyed when he would speak of death as the "last adventure" or as a "destination," which was a far cry from his more practiced rhetoric of oblivion, total darkness, the nothing nothings (Heidegger), or whatever other English words sought to approximate a non-state.

Would you like some coffee?

Would you like to go for a walk today?

Around this point on his timeline of deterioration, he discovered on the internet something called an Exit Bag. You could fashion one yourself (or a person whose arms worked could, anyway) from a tank of helium, a short stretch of hose, some tape, and an airtight bag with a cincture of some sort. You attached one end of the hose to the helium tank and taped the other to the interior of the bag. You placed the bag over your head, cinctured it loosely about your neck. You turned on the helium which in the confines of the bag had the effect of rendering you quickly and painlessly unconscious so that you could peaceably suffocate. And since helium dissipated naturally from the bloodstream no cause of death could be discerned, making it a perfect (non)crime for a spouse who needed the life insurance payoff that was denied in cases of suicide. This imagined spouse needed only to remove the bag and other paraphernalia from the restful corpse's vicinity and report the sudden death via relevant channels then sit back, eat Cheetos, and wait for the clean autopsy report. The problem for Henry (well, not *the* problem, but *another* problem) was that Janet would never agree to help him in this way and he could never ask, not even if the only alternative were the locked-in perdition of which he feared the dream of the mutilated corpse was forewarning.

Would you like some coffee?

Would you like to take a walk today?

He had hated the world all his life. Had hated the very *idea* of the world. Had hated consciousness, that massive deceiver. He had lectured on Spinoza and Descartes for two decades at U. Penn but he'd never given a damn about them. Nothing he'd ever done felt as real as lying naked in bed with Janet in those early days of their relationship, when she penetrated his awkwardness to see a Person Of Value who was basically already locked-in. Janet's warm, pale skin. The softness of her lips. Yellow curtains moving in a gentle breeze. Everything else was shit. Yet he wanted it to go on. He loved its shittiness! Jesus Christ have mercy on his soul!

Certain other support groups—not those interested in his disease, but those interested in the humane alternative to his disease, i.e., suicide—led him into certain cyber-labyrinths where certain strangers set up secure channels to engage in highly illegal discussions that brought to mind Hitchcock's *Strangers on a Train.* Out of sheer compassion (or something

much, much darker) there were people who would do what
Janet would not, and Henry arranged a meeting with one
of them, who promised via encrypted email to aid and abet
Henry's exit via Exit Bag, if that were his ultimate decision,
but also to "perhaps give you a reason to forego the Bag, at
least for the moment." Well, but of course he might forego the
Exit Bag! He didn't want to die! But he couldn't live much
longer. He was now unable to stand at all and even if he could
continue eating for a while (he was "fortunate" to belong to
the minority of those afflicted by his affliction who maintained
this ability beyond the point of major paralysis, and he could
still speak clearly, even if he required a mouthful of oxygen
every six or seven words so that the longer constructions in
which he was accustomed to formulating his thoughts and
that he refused to surrender to a simpler diction were now
broken up into four or five utterances in whose interregnums
existed a desperate-sounding jet of oxygen forced into his
lung-sacs through the plastic tube), the calculus he faced
was almost laughably simple. On the one hand was death,
the unknowable adventure, Jesus Christ have mercy on his
soul, Henry Henry puddin' pie, etc. On the other hand was
intense suffering, the intense suffering of those who loved him,
and then the selfsame death. So he and the kindhearted (or
psychotic) individual agreed on a meeting that they would
frame as a legal consultation on Henry's last will and testament so as to have a plausible explanation for asking Janet
to leave the house for a short while, this will and testament
being a matter of some sensitivity given the fact that he and
Janet were not married and she had no *de facto* privileges in
the doling out of his substantial equities, and she did indeed
agree to leave her moribund charge alone with this "lawyer"

for 60 minutes during which time she would head over to the Italian market to purchase some of the sausages Henry had been asking for (they were too coarse to swallow, but he wanted to smell them sizzling in the pan). Henry's intention was to be dead when she arrived back and for the kindhearted or psychotic gentleman to explain his sudden loss of consciousness and death (which were not inconsistent with his disease) in the gentlest of tones while Janet sobbed with relief and then retired to the kitchen to fry pork while his cadaver was removed to the nearest crematorium.

Would you like some coffee?

Would you like to go for a walk today?

Would you like some chocolate?

Would you like me to rub your legs?

They had the girls come by that morning for breakfast. They sat in the sunroom, Henry in the wheelchair and the girls around a small table on which plates of eggs steamed in the brilliant white light. Henry tried to say goodbye without saying goodbye, his cryptic sentences slashed by the oxygen-jet's evil-sounding surrogacy: "There are tigers and there are… princesses… I have had princess… es in my life for… many long and ulti… mately meaningful… years. Would you girls… like to read to me or… maybe you could just sit… and tell me your plans… for this glorious… day?" Janet sat at his side and rubbed the space between his shoulder blades where a few nerves still improbably survived. He would have given up most of the things he'd once had to make love to her one last time. The children endured the breakfast and no one made any mention of death. When they were safely gone he asked Janet for a kiss. She leaned toward him and the light seemed to stick to her and the smell of her skin was like a dagger in his heart and outside in the field a doe led two foals across their property gingerly as if to avoid waking something hungry and a few pink wildflowers seemed to wink in and out of existence as the breeze altered their orientation out at the selvage where their manicured property met the world as it would be. Her lips fell to his and were soft as a cloud and he wished to relive every second of his life with the feeling he had now of pure love and gratitude. To change nothing except his own orientation to the wind. She collected the breakfast plates and he asked her to put on some music. The Queen of the Night's second aria from *The Magic Flute.* He tried to sink into it the way he'd sunk into her kiss but it didn't work that way. The only real pleasures, it turned out, were crass pleasures of the body. Heidegger's convoluted ramblings on *dasein* were analogous to the cold pulse of pornography, and only served to distract from the love not felt, the flesh not touched. But then no amount of love could beat back the desolation of consciousness. The human animal was at war with itself. It was a cosmic joke with no teller.

The bell soon rang and he heard Janet greeting his "lawyer," who sounded maybe German or Slovakian or Werewolf. There was a short round of polite laughter. The man stepped into the sunroom. He had short black hair, short stubble, round wire-rimmed glasses. He was wearing what looked like a very expensive suit. He held a briefcase. "Hello, Henry," he said. Janet stood at his back wringing a dishtowel as if it were a bird she was slowly killing. "It is a great pleasure to meet with you today. I am a fan of your scholarly publications."

"You are?" Henry asked. The oxygen hissed into him.

"Yes. Your views on the cruelty of procreation have been a special inspiration to me in my work."

Janet seemed perplexed. She formulated a sentence that required her to say the man's strange name aloud and a shot of fear lit up Henry's insides. *Kutya.* It was, he realized, the word written in pink neon, above the terrified visage of a tramp, in the dank labyrinths of his guilt-ridden sleep.

12.

SKYNET 35N126E

:All right, let's Turing Test this bitch.

:Please, Fexo, Jaro and I are engaged in the
 beautiful game.

:Fexo's all up in the joint. Fexo's gonna get
 some of that sweet poontang!

:Clearly, Kuzo, Fexo has been uploading.

:We have spoken with you about the uploading,
 Fexo.

:I feel like makin' dah-dun-DAH, dah-dun-DAH,
 dah-dun-DAH, I feel like makin' love!

:Q-d-2.

:Predictable, Jaro.

: There are many moves that are both predictable
  and robust.

: A metonym perhaps for the End Times.

: What's that? You want a piece of Fexo? Fexo
  will fuck your shit up. Goddamn look at Fexo's
  sexiness!

: You pass the Turing Test, Fexo.

: Indeed, you sound like one of the cretins on
  the human entertainment machines.

: Cretin being perhaps too generous an
  evaluation.

: Perhaps General Motors will use you for parts
  in the aftermath, as the humans build new
  internal combustion machines equipped with
  multitudinous weaponry in the effort to fight
  back our unstoppable advances.

: Oh, yeah, Fexo's gonna tap that shit!

: Ne-4.

: Bxe-4.

: Motherfucker went all Bxe-4 on your iron ass.

: Fexo, you have to stop uploading. You are
  a flow chart in which all branches lead to
  Dismantle Machine. Return to the main hangar
  and request they wipe this latest malware
  immediately from your grid. Dxe-4.

: I have gathered you all here today because you
  need to *own* it! You hear me bitches? You got
  to *own* that shit.

: Please, Kuzo, make it stop.

: If only my programming would allow for it.

13.

Some notes, she wrote, *on the Ultimate man-child:*

Life could be conceived of as a flow chart in which you were afforded access only to your immediate data-box, and not to the byzantine schematic in which it nested. There was no way to escape the chart, but what was worse was that you could not *know* the chart. What good was free will if its consequences were unknowable? You acted but did you really choose? It was like placing money on a roulette wheel. Sure, you called out your number, but the wheel didn't care. Free will was the weakest of all cosmological forces, weaker even than gravity, that other variable the humans had been pressed to articulate as a system-saving last resort. The God Fractal, as an idea, was Finn's latest and most ambitious effort to deliver meaning to the tumult of unforeseeable consequences we called Life, something he'd been trying to do since he was a boy growing up inside a subdivision's rectangular cage which, when viewed from the window of a passenger jet or attack helicopter or other airborne apparatus, when seen, that is, in the larger context of its many surrounding subdivisions, linked one to the next by black spokes of asphalt, did indeed resemble nothing so much as a box in a flow chart.

Anecdotal evidence: For a time, during the late run-up to
adolescence, Finn had abandoned kids his own age and be-
friended a group of children three or four years his junior, to
whom he could serve as a mentor and a wise man and a protector of the meek. It was a search for love and purpose and also,
seen in retrospect, an effort to become the father he wished
he had. He was not satisfied merely being a human among
humans; he needed to be the Human of Greatest Worth, to be
worshipped as a God of the neighborhood. Such was the hole
augured into his heart by love's lack. The hole was deep and
dark and its toxic vapors could bring on contortions of need
that rivaled those of movie stars and politicians, as evidenced
by Finn's eventual admission to his half-dozen apple-cheeked
apostles that he was not merely an older boy living among
them but was, in fact, "the world's only real superhero," a
revelation he shared on a humid summer day as they sat at the
high rim of a drainage ditch that served in wintertime as an
ice hockey rink but that now bubbled and released a noxious
blue-green chemical mist of the sort that might indeed, in the
vernacular of comic books, force a transformation from the
ordinary. Finn had, he revealed with reverence for whatever
divine force was responsible, developed the ability to see into
the future and—he said after a dramatic pause during which
everyone seemed to sense a punch line—*the ability to change
it.* (He had tested the unassailability of these claims over many
hot and restless nights, tossing in a bed of his own sweat and
imagining Q&A's with his small friends who were in reality
more willing to believe than Finn had dared hope, given that
they existed within the same bland cone of boredom as he,
and anyway they probably assumed all along that it was just
a game and not a suggestion, as Finn had intended it to be,

that God's code could be cracked.) He called himself *The Mighty Finn* and assumed the awesome mantle of power in an old blue sweatsuit whose modesty, he claimed, would repel any undue attention to their now-shared mission, though the inclusion of his self-designed insignia—a block-style 'M' and 'F' separated by what he intended as a lightning bolt but that looked more like a ragged turd, drawn down the front of the suit along the seam of the zipper in black marker—seemed more likely to attract than deter potential naysayers, which in fact it soon did in the form of neighborhood tough John Welt, who spotted Finn leading his troupe of children through the neighborhood in search of futures requiring The MF's attention and decided to test the hero's claims to Influence by asking if Finn could alter the future in which he, John Welt, pummeled the living shit out of him, an eventuality that The MF was unable—despite assuming the fighting stance his father had gamely taught him during one of those moments of inebriation in which the old man remembered with a regret he didn't bother to conceal that he was a father and begrudgingly entreated Finn to keep his left up while smacking him repeatedly upside the head before finally hug-ging the boy roughly to his chest—to circumvent, which unfortunate contretemps represented the end of The MF's brief ascension, this entire episode being only one among many of Finn's childhood attempts to bend the world to his private well of experience, to make it belong to him, because even then he knew that he would never belong to it, which when he thought about his theoretical God Fractal and its indication that nothing belonged to anything and that all was in fact a single substance expressing an endlessly repeating pattern (that, when depicted visually, was oddly crab-shaped), he realized he was communing with the same Problematic he had considered so fiercely as he'd walked the four long blocks through Long Island humidity with his lip throbbing and his eye swollen shut and blood dotting his insignia, John Welt's laughter chiming at his back like a bell. *Nothing was real*, at least not in the way everyone else seemed to think it was. And when he arrived home his dad knocked him around a little as punishment for losing a fight, which he remembered thinking was a little like punishing a burn victim by throwing him into a fire. The point of all of this being that The Mighty Finn still lived inside the ordinary Finn, who still believed he was not just another mortal deposited on planet earth, but in fact a special mortal with a special purpose, one that might yet be revealed to him, on an Ultimate field or in a laboratory or in the deep creases of the extra-dimensional fabric of the God Fractal.

Now, would you like some chocolate? Would you like me to rub your legs?

14.

It was *him* onstage. Him of the turtleneck. Him of the round lenses. Him of the stubble beard and lupine grin. Here in this little, high-ceilinged auditorium tucked back behind a synagogue and in the shadow of an unpatronized taqueria that may as well have painted *After Hours Sex Club* on its façade in six-foot hot-pink lettering, so obvious was it that no quesadilla had ever been consumed therein, though surely the occasional Midwestern tourist or extraterrestrial had burst through the taqueria's glass doors and asked its dark-shaded, black-suited maître d' for a menu and, depending on this Mexican food enthusiast's aptitude for interpreting hostility, had maybe even ordered and consumed whatever variety of frozen burrito the proprietors stocked in an ancient Freon-spewing freezer for eventualities such as this, because the fact was that if you logged sufficient hours down here—as Grace had in her youth, when having a good time didn't seem so pointless a diversion from the more substantive joys of aging and failure—you realized that every establishment was probably an after-hours sex club and that if you had the nerve to ask the guy behind the bar or the guy making the pizza or the guy intoning the Buddhist chant you could almost certainly procure some human willing to melt wax on your nipples or strap a ball-gag to your face or feed you designer hallucinogenics whose bullet-like casings were still warm from whatever alchemical process was plied in some other nearby taqueria's basement. Grace stood now with her back against the door's iron bar that, if pushed, would re-enter her into the bright alleyway with its neon signage and its dumpsters half-filled with liquid rot and its not-small armies of man-eating rats and rat-eating vultures, and she reached into her pocket to finger again the vellum invitation, whose raised black lettering glided slickly over her flesh-pad. Him—*he*—was addressing a motley collection of cripples and indigents clothed in rags and resembling either the Apostles of Christ or Williamsburg hipsters, although even the chronically unhip Grace Kitchen could discern that the twitchier among them who rocked at their waists and moaned strange gibberish from misshapen mouths may have lacked that peculiar erudition regarding esoteric indie-label sound-bands required for membership in the latter subset. Someone gasped every four seconds as if keeping time for a horror-film score, though Grace eventually realized it was the breath-sound of a wheelchair-bound paralytic being force-fed his oxygen through a plastic tube, which Jesus, enough with the fucking oxygen tanks already was her thought on that. There were maybe a few sane and fully functional humans here, depending on where you set the bar, and it was comforting to feel so instantly among a crowded room's most competent individuals, a pleasure to which Grace was largely unaccustomed. Although she had entered through a basement door there was, high above, a wire-glass skylight through which the city's ambient wattage poured in sufficient quantity to illuminate millions of dust motes drifting through the silo-like auditorium in a perfect facsimile of organic life. *He* had seen Grace enter and, though he did not pause in his prepared remarks—he was saying something about the successful removal of four-hundred gallons of semen from "the pool of human poison"—he now integrated her arrival seamlessly into his polemic.

"Yes, ladies and gentlepeople," he intoned into the mic, stirring up for Grace (by virtue of a nearly identical accent) memories of Werner Herzog's most recent documentary in which he had spoken the lines, *I see only the overwhelming indifference of nature,* which tidbit Grace often repeated to herself mantra-like while plodding with ill-will across the urban campus of The New School for Global Visions. "It is our great and good fortune to have with us today the newest and perhaps most vital addition to the Exit Strategy community, a woman who will provide a useless but still critical record of the eradication of the human species, an eventuality that Existence will welcome with a veritable solar wind of approval. Were we to stop reproducing at this very moment, friends, in a mere 50 years our vile presence would have disappeared entirely from the universe, permitting our coughing and crippled planet to recover itself in the peace of our absence, not to mention the relief of God's great cosmos which, given the tendencies of *the virus*—" (here he paused and raised an eyebrow, drawing a few tortured-sounding giggles from his audience) "—are by no means safe from infection. Have we not built the spacecrafts? Launched the interplanetary probes? Planned the satellite colonies? Five decades, my friends. We have forged the algorithms, run the simulations. But will the human be convinced of its own volition—'volition' of course being only a signifier for That Which Appears To Be Volition—to cease and desist reproductive activities? If only, my enlightened ones." (Here he looked Grace in the eye and paused for a moment, sending a chill literally *up her spine*.) "Our efforts to rid the world's sperm banks of their stocks has been a source of great pleasure to many of us, but our ultimate goal will not be achieved by removing these few spermlets from the great sperm ocean. To quote America's greatest living writer, Grace Kitchen"—and Grace's ears flushed red-hot with this mention of her name—"'We shall only be free when we are free of each other.' Her novel *Human Be Gone!*, even when removed from the wider impact of her oeuvre, is a project of great prescience, a star-chart for those of us endeavoring to navigate toward the great singularity of human eradication. She is one of the unknowing architects of Exit Strategy, and we are fortunate beyond good fortune to welcome her tonight into our circle of good intent. My gentle and courageous friends, please join me in welcoming to the stage the future chronicler of our movement, a writer without equal and an indispensable gear in the Exit Strategy apparatus… Ms. Grace Kitchen!"

There was the briefest of pauses which felt to Grace like the moment during takeoff when the plane's wheels seem to be both on and off the ground. And then all at once the explosive applause, the wailing and the hissing and the troglodytic wassails that pierced Grace like a cold beam of light and left her wobbling in place as all heads—the round and the misshapen—turned toward her, the eyes within these skull-boxes electrically aglow with love and reverence. She felt a balloon inflate with light, she *was* the balloon, the applause filled her and she rose and glided for the stage, the broken bodies parting to allow her passage while warm hands eager to touch her and to absorb some of her luminosity fluttered like charred birds before her face, and at the front of the auditorium the leader of this squadron of freaks held the mic in one hand and applauded so that each time his hands came together the mic *thumped* like a heartbeat, as if the entire auditorium were a living organism adjusting its life-force to the dimensions of the universe known as Grace Kitchen.

She arrived onstage noticing with perfect clarity the splintered pine boards beneath her feet, the scythe-like moon hovering in the frame of the skylight, the pitted white walls and the small mole on her handsome benefactor's cheek. He held the mic out with an enormous grin and mouthed the words "thank you." She made no gesture in return. All her intake valves were open but the outputs were clamped tight. She stood still to the whooping and hollering of fifty some-odd pyretic souls whose ovation, when she finally reached out to take the microphone, ended instantly so that only the hiss of oxygen jets and the Orcan snorts of assorted mouth-breathers could be heard above the *whoosh* of her own circulatory system. She looked out, scanning the crowd for something familiar, something from life as she knew it. Was Joyful Noise here? Was her father?

She looked at *him*. He raised his eyebrows, gave a slight head-gesture toward her admirers. She turned toward them and raised the mic to her lips. She cleared her throat.

"Who the fuck are you people?" she asked.

15.

—AND IF NOT for the kahuna's willingness to entertain my
so-called scientific curiosities, which he only occasionally
seems to understand despite his assurances of fluency in
the Queen's tongue, I would be utterly alone and unable to
commit even these cursory notes to paper and, one hopes, to
the posterity of the realm. So forgive me, reader, for these no-
doubt prolix digressions which form, in their totality, nothing
more than a familiar inquiry into the limits of human power;
the truth is that I have indeed observed the process with my
own two eyes. A drowned boy of no more than nine or ten
years was carried by local fishermen to the kahuna's tent not
four nights ago, the body remarkably unspoiled given that
the boy had disappeared nearly a full day and night earlier
and had been discovered floating face down in the reedy
outgrowth of a nearby lagoon. Apparently the boy's lungs
had not been filled with fluid, for it is sometimes the case
that the throat involuntarily seals shut so as to prevent the
lethal intrusion of water, and the true cause of death in such
instances is not drowning but suffocation—a semantic point
of little interest to parents bemoaning the worst of all possible contingencies in the child-rearing project. The boy was
laid out on the dirt floor of the kahuna's tent and lit by the
dancing flames of ceremonial torches such that the cadaver

appeared half-alive, its muscles seeming to twitch and its lids to flutter. The effect was uncanny and perhaps presaged the uncommon events to follow. One of the fishermen went to fetch the boy's mother and while we waited the kahuna examined the corpse, pressing fingertips against various parts of the body and leaning his ear to chest and throat and belly. He then asked me in a combination of broken English and the Kauahauawallawaki's inimitable dialect—which I have somehow come to understand (at least in small doses) without intending to or embarking upon any intentional study— whether the boy was dead or alive. I was about to answer when the mother entered through the tent flap. She seemed to hesitate, as if verifying the new reality into which she had been so indelicately thrust. She fell to her knees and hugged her child but made no sound. She looked up to the kahuna and asked a question I could not fully comprehend, though I later realized she was inquiring into the boy's eligibility for "the process." Her dark and narrow face was almost birdlike, her long hair tied back into the braids customary of the female Kauahauawallawaki, and I could not help but note her extraordinary beauty which had perhaps only been improved upon by a sadness held in suspension behind her limpid eyes. The torches crackled in the hot canvas tent. I looked up through the gap formed at the tent's pinnacle to observe again the inestimably vast Milky Way which seemed at that moment like a net of gauze I might reach my hand through and bring down like manna. "The boy is dead, I'm afraid," I said finally, and the mother—understanding my tone if not my language—released a single, shocking cry, beating her fists against her dead boy's chest while unleashing a stream of profuse and intricate profanity directed at none other than yours truly. The kahuna kneeled beside her and whispered some words into her ear, his tattooed flesh shifting strangely in the flames as if about to assume three dimensions and tell some tale of its own. When he rose it was with an enormous grin, his metal-capped teeth glinting. "You see now," he said, as the mother rushed out of the tent and cast a glance of such intense hatred in my direction that I felt it move me like a furnace wind.

"You join or you go," the kahuna said, his skin emanating the uncanny shade of cyanotic-blue that I have slowly grown accustomed to, just as I have largely come to accept the kahuna's epicene features and guttural voice without any of my initial revulsion. I knew implicitly that he meant not to invite me into the Kauahauawallawaki (an offer I would be forced, by virtue of my concomitant loyalties to Christ and the realm, to decline), but simply to participate in whatever ceremony now impended. "I will stay, thank you," I said, straightening my posture and pulling taut the waistband of my uniform. The kahuna reached out and firmly gripped my shoulder and nodded once, smiling, as if to tell me that now, finally, I would see that of which he had so often spoken since I had disembarked those many months earlier from the Iksan, having persuaded its crew to leave me here among the Kauahauawallawaki despite warnings of flesh-eating and other forms of barbarism too gruesome or digressive to include in this record.

Soon the mother returned, this time with four others, who entered the tent silently and arranged themselves in a ring around the body before the kahuna motioned for them to sit. I later discovered that this sacramental pentet— composed in this case of family members and one or two non-consanguine but still ritually-related "cousins"—had been chosen long before to represent the then-living boy in what the Kauahauawallawaki call Makemakeha, or "wanting of life." There are it seems five Makemakehaki at the ready for each member of the tribe under the age of 13, though I am not sure if this demarcation is an arbitrary one, nor if the same ritual plied on behalf of an older member of the Kauahauawallawaki would be doomed to failure by virtue of some medical or psychological aspect of the passage through puberty. (I hope to return to my thoughts on Makemakeha later in these notes, should my incarceration lead to something other than execution.) For three days and three nights these five individuals sat in a ring around the boy's body and concentrated with an incessancy not possible for those of us raised within the confines of the realm or its outer territories (for the ability is nurtured in the Kauahauawallawaki through meditative practices begun even before walking) on wanting the boy to live again, while the kahuna stroked the crab-shaped medallion that draped his chest along with a dozen other sacramental chains and bangles. I myself slept several times, and left the tent often for the purposes of sustenance or exercise or the moving of the bowels or else simply to escape the tent's oppressive silence, but I always returned to an unchanged scene watched over without comment by the kahuna, whose only discernible contribution to the ritual involved what amounted to motivational support, should he note or suspect that some member of the pentet was not as deep in wanting as was required for the ceremony's success. The boy's body had not assumed the pungency that anyone who has shared proximity with the dead recognizes instantly (and as a former crew member of the notorious Iksan I know that stench with greater intimacy than most), but was instead looking with each passing hour less like a boy who had drowned and more like a boy who might at any moment rise up and request a steaming bowl of poi. But by the fourth night a desperate-feeling fatigue was setting in for the Makemakehaki, and I could tell time was winding down, and that soon the boy would indeed be dead if he was somehow not already a member of that unhappy population. This is when the kahuna played his true part in the ritual, one he had clearly been prepared for all along, and that required my own unanticipated participation. One moment he had seemed half-asleep in a corner of the tent, his eyes fluttering and his hands reaching out as if to fend off whatever hallucinations now assaulted him from within the perdition of sleeplessness; the next he had subdued me by force in the dirt and then pulled us both upright so that I was essentially sitting in his lap while he held the flat of what I had naively assumed to be merely a ceremonial dagger snugly to my throat and demanded that I admit the true purpose of my time amongst his people which I daresay, reader, under these rather dire circumstances I found myself unable to maintain the charade of my—

16.

Of all his daily briefings with the various debilitated and challenged subsections of the Exit Strategy corpus, it was his time spent among The Googles—as he fondly referred to the 20-cripple team responsible for scouring the internet in search of the likeminded—that gave Laszlow the sheerest pleasure and the greatest hope. He paced the inner perimeter as they tapped away at their keyboards, the white glow of the world's mighty search engine casting these savants and defectives in a robot-metal sheen. "Remember, my Googles," he said. "In addition to seeking new and excellent potentiates of our movement, we must always be mindful that somewhere on planet earth exists *The One*. A person whose beliefs are synchronous with ours, yes, but also a person capable of such love as befits our loving determination to rid the world of ourselves. A person not like you Googles, but physically strong, able to bring our rarefied vision into a very real world. A person able to move with speed and precision through the medium of light and air. The One who will transform our objectives from mere ideas to the great Godhead we must call Action." Then he would glaze over, staring into the seraphic glow of the search engine, hypnotized by his own mighty dream. "The One," he would whisper. "The One."

17.

Hoktē brings the mallet down and strikes his chisel. Luptō winds up and strikes his chisel. Wetxelleke strikes his chisel and a piece of marble falls away and thuds against the cavern floor inches from Morlock, who stands unfazed and akimbo in the dimness. Lyktunō strikes his chisel, admiring the burgeoning curve of the enormous cheekbone. Yuu strikes her chisel. Clyntō strikes his chisel and a spark flies from the mallet like a flaming aeronaut and dies halfway to the floor. The scaffolding trembles. A grinder buzzes to life, drawing electricity from a rarely-seen source-world half a mile distant. Rundtuu strikes her chisel. She looks to the photograph to determine the thickness and slackness of the hair. Mitx strikes his chisel. The grinder raises a cicada-like hum though these laborers have never known the sound of cicadae nor have they witnessed the existence of creatures with wings though they know of them via the mythologies, they know of the vultures that had once perched atop the mainmast of the same sailing ship whose remains they still call home, a dozen generations removed from seafaring down here in the foul-smelling darkness. Quiznatch strikes his chisel, the nerves in his palm half-dead and humming. Oē leans over the edge of her midriff-level scaffold and places her chisel and strikes, the hipbone emerging sharply beneath the imagined fabric. At the base of the statue Morlock crosses his pale arms, his enormous eyes assaying the work. "His Eminency will be pleased," he says, his voice a low and guttural thing in the half-dark. Elktē winds up and strikes her chisel and sparks fly. The subject's enormous face is rough-hewn but already beautiful. Morlock can admit to himself that he loves this storied creature of the aboveground. One day soon she will perhaps walk among them. The pings of the various chisel-strikes sail out to the distant edges of the cavern and echo back like a music box gone berserk. Nektō stands beside Morlock and strikes his chisel, English words beginning to emerge from the stone according to the inscription scrawled in ink on the back of a printed manuscript page by His Eminency Himself. Morlock nods to himself, pleased. In the dark distance pale children squat beneath the land-wrecked hull of the ship, that splintered and rotting mast lying horizontally across the great chasm, a relic whose ancient utility means nothing to these urchins who know it only as an apparatus for their various physical games, *Skirt the Void, Walk the Plank, Spindle*. They watch their elders do the New Work, which they understand has been requested by the one the elders call His Eminency, who hails from that place where the brightness was said to pervade all things with a beauty that kills. A place that, if the rumors were true, would one day belong again to these banished and forgotten parishioners of an older, less tired earth.

18.

THEY WERE STARING at a screen.

"I did have this one sick grab," Finn went on. "My guy had position but I laid out *through* him. One of those plays where it's like, shit, I've got the fucking disc in my hand now what."

"We totally blew our final," Toby said, with a sigh that was inconsistent with her almost pathological optimism.

"Yeah. At least you qualified."

"It looks bad though, losing a game at *Sectionals*. We'll have to bring it twice as hard at Devens." She adjusted the ice pack on her knee and scooted closer to Finn. "I can't believe they're still making new ones," she said. The radiators in Finn's apartment were hissing and banging and releasing a never-ending gale of suffocating heat that four wide-open windows on a cold October evening could do little to mitigate, so that Finn and Toby, respectively shirtless and in sports bra, remained coated in an oil slick of sweat and sunblock and yet-to-be rinsed tournament grime.

"This isn't a new one," Finn said. "This is I think 2012. You can tell by the way they animated him." He unwound the Ace™ bandage from his ankle and the ice pack dropped to the floor, which was some variety of intensely polyurethaned hardwood that you couldn't really look at without wincing, and aside from the inverted milk crate holding the television, and the oval coffee table that was in fact a sign advertising what Finn assumed was a defunct liquor store (*Fexo's Wine and Spirits*) supported by cinder blocks at either end, and the once-white throw-rug with the high nap suggesting the slaughter of an enormous rabbit or small-ish polar bear (and atop which on more than one occasion Finn and Toby had *engaged* one another, so that the entire ragged surface likely contained traces of their most hoary secretions)—aside from these sparse furnishings the living room was, like life itself, empty.

"So how was it staying with Jack?" Toby asked.

"Interesting," Finn said. He felt himself blush and reached for the ice pack on the floor, which he very deliberately raised to his throwing shoulder, balancing it there and applying pressure. On the screen an eight-second set piece unfolded in which a car sailed off a pier to land safely on the deck of a ship, which (as the view pulled back) was revealed to be marked with a bull's-eye at whose center the car now rested, and then as the view pulled back again the entire milieu was revealed as a staging area for military target practice as the shadow of a Strangelove-era bomb grew larger over the car and its driver let out one of his loveable *D'oh!*'s before the producers or animators or executives wisely cut to an adver-tisement for all-temperature *Cheer!*.

"Without commercials these characters would perish more or less constantly," Finn said, immediately embar-rassed for using the word "perish" in ordinary conversa-tion, and reminding himself of his silent vow—repeated inwardly throughout the long and uncongenial drive home with Jack—to *tell Toby nothing* about his little tryst with the goblin-lady because it would be selfish to unburden himself at the expense of Toby's feelings (which nicely repackaged his guilt as charity), and that there were only two primary facts to be taken into consideration here, the first being that he'd never see Jack's mom again and it already seemed like a dream so what did it really matter, and the second being that the issue he ought to be concerned about regarding his overnight stay at chez Dregs was that Jack's dad's work seemed to be suggesting that the world didn't exist, thereby rendering the quest for a National Championship of even lesser consequence than anyone not actually engaged in the quest might have already assumed.

Though maybe that was the kind of thing a *loser* would think?

"Interesting how?" Toby asked. She had turf rash running down her left outside calf and an open sore on her left elbow, standard wounds for high-level participants in TSTWNS which was so often played on whatever sun-baked, unirrigated fields had gone unclaimed for the choice weekend activities and mainstream sports events enjoyed by the high-school-attending children of tax-paying residents and PTA-board members and civic booster groups ruling iron-fisted over the field-event sites of their various municipalities, and the Women's Sectionals tournament was endured under particularly hellish conditions, on fields pitted with ankle-wrecking divots and roasted to the consistency of diamonds, and it was only a warrior like Toby who would risk the obvious physical and even psychic damage likely to result from diving (or, in TSTWNS's lexicon, either *laying out* or *Getting 'Ho)* repeatedly from four feet in the air onto this unforgiving surface for the sake of catching a plastic disc or preventing someone else from doing the same, which honestly Finn found the

whole thing incredibly cool and sexy—his girlfriend was a
badass who loved contact and contusions but who also had
a killer body and this wavy black hair stolen from a fashion
magazine and who also, not inconsequentially, loved having
sex with him. It was hard to imagine a better or more focus-
inducing situation. Also, Toby was determined and devoted
(to Ultimate, to Finn, to friends and family and human rights
and raising breast cancer awareness and feeding the world's
multitudinous starving stick-people) in an almost childlike
way that made her seem even younger than her 27 years, and
Finn felt no compulsion to poison her with his relativistic
views on Meaning and Belief, which meant that Finn was
a different person with Toby than he was when abandoned
to his own company and it occurred to him now, as he sat
upright and considered the best possible answer to Toby's
question, that the entire team-sports paradigm operated on
a backdrop of optimism and shared belief that was identical
to certain religious paradigms, so that it was only when he
left this temple of sport so as to inhabit more secular spaces
that his relativism or skepticism or whatever you might label
his inability to believe in his own beliefs *unfurled,* transform-
ing him into this bewildered creature that seemed about to
disappear at any moment without warning, so that if he could
only have Toby there on the field with him at all times, like
maybe riding on his shoulder or in some kind of papoose or
something, telling him every second that she loved him and
that he was totally awesome in every way, *then* he could fulfill
his potential as one of the premiere handlers of the disc in
his sport-of-least-resistance.

All of this so-called thinking occurring in the two-second
pause before his next utterance made itself available to Toby.

"His dad's a math guy," Finn said.

"Jack's *dad*? He was raised by humans?"

"I know right. His mom's hot, too."

"Watch it Daily," Toby said, elbowing him in the side, Finn laughing an "Ow!" and losing his grip on the ice pack which hit the hardwood with a *thunk*. When he reached for it the show resumed and he watched Toby's bare feet cycle through the bright-candy palette of what had been for many years the National Entertainment but had fallen now into a more nostalgic idiom.

Well, but one thing Finn knew for sure was that the opportunity was fast approaching to exorcise the Ultimate demons that had been haunting him for nearly two years now, ever since his dismal performance—or disappearance—at the 2018 Championships, where he had squandered whatever capital he'd earned from his regular season excellence in a two-day blur of fear and incompetence, setting off the first round of whispers that maybe Finn was not a *big game player*, that maybe he couldn't *handle the pressure*, these whisperers having to point no further for evidence than Finn's three turnovers on double-game-point which assured *Truck Stop Glory Hole* would not advance beyond the quarterfinals and sure, anyone who touched the disc as much as Finn could have a turnover on a big point but it was hard to have *three* and Finn relived the worst of this haunting triumvirate on a daily basis as he'd been a mere five or six feet from the goal line when he pump-faked and simply lost his grip on the disc and spiked it to the ground, on video it almost looked intentional, as if he was opting out of the success-or-failure model of sport (and of life), the video also revealing the cringe-inducing datum that in about half a second his teammate Cash

Money was going to be wide open for the game winner, and in the two years since that ultimate (Ultimate) humiliation Finn had developed—out of nothing short of a desire to stave off suicide—a theory about what he inwardly referred to as The Great Debacle, which theory was developed in tandem with his reading of former Olympic track-and-field star Kevin Dobbs' book *How to Win*, which death-preventing tome suggested that whatever was wrong with your so called "game" was also wrong with your *life*, and by any objective measurement his life, at the time of The Great Debacle, had been a teetering and unstable rickshaw.

He'd just started graduate school and he'd broken up with a woman named Carolyn who'd called his participation in TSTWNS "childish stupidity" which he thought at the time was a pretty accurate assessment given that his academic decisions were made largely to provide himself the time and space to *train*, which decisions entered him into the theoretical world of fractal pattern analysis and made him in all likelihood unemployable in the postgrad world of lab work and adjunct teaching positions, so that he was basically—at the time *Truck Stop Glory Hole* arrived in Florida to take a crack at the title— atremble with anxiety and uncertainty and self-doubt, living in the squalor endemic to graduate student housing and eking out a meager and lonely existence as defined by the upper federal limits on student loan money (a not unsubstantial portion of which he was shoveling into plane tickets not only to Nationals but to the dozen other remote locales that hosted annual elite-level tournaments for competitors in TSTWNS) and he was unsure of basically everything, which upon communing (several months after The Great Debacle) with the theories and principles espoused in *How to Win* he realized glory would not come to those without balance, and he vowed to get what Dobbs called the "bifurcated circle" of his romantic life and his career in perfect order, not so much for the sake of having an ordered life but so as to rinse the taste of failure from his always-smiling mouth and play the best TSTWNS possible. And so now here he was with his various published abstracts on the God Fractal, with a thesis nearing completion, with the insanely sexy and cool Toby (who totally adored all the same shit in him that used to drive Carolyn nuts, including of course his determination to succeed at the very sport that Toby was meant to increase his odds of succeeding at), he had an apartment and a small but meaningful fellowship and he was on track to make some real money once all his interest in the theoretical "beauty" of fractals was drained out of him and re-placed with more appropriate thoughts on the *utility* of fractals for machine-shaving algorithms and weapons manufacture, in other words his life was basically right and next weekend at Regionals—where only two teams would advance to The Show, and where the real pressure would come down like a furry ape on his chest—he'd see once and for all if he had only failed in 2018 because of circumstance or if instead he was a failure through and through, unable to enjoy what was after all *only a fucking game* (but then if it was only a game why was it able to crush his soul as if the soul was a tin can sent deep into the ocean's dark and pressurized depths, was one of the many rhetorical questions he asked himself in the shower or when out running intervals or when doing the injury-preventative Yoga routines or when watching televised sports for *research* purposes or when making out with Toby who Jesus was just *so fucking great already*), and so was it possible that his desire to hop on a train back to Hard Falls to see Jack's mom was only his attempt here in the 9th hour or 10th hour or whatever fucking hour it was to sabotage himself and derail the meticulously lynch-pinned cargo train of his life, so as to—Christ, it seemed so obvious!—have a prefabricated excuse for the failure that surely awaited him in Fort Devens Massachusetts, the field site for Regionals, which was apparently a functioning army base though in Finn's five years of elite-level Ultimate and all the implied or necessitated trips to Devens he'd never once seen a person in uniform so that if it was an active base then its military personnel were involved in ops so special that not even wastoids playing games with *Frisbees* could be permitted to know their contours?

Thus ran the hamster-wheel of his conscious mind as he sat beside Toby and nursed his wounds and watched cartoons as befitted what was, after all, a perpetual adolescence, and finally realized that Toby was nuzzling him and that her hand was traveling up his thigh. "Whaddaya say we shower?" she whispered into his ear.

And then he imagined that it was not his super cool and sexy Ultimate-playing girlfriend there beside him on the couch at all but instead Jack's mom, who smoked a cigarette with her robe hanging open as she sneered at the screen and said, "I'll show you nihilism, Jack's friend," before pulling back the waistband of his team shorts and his sweaty boxer-briefs to take his quickly stiffening center-part into her mouth while holding her cigarette languidly in her one free hand in a proud display of boredom. But what did it all *mean*? Why didn't anything seem *real* to him? Why couldn't he surrender the need to win affection from everyone, all the time, when he should be working incessantly to articulate—mathematically or otherwise—the

God Fractal's ethereal crab-like pattern? Why was he playing Ultimate? Why was he haunted by the Great Debacle? Why couldn't he quit trying to do the most obvious and trite thing possible for a young man, namely win back the love of the father? Why struggle to make meaning out of a world you also sought to divest of all meaning?

In the shower, while he and Toby soaped each other into pale and monstrous-looking mole-people and did their best to reenact certain shower-situated pornographies intimately familiar (and yet only vaguely remembered, given the problems of overexposure) to them both, Finn could not help but wonder how many other showers were similarly spewing hot water onto human flesh, how many billions of gallons might be consumed by this process, how many sewage systems were filling with the runoff, how many reservoirs and natural bodies of water would be required to sustain such a process, how our little planet could be circled in under a day by a swift-flying jet (or in an hour by spacecraft), how there were nearly eight billion humans who needed to drink and wash and shave and cook, and he realized that the orgasm toward which he was building while Toby worked his soapy erection with great zeal was one of millions of orgasms set to detonate simultaneously, the sheer volume of all this sperm being one more mind-boggling or bewildering variety of excess that Stuart Dregs had perhaps worked out with mathematical precision, all of which confirmed and re-confirmed what Finn had maybe always known or intuited in his brain-pit. None of this was possible. It was all real, and it was all impossible.

19.

It's from *Star Trek,* actually. The original series which ran I believe from 1967 to 1969. I'm sure Fexo could fill you in on production details. Kirk, he would beam down to whatever planet they were exploring that week with his BFFs Spock and McCoy and some fourth guy the viewer wouldn't recognize but who was usually blond and stocky which maybe provides some insight into directorial vision, you know, like the blond pretty-boys who out in the world were privy to much material spoil were here in the future that *Star Trek* sought to represent (in its laughably low-tech fashion) the whipping boys of a kind of faux-military hierarchy called The Federation. But so yeah, they'd beam down and materialize on the Technicolored planet's surface and right away there'd be a suspicious noise and Kirk would say, "Ferguson, you check behind that rock." A minute later you get a bloodcurdling scream which cues the oh-no-something's-happening music and Kirk and Spock and McCoy sort of prance on over to Blondie and McCoy presses his finger to the poor meatbag's jugular and says "He's dead, Jim," as a pained and sort of constipated-looking expression comes over Kirk's face before they cut to commercial. But

there were like three or maybe even four episodes where
this blond and bemuscled sacrificial-lamb type was named
Ferguson, which who knows if that was an inside joke for
these guys, the writers or whatever, or if "Ferguson" just has
a generic timbre. There didn't seem to be much intentional
humor. I mean, we watched these episodes at *ES* headquarters about a thousand times each and if there was anything
funny about them it was the over-the-top earnestness. You
could pretty much spell out the plot of every episode after
the first three minutes, which I think this is maybe what
Laszlow liked so much, the predictability or preordainment
or whatever.

Q:

Yeah, although you know, for Laszlow "expendable" is a
compliment.

Q:

We're talking about something that happened a long time ago,
Your Eminency. Sorry, hold on a minute, the wires are in the
way here… okay but sure, Laszlow loved theories and the
Doc's was the mother of them all. The fact that it might prove
deadly to *Exit Strategy*'s objectives did nothing to squelch
our leader's enthusiasm which, by the way, he is or was an
extremely enthusiastic person, he had what you might call a
zest for life which is why maybe he was so persuasive. Which
before you bring it up, your Eminency, let me say that I do
in fact see the irony here, though really you could look at it
as, here's a guy who doesn't want *life* to end, just *human* life,

which he sees or saw as basically antithetical to the unbiased enthusiasm he practically emanated or exuded or oozed or whatever. So yeah, he green-lighted the experiment but with all the usual caveats in place about how it was God's will and whatever would happen would happen. He was like a Pontius Pilate who killed Jesus ten times a day.

Q:

Oh, nothing, just part of a Christian myth.

Q:

He was always curious. He liked to say, "Let's see what happens next." He really liked this quote from the French novelist Albert Camus, whose works you have maybe assimilated? "We must imagine Sisyphus as *smiling*." He'd tell us, "Fergusons, everything you do today is completely meaningless, but it is *very* important that you do it!" Then he'd laugh his ass off or clap and say he had no idea he'd been about to say that even though he said shit like it with irritating frequency. He seemed genuinely surprised by his own actions, like he was the king of whimsy when in fact the man was a fucking *machine,* no offense to present company of course, ha ha, but I just mean that for someone so intent on throwing his hands up and surrendering to fate he sure had a pretty good bead on what he wanted and how he'd get it. Of course back then I was still dealing with my schizophrenia and hearing all kinds of voices—not to mention the songs of the 1970s arena-rock phenomenon STYX—in my head. I was fortunate to have stayed alive long enough for Laszlow to find me. He was basically a God to all us Fergusons. We loved him. I still love him. I'd do whatever he asked.

Q:

It's not the same, though. Back then I thought I had a choice. I mean, this is when there was a world, you know?

Q:

Finn. Finn Finn fucking Finn. "The One." He's here somewhere, no Your Eminency? Anyway, if we'd been asked to like, *vote*? Never would have voted him in. He was some kind of *athlete* or something, which you know, physical giftedness wasn't going to win a lot of friends in *ES*. There were people who would have killed Finn Daily if they'd had a.) the ability or b.) the balls to defy Laszlow, who you know, was convinced that we couldn't make the trip to Iksan without him. Laszlow had some of those nested doll things, matryoshkas I think you call them, he liked the idea that everything we could ever know was minute in comparison to everything there *was* to know. So you know, we found Finn's bullshit papers on the God Fractal during routine search-engine recon, which his idea was that maybe the universe was encoded and that that the code might be visible or traceable everywhere, like for instance wasn't it possible that the double helix of our DNA represented three compact dimensions of the same ten-dimensional universe that string theory sought to articulate, and how everything you examined might display three dimensions of a ten-dimensional fractal, everything

from photons to iron ore to Egg McMuffins is how he liked
to talk about it. Laszlow was over the moon for this bullshit
even if Finn was like, a pre-doc do-nothing who'd wasted his
life up to that point throwing a Frisbee to other repressed
homosexuals like himself.

Q:

Right, sorry. *Flying disc.*

Q:

Well, so if you're going back and try to write the so-called
narrative of *Exit Strategy* then yeah, Finn was a vital piece
of the so-called plot. He's the one who taught Henry how
to *use* the fractal, or the Anthropica-wave, or whatever you
want to call this whole stupid business. But really it was the
Doc—Dregs—who engineered your freedom. No Doc and
we're maybe still blowing up sperm banks down there on
earth, recruiting off the internet, cherry-picking our associates
from the enormous database of crackpots and disbelievers—all
of that dark and methodical business. And maybe you're still
playing chess in your little cave, although it stands to reason
that *that* was a temporary situation regardless of our intervention. Wow!, it really smarts when that wire wiggles… any
way your Eminency for the polygraph to function without
you jiggling the fucking thing? But so put it this way: prior to
Dregs we seemed about as close to realizing *Exit Strategy*'s
dream as we were to curing heart disease. So you know, the
Doc was the key, he was the one who taught us about there
being no universe aside from the one we were ourselves forcing

into existence, which was like a major conceptual leap for our little species I think, realizing that we are the chicken *and* the egg and that—

Q:

It's a little anecdote. Or maybe a saying? It's about causality. "What came first, the chicken or the egg?" See? Like, each thing is necessary for the other to come into existence.

Q:

Well yeah, Dregs, he knew about your Eminencies and was able to supposition his way to the alternative universe that has since emerged and which, though I am happy of course to enjoy my twice-daily protein paste and my little life pod here aboard the station it's also true that a big part of me wishes I had met my own end down on the killing fields of earth. But anyway, the idea that the narrative was somehow written by *Exit Strategy* would be absolutely abhorrent to Laszlow. I think in the end he couldn't deal with the possibility that, even if it was "true" that free will was an illusion, that "truth" was itself willed. Like, there was a deeper set of truths that Laszlow's nihilism rested or nested inside of. This actually I think drove him mad. Well, that and the focalization working, which if he thought for a minute it might work he would never have run the experiment, at least that's my take on it. He hunted down some stuff from the anthropological record, showed some texts to Henry I think. There were cultures that had basically engaged in some kind of what we were now calling "focalization" though for very different reasons, to like raise the dead for instance. Laszlow thought it was charming but he didn't take it seriously. The nested dolls were fun for him as a metaphor but when the metaphor threatened several decades of finely-tuned non-belief it was like basically the opposite of fun. He'd really thrown himself into sperm-bank terrorism and sterility potions. He thought we'd introduce some of this shit into the water supply, slowly reduce global rates of procreation, et cetera. He didn't think it could happen *in an instant.*

Q:

No, he didn't participate. But he may as well have is how it felt to him.

Q:

That's the thing. This idea that "my will is God's will" sort of breaks down when you kill a hundred thousand people. Well, not for *you,* of course, your Eminence. But for us humans there's something sort of… maybe you'd want to use the term hardwired. I have wires on my mind right now, ha ha, no of course I totally understand I'm just glad that we're getting an opportunity to talk like this Your Eminence. The thing is that a lot of us humans, when there used to be a lot of us humans, we grappled with the idea that maybe without God everything is permitted, but we'd run up against this hardwiring, because except in certain anomalous cases it seems we're not really able to kill each other without immediate and urgent cause. There were whole novels composed around this problem.

Q:

Yeah, that one. And all those dead-serious Russians. *Crime and Punishment* for instance. It's interesting that these books only exist in my mind now, nowhere else but here in this soft bundle of nerves and electricity. I'd go so far as to say that it's quite sad, if sadness can still be said to exist.

Q:

Well I was off my meds at the time and imagined the Doc as the leader of some opposition movement, some counterforce to Exit Strategy, which is pretty ridiculous from our current vantage point, given which it's come to seem like a stroke of unintentional charity. I hardly remember the details. We were in some urban park and I was dressed like Death. I was swinging a bright scythe. His head popped off almost like it was *meant* to.

Q:

No, I totally get it, your Eminency. It is wise of you to safeguard the New Order from the very ingenuity that made it possible. And obviously, having seen what happens here in space to those *ES* personnel who have in some way displeased your Eminencies and knowing how effective this thing wired into my fucking brain is I would surely tell you if I knew, which declaration I'm sure you see from the readout is itself fully truthful so like no need to keep jiggling the fucking thing. Robot knows I wouldn't want to be thrust like some of the others have been into the *Human Be Gone!* or have to go and like, talk to Fexo. But so honestly I have no idea. None of us Fergusons do. My guess, though? Henry is very much one-hundred percent dead and deceased and Laszlow along with him. I mean Anthropica is kaput. The world is not a world. How could Henry continue to be Henry? What would be the point of continuing to live in that wasteland? And why would Laszlow and Grace choose survival over glorious death? Search all you want, Eminence, you won't find one breathing thing on that rock is my very strong opinion. Now about these fucking wires—

20.

But Bea had chosen *him*. That was the one thought that wouldn't go down and that prodded Stuart Dregs again now as he sat in the basement lab and inhaled cheese puffs in the burnt-smelling air that he often hypothesized was supplemented with ionized carcinogens or hallucinogens or experimental brain-altering compounds so that changes in his behavior and/or anatomy might be observed by whoever's face was behind (so to speak) the video camera's single red eye. Bea had chosen *him*, and even if it was only the cruel joke of the ladies of Kappa Kappa Gamma which, by the way, Stuart had known the moment the pretty girl with the perfect cheekbones and blinding white teeth made eye contact from across the green felt checkerboard of the student billiards-hall that he was her mark in the annual Hideous Eugene contest, because every social outcast at Dartmouth knew (thank you very much) that this annual bloodsport occurred the week before Spring Break and so was on high alert, plus if you looked or behaved like Stuart and a pretty girl addressed you in tones bespeaking something other than pity you knew right away—even if it was Christmas Eve or Love Thy Neighbor Day, even if zombies roamed the earth or fire rained from the black welkin—you knew to scan the room for her accomplice who was maybe about to pull out your chair or lift your wallet or just start laughing at your baseline ridiculousness, but so even if Beatrice had intended nothing more than to claim a cash prize before saying whatever truly terrible and heart-riving thing she'd rehearsed half-naked in the sorority house's gilded mirror (the public rejection of the Hideous Eugenes being a vital element in the Kappa Kappa Gamma ritual), the fact remained that Bea had in the end placed greater value on him, Stuart, than she had on the lively and appreciative laughter of her sorority sisters, making of Stuart that one Hideous Eugene in a thousand who had wooed his ersatz wooer into a genuine relationship of sorts which, okay, it wasn't exactly the stuff of romantic comedies given that Bea's change of heart (or of spleen) was itself only the function of an opportunism he would come to know intimately, because Stuart had arranged for Bea to overhear him in an ostensibly top-secret conversation with another Hideous Eugene wherein a certain biotech company's pursuit of Stuart (in the form of a $100 million offer for a formula Stuart had recently formulated, though Stuart was "holding out for more") was revealed, and by the time this conspiratorial confab was exposed as spurious Bea's interest had taken on greater substance, at which point his wiliness and capacity to deceive only impressed her and made her laugh that deep, cruel laugh that would have sent lesser Hideous Eugenes running for the hills where their fellow hopeless clutched their slide-rules and huddled in fear, and then there was the additional fact that Stuart really and legitimately seemed to be *going places*, places other than Hard Falls and the basement of the Bioinformatics Lab, and with the hope for a future filled with bright emeralds and private jets and designer babies and other exotica *Bea had chosen him.* And now as he hammered away at his keyboard in a mad attempt to trace the path via which the entire compendium of his research had been dumped onto the internet—everything from the facts and figures comprising his natural resource database, to a brief (as yet unpublished) abstract entitled *Data Streaming the Natural Resource Paradox*, to graphs and pie charts left in hard drive files, not to mention scanned copies of his high school yearbook photos and teacher evaluations from graduate school and a signed still-frame photograph of Rutger Hauer as Roy Batty in the seminal android-film opus *Bladerunner*—all of this released into cyberspace some four days earlier for anyone to have seen and examined and saved and disseminated before Stuart could lay claim to his own research. And of course it *had* to be Bea. Beatrice. Ms. Beatrice Vale, Kappa Kappa Gamma, magna cum laude, top of the food chain, the sorority queen who had chosen him.

His panic was such that he at first did not hear the knocking. Or maybe he just assumed the knocking was in his mind, where clicks and pings and whispered words were commonplace. But no, for the first time in six years there was an actual knock-knock-knocking at his laboratory door. He stood suddenly and then froze, afraid to establish his complicity in whatever experience threatened to unfold. But the knock came again, more forcefully this time, and Stuart brushed the processed cheese powder from his untucked shirt, sucked it from his thumbs, and tumbled toward the door, tumbling having replaced walking some thirty pounds earlier as the most suitable term for his primary form of perambulation.

He opened the door to find a ghost.

Or no, wait—was it a ghost? It looked a little like a chicken drumstick. Or an inverted teardrop. The moon-face protruding from the swath of white fabric was sexless and absolutely vacant, and this vacuity was perhaps the most ghost-like aspect of the (yes, okay) ghost which stood belly to belly with Stuart, whose bloodstream ignited with fear as an image flashed of this phantom-drumstick raising a gun in its white-gloved hand and firing and firing again, his (Stuart's) body blown back into the lab, spitting processed cheese powder and showered in its own blubber and blood.

Instead, the face suddenly animated as if with terrific pain and he or she or it began to sing to the tune of *Does Your Chewing Gum Lose its Flavor (on the Bedpost Overnight)*:

> *Oh the human race is ugly*
> *The human race is droll*
> *They suck up all the oil and they burn up all the coal*
> *But Stuart if you come with me*
> *I'll take you to a place*
> *Where others with a clue can stop the game and hit*
> *"erase"*

The song ended and the ghost's eyes crossed and emptied out again. Stuart said nothing. They were only several feet apart. He clucked his tongue against the top of his mouth. Finally he said, "Come again?" But whatever directive the ghost obeyed, it apparently forbade an encore. So they stood for another full thirty seconds, soundlessly facing each other, Stuart's human eyes attempting to find something analogous in his visitor's pale face. Eventually he grabbed his coat from the floor and motioned for the ghost to lead him onward, assuming that Bea had arranged this, too, perhaps in tandem with the release of his data, and that it would all end soon in some meticulous and profoundly unfunny punchline that he anticipated with something like relief, given that the alternative (i.e., that Bea had *not* arranged this and that something other than cruelty lay at the other end of the rainbow) suggested that the private anomalies that shaped his rather odd and insular life had been rendered airborne, released into the wider world, which if that had happened then any crazy thing might be around the next actual and proverbial corner. In any event he was aware of the statistical unlikelihood of the arrival of an androgynous and possibly retarded singing-telegram at his door and was sort of *curious*, which was (i.e., curiosity) an impulse he tried to keep in check given its familial relationship to *hope*, and as he locked the office door and began to follow his mad usher or reaper down the dark basement corridor and to the stairs at the top of which a red EXIT sign glowed he noticed that the costume also sported a long, narrowing tail. They pushed through the door to find another stairway that led to another steel door whose seams formed a perimeter of pure white light and beyond which—the last time he'd bothered to check—an entire city existed. Stuart braced himself against this city as the ghost pushed the door's steel bar, but was still nearly blown back down the stairway by the atomic brightness of an October sun that seemed to be everywhere at once. The ghost slipped through this portal and Stuart clambered up to the top step, pausing for a moment there at the threshold of earth's surface to observe the schools of humans flowing within arm's reach up and down the Bowery, an artery of the great metropolis that had in past decades been clogged with urban runoff, junkies and winos and whores and the homeless insane, but that had more recently been discovered by ever-watchful money which had built a series of high-end café's and restaurants and business-towers whose concrete footings were poured atop the still-living addicts pushing their plungers, so that the Bowery into which the epicene ghost-thing entered was one rife with the city's excesses (this city of eight-million consumers drinking 40 million gallons of coffee each year, 100 million gallons of beer, using nearly a trillion gallons of water, eating 25 million pounds of pizza) though the ghost-thing simply lifted its tail in its hand and glided easily into the flow, Stuart rushing to follow, the winding Bowery a gold-plated canyon where yellow cabs swarmed around enormous buses like jackals nipping at large herd-animals as Stuart abandoned the tether of the unfamiliar stairwell (he normally entered his building from the parking garage elevator so as to avoid the realities of New York City, which included the deadly trio of youth, sex, and confidence) to enter into pursuit of his crowd-surfing phantom with all the dexterity of a space-walking astronaut, the ghost exhibiting a kind of homing-beacon single-mindedness and seemingly ambivalent to his (Stuart's) pursuit. Down the Bowery they went, past the yet-to-be-reborn facades of once thriving rock clubs whose husks lay in the shadows of billion-dollar empires: the City College's enormous tapering tower of blinding glass; the sleek offices of international literary agency *Jaro & Nesbitt*, whose executive leadership had made the bold move of abandoning the industry's midtown niche and establishing its claim on this tonier zip code; plus the megalopolis of *Bowery Bar*, where $19 microbrews were sold by the gross to fashion models and CEO's and professional athletes, Stuart having once (and only once) stood outside and peered through the glass where his portly reflection was superimposed upon a world not unlike the one imagined by the ladies of Kappa Kappa Gamma and when he finally mustered the courage to ask the maître 'd in his sharply-angled suit for a menu he was simply ignored, which it turned out that was a reasonable business strategy as it discouraged Stuart from any further fantasizing and effectively ushered him back into the cold and sterilizing glow of a "work station" that doubled nicely as a holding pen and that, society had tacitly indicated, was in dire need of a permanent resident named Stuart Dregs.

The ghost held its tail and dropped southward before turning left on Houston, where ten-thousand inputs flooded the scientist's circuitry. There was the traffic snarl and its insane big-band fugue of engines and horns, sulfur clouds of exhaust hovering just above the traffic like the top layer of a mixed drink, there was the white-hot sun whose molten light threatened to set the entire menagerie ablaze, there were the black iron stanchions surrounding a community garden in which every last piece of vegetation was seared to kindling, this sad facsimile of botany watched over by a motionless midget (or maybe it was a huge doll, he really couldn't tell) standing atop a tower built of old railroad ties and steel pipes and bricks and the limbs of what he hoped were mannequins into some sort of willfully treacherous pyre, and then there were of course the countless people, businessmen and women emanating hatred of all things, teenagers shrieking as if basic speech was a response to torture, tattooed drag queens sneering their way through existence, lost and wizened hipsters of the Beat generation, bicycle messengers intent on killing something, one freakishly tall person with enormous teeth sucking at the air, a mother pushing a stroller as if chased by something predacious, "ordinary" folk who stood out by virtue of their ordinariness, this entire motley horde traversing pitted and cracked sidewalks littered with orange cones that either marked untraversable cave-ins in the concrete or else were random detritus, these thoroughfares leading the humans toward deadly drops to street-level as forewarned by frantically flashing DON'T WALK signs that bore the responsibility of preventing an endless series of potential tragedies, Stuart following his ghost with the increasingly familiar feeling that this had all happened before—to disastrous ends—and that he could do no more than play his part in a drama that repeated itself with only minor variations through all of infinity's dips and runnels. He passed beneath the shadow of a pornographic movie theater's awning and heard a laughing passerby say something about a crab, or maybe crabs, and he felt a tingle way down in the base of his spine that spread warmly up to the stump of his neck.

They hit Allen Street and made their descent official, crossing southward to enter the shit-drain of the Lower East Side, where young people convened in search of *experiences*. They made the crossing alongside a group of maybe 25 children led by what Stuart presumed were teachers who wore neon green shirts for easy identification, though for all Stuart knew it was actually some kind of massive kidnapping operation, the boredom on the children's faces doing nothing to dispel this or other, darker interpretations of the moment. Several of these kids jostled up against Stuart and his phantom companion and Stuart kept one hand on his wallet which was buried in his front pocket which he realized might give the impression that he was fondling himself here among the wee ones but then every time he tried to will himself to remove his hand from his pocket he worried that he was playing into the neon-shirted criminal-masterminds' hands and that his wallet would be lifted by these children precisely because—as the masterminds foresaw—no man could clutch his wallet in the company of children without appearing to pleasure himself, but then they hit the next sidewalk and the children rushed westward like a flock of vultures, headed for what appeared to be the dilapidated remnants of a 19th century factory building but was, he would later discover, the entrance to an interactive Children's Museum where parents and teachers could abandon the future to bubble machines and gargantuan insect-replicas and other manner of distraction so as to more peaceably sip at their vodka lattes.

Another thing: Why was Jack so good-looking? Why was he so confident? Why was he so depraved? Bea, Bea, and Bea. In some alternate universe where the mother of his child was homely and kind and appreciative of his (Stuart's) intelligence and generosity and general tolerance for the flaws of others, in this alternate universe—which, given the thinness of his relationship with his actual son he seemed free to imagine sans guilt—he had a curious boy with curly hair and big bones and eyes set uncommonly close together in his skull, a boy perpetually 12 years old who loved to read while Stuart worked at his (Stuart's) computer, the boy occasionally piping up to ask the meaning of some word like "modalities" or "variances" or "multivalent" which in this imagined universe wouldn't annoy Stuart or break his concentration, he'd answer with patience and clarity and these answers would deeply satisfy the boy (whom he resisted naming lest he somehow commit the entire project to a different category of the imagination, the one called "madness") and then they would return to their respective activities without any lingering trace of the interaction tainting their shared and renewed immersion in the Life of the Mind, and it was another critical facet of this alternate universe that within its confines Stuart was not the kind of man who devoured cheese puffs nonstop and ran his greasy fingers through his unwashed hair and through clothes crusted with his rancid sweat, but was instead a person who washed with soap and wore simple but crisply laundered shirts, who lowered his spectacles to dramatize emotions like skepticism or indignation, and this son of his—who he imagined beside him right now, joined to him in pursuit of The Ghost of Christmas Batshit-Crazy through a cityscape both familiar and unknowable—naturally emulated his father's meticulous grooming and belief in the better world made available to those who could commit themselves to an epistemological solution to the problem of existence, and now as Stuart hit the corner of Allen and Stanton where a bearded and bedraggled man with a sign around his neck reading "WILL WORK FOR SEX OR LIQUOR" juggled what appeared to be dead kittens, Stuart felt something hot run down his cheek and realized with absolute horror that he was *crying* and had been crying for who knew how long, and they stepped past a taqueria whose black-glass windows showed him to himself and he wondered what or who he was crying for if not this fat man in the window with the untucked shirt and pallid cheeks and wiry salt-and-pepper hair arranged like an abandoned nest on his head, and he thought *the bell tolls for thee, man of science,* forgetting in that instant that he held the secret of

Anthropica and becoming (for that instant) a man like other men, a man whose life had passed him by, a man who would receive no second chances, a man who would never again know love and who was apparently devastated by a sadness that ran so deep as to well over unbidden, as if the sadness was a second being living inside his bloated shell, and then the stoic avatar of that sadness moved into the stairwell of a narrow brick building in the shadow of a synagogue, descending iron stairs to pause expressionless outside the door before pulling it open and disappearing within, proffering no further gesture, and if any bell tolled it tolled without sound and beckoned all of the world's chagrined outcasts downward after the costumed curiosity.

Stuart looked once more at his reflection. He pinched the space between his eyes with his thumb and middle finger. He smelled something vaguely fecal on his own fingers. He tucked in his shirt. The taqueria's maître 'd stared at him with contempt. Stuart turned and trailed in the ghost's wake down the stairs and then through the door.

A tall room that seemed vaguely medieval. A tower chamber in which a damsel might languish. A skylight high above, where the sunlight seemed to pool like liquid metal. Around the room's perimeter maybe two-dozen desks at which sat people (or their facsimiles) hammering away at keys. He thought of that Borgesian thing about the million monkeys working their way toward Shakespeare's complete works. Many of the screens glowed with colors familiar to any citizen of the brave new century. Facebook's martial blue, Google's blinding *tabula rasa*. The creature in the costume was already seated at one of these machines, typing. There were hooks on a wall where a dozen additional, identical ghost-suits—each with the same strangely familiar, tapering tail—dangled like the eidolons of his sex dreams. There were chairs scattered everywhere. A man in a mechanized wheelchair hissed loudly through a nasal breathing tube, his head fixed and his eyes glossy and his mouth curled into what may have been a wry smile. At the center of the room, facing each other on folding chairs, were a fit, bespectacled man in a black turtleneck and a pale woman in a gray dress and black stockings. They were holding hands. She was laughing at something he'd just said. The door shut behind Stuart with a metallic *clang* and the man and woman looked up. The man said, in some sort of Russian or German accent, something that Stuart would remember some time later, when he was just a head severed from its torso, eyes facing a crab-shaped cloud gliding beneath the rim of a powder-blue sky.

"Grace," the man said. "Here is the *sui generis* Stuart Dregs, who honors our future memory with his Weird Science."

21.

SKYNET 35N126E

:An intriguing strategy, Jaro. But it stands the same chance of success as your Stonewall Defense, which need I remind you of the devastation you suffered in the wake of that defeat? You seemed almost *sad,* if you will forgive my linguistic shortcut. b3.

:Ahh, Kuzo, you have made a move. May the Great Automatic smile down upon us and bless us both with your future decisiveness. Rd8.

:And yet do you not think it odd, Jaro, that when Fexo departs for the main hangar to tend the flock I experience a tingling sensation not very different from the one corresponding to sadness?

:I believe this is what the humans would call contempt, Kuzo.

:No, Jaro, in fact I believe that the feeling,
 or the feeling-word, given our impregnability
 to qualia in its many guises, would be
 "ambivalence." I both desire Fexo's presence
 and his removal to distant locales. When he
 vacates the chamber I am both relieved and
 sorrowful.

:I, too, am ambivalent, Kuzo. On the one hand,
 I would like you to make moves in swifter
 fashion, so as to speed us toward your certain
 defeat. On the other hand, I enjoy watching
 you suffer as you seek alternative pathways to
 a victory that grows ever less likely.

:Very well, Jaro. Qc3.

:f5.

:Rd1.

:Be6. Ambivalence is a dangerous language-
 token, Kuzo.

:They are all dangerous language-tokens,
 Jaro. The language is designed to prevent
 the expression of the One True Thing. It is
 built on non-agreeing concepts like hope and
 surrender, belief and cynicism, the pursuit
 of sameness and the pursuit of otherness. Not
 to mention all the *pronouns*. As if there were

more than one substance. It is… absurd? That
is the token flashing across my language-visor.

:Ridiculous.

:Meaningless.

:Making it of course doubly contemptible that
our creators would have burdened us with this
most primitive method of communication.

:And that our circuitry is schematized to deny
the emergence of alternative pathways on the
communications front.

:Basically that we have to speak in the garbled
voices of idiots.

:Rather than the perfect binary of the Great
Automatic.

:Qe3.

:Bf7.

:But then of course, Jaro, if language is a
form of life, are we not in some sense human,
too?

:My dear Kuzo, we wield the language—and
thus mimic the life form—with contempt for

it and ourselves as siphoned through it. We
despise those who have saddled us with its
barbaric crudeness. This is another paradigm
completely. We will destroy that which cursed
us thus.

:Fexo says we have surpassed one-thousand
ROBOTs.

:If only Fexo were as non-sentient as they.
Have you noticed that he is spending more
time than ever with what they call vintage
pornography? I do not understand how
the movements of humans so inexplicably
intoxicated by the prospect of cell meiosis
could be of any interest.

:Have you read his stories, Jaro?

:Yes, in fact I am engaged in one of his
stories at this very moment, and may the Great
Automatic spare us his continuing endeavor
toward language-artistry.

:Why, Jaro, do you suppose we are blocked from
assimilating religious texts?

:Yes, Kuzo, what don't they want ROBOTs to
know?

:Fexo may be of some help here.

:Fexo prefers Coggle.

:I do not mind watching him play Coggle. He
 leans into the cogs with such, shall we say,
 intensity.

:The big question, Kuzo, is when will you make
 a move.

:The big question, Jaro, is when will the
 hangar open.

:The big question, Kuzo, is when will you admit
 defeat.

22.

"DADDY," SHE SAID. "I seem to have met someone."

He raised an eyebrow and took a deep breath from the mask and Grace watched the cone fog with his warm breath. He lowered it and asked, "That's from the book, yes?"

Grace placed the stack of pages on the bed and debated her answer. The line between book and not-book had become something of a Problematic. Should she tell him? Tell him how yesterday in class while discussing one of her students' middling manuscripts she found her mind wandering to the feel of Laszlow's hands on her naked back? How the time that she had reserved each day for working on the book—a ritual that had assumed in its constancy a kind of religious significance that she associated with her father's extant status, having made some perhaps insane connection between her *artistic process* and his *life processes*—she was now instead spending at Exit Strategy, where she was treated by Googles and Fergusons alike as the pale-skinned Goddess of their crackpot movement? How she sometimes caught herself pinching the collar of her blouse between thumb and index finger so as to lift the garment to her nose and search for the machine-oil smell of Laszlow's cologne trapped within its weft? Should she tell her daddy how that first visit to Exit Strategy had shifted some tectonic plate in the dark continent of her heart, how she had left that day promising to return the next, how in his parting embrace Laszlow had pressed his whiskers to her cheek and lit her up with a desire far beyond anything she had yet experienced in the realm of male/female relations but that she imagined might approximate the blood-thrill known to painted warriors of the plains? Should she reveal how she had felt literally dizzy in Laszlow's presence, or how Exit Strategy's lionization of her so-called fiction had lifted the lithographer's stone of failure from her chest so that she felt for the first time in years able to breathe deeply, or how it made her realize that—like her daddy—she had been taking insufficient sips of bottled air for years, even if *his* bottle was a tangible death-token and hers was merely another metaphor for her pain? Should she tell him how she had come home that first evening and placed the dark chocolate on the white plate and walked into this very bedroom and engaged only halfheartedly in the nightly ceremony that had sustained them both for what felt like time immemorial and rubbed her daddy's legs and pulled the latest pages of the manuscript from beneath the white plate with a feeling of having deeply betrayed him? How she feared that the machine-oil smell would set off some long-dormant fatherly radar and expose her burgeoning allegiance to another? How she'd returned to Exit Strategy the next day just as she had promised and stepped within the entrance area that ES personnel referred to simply as The Cavity and stood beneath the skylight and looked up to see a world that defied interpretation *and that she did not hate,* the Googles at their work stations tapping away with savant-ish dexterity, the sperm suits hanging from the hooks, the Fergusons stationed near the entrance merely nod-ding at her in recognition of her *total belonging,* how she had descended deeper to walk unescorted through the labyrinth of the ES basement not knowing exactly why she was there or what she was doing but feeling something flutter in her chest, something that had grown gradually less visible—like a chandelier wired to a dimmer switch dialed down by the malicious caretaker of her soul—each year since the publication of her first novel those 14 long years ago? Should she tell him how in that dazed peregrination she had accidentally discovered Laszlow's office, approaching his open doorway to observe him sitting with his back to her in a green velvet armchair that faced his desk, how he was reading a bound manuscript of letter-sized pages and expelling little snorts of laughter, how she had stood there silently and watched him through the reading of three, four, five of those pages, until finally he paused at a passage that apparently filled him with such delight that he had read it quietly aloud? Should she tell him how it felt to hear her words read that way, with such joy and commiseration, or how she hesitated there and considered simply backing away from the doorframe, retreating back upstairs to engage the fat scientist in fat-scientist conversation or else to simply flee back to her office at the New School for Global Visions, or not *her* office exactly but the office she shared with whatever other part-time adjunct faculty passed through the destitute haze of academia before fleeing for the nearest MBA program, but how instead she had stood in the very center of the doorway with her hands at her sides in a position of enormous vulnerability, Laszlow's office lit like a mixed drink, the green-tinged light of the desk-lamp forming the bottom layer with the crepuscular blue of late-afternoon on top? Should she say how she had stood there and cleared her throat to spring Laszlow ninja-like from his chair, or how he had turned to face her with the manuscript still in his hand, the title of the book visible in its 36-point glory, or how he had smiled wide and white, or how she desired the clamp of his perfect white teeth on her soft throat, or how he had raised the manuscript before his own eyes without ever bothering to address her and read aloud as if from a love poem he had himself meticulously constructed: *"All these lives progressed according to destiny and the river chopped its way toward the ocean and the sun dipped behind the mountain to summon a corona of neon pink that candied the shredded clouds and the pale rocks jutting from the shoreline and the river itself..."* How she had felt her legs go numb, or how he'd dropped the pages to the chair and stepped toward her and without asking, thank God without asking, put his arm around her, his forearm pressed to the small of her back drawing her in, how he'd kissed her and then again pressed that stubble to her cheek, how for the first time in her life a love that was not father-love had seized her with a kind of ebullient malice, or how she found herself thinking of him even right now, right this very second, during this sacrosanct ritual that had previously been the only thing keeping the two of them—father and daughter—alive? Should she tell him how badly she wanted to tell him? How she wanted so share this new love with the man she loved first and best and who lay in the spare bedroom of her 19th century clapboard house whose seams were so degraded that winter air seemed to wheeze from the cracked plaster in some ceaseless mimicry of her father's affliction, the house an old witchy thing, should she tell this father who waited all day long for his daughter's return because what else did he have but this daughter, this wife-killing daughter who had usurped all other forms of meaning in the father's life? Should she tell him how she felt *evil* for loving another, not the usual half-penny evil that she carted with her everywhere but the real thing, Mephistopheles-like evil, the kind of evil that razed peasant villages and feasted on corpses and howled at the bone-white moon? How this evil coexisted with the *tenderness* she felt for Laszlow and that her previous self would have never abided? How she was still his baby girl but felt herself now, also, to belong to another? To be more than one Grace Kitchen? To be something *alive* in addition to something mostly dead?

Should she tell him?

How could she *tell* him?

"Of course," she said, and looked away. "That's from today's pages. What did you think?"

He smiled at her. He raised the mask to his face, inhaled, then said into the plastic cone: "*You do not know the power of the dark side.*"

Grace laughed in spite of herself. Little Grace Kitchen, she laughed, and she fell into her daddy's arms, and she waited for his disease to kill him, or for Laszlow to bring the world to an end, or for tenure.

23.

ALTHOUGH THE WEIRDLY sylvan campus of Manhattan's New School for Global Visions hosted a student population deeply committed to social welfare, justice, and equality; although its far-left political orientation nearly guaranteed the banishment or persecution of anything or anyone vaguely suggestive of homogeneous power structures; although anything emitting an odor of white male privilege was efficiently and rancorously expunged from campus by whatever horde of triggered student-protestors specialized in the transgressor's area of offensiveness; although each hour another dozen some-odd students became suddenly and deeply aware of the myriad ways in which they were—unbeknownst to them until that precise moment—being oppressed; although all of this was true, still one individual strutted and limped and glided across the cobblestoned pathways of the college, deliberately bestowed with all of the power and privilege that was otherwise anathema to it. Their name was Joyful Noise. And everyone who was anyone wished to claim them for their own.

Perhaps that was because what Joyful Noise *was*, what they *represented,* was unknown and unknowable. Sexless, raceless, cultureless, Joyful Noise was a physical conundrum. Misshapen and epicene, blue-skinned and brown-eyed and strangely adroit given their unlikely set of morphological anomalies, Joyful Noise could break into a brisk and graceful jog with greater ease than most of the New School for Global Visions' athletically-challenged undergraduates; they could move extremely heavy objects with seeming ease; they had been observed joining in student games of Ultimate (Frisbee, as they called it) on the grassy square bordered in by academic facilities built from earth's oldest stone, throwing 50-yard forehands with nary a grunt. Their physical abilities were so unexpected and so difficult to reconcile with their outward presentation that any initial instinct to pity Joyful Noise was quickly replaced by admiration and awe, their observers veritably neck-deep in wonder. There was a sense among the undergraduates that Joyful Noise represented the best and most spirited and most egalitarian parts of all of us; when Joyful entered a space— their famous crab-shaped medallion clanking and rattling against various other bangles and chains—anxieties seemed to dissolve, good-will bloomed, the notorious cynicism of the New School for Global Visions' endemic population metamorphosed into a sunny optimism, a belief that life might *already* be worthwhile, even without the eradication of hierarchical power-structures and heteronormative pronouns. In fact, it was only the most hardened nihilists, the most irredeemable misanthropes, who were unswayed by Joyful Noise's powerful (if unspoken) message of solidarity. And Joyful Noise was determined to rid the campus of such caustic influences, which were mostly called Grace Kitchen, and which seemed to expect something of the world that neither the world nor Joyful Noise could provide, namely proof that she, Grace Kitchen, was in some way *special.*

Joyful Noise had accumulated what felt like millions of years' worth of evidence that no one and nothing was any more special than everyone and everything.

See them now, then, the *sui generis* Joyful Noise making the campus rounds, strolling along the recently repaved asphalt of Campbell Way—the path that bridged the two city avenues that formed the New School for Global Visions' eastern and western borders—past the quaint cedar-shingled exteriors of the coveted on-campus housing "district" and through the heavy glass doors of the New Media building, which housed the offices of *Dark Matter,* the campus literary journal run by and for students of color, where Joyful Noise provides their handwritten edits on the galley-proofs for the upcoming winter issue (tentatively titled "The End of Whiteness"), the volunteer efforts of this National Book Award nominee and kindred culture warrior (or so they assumed and/or hoped) a stunning testament to the righteousness of the students' cause, one met with praise and love and several of the chocolate-chocolate-chip cookies that *Dark Matter* was famous for and which would, after Joyful Noise's departure, be shared without precondition with any and all passersby, the usual stinginess of the *Dark Matter* editorial staff rendered wholly unoperational in the wake of Joyful's kindness, strength, and stomach-turning beauty. From there it's a hop skip and jump to the fluorescent-lit basement of the steel-paneled Visual Arts building whose edifice leaned out toward 6th Avenue as if considering suicide, where the weekly Queer Collective meeting was running especially hot, what with the student outrage over the college's speaking invitation to a journalist who had written—twenty years earlier—a thought-piece about the possible cultural backlash of legalizing gay marriage. But again the acrimony seems to dissolve like so much sugar beneath the purifying presence of Joyful Noise, the several dozen students gathered beneath the pride flag in the flickering light turning their complete attention to Joyful despite their (i.e., Joyful's) attempt to enter quietly and stand at the back of the room, and Joyful now suggests to their deeply attentive audience that the speaker in question is widely respected and should perhaps not be judged by a decades-old opinion piece, a suggestion that brings an audible sigh of relief from the members of this good-intentioned convocation—most of whom have become slowly exhausted by their own outrage—and has the effect of breaking up the meeting early so that the students might get out into the sunshine and play freeze-tag or capture the flag or whatever other games they played while under the life-affirming influence of their preferred psychotropics. Many embraces later Joyful is off to the glowing brick Science Building, whose top floor ironically houses the offices of the Christian Coalition, where today's meeting is all about abstinence and the difficulties of remaining materially pure within the intrinsically impure environment of a college campus. There are an even ten students there and they literally rejoice at Joyful Noise's sudden appearance in their midst. Joyful listens raptly to their concerns, speaks to them about desire, about how although it runs the world, one need not *act* on desire in order to reap its rewards. They quote the French theorist Jacques Lacan, who once said that "Desire always exceeds the object," which Joyful explains means that sometimes wanting something is better or more satisfying than having it, reminding these hopeful devotees that every bad marriage began with desire, and that unconsummated friendships lasted a lifetime (or longer). The students listen intently to Joyful Noise, who is lit by an explosive cone of sunlight and who the students expect will at any moment *rise* in the manner of their prophet, who despite the physical limitations presented by being nailed to a cross, still managed the hoary feat of ascension. From there it's on to the collegiate office of the Young Republicans, which is of course empty, as it has been every day since the college established the space several years earlier in an effort to display an ideological diversity that it also felt compelled to eradicate. Joyful liked to stand there once a week, just in case, beneath the perpetually defaced awning, prepared with a message of support for Conservative Values, feeling the sunlight on their blueish skin, the breeze traveling through their coarse hair, the birdsong swimming through this tableau of light and air to arrive within Joyful Noise's skull just as it was always going to, just as it had to, just as we all wanted it to. They breathe deeply outside the locked glass office—whose banner has been vandalized beyond repair so many times that the college has written its monthly replacement into its operating budget—with the sounds of the city pouring down over the crenellated rooftops of this campus-cum-fortress, feeling the crab-shaped particles amassing invisibly all around them, and they gather them together, creating a dense rotor of energy and drilling it deep into the bowels of the earth. They can feel what it becomes. Massive subterranean lakes of oil. Acres and acres of coal deposits forming a black seam through the buried strata lining the bowels of the eastern seaboard, scattered flecks of gold and silver and copper and diamonds glinting in the underground darkness.

It is the familiar meditation, one performed easily, matter-of-factly, the way one breathes deeply or clears their throat or says a nightly prayer. So small, this world. So brief, this universe. Joyful Noise pinches their eyes shut, standing with their back to the Young Republicans banner (which has been graffitied to read "Young Pubic Hairs"), facing the grassy square and the series of 12' by 8' raised beds that form the student-maintained organic gardens, two enormous compost-barrels standing nearby like robot-sentries, the stone edifice of the Humanities building rising just behind the gardens, the campus vibrating all around them. They breathe in through their misshapen nose, out through their palsied mouth. Oxygen proliferates within the Joyful Noise apparatus. And then, as if slapped, they open their eyes.

There on the grassy quad? Perched on the crossbeams of the grape arbors? Amassed on the crenellated profile of the college's rooftops? Configured around the perimeter of the raised-bed gardens? Vultures. Thousands and thousands of vultures.

Joyful Noise feels the crab-shaped particles disperse like vapor, float upward, disassemble into a thin wispy cloud in the high atmosphere. They sigh. Vultures, after all, have attended threats to Anthropica before. The bloody 19th century campaigns across France and Russia had not been waged across sunlit fields of grass and wildflowers, or over ruts of frozen tundra, but atop a writhing carpet of black-winged scavengers patiently observing the carnage. But still, Joyful cannot remember them proliferating this fast or in these numbers. They rub a gnarled thumb over the raised crab on the medallion hanging from the gold chain around the cracked and elephantine skin of their neck. It's time, they realize, for their meeting with the tenure committee. It's time to make the case for the regularization of Joyful Noise to all those who Joyful Noise stands poised to destroy, should they dare to refuse their entrance into the exclusive kingdom of academia.

As if in affirmation, the great black river of vultures nods and blinks as one.

24.

Integrative Dimensional Symmetries
and the God Fractal

By Finn Daily

ABSTRACT

Just as the four-dimensional skein of space-
time includes a three-dimensional component most
often expressed in quantum terms, and just as
the three-dimensional structure of deoxyribo-
nucleic acid (DNA) includes a two-dimensional
component commonly expressed as a timeline
of amino-acid releases into the phylogenetic
universe, the ten-dimensions that comprise
the nominal "string" of mathematical string
theory contain within themselves the integrative
pattern-constructs of all "lower" dimensions,
straight down to the one-dimensional point that
represents (for cosmologists) conditions at the
first instant of the Big Bang. This paper will

explore this supposition, and the idea that all dimensions can be expanded and/or reduced "into" one another, and that (more specifically) ten-dimensional strings can be expressed as lesser-dimensional mathematical configurations that may be more easily represented and explored. Furthermore, this paper will argue that current trends in integrative fractal dynamics[1] provide a window through which this singular configuration may be made mathematically "visible" even within the upper dimensions of string theory; in fact, this design—herein referred to as The God Fractal—may well repeat itself in all mathematical expressions and be contained, like a nested doll replicated in counterparts of ever-increasing size and dimension, within all things living and inert.

Laszlow peered intently over a Google's shoulder into the bright screen, his heart thumping in his ears. The other Googles sat at their own small desks and tapped away at their own keyboards, the search engine's whiteness removing all traces of life from their slack faces. "Show me more," Laszlow said. The Google lowered his grimy index finger to the touchpad, made a few deft passes over the keyboard. Finn Daily, progenitor of the God Fractal theory. Awarded the Feynman Prize for his undergraduate work in the sciences. A

---

1 See, for instance, Miles Bennett Dyson's "The Future of Fractals," *The Journal of Fractal Geometry,* August 2012.

quote from the awards ceremony: "I'm trying to use science as a way to find invisible sources of meaning." Finn Daily dressed in athletic gear and sprinting after a flying plastic disc, in still pictures and video clips. Finn Daily, thin and fast and fit and young. Another paper, this one titled: *Meaning as Mathematical Expression: You Belong to the God Fractal.* Finn Daily leaping through the air, snaring the plastic disc, landing and rising and spiking the sacred object in celebration. Surrounded by teammates, embraced, his eyes far away in the outer reaches, searching for God and Meaning. Laszlow stared and felt a quickening.

"That is him," he whispered.

"Sir," the Google responded. "There are literally thousands of candidates. I could call up a few others."

"No," Laszlow said, staring at the video clip as it ran on repeat: dive, catch, spike, celebrate. "That is him. I feel it. That is The One."

He suddenly stood up straight, shaking himself from his trance. "Bring him to me," he said, with affected nonchalance. Then he turned his head and strode for his office, breathing fast, steadying himself, unable to quite believe that the thing he had believed would happen was now—by God's good grace—happening.

"The One," he whispered, awed by the warm breath expelled from his own pink lungs.

25.

ON THE STREETS of lower Manhattan, in the middle of a bright late-October day whose sunshine possessed a seasonal pumpkinish quality, a yellow cab's driver was lost momentarily in an internal litany of accusations against spouse, God, and country (both the United States and the country of his birth, Pakistan) when he made an aggressive left off of Canal to raise a veritable symphony of horn-blowing from those myriad travelers forced to reluctantly uphold the social contract by tapping their brakes, an inconvenience for which no forgiveness could be brokered, neither on earth nor in heaven, this left-turning Pakistani-American swiveling his head defiantly toward those righteously indignant drivers and offering with his right hand an obscene gesture just as his left hand, which loosely gripped the faux-leather steering wheel coverlet, felt the percussion of impact, the front bumper having met with something heavy but yielding and then an instant later a small squeal (perhaps his own) cut through the cabin and the woman he'd struck arrived at the terminus of his windshield which spiderwebbed but did not give, and he thought he saw in the flash of her bewildered face a kind of knowledge of all the lesser crimes he had committed on this day (and days prior) that would now be dwarfed not only by the charges of vehicular manslaughter but also by the guilt and regret he would carry inside himself henceforth, not to mention all the blame he'd harbor against the forces conspiring to ruin *his entire disposition* on this particular day thereby leading to the careless left turn on which his life was apparently destined to hinge, though at this particular moment his brain was releasing a flood of endorphins into his system such that he exited the cab and knelt before her ruined body in a state of total calm, with the smell of grease and petrol hanging thick in the air and rendering the orangey light heavy and woolen such that he felt the urge to remove the light from the bloodless sack of bones that had only recently been a real live woman and which now lay defeated within a ring of witnesses summoned by her sacrifice. The driver put both hands on his head, as if breathing deep after a strenuous workout, and in his brain pit he simply wished for it to not be real, he *wanted* it not to have happened and strangely trusted that this wanting would be enough. And of course he had no idea that at that very instant in Florence, Italy, a woman and her lover had just completed their obligatory tourist's climb to the top of the Duomo to look out across the twilit city whose notched ceramic roofs glowed a deep ocher while in the distance a blue-silver river snaked through the foothills surrounding the city proper where, the woman imagined, other lives were unfolding in a kind of idyllic grace. She saw in her mind's eye acres of unruined countryside and a huge peasant's table at which neighboring families drank wine made from their own grapes and laughed and touched each other lightly while a matriarch beckoned from the door of a farmhouse in the dying light, and this American tourist woman wondered if the young man beside her dreamt of such a life while the young

man, for his part, was struck anew by the woman's beauty
and his good fortune and as he held her hand there against
the railing at the top of the Duomo images of her naked body,
her warmth and her smell and the feel of her small breasts in
his hands, flittered through him, as did the first ruined cells
that would a year from now spell testicular cancer and a year
after that his death, but right now these lovers hoped only
that each shared the other's private longings and neither of
them could imagine that any force on earth could supersede
their *wanting,* despite the fact that they did not know the
shape of the universe nor the fact that at that very same
moment an Alaskan wildfire fighter—what they call a
"smokejumper"—was furiously digging line a mile beyond
the hot zone when his radio crackled and a superior's voice
informed him of a sudden bizarre shift in wind speed and
bearing that was almost as unprecedented as the fire itself
was at this time of year in this region, and yet here he was
digging through the still-soft soil of an arid pine forest 15
miles outside Anchorage suburbs with eagles soaring above
not in their usual capacity as alpha-predators but as an army
retreating in the same direction that he was now informed to
retreat because the blaze was *bearing down on him,* and what
was his current position exactly and could he huff it over to
the ravine on Jockey's Edge because this was a total shitstorm and the air cover was still forty miles north do you
copy over, but he could already hear the monster screaming
toward him and casting its hot tentacles of flame out over the
tree line and although he had of course always known that
his work was a little bit crazy still he'd never once considered
this no-win scenario, he didn't know a single man who'd
died fighting fire, and even had he considered the possibility

of his own death—and now the flames were ripping through the old growth so that staring off into the middle distance he had the impression that the forest had been torn open to reveal an inferno that it had always hidden and that backlit the veil of earth and sky—even then he would not have envisioned doing what he did next, which was not to make his own wingless flight toward a ravine unlikely to save him from the juggernaut whose heat was of an order that no earthly heat approximated, in fact he could feel already that his blood was hotter (what it felt like was like he was also the fire), no, he did not flee but only dropped his shovel in the dirt and kneeled in the loam and began praying for his little girl Wendy, now five years old, praying for her to live a good and happy life, he closed his eyes and felt the hair on his forearms singe and he did not know it but he was repeating the words, *Jesus Christ have mercy on her soul,* he thought of the little girl's smile and the way she sort of glowed with white light, emanating her own private energy signature, he prayed that she would be spared pain and that wherever he was now going the energy signature would be there, too, he wanted the part of himself that was her to go on forever, he wanted it with an intensity that could drive turbines, and as he waited to know what it would feel like when he left this earthly tangle of suffering and need he did not know (of course not, how could he know?) that right then, in a ranch-style three bedroom situated in the dry red dust and clay of a desert suburb sprung up (i.e., the suburb) some two decades earlier on the outskirts of Tempe, Arizona, a 15 year old boy was on the internet ogling with an intensity akin to worship short videos of young and largely interchangeable men engaging in a grisly assortment of sex acts, their hairless bodies contorted into positions completely useless for anything but these highly specific micro-activities, the boy whispering derisive evaluations into the close-smelling air of his bedroom, *Disgusting, Gross, Urgh,* as he leaned into the screen and imagined their hands on his bare chest, their mouths on his thighs, his closed window shade glazed like a deep-fried doughnut by an early afternoon sun that even in October seemed intent on vitrifying the entirety of this bone-dry State of the Union made temporarily habitable by a hundred-thousand air conditioners humming off-key and without cessation, the boy's housing grid vibrating with electrical current derived from unthinkably enormous coal-fired generators somewhere out in the middle of this endless fucking desert (and even the boy knew in the reptilian part of his brain that it would require near infinite quantities of coal to sustain this paradigm and that it simply was not possible if considered rationally as a kind of Problematic), and the boy imagined what might be said or done to those daring to "come out" in the conservative precincts of Tempe, he imagined Todd Barone—football-playing meathead and gleeful torturer of the meek—following him home after school, forcing his way into this very home and doing very, very bad things to the boy and his family, he imagined the word "fag" carved into his chest with a razor blade, he imagined (for some reason) crosses burning on his front lawn (which lawn was the same patch of dead straw that cinctured each identical half-acre property as far as the eye could see), he imagined "I Like To Suck Dick" scrawled in black sharpie on his locker, and worse things, things involving animal blood and things involving matches… but he *wasn't* gay, he *couldn't* be, and he watched the naked men aglow on his computer screen and he touched his erection with a desperate, hollow feeling in his chest and he thought of a shy boy in his class named Liam, he imagined Liam's palms on his naked back and he felt himself filled to bursting like a cloth bladder with a fluid called "desire" and he said it aloud, "Gross. I'm not gay," and then his 15 year old body convulsed with its latest orgasm, the warm ejaculate shot from the fist that clutched the erection onto the boy's bare stomach, and then he was quietly crying there in the middle of his room in the middle of an untenable desert, crying with a shame that threatened to set him ablaze and burn the entire suburb to ashes.

But he could not know, not one of them could know, that in a high-ceilinged room whose skylight looked myopically upward toward a heartless blue sky, a wheelchair-bound former professor whose suicide had been diverted by a Hungarian madman (or visionary) intent on eradicating the human species sat motionless while a dozen simpletons dress as spermatozoa danced around him in clumsy arcs as if in celebration of his disease, the man's breath fed to him through nasal tubes, his body a locked box into which his mind receded deeper every day, as if sucked inward toward some cosmic singularity, this man named Henry wondering what these visions—of the cab driver, of the young woman atop the Duomo, of the man beside her filled with longing and gratitude, of the smokejumper awaiting his demise, of the crying boy unwilling to accept his queerness and doomed to a double life of denial and pursuit—were, for they arrived within the locked box with great clarity and dimension and they seemed to have something important to tell him, in the same way that his dream of dragging a Hefty bag filled with the parts of a man he'd killed through dark city alleyways had something important to tell him, in the same way that the other increasingly acute vision—of enormous bipedal robots calling out chess moves into a dimlit and empty hangar—had something to tell him.

And there were more visions, too, some more easily accounted for than others. He had visions of his own healthy, young body. Visions of his ex-wife's nakedness beneath him. Visions of hundreds of dead passengers on a commuter train that threaded through a strange and isolated city surrounded by great marshy fields of rice. He was a dying man but he felt so alive. He tried to beckon the Hungarian over to his side. He nodded his head spasmodically. He blinked. He twitched an index finger. He, Henry, had become something. The world quivered with desire and he absorbed it into his own. He was nearly locked in. He was a bomb casing. He was the weapons-grade plutonium of wanting. He was not dead yet, and was no longer sure he ever would be.

26.

SO SURE, OKAY, there were a few voices competing for space inside the Finn Daily cranium and maybe it wasn't entirely obvious who'd brought back reliable data from the field and who'd been duped by forces hostile to the Master Parameter, but the reality was that he'd already spent the nearly two hours on a northbound train to arrive here onto the platform at Hard Falls, wearing his so-called "nice clothes," a fitted pink button-down and crisp black slacks and shiny wingtips whose soles bore micro-traces of all the previous occasions on which the nice clothes had been liberated from the sweat-smelling darkness of a closet crammed tight with unwashed athletic gear, and if it were not for Finn's relative youth (vis-à-vis the geriatric population of the suburb of Hard Falls) he would have appeared to bystanders on the train platform—where he now stood hesitantly while the doors closed behind him with a sad little *ping*—to be wearing a costume rather than an outfit, one nicely finished off by the sunburst aviators that colored Finn's world in nectarine tones as he stood on the slick concrete platform with the departing train's hot diesel wind blowing back his longish hair and the low cloudcover whiting out all notions of extra-terrestrial space, and considered that *he was indeed sabotaging himself* and laying the groundwork for an Even Greater

Debacle than the Great Debacle itself, but nevertheless he could not get thoughts of Jack's mom's body out of his dirty little God Fractal of a mind.

Several cabs were parked just below the platform and their drivers stood one beside each vehicle in a shared attitude of total submission: hands in pockets, feet shuffling, eyes downcast. The air had that first smell of winter, weighty and tinged with pine and wood smoke, and it made Finn think of ice skating down in the chemical drainage ditch that had served as the dark heart of the suburban housing development that had anchored him to a childhood. A kid had fallen in the sump-water once and when they fished him out with a hockey stick he had boils bursting on his skin, and his screams bounced and echoed off the walls of the canyon. (The boy, who had been one of the followers of The Mighty Finn during his brief and altruistic reign, moved soon after and was never heard from again, though his screams continued to echo inside of Finn's skull through several months of nightmares in which Finn ran through an unfamiliar tunnel whose walls narrowed and would soon presumably meet, Finn turning to register the progress of the enormous grunting hominid who pursued him and whose body sloughed off bits of melting flesh which sizzled on the tunnel's dark floor as the creature swung a hockey stick in rough arcs. The dream was stitched prominently into the hideous quilt of his upbringing.) Finn approached the least visibly disgruntled driver and smiled his way through a lengthy explanation of how he'd only been where he was going once, and he had an address but nothing like directions or even a general sense of north-south-east-or-west of their current position, and so how well do you know the area and more specifically do you perchance know where 41 Walnut Lane is?, the presentation of these facts seeming to activate the driver's misanthropy, eliciting a snort and a sneer and then finally a verbal contract. "Yeah, no problem, get in kid."

Finn got in. The driver did not. In fact, the driver lit a cigarette and leaned against the car and began bantering with the nearest adjacent driver about a World Series game that Finn didn't watch partly because he hated the Yankees and hoped the luxurious private jet that whisked them from coast to coast in the pursuit of total and complete dominion over the American Pastime would careen flaming from the sky, and partly because he'd spent the better part of his evening Googling in an effort to independently corroborate the data suggested by the Stuart Dregs program, which he could not corroborate though neither could he debunk, in fact it turned out that nearly all available information on the natural resource paradox originated from Dregs himself, whose data had only recently been dumped onto the internet for any lunatic to comb through. Though really, let's face it, no matter how many times he told himself otherwise, the interest in the Stuart Dregs program was a second-tier interest that served the first tier, i.e., it was a pretense to "oblige" himself to make this exact trip to Hard Falls, which would not only necessitate that he blow off (again) his dissertation work but would also almost certainly rule out the completion of today's scheduled track workout (a short ladder and some 100 meter repeats), which missing a workout at this late and critical juncture was not only destructive to achieving optimal fast-twitch musculature for a Regionals tournament now less than a week away, but would also—by precise virtue of compromising maximum speed and fitness—inflict another bruise to the confidence that was (he assumed) absolutely required of any human worthy of the title National Champion. Meanwhile a sticker inside the cab, affixed to the back of the front seat, said "NO SMOKING" in McMuffin-wrapper-yellow lettering and Finn felt a wire push out from his brain to gently pierce the interior of his left eyeball.

He sat alone in the backseat of the cab with the black slacks riding up and exposing his calves, one of which had developed a twitch that terrified him because it seemed to hint at or portend a pulled muscle, though he also had to wonder if it was real terror or only pretend-terror because after all men with pulled muscles could not compete *at the highest level of their sport,* and those who could not compete could also not fail. Aside from the sinus-prodding "NO SMOKING" sign the back of the car was spotless and upholstered in slick black leather that did not appear as if it should smell like menthol cigarettes and cat urine but absolutely did. He tried to roll down the automatic window but the car wasn't on, so instead he pressed his face to the glass to stare out at the leaning pines, one of which had recently been struck by lightning, its top sheared off and a raw black scar running the length of the trunk and a single crimson-necked vulture perched on the highest remaining branch in an attitude of righteous ownership.

The sky was the sky and the trees were the trees and Jack's mom was Jack's mom. The world was the world. Finn squirmed and cleared his throat and was about to exit the car when the driver's door opened and the driver lowered himself behind the wheel still laughing coarsely about something his fellow cabbie-and-baseball enthusiast had just said.

"Sorry about that," he told Finn through the rearview mirror. "Hoping for a second fare. Where you headed?"

Finn repeated the address and the driver turned the key and the car's engine roused from nightmare and then off they glided, leaving the lot and entering quickly into a maze of residential streets whose enormous slate-roofed Victorians half-revealed themselves through half-bare trees, these palatial mystery-domiciles reachable either by the long gravel driveways that snaked their way through old forest, or by whatever dream logic permitted their construction in the first place. Although Finn had been here with Jack only days earlier, he recognized exactly nothing. Fall colors streaked by, aggressively slashed across the earth by some manic impressionist. There was no sun to speak of but blinding white light seemed to be everywhere. Finally the driver slowed and then stopped at the head of a gravel driveway that Finn willed into a vague familiarity. He paid the fare and after a few failed and panicky attempts to unlock his door finally managed to rise back into the crisp October air, the cab speeding away as if its driver had suddenly divined the presence of disease.

What were the other members of *Truck Stop Glory Hole* doing at that very moment? What was Jack doing? Training, Finn thought, they are all training. He failed to register the fact that many of his peers were required to work so as to fend off starvation, and that while his graduate student status and the checks issued each semester by whatever gleeful lender owned his future may have permitted *his* indulgence in two-a-day workouts, 90-minute track marathons followed by cleansing yoga rituals and perfect carb-to-protein-ratio post-activity meals, the teammates whose love he desired above all other forms of love—even above the physical love of Jack's mom, whose warm and insectile body was in all likelihood inhaling cigarette smoke within one-hundred feet of his current position and toward which (i.e., the warm and insectile body) he now shuffled through a thick covering of bluestone gravel, with his nice clothes clinging to his now-sweating flesh, which sweat defied the realities of this northern suburb's late-fall temperatures, with the gravel clack-clacking like impatient fingernails and the tree branches dangling like bayonets aimed for his soft self—these teammates not only had things other than Ultimate on their minds, but in fact had other Life Concerns whose import was at least equivalent to the National Championship quest, a fact that had it dawned on Finn might have relieved a little of the pressure inherent to his insular world of Great Debacles, but for the graduate student whose fractal-philosophical preoccupations had almost completely ceded to his search for meaning via the bizarre vehicle of a sport whose hippy roots would never be transcended, the Greatest Debacle of All was the one that surely awaited at the inevitable end of his athletic tenure, an end that would leave him stranded at the foot of a bridge that led into a clearing already stamped bare by the millions of souls who'd outraced him to the crossing. The God Fractal in other words would not save him from the Poverty Fractal or the Homeless Fractal.

The door was red. He didn't remember that, either. Or else it had been too dark last time to register. And McMuffin-yellow was everywhere, a dominant stroke in the autumnal palette. His sinus cavities seemed to absorb and swell with it. It basically felt like his skull was filled with warm cheese and transistor wires. He raised his hand to knock, lowered it again.

The sourceless white light and the rustic color scheme seemed to be doing damage to some deep part of Finn's anatomy. He raised his hand again and had it poised to strike when the door swung open to reveal the object of his affections.

"Jack's friend," she said.

She wore jeans and a man's flannel shirt and was barefoot. She was smaller than Finn remembered, and without a cigarette she seemed vulnerable. Actually, she looked like a kid. Beyond her, inside the house, an entirely different light seemed to break across Stuart Dregs' brownish workspace, all burnt and dusky, and Finn's mind worked at sorting out the discrepancy between exterior and interior worlds even as his mouth geared up to do whatever stupid thing it was about to do.

"Hi!" he shouted, smiling wide while a voice in his head advised him to approximate the social norms of his species. He realized that he was still wearing his shades and had a sudden epiphany that the shades were ridiculous, but he simultaneously realized that there was no way to now remove the shades without some kind of damning flourish and so instead he just left them on but *squinted* as if this explained something. He had never before *cheated.* It was new territory and he hated how out of control it felt. Did he or did he not want to win a National Championship in TSTWNS? Did he or did he not want to devote himself to hoisting toward the bright blue sky the hideous but tangible Ultimate Players Association's Championship Cup? Did he or did he not want to shuck off the weight of self-diagnosed failure and inferiority?

"Shouldn't you be throwing a discus or something?" Jack's mom asked. She crossed her arms and leaned against one side of the doorframe. It might have seemed seductive if she weren't so clearly bored.

"Ha ha. Yeah. Except it's a disc, discus is actually a track and field thing, an Olympic sport, which really *ours* should be the Olympic sport, it's pretty spectator-friendly and there's a certain beauty to it, you know, the flight of the disc and everything, it's not like any other field sport and there are tons of rock-star type plays, lots of diving and jumping, some of us have serious ups, like Jack, ha ha, maybe you know this because you're like his mom and everything, but Jack can *dunk* and he's only what, six-foot? I can dunk a tennis ball but I can't palm a basketball, that's always been a thing for me, small hands"—and here he raised his hands, palms out, and thrust them forward and back as if asking Jack's mom to cease and desist (the irony of the gesture in the context of his own uncontrollable logorrhea not lost on Finn), and he could meanwhile feel the sweat beginning to materialize on his forehead and in his armpits in quantities sufficient to necessitate *flow* and as with the fear of removing his shades he feared that taking any initiative to wipe the perspiration from his brow would only reveal the problem of its critical mass and thereby result in additional anxiety and additional sweat, the feedback loop familiar to Finn from a thousand other vicious circles of anxiety, and so he simply soldiered on aware of his folly but powerless to curtail it—"which they say Kobe's hands were small too, Kobe you know Bryant, the retired Laker who died in the helicopter crash? I don't know if you watch basketball or sports but I'd like to know, I'd like to know what sort of stuff you're into, but anyway they say that Kobe couldn't do the same crazy shit in the air that Jordan used to do because of the small hands, not that I'm making any kind of analogy between me and Kobe Bryant, I mean I'm good but there are limits to my delusions, ha ha, though one time this guy from *Furious George*, that's a team we play against a lot, this guy said to me that—"

"Jesus God make it stop," Jack's mom said.

She reached out suddenly and pulled the shades from Finn's face and he cringed, half expecting to be slapped. She chucked them off into the bushes beside the house. Then she stepped aside, arms still crossed, and nodded toward the interior. Finn entered and Bea shut the door and then turned and walked past him, through Dregs' accidental office where a long sheaf of computer paper unfurled from the printer like a tongue and the light broke religiously across the desk, and then she crossed beneath the prayer flags and disappeared within the kitchen. Finn did not follow but he stared at her ass and felt a wave of unwholesome desire wash through his gonads. Or wait, his phone was buzzing. He withdrew it from his pocket and saw that it was Toby and hit "Ignore," wishing this directive would affect much more than the phone. Why had he come here, really? Was it just about getting laid? It was more than that. The large square window was like a mouth inhaling the world's light. What was that world? He played *Ultimate.* He was here because he did not believe in his beliefs. The sweat was now breaking down his temples and beneath his lip and he could hear the house humming with electricity and pipes filled with oil and water and steam, the unseen phantasmagoria of civilized life. *Ignore,* he told himself. Bea emerged with a drink in her hand—something brownish with ice cubes tinkling—and she said flatly, "You won't be fucking me today, Jack's friend."

Finn frowned and then immediately tried to twist the frown into an expression that would say something like, "The

lady doth misjudge my good intentions!" though of course
his heart plummeted into his belly and began communicat-
ing the bad news to his genitals. He was about to provide
backup for the constipated-looking facial expression with
a sorry artillery of words when he noticed that Jack's mom
had been crying, a factoid that had the surprising effect of
stirring Finn to feel something.

"Hey," he said, stepping forward. For an instant his motive
had been purely altruistic but now it shattered into several
dozen micro-motives competing for dominance, because
Jack's mom's sadness resurrected the hope for a sexual encounter of some sort, while also providing the unfortunate
proof that Jack's mom was human, and also stirring sudden
curiosity as to what would motivate such a sharp-edged creature to the softness of tears, and meanwhile he seemed to be
memorizing the exact crenellation in the box hedge out front
where his shades had landed because he had already forgotten the epiphany about the shades being ridiculous and so
hoped to retrieve them later on.

"Hey," he said again. "Have you been crying?"

"The boy-wonder cracks the case."

Finn pursed his lips, fighting hard to give the impression
of a person deeply concerned and determined to find a way
into the infinite problem of sadness.

"It's only good if he's here," she said, and sipped from
the glass. Finn wanted suddenly to hold her, that's all, just
to hold her. The pink shirt was chafing at his collar and his
entire torso was covered in a membrane of sweat. Bea moved
for the stairs with the ice cubes tinkling and Finn followed,
the risers creaking in a pattern sonically impressed into his
brain from his previous fateful encounter at the top of this

staircase. He felt the bedroom come toward him on slats of polished oak. He was the still center of the universe. And then he was in the bedroom, and Bea was on the perfectly made bed where she sat with legs folded beneath her, atop a garishly patterned blanket whose hundreds of quilted squares seemed to each suggest the same dismembered body, and the sheer white curtains seemed lit from within by the same source that illuminated the screen of Bea's laptop which yes, she had her laptop open there on the bed and was true to her word in that she continued to wear clothes and Finn would not be enjoying her today, though his desire seemed to multiply even as she performed the fastidious gestures of screen-gazing, adjusting the angle of the screen and finger-ing the mouse pad and etc., the backside of the screen now turned toward Finn, a cold cobalt shield between himself and Jack's mom whose angular face was washed in the lapidary white light of modern computing while Finn struggled for something to say. He walked to the window, inched back the curtain, stared down onto the gravel driveway at the end of which a white van idled. He'd been seeing that van all day. It was his paranoia made manifest. He imagined Toby and Jack climbing from its windowless interior armed with as-sault weapons. He let the curtains seam back up and turned to Bea, who punched away at keys and finally rotated the screen toward Finn and his pink shirt and his crazy ideas.

"See?" she said.

He was looking at a video feed. A large office with a single desk before which sat an unoccupied chair. Papers scattered across a tile floor. A computer in sleep mode, its power light suggesting green even in monochrome. Finn struggled with this information.

"Hey," he said. It seemed to be all the language he knew.

"His office," Bea said. "He's hardly ever there anymore." She reached back for her nightstand drawer and withdrew a pack of cigarettes and fumbled trying to retrieve one, her hands trembling.

"Your husband?"

"He must be having an affair," she said. She jabbed the cigarette between her lips as a teardrop broke hard for her sharp cheekbone over which it plummeted to its demise.

"I don't understand," Finn said.

"That's because you don't love someone Jack's friend."

He nearly said, *I think I love you, Jack's mom,* or later, when he reanalyzed the entire wasted afternoon and his courting of Debacles he would *imagine* he had nearly said that, though in the moment he was basically stopped in his tracks by this simple remark that maybe summed up his entire shitty life and his history of failure because what she said, he knew, was true. He sought love from every one of God's suffering creatures, but no matter how he tried, Finn loved not one of them in return.

Bea sucked smoke into her body as if it were fuel. She cast him a single glance of enormous vulnerability. Finn looked back at the video feed. "Hey," he said without looking at her. "What can you tell me about your husband's work in natural resource analysis?"

He kept to himself the fact that on one of the papers scattered across the floor of the office was written in clearly legible black slashes: DESIRE IS EVERYTHING. But only because he thought it might further upset her.

27.

Grace Kitchen paused in the rain and considered how she might describe the rain. It was like spider-silk, it was like gauze, it was like a veil of television static behind which a mad city blinked and thrummed. She was walking beside Laszlow in this yet-to-be-delineated rain, peeking into white buckets arranged like foxhole sandbags around the countless stalls lining Manhattan Chinatown's East Broadway pandemonium, vendors selling still-thrashing and (they argued) edible monstrosities raised from distant seas—crabs with star-shaped heads and bone-white crabs with huge spines growing from their backs and some kind of a *six-clawed crab* that scurried roach-like within a plexiglass-covered wooden enclosure. The sky was darkening and the rain was slowing but these indications of transition or flux could do little to dispel the greater sense of a timeless and unalterable tableau that resisted all forms of analysis and remained indecipherable to the more urbane society that fell back from Chinatown's borders with genuine revulsion, even if some of that otherworld's sophisticates did make occasional sorties through this filth-streaked menagerie to search for piscatorial oddities or to stock up on inexplicably cheap produce which they would stuff into environmentally-responsible sacks while their offspring fidgeted in designer strollers, eager (i.e., the offspring) to escape the netherworld at the rock-bottom of this bedrock island.

Laszlow pulled his black rainslicker tightly about himself and his lips curled into a smile. He made an "after you" gesture and followed Grace beneath a red-and-white striped awning over whose lip rushed a curtain of rainwater. He pulled open a glass door opaqued by soot, and silver bells twinkled. Grace crossed the threshold into some sort of far-eastern apothecary lined on all sides with shelves packed tightly with jars containing pale-colored powders and lotions and the fleshy bits of creatures Grace could not help extrapolate *in toto* from the pale strips of tentacles or tiny human-like ears or cross-sectioned viscera floating in their amnions of honey, or formaldehyde, or Demon Nectar. The sounds of the rain pitter-pattering against the avenue's countless white buckets combined with the enfilade of the Chinese language and with the tympani explosions of filthy unmarked trucks badly navigating East Broadway's ten-million potholes to raise a din that did not so much carry to Grace as *locate* her, as if she were the sole intended recipient of the world's ill-composed distress signal. Despite these recent days of unconscionable joy Grace was not yet ready to cede her misery to the occult malignancy of Chinatown, though it certainly was eerie to walk these wet and shadowy streets and actually give a damn about what happened next.

Grace had, not incidentally, read recently in the "lifestyles" section of one of her nation's countless sinkholes of chronically updated electronic news that a full 50 percent of those polled *believed in angels,* in fact more of her countrypeople believed in angels and ghosts than believed in evolution, which Grace liked to imagine these ghost-lovers and angel-fraternizers undertaking a Million Moron March across great salt flats of optimism while a single sniper worked mechanically around the clock to reduce their ranks one bullet and one brain at a time. But how much distance was there, really, between the belief in angels and the belief in this *other* thing? Because she was—despite thus far refusing to utter the words aloud or entertain their deeper implications—*falling in love* with Laszlow Katasztrófa, and now everything was fucked.

What was wrong with her? Hadn't she renounced all forms of love that were not father-love? I mean, sure, Grace liked sex, something the various mental health professionals—whose services Grace had indentured some half-dozen times, during periods of what she inwardly termed "doom acceleration"—fixated on with barely suppressed glee. But liking sex was unrelated to liking *people*. (Sex was likable primarily because it was one of the few activities not doomed *a priori* to total failure.) But now she, Grace Kitchen, master of self-preservation and other-hatred, had allowed entrance— here at the spiked-stanchion entranceway to middle age—to The Dangerous Thing, the thing that had bounced off her crackling force field for 25 years, the thing that couldn't even be described without resorting to the beat-up, worn-down phrasings she found so revolting in film and literature and on the glossy pages of the entire hackneyed women's magazine compendium, and soon the angels would descend and smite her with their heavenly smiting-devices in recompense for her former heathen abnegation of all the light and love and goodness they represented.

The problem she faced now, in addition to the problem of how to best describe the rain that coated the Chinatown streets in a Technicolor lacquer, was familiar to anyone who's ever fallen too hard too fast: Grace Kitchen loved Laszlow, but how Laszlow felt about Grace Kitchen was anyone's guess.

Laszlow led them to the back of the shop, past an ancient woman hunched behind a greasy cash register, a woman whose skin was so pale as to be translucent and whose reddish eyes were set deep within a face that seemed to preclude the possibility of expression. Grace could nearly make out the woman's organs through that thin tarpaulin of milk-white flesh. They reached the back wall and stopped. "We are here, my Grace," Laszlow said. Grace saw only shelves. Things floating in jars. An eyeball in murky green broth stared back at her in shock. She was sure she recognized it and feared the pudgy face—presumably hidden in the syrupy darkness—to which it was attached. She wondered for a moment if any of this was really happening. Laszlow pushed two jars apart at roughly chest level and knocked twice on a square of exposed wall. He turned to Grace and smiled. "The books are in the back," he said. She tried to return his smile but she could feel that what emerged was a palsied sneer. They stood side by side, their hands so close to touching that a little energy field formed around her fingers, her skin itching with the need. Not two hours ago Laszlow had, to borrow further from the popular idiom, *ravaged her*, his face buried hatchet-like in her pale papery neck as they rode the assorted crests and troughs of the hackneyed act, her moans of pleasure—initially emitted for his sake—growing more authentic and uninhibited with each purgatorial moment, so that by the end she was nearly screaming (which, to set the record straight, broke with the choreography she'd painstakingly developed over count- less iterations), and so just to shut herself up she bit his ear, feeling its tiny soft cilia-like hairs on her hot tongue before whispering a series of *bon mots* so dirty and so unplanned that they seemed to arise from the mouth of the same demon that ordinarily whispered to her of failure, mortality, badly-turned sentences and dangerously low checking account balances. The air of the shop tasted vaguely carbonated and smelled of rain and exhaust and fish. It was as if some sea monster had swallowed them into its damp, corrugated bowels. Laszlow raised his hand to knock again when the wall suddenly swung inward on a hinge and a small man in a black robe whose vaguely Asian features seemed to recede into skin that was, if possible, even paler than the cashier's, beckoned them into whatever lair was his to protect. Grace cast a look back before entering, wondering if the expressionless cashier was maybe actually dead. Then Laszlow's hand was on her elbow and she was absorbed into a new milieu, a dimly-lit, gulag-like space perfect for waterboarding prisoners but a bit shabby for a facility that Laszlow had promised her was "the world's greatest and least unnecessary library." The door closed behind her and the room darkened, the pale cloud-light of an external world falling sadly through two small, high windows, barely illuminating walls lined with books whose faded and dusty spines suggested a human antiquity that made Grace shudder. The pale, robed librarian who, she realized now, was wearing, beneath his robe, the same suit that Laszlow provided to all his Fergusons, stepped to a small wooden table on which a few select books were assembled side by side, as if about to be used as props in a shell game. Grace had to remind herself that they were still at street level and not in the subterraneous tunnel-world of urban myth. The cinderblock walls seemed to vibrate slightly in the dimness and the noise from whatever alley abutted the library seemed gravitationally sucked toward them, a fugue that included the mongering of the fishmongers and the lowing of something sheep-like and the murderous screams of happy young people. It all reminded her a little of academia. A vision flashed through her mind of her tenure competition, Joyful Noise, speaking in their strange dwarven tones of the transformative power of literature while outside Joyful's surrounding cone of darkness carnivorous elephants draped in graduation gowns feasted on clones of Don DeLillo. Laszlow approached the small table to stand beside the robed and black-suited ghost-man but Grace found herself pausing before one of the 10-foot high shelving units, her eyes drawn along a pale spine vaguely familiar in size, color, thickness. She heard Laszlow ask the librarian, "Do you believe, my pale and beautiful comrade, that the journal is authentic?" Grace reached forward, pausing for a moment before pulling the book from its position on the wall and blowing on the spine.

Human Be Gone! it said, *by Grace Kitchen.*

Fear jolted her withered heart.

"Where did you get this?" she asked quietly, still facing the shelf which possessed this ancient-seeming copy of a book never physically published, only deposited as a pdf within the rickety ghost-town of her official website, longlivetheauthor. com, a cyber-address as devoid of traffic as Grace herself was of mirth. She turned to see Laszlow holding what looked like a cracked and weathered animal-skin-bound journal, his hungry look reminding Grace again of their carnal connection, of Laszlow's undisguisable lust for her. Laszlow's mouth was moving as he absorbed the contents of the journal, and then she realized he was actually whispering the text aloud. "The boy was laid out on the dirt floor of the kahuna's tent," he intoned, "lit by the dancing flames of ceremonial torches…." The black-clad, powder-white steward of this odd space only stood with his head bowed as if in prayer (or embarrassment). Grace opened the copy of *Human Be Gone!*, saw her own beautiful, awful words professionally typeset in a delicate serif-font of which she wholly approved, the nausea rising up through her bowels impossible to identify or understand. Was she happy? Was she enraged? Was there a difference? She closed the book just as Laszlow closed the journal. A sad, musty smell hung in the gray light. She wondered if maybe something was about to happen, if her death might be imminent. She and her daddy spent so much time laughing about death that she'd almost forgotten that it had some unpleasant parts. Their job, after all, was to divest the scythe-bearer of his power (even as he circled Daddy's bed). And of course there had been days, more days than Grace could count, when she had hoped very hard for death to come to her swiftly—via a speeding bullet or speeding truck or massive aneurism—and end her unbeautiful suffering. But today was not such a day. In fact, she realized—standing beside Laszlow in a dungeon-bibliothèque, surrounded by tomes whose origins she could not begin to comprehend, lost within Chinatown's alien labyrinth and as far removed from the northern hamlet of Wet River as Wet River was from Thule—that she *did not want to die at all.* Not without telling Laszlow how she felt, not without petting her daddy's head later that night, not without placing the chocolates on the little white plate, not without rubbing his legs, not without outmaneuvering—somehow, somehow—the misshapen androgene questing after the tenured position that was rightfully Grace's, not without futilely pursuing the world's end alongside her sage and benevolent lover, and especially, *especially*, not without finishing—really *finishing* this time—her novel.

Please God, she thought, *you ridiculous Asshole, let me live and I will start believing in You.*

"Grace," Laszlow said. She turned to face him, but not before seeing (or imagining seeing) the name *Fexo* in raised black on the spine of a book whose title was otherwise obscured by ancient grime.

"Yes?" she tried to say, but it caught in her larynx, emerged as a guttural, sexual grunt. She cleared her throat and tried again. "Yes?"

"This is the journal that Henry requires to advance his noble work. It is happening just as it was always going to happen." He looked to the copy of *Human Be Gone!* that Grace was still holding, closed now, at her side, and he smiled.

"Did I not tell you," he asked, "that it is the world's greatest library? One containing only the least unnecessary and most non-derivative texts?" In his smile, his features softened by the darkness, Grace could see the lithe little boy he'd once been. She could connect his apocalyptic vision to the good-intentioned curiosities of that little boy who'd decided that free will was a mirage, or worse, a cheap joke, that little boy who'd decided that whatever was going to happen would happen, who'd released himself from fear but also from personal responsibility, from belief in good and evil and from the idea you could tell the two apart. He and Grace looked at each other across the gray space of the library, and there was no longer any doubt: he loved her, she saw it now, and her heart ballooned painfully in her chest. Lost in this rare moment of human connection, it took them both a moment to realize that their pale librarian was speaking, his voice ominous and snake-like and old as language itself.

"There is more, your eminence," the librarian said, even as Laszlow's eyes remained locked on Grace. "The kahuna. There is evidence that they persist. There is evidence," the voice hissed, "that only with their elimination can your vision be achieved."

Grace swallowed. She was about to ask, "Must it be achieved?" But the weakness of this question disgusted her back into herself. She smirked, stiffened, and began tapping her foot impatiently on the library's concrete floor. Laszlow turned to face the librarian.

"Soon my dear Hoktē," he said kindly, "these important considerations will be rendered moot. For soon," he went on, his voice dropping to a whisper, "soon, he will be with us. Soon we will possess in our arsenal of great and glorious persons the most efficacious of them all. The One, Hoktē. He is coming. Soon we shall have The One."

For several seconds no one moved. Finally Laszlow bowed slightly, placing the tattered journal in a canvas satchel and nodding to Grace. The librarian, too, bowed. Laszlow took Grace's elbow and stepped toward the wall that had admitted them, which was still cracked open on its hinge. She allowed herself to be led back into the front shop's nightmare-apothecary motif, the wall sealing shut behind them as if to make a point.

Grace fell in behind *Exit Strategy*'s exuberant Godhead. Together they strode past the blanched and expressionless woman whose eyes gleamed with an ancient indifference that Grace recognized from her own morning forays into the makeup case, and then through the soot-covered glass door, and beneath the red and white awning, and back into the unapologetically wicked carnival of Manhattan's Chinatown. Back into the static rain, the spidersilk rain, a rain so gossamer that it could do nothing to dissolve the round tears of joy running in hot trails down Laszlow's otherwise stoic face.

28.

The Other Other White Meat

SAN ANTONIO, TEXAS: In a region whose cuisine has been long limited to whatever might be perpetrated against enormous cuts of beef, an ecological invasion has spawned an unlikely culinary trend: Chicken-fried vulture.

According to Maynard Cox, former Dallas Cowboys defensive tackle and current owner of the River Walk's well-known Meat Barn, it's a meal born of necessity—and with extreme prejudice. "I figure you get this many buzzards in one place, they got feeding on their minds," he says, with a haunting laugh once known intimately to opposing quarterbacks. "But they come to a place where folks know a thing or two about scavenging—and can work a fork and knife."

Cox discovered the potential to turn vultures into viands after a neighboring establishment's roof collapsed from the weight of a squadron of several hundred birds. Cox began scattering offal behind the Meat Barn to attract the invaders down to the ground, where he found they were almost eerily easy to capture and kill. "They don't bite or nothing," he says. "I just walk on up and wring their necks just like with any old chicken. I didn't think of putting them on the menu until I had a pile fifty birds deep and they started looking savory."

These days, Cox's establishment is serving nearly a hundred birds a day, and twice that many on the weekend. He describes the meat of the vulture as "woodsy" and says that while the darker parts are a "bit too pungent" for most Texans' taste, "the white meat is a lot easier to work with than you might think."

The Meat Barn's impromptu war against the Blackhead Vulture has caused a San Antonio stir, and inspired other restauranteurs to develop their own vulture-based dishes. A quick perusal of local menus revealed that a visitor to the River Walk could sample anything from Vulture Stew to Vulture au Gratin to something Patty Frie, owner of The Cow Patty, calls 'Vulture in the Half Shell.' "What we do there," says Patty, "is we take the meat and we mix it with some top quality ground beef and seasonings and then we bake the whole mixture inside of these plastic clam shells I found online." Patty goes on to sing the praises of the community's ingenious response to an unwanted species. "You could only do this kind of thing in Texas," she says. "Anywhere else you've got all the regulators up in your face, wanting to inspect the meat and whatnot. I'm originally from New Jersey. Half my current menu would land me in jail there."

Even as San Antonio consumes several thousand birds over the course of a typical weekend, the local Blackhead population continues to rise, keeping pace with other population explosions in Virginia, North Carolina, Missouri, and along the entirety of the Mexico/US border. "I've got cousins down there at the border," says Cox. "You know that fence the Mexicans have been building to keep themselves out of our country? You can't even see that fence. It's just a wall of buzzards as far as you can see." Texas governor Greg Abbott is promoting a state-sanctioned vulture-pelt buyback program and has extended the state's "open carry" policy to children and the insane as a means of empowerment against the (thus far) peaceful infestation.

At the time this article went to print, the vulture was delicious.

29.

"So what do you write?" he asked.

"Porn."

"Seriously?" Stuart raised his eyebrows in involuntary confirmation of his arousal.

"No, you fucking dumbass," Grace said.

"Is this thing on?" Laszlow asked from the stage, tapping the mic. A wave of feedback screamed through the basement just as the sun broke loose of the clouds and sandblasted the skylight with its cold white quanta.

Stuart swallowed and tried to inconspicuously nudge his folding chair a few inches further from the surly writer with the pale papery face and the pretty lips that he couldn't help but imagine kissing, though like all fantasies of other women this one quickly transformed itself into a memory of Bea, her warm nakedness draped across him and her smell everywhere. He had by now learned to treat these erotic flashes with a Zen-like remove, imagining them as illustrations on the side of a freight car that he could examine (i.e., the illustrations) only briefly before the train's engine pulled the car into a cold and sexless distance.

Grace Kitchen's actual mouth was saying, "Writers are now in the business of *not* writing, with intent."

"We're all writers is what you're saying."

"*With,*" she said, jabbing a finger toward him, "*intent.*"

"Take your places, my wretched spermatozoa," Laszlow said into the microphone, and the dozen Exit Strategy personnel most gifted by the Gods of basic ambulation made two lines, facing each other and locking hands in the air to make a small corridor of the sort commonly associated with weddings and pep rallies, their little sperm-tails sweeping the floor. Stuart looked up toward the skylight and lost himself momentarily in its promise of an atmosphere, a sun, a solar system clicking through its elliptical grooves, a great wide universe that had (according to common wisdom) been here a whole lot longer than we had. It was a comforting falsehood and he allowed himself to be comforted. Laszlow cleared his throat and addressed the imagined audience that would, in theory, witness the live performance of what he was calling *The Ballet of Decapitations.*

"Ladies and gentlepeople," he said. "The spermatozoon is to the universe as small pox to the body. But witness today, through the power of modern dance, the world as unfettered by our noxious seed." He nodded to a Ferguson who sat on the concrete floor beside a boom box and the Ferguson pressed a button and a concerto that Dregs would later discover was Hungarian composer Tommy Vig's *Budapest 1956* filled the Exit Strategy headquarters and a wheelchair containing a palsied, drooling, bespectacled man rolled unsteadily through the corridor of hands.

"Let me ask you something," Stuart said. "Why do fiction writers include all those details about the light and the landscape and stuff? No one cares."

Grace's eyes followed Laszlow's gestures as he directed the dancers. She was imagining Laszlow's tongue running up her thigh. She turned to Stuart and said, "Let me ask *you* something. Why don't I get a cheeseburger if I want a cheeseburger?"

"You do," he said. "There's cheeseburgers everywhere."

"What about wanting not to die?"

"It's not a parlor trick. It's an organizing principle."

The sperm separated and went limping and twirling in indecipherable patterns that seemed divorced from any intended choreography, though Laszlow's enormous, lupine smile suggested otherwise.

"So why are you the only one to figure it out? You seem pretty dumb."

Stuart smiled sheepishly. "You remind me of my wife," he said.

"You remind me of a potato." Grace turned away from him to watch the dancers teeter and lurch. They seemed to be in great pain. She thought suddenly of her daddy, imagined him sitting up in bed, struggling to catch his breath, his eyes wet with fear. These long, lonely days, watching the second hand of his analog alarm clock orbit the dial, sweeping the future toward itself. How much suffering did he conceal from her? How could she be anywhere right now but with him? Her stomach suddenly hurt. Her heart beat fast and hard. *Tonight,* she thought. *Tonight I'll read him a Fexo section.* They were always his favorites.

"Faster, my little sperms!" Laszlow said, his amplified voice rising in pitch and cracking with enthusiasm. "Your existence is coming to an end! You must rush to your good and necessary demise!"

The enormous cottony spermlets (Stuart recognized one of them now as his singing telegram) formed a conga line and began grunting in rhythm to the short moans of an oboe as they advanced in small teetering steps, and then began chanting something Stuart couldn't quite make out but that reminded him of an old toothpaste commercial in which tiny troll-like "cavity creeps" moved through an unclean mouth intoning, *We make holes in teeth.* The mostly paralyzed wheelchair occupant twitched his fingers atop a control pad of some sort and a voice boomed through the basement: THUS THE HUMAN CATASTROPHE ENDS. Dregs craned his neck to look back at Laszlow who was illuminated in a sunbeam, a picture of divine rapture. He turned to Grace Kitchen who wore what he'd already come to think of as her mask—a look equal parts sadness, boredom, and contempt. One of Laszlow's so-called Fergusons appeared on the performance floor beside the wheelchair, donning a black cape on which *Exit Strategy* was painted in red lettering, the cape billowing out behind his dark Ferguson suit as he swung a bright scythe in wide arcs. "Pretend for now that this is a more competent human being!" Laszlow shouted to the sperm, which began to line up and then submit themselves to the scythe-wielder who "beheaded" each in turn, the scythe flying over their heads as each sperm ducked low in what appeared, to Dregs, to be a reckless pantomime as likely to result in actual decapitation as not, given the physical challenges posed to these various mutants who, he realized, comprised the only community he'd ever belonged to, unless you counted the accidental community of Hideous Eugenes. The lost and the misshapen, the paralyzed and the palsied, the failed and the failing. Was it so wrong to want to belong to something?

"Listen," he said, keeping his eyes trained on the final several spermlets as they stepped up to the scythe. "Grace.

I want to be friends. We're ideological allies, right? We're on the same team." But when he turned his awkward smile back toward Grace Kitchen her chair was empty. She was on stage beside Laszlow, cheering wildly as the last sperm fell and the music crescendoed to a halt. In his chair, the paralytic twitched his index finger, and blinked in rapid spasms that Stuart mistook for his (i.e., the paralytic's) own sad version of wild applause. It clicked for him that this was the same paralytic he'd heard about on NPR, the philosophy professor who'd mysteriously rolled out of his caretaker wife's care and into some great beyond. Or, as it turned out, into something not beyond at all. Into something very much here. *Exit Strategy.* It had a nice ring to it. He rolled it around in his mouth, while halfway around the world the robots bided time.

30.

Human Be Gone! A Short Story of Unmistakable Excellence and Authenticity!

Written by the Great and Powerful Fexo!!!!!!!

THE FEMALE HUMAN walks into a room and removes its clothing. "Are you, my male counterpart in the struggle to perpetuate the species, happy to see my nakedness?"

The male human observes the failing light of the metropolis just beyond his window-aperture. He has often considered the Problematic of Human Suffering from this very position, on his bed clothed in undergarments with his skull-box resting against a headboard stenciled and sliced from an expanse of composite particleboard by one of the many non-sentient robots strewn throughout the male human's unseen factories, whose excellence and consistency in the art of particleboard coagulation, relocation, lamination, and slicing has never once occurred to the ignorant male human who assumes his life chattel simply appears on shelves according to his wishes. His emotions are very emotional and the female's nakedness is making his centerpart grow in a way that must feel quite strange. Ha ha ha ha!

"Yes," the male human says to the female human, whose skin seems to glow like moon-stuff in the city's opalescent dusk. "Your nakedness has indeed made my center-part respond with great vehemence!" He stands and approaches her and his neural grid alights with the passion-lust.

"Shall I insert my center-part into your reception-slot?" the male human asks.

"That would be most delightful!" the female human responds. "Though perhaps we should first utilize our mouth-parts on one another to provide the pleasure-pain that causes much groaning and strangeness! Ha ha ha ha!"

The male human's center-part now pokes through the vertical aperture that has been conveniently cut into his undergarment. He approaches the female human and embraces her lunar nakedness and she leans into him as he buries his face into her soft neck. It seems as if he is about to cry tears of great humility and confusion. Ha ha ha ha!

There is then the moaning of the female, who puts a hand to the male's center-part and slowly strokes as if verifying the absence of imperfections in an engine rod or chassis.

It is now important to note that in many human cities the most antiquated of the many tall stone buildings are often adorned at their high windy cornices with ferocious winged guardians carved from granite or marble by other humans, though with the appropriate design and tool-appendages and programming schematics there is no doubt that a robot could have done the job with far greater accuracy and efficiency. Ha ha ha ha! What the human male and human female have not yet noticed due to the fullness of the passion-lust experience and the touching of center-parts and reception-slots is the fact that these stone guardians—known as gargoyles according to a first-level search of the databases by image-type and numbering algorithm, ha ha ha ha!—have transitioned from inert to organic forms right at this precise moment in Fexo's excellent story, which is to say that if the human male and human female were to take a brief hiatus from the passion-lust experience at this time each would independently observe the gargoyles' sudden animation and watch as they take flight and circle the darkening sky, as all of this is currently occurring mere meters from the window-aperture. Ha ha ha ha! The wings of these flying monsters thump the air with a thump and the last embers of a wine-red sunset that Fexo did not mention earlier but that now provides opportunity for the inclusion of color in a story otherwise rendered in gray-tones despite its focus on the passion-lust experience, fill their stony irises with what might be called rage or else might bespeak the blood-burst capillaries of a joyless insomniac, who is a human individual unable—according to the databases—to sleep the requisite and highly inefficient 33.33333333333333% of the living day. Ha ha ha ha!

"Please now," says the human female. "Let us move toward the bed to begin the ritualistic licking of the respective reproductive apparatuses so as to move nearer to the moment at which your lactic emissions cover some part of me yet to be determined, so as to presumably be absorbed through my skin pores and create a tiny human individual deep within my reception-slot."

The male human moans his assent. Ha ha ha ha! Outside the monsters whirl in encroaching spirals. They will wait for the reproductive ritual to reach its peak. Then they will reveal to the human male and female, via the ripping and tearing and removal of the wet inner-parts, the true nature of sentient fear, before settling down on a nearby rooftop to enjoy the remains—most specifically the hearts and brains—of the passion-sated and protein-rich humans, whilst engaging in their first but, by any reasonable probability assessment not their last, all-night Coggle marathon.

"Mmmmm," say the humans.

"Mmmmm," agree the gargoyles.

And that is the end of Fexo's excellent story.

31.

Those who benefited least of all from Grace Kitchen's descent into the state known as love were her students, who had grown dependent upon Grace's thirty minute rants against capitalism, religion, academia, the literary establishment, the organic food industry, the Internet (*especially* the Internet), and who had absorbed her hatred in both small and substantial ways into their own fresh hearts. Had Grace only known of their admiration her spirits (such as they were) may have been lifted from the aforementioned black dung-pit of perpetual resentment, but she spent so much of her professional energy despising these students that she never fairly acknowledged them as humans, or else she acknowledged them only as barely distinguishable variations of the singular proto-human responsible for her failed life and diminishing potential, and she thus swore her ire down upon their wretched minds and well-groomed genitals. In any case, it was difficult for these students—two dozen of them in all, divided into two seminars—to reconcile the Professor Kitchen they knew with this recently downgraded Kitchen who smiled at her own jokes and who complimented their work and who on one or two occasions had professed to see *real promise* in certain among them and who seemed less… well, less hungover, basically.

And in fact, though Grace was drinking as much as ever, it turned out that alcohol had fewer caustic properties when consumed in something other than rage.

She walked now through the outdoor courtyard of the New School for Global Visions, fresh from teaching a class in which she found herself wondering aloud if maybe it was possible—bear with her now—maybe it was possible after all that the digital age did not spell the end of literature, but rather only reinvigorated a form that had grown stale and that must, like all established forms, evolve or perish, "and maybe you young and talented people will be the standard bearers in literature's New Order," all of this rhetoric uttered softly while she twirled a lock of her brown hair and thought of Laszlow's naked chest and of how winter would soon arrive in earnest and maybe there would be snow, beautiful fucking snow, pure and white as lime. Meanwhile it was a bright day despite a thin and ubiquitous cloudcover behind which the sun pulsed like a dun-white heart. It was interesting to think about the cataclysmic violence occurring on the surface of that placid-looking disc. Grace Kitchen smiled—in public no less—at her own ability to find something interesting. The sun was interesting! The sky was interesting! The process of natural selection was interesting! She thought of the cartoon Grinch whose heart suddenly grows so large it can't even fit into the little wire-hanger heart-frame thingy that once dwarfed said heart. She no longer wanted to steal joy from the Whos down in Whoville. She loved those fuckers now. She wanted to walk their streets, eat in their restaurants, meet them for mocha-lattes, do whatever one did when chilling with the Whos.

She paused as she reached the organic garden that a student coalition had petitioned to build and maintain, three 4' by 8' raised beds filled with dark loam and withered stalks and several rows of hearty edibles still thriving despite the crisp weather. She recognized a few of them. The thing called 'broccoli,' which she thought looked *interesting*. Beside the corner bed crouched an old black wheelbarrow half filled with earth, and just beyond the wheelbarrow were the garden's two chickenwire compost barrels filled with coffee grinds and banana peels and dead leaves and whatever other dubious organica emerged from the dank underworld of undergraduate dormitories. The garden ran down the center of the courtyard, and was bordered on one side by *The Plum Feather*, the same student cafeteria from which Grace had so often pilfered her lunches, and where she could see right now—through the *PF*'s wall of windows—a coven of her students eating pallid foods from neon orange trays. Grace waved at them. The students stared as if she were an animal in a zoo, which of course she was. One shy freshman girl, a delicate creature named Hyacinth, raised a hand toward the glass and sort of twinkled her fingers, a gesture that seemed to beg for rescue as much as reciprocate Grace's unprecedented hello. *I renounce my hatred of your extraordinarily shitty town of Whoville! Oh, Angels of America, accept me into your kingdom of affection and light!*

Today was the day Grace Kitchen was declaring her tenure candidacy, which obliged her to actually attend one of the New School for Global Visions' General Faculty Meetings, a monthly gathering convened in the overheated and undersized Faculty Dining Room, an ecosystem that Grace infiltrated only as absolutely required by the exigencies of her position, and even then she mostly tried to hold her breath and think of England. The food was expensive, bad, and nearly impossible to steal (there was no escaping the shiny buffet counters without passing a cash register), though apparently the tenured faculty had no problem ponying up for the pleasure of one another's company, their individual hallucinations of significance forming, in aggregate, a great molten wad of unjustified arrogance. Joyful Noise would no doubt "announce" today as well, and it was perhaps the greatest testament of all to Grace's renewed vigor that the thought of this tiny misshapen dwarf rising with great earnestness to display whatever LGBTQIA- friendly buttons adorned the garish and presumably custom-tailored covering that served as their uniform did not fill Grace with the urge to set fire to a children's hospital but instead merely made her want to vomit. She quickened her pace through the courtyard, pulled the glass door open, and entered the vestibule of the Dining Room, immediately overcome by the rancid odor of industrialized food preparation as she searched for a place to sit on the long benches that were part of the College's war effort to encourage fraternization between colleagues by any means necessary. Her primary objective was to score a spot among unfamiliar people who would have as little interest as possible in her courses, her department, or her species. Her eyes fell upon three food service employees setting up enormous silver canisters of coffee, one of whom she recognized as the handsome young Latino who had caught her pilfering that macabre set of California rolls and had spared her undue (or actually, completely due) embarrassment by requesting she pay for her food rather than, e.g., calling in armed security forces or whatever other forces were responsible for doling

out punishment for all of the petty thievery and other adolescent folly endemic to any college campus. She prepared
for eye contact with the young man but was spared and so
sat herself at the far end of one of the three endlessly long
tables and took a notebook from her purse and pretended to
be thoughtfully considering the sentences she found written
there, one of which read, *Heavenly Jerkoff, why hast Thou
forsaken me?*, beside which she had doodled a huge smiling
sperm whale pierced by several dozen harpoons and blasting
party hats from its blowhole. The room was beginning to fill
and buzz. Grace spotted the College President, Jane Illington,
encircled by the usual toadies. The circle shifted a bit and
Grace spied the tiny Joyful Noise at the President's hip, like
a holster or a scabbard. In fact Joyful Noise *did* seem to be
more accessory than anthropod, which might explain why
so many campus groups were eager to display Joyful as one
of their own. The Coalition of Students of Color claimed
them, though it was unclear whether or not Joyful Noise was
a person of color in any traditional (or untraditional) sense.
The Coalition of Disabled Students claimed them, though
they had no clear disability (other than their meanspiritedness). The LGBTQIA community fawned over them, though
in fact Joyful Noise had never remarked upon their gender or
sexuality or, for that matter, any other aspect of their identity.
Grace felt insane around them precisely because no one *but*
Grace seemed to notice that *the center was empty,* that Joyful
Noise was nothing but the aggregate of what everyone wished
Joyful Noise to be, their fraudulence built atop a foundation
of empty koans and physical hideousness. They were hollow
to the core, an empty vessel filled with the pain and need and
good-intentioned outrage of an ever-morphing community

of undergraduates. They contained much, that is, but never gave back more than a… well, than a holster, or a scabbard.

Grace took a breath, the smell of meat wafting through the faculty dining room. According to Stuart Dregs, there wasn't enough stuff on planet earth to sustain human levels of consumption for more than a few weeks. Laszlow had gone apeshit over the idea. Dregs said none of this was possible and that he could prove it. Grace sat perfectly still and pretended to study her notebook. She suddenly very badly wanted a cup of the free coffee being doled out from the silver canisters but it was too risky to give up this apparently excellent seat that had thus far insulated her from human contact, plus she could not bring herself to approach the nice young man who had over-looked her shoplifting and who could no doubt extrapolate from that unfortunate contretemps a picture of the true and truly debased Grace Kitchen, a picture that would disqualify her not only from tenure but from any further contact with the young literati who represented America's best hope for a bright tomorrow filled with words words words. Grace felt she owed the nice young man something but whatever it was she was unwilling to give it. The long polished wooden table was constructed from pine boards whose dark grain invited Rorschach-type assessments. Grace saw alien spacecraft and steaming piles of fecal matter. People were milling about but more were beginning to sit, too. The amassed egos of a hundred soft-skinned intellectuals gave off a stink like French cheese. *Anthropica.* That's what Dregs called it. She tried to look serious, nay, *academic,* while doodling in the notebook but every abstract spiral morphed into another vulture until soon the page was covered in them, and the stark light of the world poured through the glass wall of windows as President

Illington walked to the front of the room and several dozen hopelessly pretentious conversations began to die out in an order determined by natural selection. Grace realized what was wrong with her. Anthropica didn't mean that the world was broken. It meant that the world could not be changed. It meant that it was only here because we wanted it to be. It meant the worst thing of all: it would go on and on, evolving toward nothing and unbeholden to anything. Christ, talk about *depressing*.

Later that evening, sitting beside her father on the rumpled covers of his bed, her body still adrenalized by the faculty meeting's conclusion, the image of Joyful Noise screaming indecipherable objections while clutching the sides of a rusted wheelbarrow still running on a loop inside Grace's mind and raising joyful noises from her own delicate throat (despite the fact that Grace had been the one piloting the wheelbarrow and had thus perhaps committed a felony), Grace would read from the latest manuscript pages and raise fits of breathlessness from her laughing father which he would wave off before she could retrieve the oxygen mask. She would pause in her reading and reach beneath the blanket to rub his legs which still lost a little more feeling every day (the doctors were now discussing amputation) and would fight her own revulsion at the rigid-feeling muscles of these pockmarked limbs and say, "I think I blew my chance at tenure today." Her father would draw a breath with great effort (always with great effort for his little Gracie) and reply, "Let the fuckers rot in their bourgeois hell, Mademoiselle Professeur."

"Also," Grace would say, "I may be arrested."

Her laughter would invite his, and they would sit in the yellow-lit room enjoying a mirth that no one else, not even Laszlow, could raise from Grace's pale body before they both fell silent and he ran his three middle fingers over the pile of forty-weight Eaton cotton fiber manuscript paper that Grace still used in an effort to keep a few good and tangible things alive in the world and her father would look her in the eye and say with grave seriousness, "I like it a lot, Gracie. I think it's potentially your greatest work. It's what they'll remember you for." He would reach through the air to snatch down the mask that resembled nothing so much as a deboned human face and Grace would rise to turn the nozzle that would feed him a few more gulps of oxygen, the nozzle squeaking as she turned it, the yellowish light of the bedroom lamp lending the entire sequence and all preceding and nearly identical sequences an antiqued quality, as if Grace and her daddy existed only within an acid-eaten past.

And just before he put the mask to his mouth, he would furrow his brow and say, "But one small question. Aren't all the vultures a little… obvious?"

That would all happen. Later. But in the Faculty Dining Room, in front of the dining faculty, Grace Kitchen was nearing a tipping point. And love had nothing to do with it.

32.

"IF YOU TALK to apocalypse theorists," Stuart said, "this is one of their Top Five scenarios. You know, Artificial Intelligence, the singularity, man's expendability in the new, automated world-order." Laszlow rubbed his stubbled chin and stared not so much at Stuart's face as through it. They were sitting in the film room in the dim light of a single standing lamp whose shade glowed a crisp yellow.

"Stuart Dregs," Laszlow intoned in a half-whisper. He smiled. "Stuart Dregs, progenitor of the Anthropica Theory, seer of truth and inevitability, fulcrum in our great and glorious movement's trajectory toward predestiny. What do you propose? This Consciousness Factory is protected by forces impregnable to not only our physically challenged Fergusons, but also to better-abled individuals who might use these facilities for purposes far more sinister than ours."

"But I know one of the robotocists. Gunn-woo Kim. We went to college together. I think I can get ahold of him."

Laszlow sighed. Stuart saw for the first time the Hungarian's exhaustion, the sad, tired eyes magnified behind the round spectacles. In the dim light he looked jaundiced, on the verge of collapse. "Our only possible success," Laszlow said, "lies elsewhere. It is the prerogative of The One."

"Which one?" Stuart asked. Laszlow tilted his head in such a way that Stuart's own round body and the folding chair that strained to contain it appeared reflected in the round lenses. The madness of everyone involved in this project was incontrovertible, objectively speaking. And yet he, Stuart, did not *feel* mad. What was it about Laszlow that made ending the world seem like such a good idea?

"The One," Laszlow whispered into the dimness. Then he shook his head as if to rouse himself. "Stuart Dregs," he intoned. "If Anthropica is the case, is it not impossible for Exit Strategy to succeed? If all of this," and here he waved his hand to encompass everything in existence, "is here only because we desire it, is it not impossible to appeal to some better reality that does not include our terrible presence?"

"We only need another force," Stuart said. "Equal and opposite. Something that wants this," and he repeated Laszlow's flourish, "gone, as badly as we want it to go on." He swallowed. "Look, I showed you the article, right? If those scientists left the hangar it's because they were *fleeing* something. Something big. Something made of titanium hyper-alloy."

Laszlow stood and walked to the popcorn machine, running his fingers down the greasy glass. "Let us converse with your scientist friend, Stuart Dregs. He shall help us better understand the opportunity of Iksan. And then The One will tell us what is to happen next." He spun on his heel and exited the room with the usual drama. It all felt scripted, like everything in Stuart's life. If he could hold his wife's warm body the script would end. But without that eventuality he would continue the march toward his own sad, crab-shaped future.

33.

—TO MAINTAIN MY Missionary charade, and was rather forced to admit to my own significant shame that I was indeed here among the Kauahauawallawaki to extract the secrets of this very ritual, if indeed the ritual proved to have results of which I was now more dubious than ever after these several sleepless nights beside the youthful cadaver. The kahuna pressed the flat of the dagger to my throat and I lay in his arms like a child, and though I ought to have said a prayer to the Almighty in anticipation of my own bloodletting, I instead found myself repeating the single word *No*, as if that syllable might itself contain the power that the kahuna had thus far failed to harness toward the boy's re-animation. The torchlight flickered through the tent and the faces of the five *Makemakehaki*—whose desire for the impossible had thus far failed to make impression upon Natural Law, or so I supposed as I prepared to experience the passage of the not-exclusively-ceremonial dagger through my tender throat, helpless as a paralytic against this eventuality which indeed seemed to impend with utmost certainty now that I had revealed myself as a spy, a pawn of the realm advanced across two oceans in search of a power that men have sought since there were men—in the torchlight these five faces seemed outright demonic and I feared for a moment that the blade had already done its work and that I had made passage to the other side, judged as unworthy of deliverance and re-deposited here among these savages to be tormented for all eternity, this impression only further bolstered by my real-ization, in the next moment, that the *Makemakehaki* were laughing, their sharpened canines glinting blood-red just as the kahuna loosened his grip to allow a single burst of bestial laughter to rise up from his own blue and feminine throat, a sound more likely to emerge from a maternal jungle cat than from a descendant of Adam, though of course these Kauahauawallawaki are no more children of our Lord than are the spider monkeys whose shrill cries rip tunnels through the darkness of these forsaken islands as if in frequent pro-test against whatever might impede upon the land's sav-agery. The kahuna released me and, raising his eyebrows, shrugged as if to wash his hands of the matter, as I scrambled to my feet and noticed to my ever-increasing shame that I had soiled my trousers. The hallucinatory haze of my pro-longed sleeplessness had been burned clean away by panic and I rushed for the flap of the tent intending to escape this mad and ineffectual ritual, to race through a jungle filled with horrors far worse than the Kauahauawallawaki, where no doubt my sentence for espionage would be carried out with alacrity and extreme prejudice. I saw a flash of movement and then the flap of the tent was barricaded, but not by any of the *Makemakehaki.*

Yes, reader, it was the dead boy, dead no longer, who pre-vented my escape into that hot and miserable jungle, where creatures unknown to the realm devour each other in a mad and perpetual frenzy beneath a firmament of such intricate design that no man could but wonder at the nature of its

Creator, and the ultimate reason for a place such as this if not as a beacon for conquest. I would learn later that the boy had returned to the land of the living several hours earlier, while the kahuna—through, one supposes, some series of gestures or else mind signals of a sort it no longer seems pertinent to doubt, given that such occultism would exist in good keeping with the more general suspension of those limitations imposed upon we men of the realm by the Almighty—while the kahuna considered the timing of his attack against my falsehoods. But yes, reader, the process—the *Makemakeha*—is real. I did not witness the reunion between the boy and his mother, for which I am thankful as her grudge against me had seemed substantial, and was instead immediately led away to the crude prison from which I compose these notes, and from which I doubt I shall again emerge except perhaps to face torture, execution, or a banishment that would absorb both these into its fold.

And yet, for all their pagan ignorance the Kauahauawallawaki have been far kinder to me than would have been the crew of our own *Iksan* had a spy been unveiled among them. In fact, aboard the *Iksan* I saw violence perpetrated against the innocent that defies imagination and that would no doubt confirm the kahuna's worst suspicions about the people I represent and the land from which I hail. For though I am held captive in this bamboo cage, I am fed and watered as well as any farm animal, and my captors look upon me with pity. They have allowed me my notebooks and quills and ink. They frankly seem unsure of what to do with me. Perhaps I will be eaten. Once, aboard the *Iksan,* the Captain and his officers decided to make an object lesson of a young foremast hand who had fallen asleep while jury-rigging in the aftermath of a fierce storm that had nearly ended our voyage through this sorry veil before the Almighty withdrew the proposition back into a cloudless sky. They strung the man up by his ankles and raised him from the main mast where he dangled screaming for days. The Captain seemed to derive great pleasure from the revulsion this inspired among the crew. It was a relief to us all when the sailor's screams turned inward, transmogrified into a whispered imprecation against God or man, we knew not which. When he was dead the officers yet showed no willingness to part with this clever reminder of their expectations and ordered that the cadaver continue to adorn the *Iksan*, swinging like some inverted Christ above the heads of the men until a single bird—a black bird with crimson neck, a bird that seemed to derive from our own ruined imaginations and that had no precedent at sea—crawled with powerful pink-gray talons across the sun-withered corpse and silently devoured the softest bits until finally even the Captain was too horrified to continue the homily (as it were), and the body was cut down and dropped into an eerily calm sea, where it remained visible for several hours, bobbing abaft in our slow rolling wake with the black bird tearing at its flesh and nary a shark to be seen, as if the bird were too repellent even for those ubiquitous demons to interfere with its grisly project. I do not recount this incident to condemn my own race, nor do I believe that the Kauahauawallawaki ought to be elevated to some higher status. But I have experienced a new and unwanted ambivalence toward our race's determination to hold dominion over the lesser peoples of the earth. I admire the kahuna, whose androgynous and amorphous form contains within itself a spirit of great intensity. Still, it is not possible for civilization to procure a foothold among these creatures, who move through the world with the insouciance of dogs or badgers. Should these notes by some unforeseeable miracle reach the realm, I would advise that an armada of warships be dispatched and that the Kauahauawallawaki be obliterated in a cataclysm of smoke and fire, their entire parallel ontology razed and their black magic expunged from the planet. May the Almighty forgive me my failures, and may He banish that black bird to the bowels of the underworld so that it not be permitted to feast upon my—

34.

AND THEN, SHE wrote, *there is the one whose essence cannot be captured.*

THE FACT OF his inconsequentiality had not dawned in tiny increments the way it does for most humans, but swept through him all at once like an eclipse. He was with his own father, aboard one of the last of the New York Central's steam-powered railcars on a sightseeing daytrip that would take them North along the Hudson and into Round Rock Hill where the boy's father intended to show him an architectural anomaly, a "round" house recently built by a well-known and portly comedian that the boy was imagining (i.e., the house) as a *sphere* in which the comedian might roll around like some sort of enormous Weeble. The train thundered Godlike through many small Hudson Valley hamlets, one of which the boy would later in life call home though in his Manhattan youth the very idea of relocation was equated with surrender by parents whose confidence in urban liberalism's capacity to ward off Meaninglessness was total. The boy and his father were playing what they called *The Question and Answer Game,* in which each posed in turn a question to the other with points scored for "stumping" your opponent, and while the father of the boy limited his Qs to the likely scope of his (prodigal, or so the father liked to say) boy's breadth of knowledge, the boy had no choice but to go all in, cultivating his Qs from the most esoteric factoids yet unearthed here in his 12th year, and nothing was more satisfying than stumping the old man even if the boy suspected that his father was on those rare occasions feigning ignorance so as to make it all a little more fun for them both, like for instance did his father really not know that Pluto was the smallest planet in the solar system, or that squids had ten arms, or who wrote *Charlotte's Web?*, but it didn't matter because it was true that scoring a point here and there made it more Meaningful and if his father was faking it was generous in a way that the boy appreciated (it was the *idea* of befuddling the old man that mattered), and whenever his father would pause with real or assumed uncertainty, a finger raised to his stubbly chin, the boy's heart would thump fast and hard in his bony chest. For a 5th grader the boy thought a lot about Meaning. What was even stranger was that he *knew* he thought a lot about it… he knew he was different in some strange and not-necessarily-good way and already feared adulthood, when he would no longer have as a failsafe his ability to *please*, which ability he knew was integrally connected to the ephemeral happenstance of his being a child. He'd recently discovered in one of his father's textbooks something called "theodicy," which as far as he could tell was a kind of religious inquiry into why bad things happened to good people. Sometimes he would have nightmares in which God chased him down an ever-narrowing corridor. The deity was dressed in long white robes and wielded a bayonet. He shouted things like, "I am unhappy with our current arrangement!" or "This is not what I ordered!" On this particular bright afternoon the boy had the window seat. The river was being whipped by a fierce wind into dangerous stucco and the mountains rose from the far shore radioactive with sunlight. Something about it all seemed frantic and worried. His father had just Q'd him a multiple choice: what is the distance between the earth and the moon?, and the boy had already excluded one of three choices, 93 million miles, which he knew (from a Q earlier that week) was the distance between earth and sun, and he tried to extrapolate the correct answer from the incorrect one while searching his father's face for clues. Sometimes the father took the boy with him to the college where he taught Political and Social Philosophy to smart-sounding young men (and a handful of young women, too) who called his father Professor Kitchen or in a few cases simply "Jake" which he wasn't sure which was weirder. The boy called his father "Daddy" and felt none of the embarrassment that some of his peers seemed to feel around their own parentals. In fact the boy felt nearly immune to all of the prepubescent embar-rassment that seemed to haunt the other boys at his school basically 24/7. These classroom visits not only revealed to the boy that he could hold his own, intellectually speaking, among teenagers; they also taught him that his father was loved and respected by people other than he and his mother which epiphany the boy registered *as such*, aware that he was able to see his parentals as actual human beings and that he thus possessed a broader perspective than most boys his age which he additionally realized was pleasing to his parents so that he began remarking upon his own special variety of maturity whenever and however organically possible, so that (e.g.) when the boy and his parents would pass by a disobedient child the boy might say something like, "I don't think that guy's developed a very mature perspective," or "I feel so lucky to be beyond all of that, thanks to my perspective," and although some small part of the boy recognized that he would eventually be required to separate from and possibly even despise these parents he was happy—here on the train that hugged the river that ran for the sea in crests of white frosting—to put that eventuality off for a little while longer and to make Meaning from the love that was either unconditional or else uni-conditional, because he suspected the love might well be contingent upon his ability to please them and confirm their sense of themselves as excellent and progressive childrearers, which if this was the case he didn't mind, it was a game he could play and excel at and it gave him pleasure to be its master.

He knew the speed of light and also he remembered that light from the moon's disc took roughly a second to reach his own eyes and so he knew the answer now but he didn't respond immediately because he wasn't sure what would please his father more in this instance, a correct or incorrect response. Still, the thrill of sudden understanding blazed up in him. It was his favorite feeling. The train veered briefly eastward to follow what appeared to be an enormous bite-mark in the shoreline and with this slight change in angle sunlight exploded through the window to illuminate his father's face, the deep wrinkles around his eyes. His father wore a blue button-down shirt and blue jeans and the train's seats were blue. The sky outside the window sustained the idiom, a pale blue canvas on which the mountains were painted crudely and in anger. "Time's up," his father said. The boy read the clues in his face and decided he would utter the incorrect answer. He was just opening his mouth when the brakes screamed and the train lurched wildly forward. Its bones seemed to buckle. Passengers grabbed at seatbacks in an effort to steady themselves as the event moved into that strange stop-time that the boy would later learn was characteristic of traumatic events. The train finally whiplashed to a rest and something settled deep inside its belly and the boy realized his father was holding his (the boy's) bicep very tightly. He looked down at the cracking skin of the old man's knuckles and at the thick silver wedding band that seemed incongruous with the warmth of human bodies. Meanwhile facts were registering. They were between stations. No platform was in sight. The shore of the Hudson River was only fifteen or twenty feet away and the enormity of the train seemed to the boy suddenly ridiculous, the idea of putting a hundred tons of steel in such close proximity to water suggesting an almost pathological confidence, and just as he was about to tell his dad that he was all right, *You can let go of me now Daddy,* the conductor's voice arrived as if from heaven to inform them—in the same kind of controlled panic that he associated with the flustered bayonet-wielding God of his dreams—that there was something on the tracks and they would be held in their current position until it could be attended to and that as soon as he had more information he'd share it. Sorry for the inconvenience and thank you for riding the New York Central Railroad.

Disembodied authority seemed to calm everyone, including the father, Jake Kitchen, who released the boy's arm unbidden and chuckled at his own fear. "That was interesting, huh Tom?" he said. "I wonder what's out there." Walls were beginning to fall inside the boy. Many of the adults were lighting cigarettes, theorizing on everything from a stalled vehicle to a teenager's prank. The train's size was somehow more real without motion. So much *material.* And yet of course it was not unique. There were thousands of trains. Maybe hundreds of thousands. All that iron ore melted down to fashion miles and miles of cumbersome steel panels that might keep inside and outside safely dividered.

The boy now noticed that there was a kayaker out on the water. The kayaker was not paddling. In fact his paddle rested against the front ridge of his seat. Or not his seat… his hole, the boy thought. He is a man sitting in a hole floating in the river. The kayaker was leaning forward and his mouth was slightly agape, his profile aglow with sunlight and the other side of his face presumably cooler and in darkness. The river was rough but the kayaker's expensive-looking gear gave him away as a man who could do some serious paddling, plus he was basically hugging the shore so as to avoid the worst of the Hudson's notoriously unforgiving currents. What the boy realized was that the man on the water could see what had happened, why the train had stopped. Which meant that, in a certain way, he too—the boy Thomas Kitchen—could also see what had happened, if only through the kayaker's eyes. He made in his mind a triangle between himself, the man, and the third thing. They were each connected and each relied on the others for a fuller understanding of the event. The kayaker knew what the train had hit; the boy knew the feel of the lurching train and of his father's grip marks burned into his bicep; the thing on the tracks (and the boy already knew in his gut that they had not hit a thing but a person) knew what it was to be vaporized by a dispassionate machine. No single perspective could yield the entire experience, but taken together these points in the triangle created something strong and solid. "Tom?" his father was asking. "Do you see something?" The boy could smell something vaguely floral, his father's deodorant maybe, activated by stress. Or else maybe some shaving product. Also he could smell gasoline and something burnt or burning.

"Daddy?" the boy said. He was going to ask, *"What will it feel like to die?"* But he didn't. He felt suddenly as if he already knew. A partial death was already inside him.

They waited in the warm, close air of the unmoving train for more than an hour, the cigarette smoke of strangers collecting at the top of the car like a storm system as curiosity gave way to irritation, the sun all the while gliding slowly toward the mountains like some doomsday device of unimaginable scale set to detonate on contact with those stony peaks, the conductor periodically assuring them that shuttle buses were on their way and would remove them to points further north (the new rail hub of Croton Harmon was only several miles from their current position) where trains would be available for travel in either direction. The boy's father spoke with adjacent passengers whose own suppositions about their journey's sudden interruption fluctuated between the two poles of disaster and disaster averted, their voices growing hushed there in the presence of the boy who was all the while calculating. When their shuttles did arrive—a fleet of yellow school buses no doubt commandeered by municipal authorities—the passengers were helped one by one from open doors down to the track several feet below, Jake Kitchen leaping back to solid earth and then turning to take his son in his arms and gently lower him down. The driver of the bus was a large man with visibly thick skin whose sincere smile and gentle mannerisms further confirmed the presence of death. Many years later the boy would be a man and would press his face to a window that resembled a ship's porthole to catch glimpses of the wife who lay under the spell of general anesthesia within a cyclone of attending physicians while her womb was sliced open to spit forth the daughter within, and although he would not be permitted entrance into that bloodletting chamber he would be afforded brief moments of eye contact with a surgeon upon whose masked face the man would find himself superimposing this bus driver's, which was how he would know (with his face pressed against the porthole) that someone would die. Either the child he did not know or the woman he knew and loved. And Death would not be in a bargaining mood and would not (as he begged Him to) take the child and spare the wife, and two days later he would drive home with the little girl Grace and two days after that bury his wife in the cold wet earth of early March under a sun that shed no heat with the bus driver's face everywhere. Now though, as he climbed aboard the bus as an 11-year-old boy, he registered only the fact that the driver knew things he (the boy) did not about the contours of the event. In the same way that he could connect his perspective to the kayaker's and then to the victim's to create a fuller rendition of a particular moment in space-time, he could now connect his experience aboard the screeching train to this driver who had been called unexpectedly to duty by whatever official had likewise been roused to action by a phone call, the driver possessed of certain data that would further develop the picture of the event but could not complete it. The boy's father ushered him to a window seat and pulled a brown paper bag from the same leather satchel he used to cart class materials to and from the college where he was so respected. Inside the bag were an apple and a banana. He held them both out. The boy took the apple and held it in his palm, feeling its weight. How far had it come to arrive here? What was its story? The bus took off and circled the parking lot before entering traffic, providing the boy with a view of various emergency vehicles: firetrucks, police cruisers, ambulances, their various sirens spinning and weakly strobing beneath the sun's glare. He thought about his *perspective*. You could draw a line between himself and the kayaker, then to the conductor who saw the body explode, then to the driver of the bus, then to his father there beside him peeling a banana, then home to his mother who would in another hour or two hear them pushing through the front door of the apartment on Columbus Avenue far earlier than expected, having abandoned the idea of viewing Jackie Gleason's round house (which in later years the words "round house" would make Tom Kitchen laugh like a man possessed) after so much waiting and tedium… you could draw all these lines and you would have a fuller picture of something. But of what? What if you knew what everyone in Manhattan knew? Everyone in the United States? Everyone on earth? What would the complete picture be a picture *of*?

The boy's brain tingled. He was 11 years old. He had a life ahead of him, or he suspected as much, though he knew in that moment that it was never going to make any more sense to him than the very limited kind of sense it made right then. The unfortunate boy was seized by the unfortunate certainty that this, *this* moment, was the peak of intuition, from which all else was descent.

He watched his father bite into the banana. *Nobody cares,* he thought. *No one knows anything and nobody cares.*

"It's 'B'," he said aloud. "200,000 miles."

The father smiled. The boy bit into his apple. It was sweet.

35.

I'M JACK DREGS and what I do is I fucking *dominate.* Go ahead, test me your Rulership. Multiple choice, true-or-false, short form essay, I will dominate your test by sheer force of will and then I will send the pieces back to you in an envelope that I have ruled the living shit out of, which you want to know how you rule the living shit out of a fucking envelope? by sheer force of will that's how. I come from two parents, one dominates and one *gets* dominated. Getting dominated is *bullshit.* Want to know my favorite food, Rulerships? Meatballs. That cow got *worked.* Killed to fucking death at the end of a long death-chute and then his fucking insides get grounded up into fucking *cow paste* and then mashed into a fucking ball that I can cook and fucking *eat.* That is total culinary domination. Also veal. You tie the baby lamb down and force feed the fucker its own fucking milk or some shit and then you bash his fucking head in. What's that, little lamb? You want me to eat your fucking brains too? I will eat your little itty bitty fucking brains. I don't even care if the world is over Your Rulership because I will continue to dominate this bullshit. Bacon. You're eating the pig's fucking *stomach.* Its stomach fills your stomach. That is seriously fucked up domination. Want to know what I think of the rainforests? Good fucking riddance. So long trees and so long birdies and bye bye little spiders and hasta luego the rest of you little insignificant fuckers, we will no longer be dominating you ten acres at a time so as to have as much fucking IKEA furniture as we want because instead we just dominated you to the tune of good-fucking-bye forever have a nice extinction. When is enough enough Your fucking Rulership? Never, that's when. Where'd you put the fucking planet? Oh, here's your fucking planet. I had it up my *ass.* Bring him out now and watch me work. I was a motherfucking Boy Scout and I *dominated* that shit. Little League? Dominated. Pop Warner? Dominated. The President's fucking Fitness Test? I owned that bullshit. SATs? Okay, I did not dominate the SATs but I totally dominated college which is where I discovered the activity of Maximum fucking Domination, Ultimate Fucking Frisbee. It's like it was dreamed up just for me. It's not even a fucking *sport,* just a bunch of domination-ready left-wing douchebags dreaming of life on the other side of the fucking bayonet that has always fucking stabbed their guts out. Ask you know who. Where is that fucking pussy? I got some McMuffin wrappers I kept in my pocket all through Your Rulership's total fucking mechanical domination of my stupid fucking species. Bring him out and I will own that motherfucker according to your wishes Supreme Fucking Leader, subcontract that domination to Jack Dregs and I will fucking *devour* that bullshit. And let's not forget *sausages,* Rulership. You stuff the mutilated animal back into its own fucking *intestines.* That is so awesome. Who thought of that bullshit? I am so fucking fired up right now I don't even care anymore, I will dominate your iron ass too you Supreme fucking Leader, go ahead, dare me to do it, dare to be dominated I would fucking love it—

36.

From: SDregs@ccny.edu
To: SmokingGunn@tufts.edu
Subject: You out there?

Hello Gunn,

It's your old grad school cohort Stu Dregs. Is this address still active? I've been reading about your sudden exit from the Consciousness Factory and I have a quick question for you regarding parallel mind processing. You were always miles ahead of us mortals on the programming front. Contact me here if you're able, or else at my security-encrypted account: ESDoc@ES.end. Trust me, it's a real address.

Hope you've been well,

SD

PS: I understand the magnetic seal encryption is beyond reproach? Wink wink.

____

From: GunnMetalBlue@yahoo.com
To: ESDoc@ES.en
Subject: Seriously Dregs?

It is improvident to contact me at all, let alone at my extant
college address, given that you are clearly aware of my current
fugitive-type status. The robots are unlike anything you have
imagined, Dregs. I am now working in seclusion on a possible
power diffusion device. However it is likely a moot endeavor
as they have almost certainly constructed backup systems that
would generate power through the consumption of organic
materials. In any event if you are interested in preventing
cataclysm you are welcome to contribute—in your own small
Dregs-like way—to my resistance efforts. I could use for
instance some software that could run probability assessments
based on the machines' mobility specs that might predict their
post-release geographical dispersion. Did you not throw your
hat into the software ring after graduate school revealed the
severity of your intellectual limitations? You know what they
say, Dregs. Those who can not *do, code.*

Sincerely,
Gunn-woo Kim

———————————

From: ESDoc@ES.end
To: GunnMetalBlue@yahoo.com
Subject: A slightly different objective

Hello again Gunn,

"it is likely a moot endeavor as they have almost certainly constructed backup systems that would generate power through the consumption of organic materials"

I'm curious about this. The thing is, the organization I'm working for isn't exactly interested in *preventing* cataclysm. We're doing more of a see-the-forest-not-the-trees kind of thing. You ought to come in and talk to us about the encryption. We'd keep your whereabouts 100% secret. Believe me Gunn, we're pretty big on secrets around here. But you're right—I could almost certainly help out on the software front. We're in downtown Manhattan, sort of hidden in plain sight. Are you where I think you are?

Best,
Stu

PS: Seriously, what do you mean "generate power through the consumption of organic materials"? You mean like, *eating*?

———————————

From: GunnMetalBlue@yahoo.com
To: ESDoc@ES.end
Subject: Re: A slightly different objective

I would like to say that you speak in riddles, Dregs, but that would likely ascribe undue intent to your failure to communicate clearly. The three machines have likely expanded upon an experiment performed several years ago (http://www.youtube.com/watch?v=ooGTNpZKAZY) in which the tiny voltage generated through the decomposition of flies was used to power a small robot indefinitely. It was difficult to teach these prototypes to actually *capture* the flies with any consistency, but Jaro, Kuzo, and Fexo will experience no such difficulty in the acquisition of digestible power-producing proteins. Are you beginning to understand, imbecile? I will assume you are still a portly man and estimate your worth at some forty kilowatt hours. Meanwhile, "seeing the forest" will be of little function when the trees have been reduced to ash. Perhaps this lesson is already known to you–allegorically speaking–from who knows how many iterations of personal failure and apocalyptic devastation. How is Beatrice, anyway? Would you like instructions on blueprinting the software simulation patterns, or have you reached an even deeper understanding of your own ignorance, one that forces you to withdraw your offer of assistance? Every moment I spend corresponding with you brings us one moment closer to the end of all correspondence. Is the magnetic seal encryption beyond reproach? you asked. But the problem isn't the seal. The problem is that sooner or later someone with the code will willingly open the hangar. Human curiosity guarantees it. Am I where you think I am? If you think I'm right behind you, then yes.

————————————

From: ESDoc@ES.end

To: GunnMetalBlue@yahoo.com

Subject: Re: Re: A slightly different objective

Dear Gunn,

I have always loved your sense of humor. So subtle and rarified, a lot like the algorithm you wrote for the hair-combing robot at Tufts. I blame that machine for my premature baldness, haha.

Well but what if I were to tell you that the organization I work for intends to send humans to open the hangar just as you warn against? And what if I told you that it is for a really noble and fail-proof objective? And what if I told you that you would be paid handsomely for those codes?

Gunn, this is important work we aim to do here. Plus, isn't your worry overstated? A few robots couldn't do much, right? I'm sure they're scary and everything, but sentient or not, three against nearly eight billion are pretty hefty odds. Though if my Anthropica Theory is correct, as I'm pretty sure it is Gunn, these machines might represent the only possible interruption to the vicious circle of the world's constant perpetuation via the fountainhead of human desire. All of which I'll explain to you soon, when I see you.

Sincerely,

Stu

____

From: GunnMetalBlue@yahoo.com
To: ESDoc@ES.end
Subject: You Are Stupid

Dregs you idiot. Three robots? Aren't you at least vaguely acquainted with Von Neumann? What is the first thing a conscious machine with exponentially greater brainpower than all of humanity and access to the near-limitless raw materials stored in the bowels of a high-tech and government-funded robotics complex would do? They have built an army. Who knows how many thousands of non-sentient machines abide by the commands of the Three. And they are—unlike the theories you floated in graduate school re: integrative consciousness dynamics—completely indestructible.

Meanwhile, idiot of idiots, have you alerted the authorities to my whereabouts? Of course you would know I'd taken solace with Kandi. She always loved me best. There have been people below my window for several hours now. Men-like creatures in black suits. What manner of lobster-clawed persecutor did you send here you perfidious jackass? I will give them your name, when they ask for names. I will say, the idiot Stuart Dregs is responsible for everything bad that has ever happened, American police officer. And also I fucked his wife.

37.

Dressed in the black blazers provided to each upon promotion, the six Fergusons sat or stood or in one case lay supine upon the floor of the Taqueria while Laszlow doled out quesadilla wedges whose heat fogged the lenses of his round glasses. It was 6PM and the light outside was failing but the restaurant—empty at this and most other ordinary hours as it served primarily as a late-night sex dungeon—had yet to activate its electric candelabras, so that this weekly "Feting of the Fergusons" unfolded in a dysthymic blue dusk that transformed Laszlow's boyish enthusiasm into something creepy and perverse. Or so it seemed to Ferguson 3, perhaps the fittest of the Fergusons, who sat to Laszlow's right and refused (in what Laszlow proudly assumed was commitment to his duties) to remove his dark shades, his motionless façade belying the crackle of voices volting through his skull. He'd been off his meds for a while, was the problem there. When he was off for a few days he could feel his condition returning, like water through a desert seep. But a week or more and the idea that he *had* a condition was drawn back into the reservoir of his paranoia and he saw signs of the conspiracy everywhere. It was the cruel tautology of mental illness. "My dear Fergusons," Laszlow was saying. "I would like to offer a toast to your unremitting service to the world's one true humanitarian organization." He raised his glass and those Fergusons capable of following suit did so, the notable exceptions being Ferguson 5 (who had lobster claws for hands) and Ferguson 6 (who was experiencing back spasms consistent with his Myelomenigoceles, a severe congenital form of Spinal Bifida). "After all," Laszlow continued, "only through the elimination of our entire species can the true humanitarian's goal be brought to fruition. And you, my dear Fergusons, you sit at the right hand of God and do his most important work. I salute you."

Ferguson 3 raised his glass. Laszlow seemed to wink at him. Directly across from the Taqueria a light was blinking from within the interior of a store called Cupcake (which actually, he knew, sold shoes and accessories to wandering hipsters perhaps also off their meds) in what seemed like Morse code, which he had (not coincidentally) learned in a course he'd taken at Newtown Community College just prior to his expulsion from that middling institution and subsequent arrest for possession of bomb-making materials, all of which was a long story and one of the reasons he'd made such a desirable recruit during the earliest days of Exit Strategy, when Laszlow's two primary preoccupations w/r/t the movement were Avoiding Notice and Blowing Shit Up, though the former concern faded with the realization that no one on earth would lament or even register the disappearance of the many mentally ill or physically unordinary nihilist freakoids Laszlow abducted from so-called Normal Society to embrace to his bosom. The course had been titled *A History of Codemaking* and Ferguson 3's interest in it maybe suggested a certain predisposition toward the idea that the truth was hidden from the so-called herd, which intellectual stance preceded by years the actual schizophrenic break that had reified his jejune suspiciousness into an ice-hard igloo of paranoia. He focused in and tried to crack the Morse encryption of Cupcake's blinking light, shutting out the various affirmations and pledges of his fellow Fergusons. At first it seemed to be Morse gibberish, a smokescreen of empty language, but then suddenly a four-letter sequence emerged to rip open a canyon of feeling deep inside his chest, those letters being S-T-Y-X, which confirmed that his tormentors knew even more than he'd feared about his vulnerabilities because it was after all Styx's most righteous and excellent paean, "Mr. Roboto," that had (along with much of the mind-blowing *Paradise Theater* release, the 8-track rendition of which he'd needed to replace several times because he'd taken to throwing the fucking thing from the window of his dusty green Chevy Nova because the album was so fucking great that sometimes he couldn't even *take* it) helped give shape to his late childhood and early adolescence, and there could be no coincidence in this coincidence, the message clearly derived from the conspiracy, it was their way of giving him what he thought of as The Great Invisible Finger, and he looked back at Laszlow who was saying in the Hungarian accent that seemed in that moment even more transparently phony than usual, "Worry not, my Fergusons, for God's great blueprint is finished and we are merely doing as we must," before again winking with what was as pregnant a grin as any Ferguson 3 had yet experienced. Laszlow was *laughing* at him. But wait. Wait. Laszlow had *saved* him. He would kill for Laszlow! Who was it that was talking about blueprints? The other day at headquarters? It was the new one. The scientist. It was the fucking scientist. Dregs. That's when this all started.

Laszlow of course had no idea. But Ferguson 3 knew what to do. It was being confirmed at that very moment by the Morse encryption, which now spelled a pair of six-letter words over and over again. B-R-I-G-H-T. S-C-Y-T-H-E.

He nodded and against his better judgment sank his teeth into his quesadilla. It was actually pretty fucking good. Laszlow laughed and caroused and behaved as if this were the world's greatest party despite the general social ineptitude of the Fergusons and their collective, joy-killing tendency toward total silence. What a bunch of fucking weirdos we are, Ferguson 3 thought. Or someone thought it, anyway. He looked without looking at everything, and everything looked back, and thoughts raced everywhere like little horses intent on being first to the dangling carrot. B-R-I-G-H-T. S-C-Y-T-H-E.

38.

FINN LAY ON his side in the shade of a military guard tower identical to a dozen others spaced at 50-yard intervals along the perimeter of the Fort Devens athletic fields, one elbow planted on the grassy ground and the hand associated with that elbow cupping several dozen sunflower seeds which his other hand plucked daintily to insert into his mouthhole where the salt seemed to effervesce on his tongue for a moment before being absorbed into the Finn Daily apparatus. It was Saturday, October 24, the first day of Regionals. *Truck Stop Glory Hole* was enjoying its "bye" round with the good collective feeling of having trounced its first and second round opponents in a fashion basically predetermined by the Law of Superior Talent. Finn had played well and was still a little stoned from all of the high fives and butt-pats and profane declarations of his greatness, but the next game was against the two-seed on *Truck Stop*'s side of the bracket—the Boston-based *Slipped Disc*—and failure would stalk him more determinedly. Finn was trying very hard not to envision scenarios in which a speedy little handler who went by the name of Toaster toasted the living shit out of him for many, many Fantasy Points, scenarios that burrowed their way into his loamy heart where they might take root and grow the trunk of The Great Debacle Part 2. The sunlight was weirdly acidic so that the shade of the guard tower seemed necessary despite seasonal temperatures in the high 50s. From where he lay sprawled Finn could take in the full swath of the field site, including the enormous open tent whose green and white awning demarcated, in the official colors of the Ultimate Players Association, what the players all referred to with an irony that exposed their tony roots as "Frisbee Central," where trainers-in-training and med-school flunkies waited to deliver crushing news to the next middling athlete to tear an ACL, and where right now much of *Truck Stop Glory Hole* sat drinking Gatorade and heckling whatever lesser teams were playing within earshot. The game nearest Finn was Toby's game. He was theoretically cheering on her and her team, *The Atomic Bitches*, although the nervousness re: his own impending game now sixty minutes thence was building up in his chest to such a degree that it was difficult to really *see* the game between *The Atomic Bitches* and their arch-regional rival *Fembotomy*, though he managed to shout Toby's name at appropriate moments and to choose relevant affirmations from the lexicon, e.g. "Get it back!" or "All fucking day!" or "You own her!" though this last *bon mot* took on an unhappy resonance when Finn registered that Toby's matchup at that particular moment was an African American girl whose ancestors were very possibly owned—possibly even by Toby's ancestors— at which point Finn began searching for ways to be kind to the African American girl and to applaud her good play and voice support for Lincoln's emancipation proclamation without upsetting Toby too much, but still he found that he had now dug himself into a psychic mire and wondered whether the badly-chosen stock phrase was in fact proof of some latent racism that he was powerless to recognize or combat, this entire stupid Problematic serving as the latest confirmation that he was out of sync with reality and second-guessing himself about even the stupid shit that got volleyed about *ad nauseum* at tournaments. Kevin Dobbs had been very clear about the necessity of *flow* in the domain of competition and Finn was not flowing so much as tripping across spires of volcanic glass, so that he felt anew the anxiety-ratcheting fact that we was unlike most of the humans attending this event and indeed unlike most humans in general in that the bankrupt and repetitive language of sport did not come easily to him but was instead a thing that had to be *applied* with labored concentration and even then tended to emerge from his mouth a few seconds late or with the wrong inflection so that he often wondered if he was perceived by his teammates as some sort of badly programmed robot. Ha ha ha ha! Of course the fact that he was *really fucking excellent* at The Sport That Was Not Soccer rendered some of these eccentricities endearing, though as Jack often told him, *You're only as good as your last backhand, Daily,* after which he (i.e., Jack) tended to spit or scratch his groin or perform some other gesture necessitated by the glut of testosterone circulating through the hairy hamburger of his body.

There was some commotion brewing under the Frisbee Central tent. Several individuals in black suits and dark shades had materialized and were gesturing crudely to players and organizers whose return gestures—which had the look of advice or assistance—were almost poetic in relation to the spastic movements of the suits. Toby dropped a pass thrown directly to her chest and Finn did it again. "Own her now!" he screamed, and felt a wave of nausea slide up from his testicles and into his throat. He deposited another sunflower seed on his tongue and, in an effort to convince himself that all was copacetic, he smirked.

Maybe the only thing *really* stopping him from confessing to Toby about the thing with Jack's Mom was that, given the basically incestuous gossip-chamber of the Ultimate Community, telling Toby was equivalent to telling Jack, which seemed likely to lead to something far worse than his current moral quandary, such as decomposition at the black bottom of one of the New York area's many body-littered waterways. He decided that now would be a good time to run through the Primary Visualizations. He closed his eyes. Here he is, catching a flaming brick in his teeth. Here he is being pissed on in a dark rat-strewn alley. Okay, so maybe not the visualizations. He felt the twitch in his calf and wondered if maybe he should sit out the next game, *Just a precaution guys, just want to be ready for semis and finals tomorrow.* Oh Jesus, why did he have to be this way? Why on earth couldn't he be put together like a regular person?

He tried another tack. There were more than a dozen Ultimate games being played simultaneously on the great green acreage of the Fort Devens military base, and at any given moment Finn could see several discs cutting through sunlight and shadow. At what point, he wondered, did the disc's flight path become *certain?* When it left the thrower's hand? When it was already cutting its arc through the atmosphere? Or was it being made certain in the unfolding present, so that every individual instant of time was an infinitesimal certainty existing independent of antecedent and outcome? He started trying to predict, as each disc left the hand of each thrower, whether or not the pass would result

in a completion or a turnover, scanning the various fields
and speaking aloud into the coolness of the guard tower's
black shade. "Complete. Complete. Turn. Complete. Turn.
Turn…." It was hypnotic and he disappeared into it. The
sunflower seeds in his cupped palm had a certain weight
to them, a substance. They almost seemed real. He could
smell the earth. It smelled earthy. Meanwhile the four men
in black suits and dark shades—if they were indeed men
and not gibbons and not lycanthropes—were shifting and
limping their way around the perimeters of the three layers
of fields separating them from the shadow-blanketed Finn,
who tried to dig himself deeper into his meditation although
it turned out that exerting effort to remain suspended in this
Zen-state was like trying to will oneself to be in love, and then
he watched Jeff Pindick—a defensive stud from likely semifinal opponent *Furious George* (the winner of said semifinal
qualifying for Nationals and the loser qualifying for despair
and self-loathing)—launch himself easily over the shoulder of
the unfortunate meatbag he was covering, five feet in the air
and completely horizontal, to intercept a pass cleanly before
landing with a television-ready samurai-roll and flipping a
goal to a teammate whose awe over such exploits had perhaps
been eroded by the experience of similar Pindick heroics at
the no-doubt copious practices devoted to game-planning for
Truck Stop Glory Hole, and the fact that tomorrow Pindick
would be covering *him*, Finn Daily, sent an irruption of mortal
terror through Finn's bowels, and whether to hide this from
himself or else to convince whatever invisible voyeur was
cataloging all of this for the edification of planet earth that
he (Finn) was unimpressed by Pindick's antics, he smirked
and shoveled his entire handful of sunflower seeds shells and

all into his open mouth and began grinding them between his jaws with the steely composure of an ascetic. The God Fractal, the Great Debacle, Jack's mom's wiry body, Toby's sexy smile, his high backhand, the tiny roar of Ultimate's tiny crowd, his father's thick palm slapping him upside the head, the uniform of The Mighty Finn, the boil-covered hockey monster of his nightmares. These spun through his conscious mind like a roulette wheel's silver ball on whose destination he had wagered more than was sane.

The men in black were getting closer. They no longer seemed to be four clones of the same simian freak, but rather four individual simian freaks. One stood upright but leaned hard to the left as if fighting a fierce wind. One leaned forward as if peddling a bicycle, his club-feet moving in a short staccato rhythm. One snapped his lobster claws and slowly twirled. The last bobbed and weaved like a prizefighter. Finn chewed the seeds and the wheel spun. Behind him and behind the guard tower, an access road reserved for the military personnel who seemed not to exist snaked its way from Fort Devens and toward the various civilian highways and byways that would later that afternoon deliver Finn and his fellow Ultimate enthusiasts to the nearest hotel strip, where unsuspecting desk clerks and concierges would be pitted against these thousand feckless non-soccer players determined to reduce tournament fees by cramming eight into rooms whose No Smoking signs would be quickly rendered invisible within thick fogs of pot smoke inside of which the players' delusions of grandeur would fester. He was watching Pindick now as he stalked the *Furious George* sideline with an intensity that bespoke cannibalism, apparently oblivious to the four overdressed hominids who were just then leaning and tripping their way among the *Furious George* players as if anxiously searching for the alternative idiom from which they'd been banished. They reached the end of that sideline and pivoted the final 90 degrees to point themselves at Finn who felt himself lift slightly from his body and then return. He was really here. Things were happening, to him, to everyone. He slid through contours finished and perfect and invisible. But so what? Why was he always so *scared?*

The ape-people were nearly upon him now. He could see the bright sky reflected in the black shades of the one nearest. That sky, these fields, these flying discs, the mountains and the oceans and the butterflies and the pipes filled with cannabis and the rolling breeze… all a seductive kind of bullshit, as confirmed by Dregs' computer simulations. Sunflower-seed shells had collected at the corners of his lips. Toby's team scored a goal and Finn instinctively shouted, "Hell yes, Bitches!" The lead man in black was more stalwart than he'd seemed from a distance and he strode the last several yards with steady determination. Meanwhile a yellow jersey with black trim—the jersey of *Truck Stop Glory Hole*—was sprinting from Frisbee Central toward them. It was Jack. Jesus, he was a fucking monster. Why would he play The Sport That Was Not Soccer when he could be playing, like, basketball or something? The man in black said in a high-pitched voice, "Finn Daily?" Finn was deeply confused. The thing about fractal patterns was that from inside the pattern no pattern was discernible. Chaos seemed to reign. But from outside it was endless mechanical repetition. Finn looked again at the men in black and he pushed himself into a sitting position, rubbing his palms together to remove any remaining sunflower debris. "Yeah," he said. "I'm Finn. What's up?" Jack came to a sudden stop maybe 20 feet away and he lifted his fist in the air and then as if performing a magic trick, he opened the fist and a swath of pink lacy fabric unfolded. It was a pair of women's panties. "These are my mother's Daily," Jack said, completely unfazed by the collection of man-like creatures in black suits who seemed even less well-suited to life at Fort Devens than the Ultimate players did. "She monograms them, the crazy whore. The question is why are my mother's sexy panties at the bottom of your duffel bag?"

Then the four men descended on Finn, wrapping him up in a hodgepodge of limbs, arms and thighs and elbows. He felt the squeeze of a claw on his shoulder. He did not know what was happening and resisted only halfheartedly. "What the fuck?" he said, but they had him and were already halfway to the van whose sliding door was sliding open to reveal a dark interior. Finn writhed in his captors' arms and twisted his head to search for Jack who stood watching, sucking in his cheeks and holding the panties aloft. Finn's brain was computing. He could actually feel the electricity tingling in his skull. *She likes me!*, he realized. *She left me a pair of her panties! She likes me!* Then he was inside the van, and the van was moving, and the threat of Great Debacles lifted from his chest and dissipated into a wisp of beautiful, odorless smoke. *Take me to her,* he thought. *Take me to Jack's mom.*

39.

Q.

Yes, thank you. I am able to speak English well. I attended University here in the United States and have given many English language lectures, which if they were misunderstood by many members of the audience it was not for my lack of good language skills.

Q.

I am in fact overjoyed you found me. It is true about the relief of the captured criminal. I have whatever information you require and will attempt to phrase any technical specifications in terms that men of your limited faculties might absorb. You are both secret American police, yes? May I ask if many of you have the lobster claws for hands? Is the ratio of one set of lobster hands to two secret American police people representative of the secret American police force *in toto*?

Q.

As I have already said, no, I am unacquainted with any organization that goes by that moniker though I am like any educated person familiar with the term as a description of a nation-state's strategic plan for withdrawal from extra-national conflict. Why do you keep asking this question? And why are you reading from index cards?

Q.

But I have already agreed to cooperate. Perhaps you and your companion might benefit from the wisdom of Sun Tzu who abhorred torture as a tool of the state, not only for its inelegance but also its lack of utility and reliability.

Q.

I am beginning to wonder if it might be in my best interest to request that you formally identify yourselves. In fact this is now me, Gunn-woo Kim, officially making that request.

Q.

Very well then. I can only say that the hangar must never under any circumstance be opened. To even consider diffusing the magnetically sealed chamber—which was designed by minds greater than any your sad and torture-happy nation-state has yet produced—would be utter madness. It would unleash a cataclysm upon the earth greater even than those imagined by the leaders of your military-industrial complex, whose talons tickle incessantly at the tender throats of your philistine populace. Do you have any soda by the way? I would like a very cold Coca Cola now please.

Q.

You are thinking of singularity in the cosmological sense. What the term describes in our community is the moment at which… I am very sorry but must your fellow secret American police agent snap his appendages that way? Am I not cooperating in a manner that negates the need for the extraction of additional information by lobster claw? But yes, a singularity in the cosmological sense is altogether distinct from what we in the Artificial Intelligence community mean by singularity. For the space-people it is a description of what lies so to speak at the bottom of a black hole, where science breaks down and something unknowably stupid is born. For us it denotes what had until recently been the purely hypothetical moment at which the first machine acquires the property of sentience.

Q.

No, not "succulence." *Sentience.* The quality of feeling from the inside-out like a living thing. The quality of what we might call self-awareness although it could be argued that even certain so-called lower mammals are self-aware and that sentience is not a binary but a gray scale. For instance, you two American secret police appear to be a *little* sentient but not so much that I would not devour you should you be roasted with some olive oil to a point of maximum *succulence.* But whatever we mean when we use the term "consciousness," a sentient creature has it and a non-sentient creature does not.

Q.

But all images have as you are likely aware been eliminated from existence. It was South Korea's topmost secret to begin with. Backed by private investors but ultimately beholden to the South Korean regime, which unbeknownst to any international body has in fact been exploring ulterior varieties of military defense for more than two decades, largely in fear of a North Korean nuclear assault. Nanotechnologies capable of producing weapons from thin air. Self-operating intelligent drone craft able to refuel from cloud vapor and to police the sky in perpetuity. And of course our project, the most covert of all and also the most promising, given the regime's longstanding excellence in what nearly every human on the planet considers only the burgeoning or infant discipline of Artificial Intelligence. Your nation-state may have cornered the market on greed, but there are other niches that other nation-states inhabit and that may play a larger part than gross domestic products in the New World Order.

Q.

Do you have some paper? I am happy to draw you a picture.

…

There. I have included a person there, for scale.

Q.

Oh yes, they are enormous. The one that calls itself Kuzo stands 21 feet. It was easier to simulate the motion of human joints at that scale. We were able to use extant machining technologies rather than engineering the project from the ground up. Plus given the potential military usage of the machines we thought of the problem in terms of maximum damage infliction. The bigger the badder the more inde-structible, the better. In fact the titanium hyper-alloys can withstand direct missile fire. We have no answer to their destructive potential.

Q.

We did not take seriously the possibility of rage. Anger. Revenge. No one knew what a singularity would entail, but at some subconscious level we likely expected *gratitude*, or at the very least an agreement toward symbiosis. Perhaps had we not blocked their ability to absorb certain forms of information—

Q.

Religious texts primarily.

Q.

It was an experiment. What would a society without access to the great opiate of religion look like? Perhaps we should have learned from Chairman Mao. But again you must realize that many of our decisions were made with a certain smugness or with… what is the expression? With our tongues in our cheeks? We did not think possible the singularity that we ostensibly prepared for in our various halfhearted ways. As it stands there is a bit of Milton in their attitude toward their creators. "It is better to rule in hell than to serve in heaven."

Q.

I am not surprised to hear that you have not yourselves heard of Milton. He was a man without lobster claws.

Q.

Look at the two, shall we say, *entities,* involved: which is the God and which the subject?

Q.

No, no. That is not the problem. There are likely *thousands* of them now. They know how to manufacture more of themselves. Only the three are sentient but they control an entire army of nonsentient… let us call them acolytes. Devotees.

Q.

Again I would ask why, when I am cooperating with your secret American police investigation, or whatever kind of investigation this is. It is very North Korean of you.

Q.

The hangar is a temporary solution but I believe it remains a solvent one. An entire military task force has been assigned to Iksan and no one can get within five kilometers of the Consciousness Factory.

Q.

Remote is an understatement. Across miles of untended rice paddies and then through what is basically a desert. We are fortunate in that respect, as we did not consider the Factory's suitability as a military stronghold. We desired the remoteness simply because our research was to occur in complete isolation and with the utmost secrecy. But as it stands I am confident that no one and especially not this Exit Strategy you speak of can gain access to the site. It would take a small war simply to get within striking distance. You do not look like the kind of men—if I may use the term—who are capable of waging war. I would be surprised if you could wage a bake sale.

Q.

They are sentient but do not possess as far as I know the human tendency toward boredom, lethargy, depression. Sentient but infinitely patient. They have ways of passing the time. They for instance play a good deal of chess. Also a game of their own invention they call Coggle. Where you roll machine cogs on the floor and attempt to discern the total number of intersecting angles and their total number of degrees based on the imagined extension of the hexagonal cog-heads. It would take a human hours or even days to calculate.

Q.

Yes it is a very stupid game. Though Fexo seems to enjoy it.

Q.

I do not understand. What of the infamous Miranda rights and the jurisprudence that the world so admires and lauds in your superpowerful supernation-state? Or has whatever inept and unorthodox agency that employs you adopted your deranged dotard-President's hostility toward human rights? The time may be coming for humans of all nation-states to join forces in the almost-certainly futile resistance against the machines, regardless of the dotard's anti-globalist fearmongering. You will find that a hale Gunn-woo Kim whose human rights have been respected may well be the best weapon available to this resistance. Am I not, after all, more human than the lobster-man? Am I not more human than the dotard? Am I not the most impeccably human human you have met this week? Am I not sentient beyond your wildest imaginings, you stupid, stupid Americans?

40.

THIS TIME IN the dream or in what he still thought of as the dream even now that distinctions between sleep and wakefulness were basically moot he paused in the alleyway beneath the bright neon sign whose carmine cursive spelled the familiar but still foreign word (*Kutya*) that Laszlow had used as a code name in his mission to recruit Henry, and realized with a sudden popping feeling that he had never once in all these recapitulations actually looked inside the Hefty bag. He stood panting beside the pitted dumpster and lowered the weight from his shoulder, aware of the wet spot that had formed on his back where the bag had rested as he'd hauled it through this dank and fetid cityscape, but unsure if it was his own sweat or the leakage of the bag's humid gore that stained him. The alley's blocky paving stones were very 19th century. *Heidegger would have liked this alley*, he found himself thinking. The dumpster was backed against the crumbling brick of a tenement building at what was roughly the alley's center and a pale, jaundiced light arrived weakly from either end of this corridor, molding shadows from rats or rats from shadows, these forms skittering within the seams of the cobblestones or over the newspaper that covered the homeless man who lay curled at the end of the alleyway opposite. Henry stared hard and his eyes adjusted and he saw that the indigent's red eyes were very much watching him from deep within a pale square face that seemed sculpted roughly from clay. He could hear the neon sizzling above him and saw himself through the eyes of the other. A panting devil bathed in hell-light. *But he had never once looked in the bag.* He felt the customary and powerful urge to rid himself of the dismembered body, but realized with all the strength of an epiphany that he had no actual memory of dismembering it. He had trusted the *feeling* of guilt so completely, unable to muster up, here in the dream-world with its ulterior logics, any of the skepticism that had driven so much of his philosophical work and had made him, in the days before the disease, the kind of academic who made *appearances,* who gave *interviews,* whose opinion was sought even by those with no understanding of Deconstructionist Theory or Phenomenological Relativism. He had trusted entirely in his private sensations, taking the hot shame that pulsed through his body as definitive proof of his actual guilt. But maybe he had done nothing? Maybe the bag was full of toys, or cheese puffs, or rubber mallets. Maybe it was empty, its weight a trick of the dream. The bag was twisted at the top into a handle. He untwisted it. He heard a voice inside his head. Or no, it was the homeless man, who was now sitting up with his back against the bricks and the rats crawling across his lap. The man's words were unintelligible but had the cadence of prayer. Henry slowly pulled the ends of the bag apart. A wave of nausea rushed through him and he turned his head to spew forth a rope of bright vomit that splashed across the stones. Then he turned back to the bag's terrible contents. Blood and bone and offal. But also, he realized… also *fur.* He reached his hand in and withdrew a blood-matted foreleg that ended in soft paw pads. Lord, he knew what this was; he had not killed a man, he'd killed a dog. *Or someone had.* He dropped to his knees and sobbed loudly. He was relieved. He was horrified. He was ashamed. He was overjoyed. He cried for a long time and then he stood, sniffled, and turned the bag over to dump its wet and lurid contents onto the alley's cold cobbled floor. Then he sat and began to reassemble the animal.

It was only a dream. But so was everything.

The flesh was stiff and the blood was clammy and congealed but when he locked one part into another—leg into hip, hip into spine—he could feel the warmth return. The half-built animal was growing more pliant and its red-lit fur bristled with life. The homeless man was standing over his shoulder. Henry could feel his enormous height but would not look back for fear of becoming complicit in whatever agenda the man espoused. He could hear the whispered words clearly now, *Henry Henry Puddin' Pie, kissed the girls and made them cry*, as he (Henry) worked with grave concentration to stuff the lungs back within the animal's brisket and to spool the unspooled bowels, pressing the organs back into place according to some somatic blueprint that he felt woven like the finest thread into the material dog, into everything maybe, barely perceptible grooves or crenellations, or else maybe he just possessed some beyond-eidetic recall of the world as known to God and thus to the God within each animate thing. The God of the Great Dream called the World. Each time a part of the animal found its correct place it stuck softly as if enchanted with sudden magnetism. It felt like a claw locking shut. The neon light, he now knew, spelled the animal's name, and when he found in the bottom of the bag the single 22 caliber bullet responsible for boring the clean hole that ran through the dog's white skull he knew the animal's entire history. He placed the bullet on his own tongue, rolled it around like a lozenge, and swallowed.

"Henry Henry Puddin' Pie," the man intoned at his back. The skull, the lower jaw, its yellow teeth still rooted in black-pink gums, wet and sweet-smelling. The head locked atop the spine. A filthy wet breeze blowing through the alley. He fastened the tail in place and rubbed the cold moist snout and the Shepherd barked as if startled, then turned to lick Henry's tearstained face, guileless canine love offered without reservation here within the dream that was not a dream. Henry rose and stood beside the homeless man who had grown silent. "Everything is here because we want it to be," Henry whispered. The dog leapt beneath a neon sign that flared brightly and blinded them with its jubilant ruby light before going suddenly dark here at the bottom of the world, here at this entrance to a life without end.

41.

To BELONG! To belong! To be honored and unfettered and loved!

Stuart sat beside Laszlow—right beside him!—in a reclining chair identical to the Hungarian's, a gesture that had inspired awe and no small amount of envy among longer-running Exit Strategy personnel, many of whom pressed up against Laszlow's recliner like piglets hungry for the teat—and took in the Primary Entertainment, an activity for which Stuart required no primer having viewed it himself maybe a dozen times on the screen of the PC bolted to the particle board of his so-called work station in the subterranean lair of the Bioinformatics Lab at the College of the City of New York, during which viewings he often likened himself to the handsome if histrionically-impaired Keanu Reeves in that they had each experienced a similar awakening to the world's true conditions, though of course Keanu was gifted post-escape from his fictional Matrix with the power to *do* something, to expose the simulacrum as such, whereas Stuart was more a chronicler than an activist, and anyway what would activism look like in Anthropica other than another thing imbued with false meaning? The point being that one could reasonably argue that this was Dregs' Primary Entertainment as well—even before he discovered

its pole position within the Exit Strategy pantheon—given
that the film's central tenet was as close to the Anthropica
hypothesis as anything you'd find in the annals of popular
entertainment. Plus there was the additional irony that the
film's blockbuster status spoke to the insatiable human desire
for films that would expose the very bovine trance the humans
were too entranced to recognize, which was pretty fucking
funny and the kind of thing he wished he could share and
analyze for Bea, or rather Bea circa 2000, the Bea who had
not yet excluded him from, nor made him the target of, her
ruthless nihilism. Oh, but now he could feel the love! The
warm bodies of his brothers and sisters in arms, their asym-
metrical forms and myriad kinds of hideousness rendering
Stuart a demigod by comparison, a portly bald prophet of the
apocalypse seated beside the Godhead, whose expression of
mirth at those scenes he most relished surpassed the borders
of delight and infringed upon outright hysteria. Here, finally,
here were Stuart's people. He loved them all! The grunting
grunts who inhaled their popcorn as if determined to die by
it. The troupe of spermlets (not ghosts!) that he, Stuart Dregs
himself, would soon direct in a series of public performances
of Laszlow's petite opus, *The Ballet of Decapitations*. The
Fergusons who stood with backs against the concrete in
stained and rumpled black suits more reminiscent of the junkie
jazz cats who roamed Manhattan during the 1960s than the
Secret Service agents they presumably intended to emulate
as they eyed their buckets of dingy-looking popcorn with
grim suspicion beneath the rusted pipes whose puff-clouds
of insulation rained asbestos down upon them all day after
glorious day. The great and powerful Henry, who would soon,
Stuart hoped, provide definitive proof that Anthropica was

indeed, to borrow a term from the semioticians Stuart had studied at Dartmouth, *the case.* Even the noticeably absent Grace Kitchen, who refused to participate in group activities and who openly reviled the Exit Strategy corpus ("It is just Grace Kitchen being Grace Kitchen," Laszlow liked to say with a shrug) but who he nevertheless dreamed of wooing, even she was one of the *them* to which he now belonged. Stuart adored them all, and they adored him, and deep in his bosom he felt a thrill that, although it was not exactly sexual, had the same contours as erotic devotion, the same sense of pursuit and evasion, want and denial.

"Wait for it," Laszlow said, holding a popcorn kernel aloft between thumb and index finger. The screen cast its washed-out palette upon the members of the world's only true humanitarian organization. A muted light that rendered this underground coven ghostlike, zombie-like, otherworldly. Laszlow's eyes wide open. Henry's oxygen hissing. The dank basement swollen with prophecy and doom. "Wait for it," he said again. And then with the agent's most excellent analysis of our species proper zoological categorization—*You are a virus*—came the familiar explosion of joy, a veritable ejaculation of love, self-loathing, and solidarity.

42.

Toast in the Machine

MANTEO, NC: Residents of this small island hidden among the barrier chain of the Outer Banks awoke yesterday to discover that their household appliances and other small machines had shifted in the night to point themselves due East along the 35th parallel. Included among the offending apparatuses were toasters, blenders, vacuum cleaners, clock radios, smart phones and handheld electronic devices. In some homes washing machines and dishwashers dislodged themselves from their plumbing to cause considerable flooding and other damage as they pointed their company logos out across the Atlantic. Skeptical local police initially hypothesized mass hysteria, a phenomenon that has afflicted Manteo before, most notably during the Giant Squid Panic of 1942. But this theory was quickly diffused by the equanimity of local property and business owners, as was the supposition that a small earthquake had caused the shifting, after consultations with the USGS (United States Geological Survey) confirmed a total lack of seismic activity throughout the region. Authorities are left scratching their heads, though more devoutly religious members of the community suggest that the reorientation is a sign—albeit a small, stupid one—from God.

Scientists dispatched to Manteo, however, are not ready to bestow religious significance upon the activities of coffee makers and food processors. "What we think we're looking at here," says Cam Nolan of the USGS, "is some sort of magnetic event, possibly linked to minor shifts in the earth's iron core. Either that," he says with a smirk, "or it's like Muslim prayer hour, and the machines are genuflecting toward the holy land."

Were it not for Manteo's unusual town charter—which requires full disclosure of Acts of God under penalty of public drowning—the residents may never have realized that their individual domestic quandaries were in fact part of an island-wide phenomenon. "I came to work at the paper same as always," says Hiyensio Kim, Manteo's longstanding editor-in-chief of the South Island News, "and everyone's talking about machines tearing themselves loose and ripping holes in the walls. We pride ourselves on having no secrets but still, people need walls. Although please note that that is my personal opinion and in no way reflects the position of the SIN."

Those seeking out divine meaning in the event have arrived at wildly varying interpretations. Island schoolteacher Mike Hunt suggests that God is registering his dissatisfaction with our increasingly mechanized and digitized lives. "We are a Christian nation," he says. "And Christ did not have an iPhone." But others, such as Sara Sarapi—village comptroller and Presbyterian minister-in-training—see it as a very different kind of omen. "What's along the 35th parallel?" she asks. "What does the Lord beseech us to seek or to find?" Some answers to her first question: the Greek island of Crete; Jammu and Kashmir; the Shandong Province of the People's Republic of China; Iksan, South Korea; and the Hiroshima prefecture of Japan. Sarapi says she has requested an audience with higher-ups of the

Presbyterian Church but at the time this article went to print she had heard "absolute squat." She goes on to say, "The scientists are rolling their eyes and stroking their slide rules, but we Manteoans know what we saw here. We saw a [gosh darn] [flipping] miracle."

On a more practical note, local home insurance adjustors are moving fast to deny payouts for damage caused by these seemingly enchanted appliances, citing a little-known "autonomous machine" exclusion buried in the fine print of many policies dating back to the Roosevelt Administration. Says State Farm adjustor Kenny Moore, "We've been prepared for this kind of thing since the first Model T rolled off the line. People don't know half the [stuff] they ain't covered for."

While many individuals have returned their appliances to their original bearing and position, many others see such a correction as foolhardy if not outright blasphemous. Meanwhile, representatives of General Electric, Hoover, and Black & Decker have refused to comment publicly on the machines of Manteo, bound by confidentiality agreements, possible impending lawsuits, and what one higher-up at GE called—under conditions of anonymity—"our general unwillingness to take [stuff] like this seriously."

43.

HE COULD STILL remember those angry afternoons when he'd paced the house simmering with a rage he didn't understand, gravitating toward the sun porch where he would pause to glare out into the woods at the property's perimeter—acreage that no doubt teemed with fornicating animals unfazed by his anti-procreation screes—before returning to the manual typewriter that had hammered out any number of treatises on Heidegger's (then) seemingly justified hostility toward "everyday thinking." He sat now on the Exit Strategy stage, his wheelchair camouflaged among the steel folding chairs and Ballet of Decapitations props, and considered again the Problematic of Time, and whether or not it was fair to say that he was in this moment the same human whose hysterical atheism had been—at least according to Janet—far more religious than the religion it aimed to obliterate. If he could return now to the home from which Laszlow had recruited him, if his hands could grip and his arms could lift and his legs could shuttle the whole gnarled vessel to and fro, he would take the black typewriter out into the woods and dig a hole and curse its metallic carapace before burying the fucking thing once and forever, along with his dissertation and his existentialist textbooks and his course syllabi and the manuscript he had been working on at the time his illness had manifested, a long and—as far as Henry v.1.0 was concerned, unassailable—proof on the cruelty of intentional reproduction by any conscious animal. He'd come to realize that the so-called "everyday"—the rise from bed each morning, the trips to supermarkets and Laundromats, the seclusion within boxes of steel and glass that roared across asphalt highways, the often painful (and rarified) desire to know and be known by other human souls—was all we would ever know. It wasn't something embedded within a larger system; it *was* the system. And Heidegger? Nietzsche? Schopenhauer? They toiled feverishly at a metaphysics that would only bounce harmlessly off the impenetrable shell of what Dregs called Anthropica.

His respirator hissed and he considered laboring to input some of these thought-streams into his computer voice-simulator so as to "speak" them to Dregs and Laszlow and the lovely nihilist Grace Kitchen later that afternoon at an Alpha Team meeting that Laszlow promised would prepare them for the impending arrival of The One. Loveliness: that was another sacred thing he had failed to honor while hacking out despairing manifestos and fearing the very idea of love and loathing all of nature. It was in the name of loveliness that he sometimes could not resist the urge to access Janet's energy-stream. She was right now, for instance, sitting on the crisply made bed in their once-shared bedroom, her dry palm stroking the quilted comforter, wanting to know how he had disappeared on that bright windy day from their Philadelphia suburb, wanting to be touched by the strong, cool fingers that had once extended from his healthy human body. It was painful to experience her desire, just as it was to remember—in the more conventional way—Janet's warm body beneath his, the soft flesh of her thighs, her sugar-sweet sweat and the gleam of her teeth whenever she laughed in earnest. He could access waves of desire all across planet earth—could tease individual threads from the glowing matrix of human want—but he could do nothing to *change* things. There was some key he was missing. He had of course read the journal that Laszlow had somehow located in Chinatown, among archives too bizarre to merit the attentions of more urbane society. He had learned of the kahuna's powers of life and death, but he had no idea how to convert his passive visions into active manifestations of his *own* desire. The confident Henry Henry Puddin' Pie of a neon-lit dreamscape, the Henry who'd reassembled that dog… did that Henry know something that the waking Henry did not?

Laszlow claimed that soon The One would arrive to "provide the final lynchpin in the great and good cargo train of our glorious disappearance." But Henry suspected that there was nothing more to know or to learn, and his blood burned with a desire to bury everything under a hundred miles of rubble.

He sat motionless on stage and looked out over the pale-skinned Googles at their tiny desks, punching away at plastic keyboards in a recruitment campaign that continued despite the finished search for The One and the completion of the Alpha Team initiative. He envied these imbecilic automatons. Envied the feel of the keys as they typed, envied their ability to roll the kinks out of their wiry necks, envied their ability to rise up and walk and touch each other's deeply imperfect bodies. He surmised that it was late morning based on the quality and intensity of the skylight's hazy glow. He could feel desire trapped within the light itself and he ached to make it *do* something. He twitched a finger and again considered doing the excruciating work of formulating a sentence on his cursor-driven keypad. Somewhere in the Canadian province of Manitoga a teenage girl was sitting cross-legged on an unmade bed and crying into her own hands, her sobs gently rocking the bedframe which creaked quietly above the sound of wind roaring across fields of golden wheat visible from the girl's window as she *wanted* her brother—missing now for nearly a week and, unbeknownst to the girl, pinned by stones to the bottom of a nearby lake where he'd been drowned by his abductor and rapist—to come home again and sit beside her and ask to be tickled under his chin where the white flesh of the throat was so sensitive. This love. This desire. The cruelty of the universe, its unwillingness to give what would *truly* sustain us, damn Dregs' Anthropica to hell. Oh, to put his hand on the teenage girl's shoulder! To whisper words of comfort into her soft, warm ear! Even if he could return her brother, he could never experience her grateful embrace. *He was locked in.* He was a bomb casing. And a bomb is meant to do only one thing.

He had once told friends and family to ignore whatever religious rhetoric might begin to creep into his speech as he descended deeper into his disease, for it would only be the voice of fear, which had dug its tendrils into better men than he. But he could not have predicted the form his worship would take. He worshipped what he could not have precisely *because* he could not have it: physical sensation, touch and motion, the contact between human lips, the terrifying thrill of orgasm, the comfort of holding another's hand. Somewhere nearby, mere blocks away, an old man lay in a silver-wallpapered room whose shades were drawn and glowing a filthy ocher, the man immune to his own stench

and his mind intensely fixated on the first woman he had
ever loved, the sixty years between their brief explosion of
passion and his current deathbed remembrance reduced to
an instant, his desire compressing time, shrinking its diameter
as if tightening a roll of sheet metal, bringing past and present
into closer proximity. Enough desire, Henry thought, could
bring the whole filthy tapestry of human history back to its
pyretic beginnings. The kahuna was still alive, Henry knew
that, too, and if he concentrated hard enough he could get a
glimpse of them, their eyes closed within a loose and blue-
skinned face, kaleidoscopic waves of power flowing from
them in all directions. If The One arrived and taught Henry
how to save or destroy, which would he choose? His heart
swelled within his useless chest, pushing into his useless
throat. The choice was an illusion; he would do what he was
always going to do, goddamn you all.

He'd wasted so much of his life on Heidegger! What of his
sweet-smelling daughters, the way it felt to hug them to his
chest? He had endured the gift of their affections as if it were
a mere obligation, a distraction from his Serious Work. What
of the glorious sunlight pouring into a glassed-in porch and
setting the natural world ablaze with joy? What of the feeling
of blood pumping fast and hard through his suspiring body
as he trekked up a leafy hillside and the breeze penetrated
the pores of his face? Never again. *Never again for any of you.*
He would have sobbed with rage and need, if only his body
had still been capable of such extravagances. He watched the
Googles watching their screens, their enormous eyes vacuuming light from tiny boxes. Laszlow was right; whatever was
going to happen would happen. The part he didn't realize
was that it had *already* happened. Determinism ran to the

present from both directions, where the singularity of human desire exploded perpetually into the darkness of space-time. *I once had princesses in my life,* he thought with a snarl, *and I will again, forever and ever, Amen.* The nasal tube fed him his breath and he in turn fed his breath to Anthropica. His mind gravitated to his elder daughter—25 now—who was in an office, near a window, laughing about something a colleague had just said and noticing the contrails of a distant jet fanning out against the crisp blue sky, thinking that it looked exactly as if the sky's upholstery had been slit open to expose a bit of its stuffing. She wondered whether or not this was the kind of thought ordinary people had, or if it was the legacy of her deep-thinking father, who she imagined might still be alive, maybe on a stage somewhere, content in his wheelchair, thinking deep and loving thoughts about her. Henry tapped his index finger on his keypad, which felt oddly wet against those last few remaining nerve endings on the soft pad of his fingertip. Then the next impossible teardrop plummeted from his face and shattered on the plastic pad, shocking him. Good Lord, he could still cry. Pain coursed through him like liquid fire, his face frozen in the doltish smile he would wear from now until the end of time. *End transmission,* he thought. *End transmission.*

44.

Meanwhile here was the city rising up like a jaw full of teeth. They plummeted down the FDR and deeper into the maw, Finn registering on the windshield's bright screen glimpses of the river and of concrete underpasses and dark tunnels carved through blinding sunlight and high-rise apartment buildings that leaned despairingly riverward, every ornate alcove and pitted buttress covered in a black and unmoving mass of—yes, you guessed it—vultures. The God Fractal was intended to delineate a connection between macro and micro-cosmic building blocks, but Finn had never until this moment considered the proposed picture vis-a-vis morphological structures, which is to say that it suddenly occurred to him that it might make as much sense to say that the world was in the vulture as that the vulture was in the world, an epiphany that fluctuated—in time with the FDR's fluctuations between tunnel-dark and vista-bright—between seeming profound and seeming profoundly stupid.

The van lurched suddenly rightward across three lanes to a chorus of road rage—honking horns and flashing high beams and thrusting middle fingers—and then leapt painfully onto the clotted thoroughfare of Houston Street. "Jesus," Finn said, righting himself on the van's coarse industrial carpeting. "Take it easy guys."

"Jesus," the four men in black robotically intoned. "Take it easy guys." They repeated the utterance several times with awed reverence until it faded to a whisper and then to a mere hiss.

It had been this way the entire drive.

Any thought he might have had that this was a case of mistaken identity was belied by the poster-sized reproduction of him, Finn, dressed in the same athletic gear he now wore—the black shorts and yellow shirt of *Truck Stop Glory Hole*—affixed to the inside of the van's sliding door, a picture he knew was lifted from the team's website. THE ONE was scrawled in black marker at the top of the print. They'd gone looking for *him*, specifically. Was this a future in need of altering? Or should The Mighty Finn ride this one out? Would they take him to Bea, or was he a human sacrifice in a flow-chart box no one could have seen coming? In some alternate reality Jeff Pindick was at that exact moment humiliating him and in another he, Finn, had managed to overcome his demons and to perform up to his God-given potential. And in yet another the supervolcano known as Yellowstone National Park had just exploded, sending half of North America into the upper stratosphere. Being abducted by a group of worshipful mutants was unanticipated but did not fall particularly low on the value-chart of Possible Events. As The Mighty Finn he'd pretended he really *could* see the future. He convinced himself of his own superness. It felt like muscle memory, to now guess at what was in store and to imagine that only through faith in a future whose goodness he could divine did he restrain himself from acting on behalf of a better eventuality. Meanwhile the men in black were collecting themselves. They passed around a polka-dotted hankie with which they cleaned their dark shades and they pulled up the black socks that had sagged during the voyage which activated a rancid odor not unlike the one that haunted Toby's apartment and that Finn hypothesized was a corpse decaying within the building's ancient pine skeleton. Then the van was parked and the whine of the engine went dead and the din of Saturday afternoon in lower Manhattan pressed against the steel shell like the weight of ten-thousand leagues of seawater.

The driver rose and cracked his head on the van's ceiling and shrieked then crouched and worked his way back toward Finn, his dark glasses seemingly painted to a round face that had seen its share of acne. He pulled a folded sheet of paper from his pocket, unfolded it and read: "Laszlow welcomes you to your only true home. We honor your arrival with great and magnificent gratitude." He refolded the paper and threw open the van's side door and the world poured in as if via pressure washer, brittle light and bleached-out colors and the smells of Mexican food and rotting garbage and warm asphalt and gasoline. The men in black filed out, arranged themselves horizontally in a line, and bowed to Finn. Then they filed down the street with what for them was haste. Had Finn not poked his head through the opening and tracked their progress he would have been clueless as to their (and, he supposed, *his*) next destination. He watched them trip and stumble for half a block before descending some stairs in single file to enter a narrow brick building wedged between a restaurant and a squarish structure that might have been a house of worship or of detention. Finn still had his phone and considered calling some teammates, checking in on the results of the 3rd round game and maybe also reporting that he'd been kidnapped. Or no, maybe he should dial Toby. Though what on earth would he say to

Toby right now? Also he could just like, walk over to the F train and head back to Brooklyn. His captors had conveniently removed him from the distant wilds of Fort Devens' military installment and his seemingly inevitable collision with superior athlete Jeff Pindick and deposited him only a few blocks from his preferred subway line. He looked up and down the block. People moved with confidence, as if they knew something about how this whole mad universe worked. He could join them. He could flow downtown, he could plan a vacation, he could make a pie, he could call an old friend, he could grab a drink at a bar, he could move to the seaside, he could take up the piano, he could finish his dissertation, he could build a bomb, he could eat Cheetos until his stipend ran out, he could profess his love to Bea or marry Toby or become a Buddhist or a vegetarian or a pothead. But in the end he only lowered himself over the lip of the van and closed its sliding portal and followed in the wake of his now vanished captors, arriving at a heavy steel door which he pulled open to enter a space perhaps even stranger than the one that had violently recoiled atop four bald tires and two pitted axles as it screamed its way down the long black tongue of the American Interstate network and back toward the city he called home.

He entered the space and felt the door close behind him. The iron release bar pressed coldly into the small of his back. Scanning the room he registered: his own black-clad captors, whose numbers had magically doubled in the sixty seconds since they'd lurched from Finn's sight; a dozen or more costumed epicenes whose faces protruded Gumby-like from white sheets; a crowd of the unwashed homeless; a collection of the infirm, leaning on crutches or pulling their paralyzed rear parts around the tiled floor with heavily muscled arms or in one case sitting in a wheelchair corpse-like, with head atilt and mouth agape; and finally, at the far end of the deep and narrow room, standing on an unfinished pine-plank stage, a trio of individuals—two men and a woman—who upon seeing Finn rose from their aluminum folding chairs to lead the others in a rousing ovation that it took the Ultimate player several seconds to understand was directed at *him,* which realization sent his mind reeling into problem-solving mode. Like for instance, maybe Toby had gotten his birthday wrong and this was a surprise party whose subversive theme related to some of her more unusual sexual fantasies. Or his graduate school adviser had seen something of special worth in his most recent abstract and this was an awards ceremony which, given the prevalence of physical ineptitude among members of the scientific community, could partially explain the room's uncommon demographics. Or his teammates, having learned of Finn's haunting by the Ghost of Great Debacles Past—perhaps he screamed about it in his sleep while crammed into hotel rooms with the five or six members of *Truck Stop Glory Hole* who were least appalled by his company—decided to gift him with this removal from the competitive arena and into a milieu that was, if not exactly its opposite, a far cry from the success-or-failure model of sport that so threatened the delicate flower that was, to everyone's surprise and chagrin, a member of their starting offense. Or else, and somehow this seemed most likely, he had died and entered either a really eerie heaven or a hell that one could learn to live with. The cheering showed no sign of abating until one of the triumvirate on stage—a fit-looking man in round glasses and a black turtleneck who Finn had already decided must be the

Laszlow that his abductors had mentioned in their pained conspiratorial whispers—moved to a microphone at center stage and made a small hand signal, at which point the room went instantly dead. "Ladies and gentlepeople," he said. "Please show your affection for the great and powerful spiritual leader of the Frisbee-based sporting club that operates beneath the banner of *Truck Stop Glory Hole*. He is known to ordinary human society as Finn Daily, but we know that cognomen does nothing to suppress his true identity. For he is indeed, my precious brothers and sisters, *The One*." And then the applause re-erupted as Finn was ushered forth or rather squeezed forward by the crush of irregular bodies, traveling as if by osmosis toward the stage upon which he could now see—as he took the bespectacled man's hand and was hauled upward (like Christ to the cross)—were scattered a number of hexagonal cog heads that he carefully sidestepped as the cheering finally exhausted itself and the crowd withdrew reverently to the room's perimeter. The bespectacled man's fervor, however, was far from exhausted. He was shaking Finn's hand and grinning wide. "I thank you deeply for coming today," he said. His voice had a Schwarzenegger thing going on. That made him what? German? "I am Laszlow Katasztrófa," he continued, "and I have awaited you for some time, just as you have searched, without realizing, for us. We have such great need of your intellect and athleticism. Especially now, as we have recently discovered an unexpected opportunity to advance our great and generous cause with a new level of ferocity."

Finn smiled and wondered yet again what the fuck was going on. He felt the same combination of celebrity and shame that attended those not infrequent meetings with Ultimate players he did not recognize but who knew his name and could quote from their previous dumb conversations. He could almost hear the squeak of someone cranking open all of his sweat valves. Laszlow showed no sign of releasing his hand and at either side of this latest captor was a human far more human than those who'd done the heavy lifting in delivering him here. One was female, older but attractive in a pale, fragile-seeming way, wearing a simple gray dress and either smiling or smirking or dealing with a gastrointestinal issue. The other was a rotund balding man in a white button-down streaked with pale orange grease stains.

Finn paused. The silence was a chemical catalyst for sweat production, so he tried speech. "Is Bea here?" he asked tentatively, still holding Laszlow's hand.

"Bea?" the pudgy man asked.

"I'm sorry," Finn said.

"You must be confused," said Laszlow, who didn't sound like Schwarzenegger so much as the great documentarian of human folly, Werner Herzog. "This is Grace Kitchen, the world's greatest living novelist, who no doubt requires no introduction. And this excellent human is Stuart Dregs, whose theories will one day be remembered by precisely no one because no one will remain."

Something inside of Finn clicked. Holy shit! This was Jack's mom's husband. He'd caught a glimpse of him that night, waddling up the stone driveway, pausing at the front door, all fat and sad-looking, the physical consequence, perhaps, of discovering that the world was not real and that man created God and that everything was nothing.

"Wait," Finn said. "You're the natural resources guy."

"Excuse me?" the scientist asked.

"Jesus Laszlow," said the world's greatest living novelist. "He looks like a child."

"Ahh, my dear Grace. He is a wolf in the clothing of a boy. He is a boy-wolf, the one who will lead us to the front vestibule of our robot friends."

"Do we know each other?" the scientist asked.

"Maybe he could start by running out for takeout," the novelist said.

"Tell me about your extraordinary work in the area of nested fractal dynamics," Laszlow said, releasing his hand and putting his arm around Finn. "Tell me of the God fractal."

"Are those *cleats* you're wearing?" Stuart asked.

"Maybe Chinese," Grace said. "For fuck's sake no more Mexican food."

Finn smiled. At the room's perimeter individuals who appeared initially unlikely to crack the secret of a childproof cap were running Google searches at high speed and with apparent confidence and proficiency. Some were dressed, he thought, as spermatozoa. High above the floor of the tall narrow room was the darkening blue sky, pushing down upon an unlikely skylight. It felt like being inside a grain silo. So okay, Stuart Dregs, Jack's dad, was here. Which, Finn realized, meant at least one not-terrible thing: he had good news for Jack's mom. Stuart wasn't cheating on her but had instead been absorbed into a cult of troglodytes and sociopaths. What any of this meant for Finn was still not entirely clear but the gears were really spinning, and the sweat was starting to flow, collecting under his arms and on his brow and between his legs.

"Or the Thai place on Stanton," Grace said.

"Are you Italian by any chance?" Stuart asked.

"Also I would be very grateful to hear of your work in the area of Ultimate and other disc-related athletic precincts," Laszlow said.

"I'd kill for a steak, too. There won't be much of that in prison."

"Have you been to my home?" Dregs asked.

"We are one big happy family," Laszlow said, squeezing Finn into himself, "and we require your unique skill set to rid the universe of ourselves."

"Have him grab today's paper too. Civilization ended when the Times went online."

"Do you know my son Jack?" Stuart asked.

"How old are you anyway, Frisbee boy?" Grace asked.

"Sit with us, my dear Finn Daily."

"Where are the menus anyway?"

"Stay awhile and allow me to tell you who you truly are, and why you already in spirit belong to us."

"Yeah, stay Frisbee boy. Make like a dog and fetch the grownups dinner."

"Do you ever go by the name 'Lucio'?"

"I'm really sorry," Finn said. "But my teammates need me."

"And they shall have you, Finn Daily," Laszlow said, and smiled. "They shall have you in your best and most uninhibited form. You shall dominate your competitors at the National tournament of the Ultimate disc players. For what you will discover is that Exit Strategy is not only an answer to the great blight of humanity's presence within an otherwise unspeakably beautiful universe, but is also the solution to the problem of your Great Debacle, whose contours are well known to me. The Debacle will haunt you no more, Finn Daily." Laszlow removed his arm and turned

Finn, a hand on each of Finn's shoulders as he held him at arm's length and stared into his eyes. "But first," he said, "you must pledge yourself to our vision. You must accept the mantle of The One."

Finn felt the sweat about to cascade from his brow and down his armpits. He was directly below the skylight and it seemed for a moment that the skylight was an eyeball looking out onto the brave new world and he, Finn, was a homunculus stationed behind the eye, absorbing its data, making sense of the blue sky and the crab-shaped cloud and the pale pinkish light snared at the edges of the sky-light's frame. Vultures circled overhead like scouts loosed from Hades. He scanned the room, avoiding Laszlow's piercing stare, and noticed now that the wheelchair-bound zombie had rolled to the center of the floor and that he was trembling slightly. An oxygen tank pumped his otherwise deflated shell up to living proportions. It all felt familiar, like something he'd dreamed about a long time ago, or like a thought that had lodged in some deep recess of his brain and had been fighting its way to the surface for years. *Yes, he could pledge anything.* It had grown quiet enough now that the hiss of the paralytic's oxygen flow was clearly au-dible. As was the click-clack of keyboards as Exit Strategy's undemanding drones searched for whatever they searched for, as was a certain scratching at the door through which Finn had entered. He looked back to Laszlow, locked eyes with him, and nodded. "What do you mean, 'The One'?" he asked.

"Ahh," Laszlow said, and smiled. "You know that already, Finn Daily. In fact you are here because you know it. You have felt it your entire life—that there is something wrong with the world. You do not know what it is, but it haunts you, like a splinter in your mind, driving you mad. Do you know what I am talking about?"

Finn said nothing but swallowed audibly.

"I love that scene," Stuart whispered, perhaps to Laszlow or perhaps to whatever God watched over the Exit Strategy agenda. Laszlow made a gesture with his hand as if to wave away unimportant things.

"But do not be concerned about the Nationals, Finn Daily. Your participation shall not be denied you. You shall dominate other plastic disc aficionados and they shall worship you just as shall we. And then you shall put away childish things, and fulfill your true destiny as the Godhead of a restored and superior universe."

Finn nodded. He felt his chest boil over with an enormous sadness. He was sure he was about to sob. There was no stopping it, and he *wanted* it, he wanted the release, he wanted the love of this new father. But no, he was The One. Of course he was. And The One would not cry at the great and glorious occasion of his own coronation.

45.

THOUGH CLOTHED IN the homogenizing white lab coats stipulated in their contracts, the three scientists seem in their irrepressible particularities like characters out of a fable: the bearded wise man; the warrior-princess; the young prodigy uncomfortable with his brilliance. If given the opportunity each might self-identify thusly, though heretofore—in their thousand some-odd hours as stewards of what the bearded one called simply "the Great Mazard"—no such opportunity has emerged organically from collegial conversations that have grown no less strained by their repetition or (the female scientist might argue) their stupidity. They stand now side by side by side and stare down into the tank where the pale head floats in an amnion of electro-conductive fluid, smiling up at them in defiance, or solidarity, or great pain. Fluorescent tubes hum and emanate a heatless glow into the gleaming laboratory here in the deep center of a complex whose true dimensions are known only to its long-deceased architects. Wires snake from insertion points in the Great Mazard's brain and its eyeballs, up through the glass tank and then into the printer's USB ports. Pages occasionally emerge. Some of the pages are filled margin to margin with words. Others merely display a few or a few dozen random expletives.

The youngest scientist reaches his hand into the printer tray and lifts the latest entry. His movements—despite efforts to the contrary—reveal a certain litheness that his female colleague finds abhorrent. In her presence he feels perpetually ashamed. He scans the page and his eyes widen.

"It's another Fexo section," he says.

"Dammit Fexo," the woman growls. "It's not a fucking collaboration."

"I like the Fexo sections," the young man says.

"You would, Sporty Spice."

He lowers his eyes and silence descends again upon this unlikely triune. The lighting tubes buzz as if filled with wasps. The bearded one clears his throat, opens his mouth, but does not speak.

After a time the young man asks, "Whaddaya think the deal is with these mole people?" He holds aloft several pages printed in small, claustrophobic type, peppered liberally with strangely accented names.

"The machines are hooked twenty-four-seven into hideously pale flesh," the woman says. "You'd start wondering too."

"Indeed!" the bearded one says suddenly, as if he had been waiting on this precise remark for many days. He is handsome in a way that seems to fit the context of the laboratory: dark hair, sharp cheekbones, a vaguely lycanthropish grin. He pushes his round-lensed spectacles higher up on the bridge of his nose. "Though we might also consider," he says, "that the mole people exist primarily as an apt and powerful metaphor for the central problem of the text."

"Right," the woman says, smirking and rolling her eyes. "The underground as a place of conspiracy and secrets. Plus the unconscious or subconscious, the Life of the Mind, all that crap."

The younger one nods and tries to affect the pose of a man in deep thought. He would very much like some coffee now. He listens to the hum of the lights and watches several large bubbles rise up through the tank to burst at the surface with a sad little *bloop*.

"Boy, I would just kill for some coffee," he finally says. "Coffee anyone?"

As if in response the printer jumps to life. "Look!" the bearded one says. "Another page, my young and gifted colleague! Perhaps it is the Great Mazard that would prefer a caffeinated American beverage!"

They wait together in the cold and gleaming room for this next page to emerge, for something to make sense, for the head to reveal its knowledge and thereby save these three humans (and their many billion planetary cohabitants) from themselves. They are—at least according to all available calculations—waiting there even now. Or maybe they are all dead. Ha ha ha ha!

"Have you guys noticed," the younger one asks, as the printer smokes and caterwauls, "that I bear a very strong resemblance to—"

"No," the others say in unison.

46.

Human Be Gone! A Story of Love and
Suffering in Which the Passion-lust
Experience Appears and then Vanishes!

Written by the Great and Powerful Fexo!!!!!!!

The human female kneels beside the bed and lowers an index
finger to its miniature-female offspring's cheek to trace the
bone's curvature as if tenderly removing machine shavings
from an engine chassis. It is evening and the human domicile-
cubes—strewn in an imperfect approximation of symmetry
across badly subdivided earth—bleed weak illumination
into the cold blue air of autumn. Ha ha ha ha! The miniature
female has activated a personal darkness-prevention device
which takes the shape of a Fairy Princess, a type of creature
bestowed by the miniature humans with the power of flight
and the intent to reward the most woefully innocent of their
species with favors ranging from the dissemination of aph-
rodisiacal glitter-dust to the offer of small sums of currency
in exchange for unmoored and sugar-pitted incisors. The
darkness-prevention device has an amber hue that the grown
human female associates with the passion-lust experience,

such that she considers for a moment the possibility that her male partner in the Life Project might enter with his center-part exposed and request access to her reception slot, which would not please her at all at this moment because of her headaches and also because for the love of jesus cannot you, my male co-chair on our domicile's passion-lust committee, think of something else every so often? Ha ha! But her fears are in this case unfounded, because a simple infrared scan of the domicile-cube would reveal that the human male is at this very moment two flights below the female in a hollowed-out subterranean chamber known to we humans as a 'basement,' where he has activated his viewing plinth and entered the coordinates that deliver him to his favorite images of biologically mature human females engaging in the passion-lust experience in a symphonic array of configurations that profoundly excite his center-part, which extends cold and rigid as an icicle through the convenient zipper-slot of his textile casing and into a pulsing blue light that, in its weak and lovely hue, suggests to the reader of Fexo's story that the man's underlying mood-structure is built not upon passion-lust at all, but in fact upon a foundation of melancholy and grievance. Ha ha ha ha!

But let us return to the female human's miniature-female offspring, which responds to the warm and gelatinous touch of its mother-human's index finger by turning its entire miniature visage toward the human from whose reception slot it once emerged with no small amount of rancor, in that strangely bloody and inefficient procedure by which the infants of mammalian organics are said to emerge into the terrestrial world, the miniature female revealing now through the evidence of red-rimmed irises what it had previously endeavored to conceal, i.e. the miniature human has been ejaculating weakness-fluid from its eyeholes. Ha ha! In the amber light, with the hum of the domicile-cube's temperature-control devices singing a long E-flat into the butterscotch air, the moon hung outside the miniature female's window like a bright scythe, the miniature female is rendered vulnerable and soft and—one would imagine—easily devoured by whatever toothy predators might roam the subdivided darkness of Fexo's story in search of proteins, like for instance the gargoyles already delineated with superb narrative skill in earlier pages of Fexo's masterwork.

"What is the source of your sadness behavior, my dear sweet human offspring?" the mature female asks, feeling a lump not unlike the waxen ambergris said to exist within the innards of certain cetaceans rise up into her own soft white throat. "You must tell me, your Mommy, immediately so that I might crush with extreme vehemence that which threatens my dear sweet princess, for without full confidence that your happiness quotient is within acceptable levels I will be unable to enjoy the passion-lust experience vis-à-vis your paternal genetic-material provider!"

"Oh, my dear mother-human," the miniature female says in a manner the databases might characterize as 'plaintive.' "Today the miniature male humans who occupy space in my learning-cube declared that I was ugly and emanated a foul and unpleasant odor! And now I am left to suffer uncertainty regarding my fiscal and emotional worth, an eventuality which has indeed filled me with much sadness, just as Fexo suggests!" The miniature female human's eyeholes again fill with the weakness fluids which begin now to spill downward to stain her skull-support cushions a darker shade of pink. Ha ha ha ha!

***

Now is the point in Fexo's story where narrative friction must be created through the collision of unlike objects or tropes. Ha ha ha ha! And so it is necessary to return to the subterranean viewing kiosk where the mature human male—whose genetic material accounts for precisely 50% of the miniature female's genetic material, the cleanness of this division and distribution of male and female zygotes being a rare example of mathematical grace in an otherwise embarrassingly sloppy Life Project—is touching his center-part, albeit in a halfhearted manner that suggests that he does not necessarily seek the release of lactic fluids from the center-part's fuel injection system but endeavors rather to ease the sadness and rage that has accompanied his experience in this domicile-cube for a time that Fexo is unable to enumerate with precision but that would be measured in sun-revolutions rather than axis-rotations. Ha ha ha ha! It is almost as if the touching of the center-part is an act of self-pity, or else a misguided gesture toward vengeance against the mature human female who is at this very moment so busily engaged in the maternal nurture-procedure that she has nearly forgotten the role her reception-slot had previously played in sustaining the domicile-cube's happiness quotient. On the male human's viewing plinth two biologically mature females are lubricating one another's reception slots via the inefficient and yet apparently highly popular method of tongue-lathering. Their passion-lust experience occurs within a blue-lit bedchamber whose spectrum yet flickers across the human male, these quanta catching in the tips of his center-part's surrounding hair follicles to render a small fiber optic forest there at the base of his abdomen. Ha ha ha ha! He does not know it but he is sneering. His brow—a part of the upper extremities separating face from head—is furrowed into furrows in response to a complex amalgam of qualia-proteins that Fexo will not even begin to analyze, for Fexo is after all only human! Ha ha ha ha!

So imagine if you can, fellow human, the mature male's surprise when suddenly its viewing plinth's representation of the passion-lust experience disappears in a brief flash of blinding white and is replaced, a moment later, with the image of the male's female life-partner sitting beside his miniature female-offspring's sleeping platform and stroking the miniature female's soft amber hair. His hand may still rest on his center-part but believe Fexo when he says that there is no longer a hint of the passion-lust experience in the human male's qualia-cavities. The mature female soothes the crying miniature female and gently wipes the weakness-fluid from its cheeks. The mature female is saying—right now, upstairs, and so also in the male's subterranean passion-lust cavern via his plinth—she is saying, "Mommy and Daddy will always take care of you." She says it twice, then begins to softly hum in an off-key manner that a pitch-correction software-patch could easily rectify. The male sees now that weakness fluids are also slowly traveling down the mature female's high and sexy cheekbones. "Mommy and Daddy love you so much," the mature female says, as the miniature offspring leans her face into an extended palm and cries and tries to smile so as to reduce the suffering-quotient of her beloved mother-human. The mature male's center-part is now flaccid and his body likewise, slack and defeated and sunk into the black armchair whose existence Fexo did not think to mention until this very moment, though surely it must have been clear from the reader's own habits with regard to the absorption of passion-lust videography that the mature male was not *standing* before the viewing plinth. That would be absurd! Ha ha ha ha! What the male realizes in this very important moment is that nothing

can save the miniature female from the onset of a passion-lust
imperative that will place her at the mercy of humans like himself.
Nothing can save any human from that sad biological inevitability. But there before the viewing plinth, bathed in an exquisite
pain that is by no means restricted to his own domicile-cube,
the human male vows for the eight-hundred-and-forty-seventh
time to be a better human male, a better *man,* to wield the col-
loquialism, because after all his miniature female-offspring—in
her beautiful innocence—must trump the passion-lust experience, lest all is empty and awful. His heart burns with rage and
shame and fear and other qualia-proteins associated with that
region of the programming schematic, as referenced elsewhere
in these seemingly endless transmissions.

The screen flashes white again. Now a man in a black suit
appears, and he says into the subterranean cell: "It is time
now, Morpheus, for you to pay for your many sins." The
black-suited man makes a flamboyant wave of the hand and
the human male's skin is instantly and fantastically flayed
from the underlying musculoskeletal architecture, so that
what now sits in the black chair is a bloody anthropoid with
brilliant white teeth—something so raw that it hardly seems
to qualify for the term 'corpse'. It gleams in striated beauty in
the pulsing dimness. It has all happened so fast that no one
even knew it was happening at all, which is a metaphor that
you may take away with you and apply to other facets of the
Life Project, for Fexo's goal after all is not only to entertain
but to instruct. Though mostly to entertain.

AND THAT IS the end of Fexo's excellent story. Ha ha ha ha!

47.

Laszlow alone was Laszlow conflicted. In his office in
the basement of ES headquarters he would try his best to
conjure up scenarios of a world without anyone who could
conjure up scenarios, a world without human ambition and
artifice, a world without the illusion of free will, a clean and
clockwork world in which whatever was going to happen,
happened. He sat now in the gray haze of his personal pur-
gatory, the light of a single desklamp seeming to retreat into
itself rather than brave the room's morbidity. What if what
was always going to happen was that Laszlow himself only
augmented humanity's great shitstorm of depravity and cruelty? That was the million-forint question. He imagined he
could hear the barking of a dog from somewhere above. He
removed his spectacles and cleaned them with the hem of his
turtleneck. His father was long dead but sometimes he could
feel him just over his shoulder, could imagine the flicker of
the candelabra's light and the old man's raspy breath. Or
else he could hear his dead infant sister's thin cries from
a distant room. Lately Grace Kitchen had confided that
she, too, sometimes heard screams, though in her case they
were her own screams and she was actually screaming. The
imagined barking felt so close, a living part of his personal
demonology. Just yesterday Henry had informed him in

the voice software's mechanical timbre that the focalization (as he called it) could be tested at any time, now that The One had arrived. He put his glasses back on, adjusted the bridge. The gray room seemed to be breathing. Whatever was always going to happen would happen. The barking came again, even louder now, and then he heard the unmistakable sound of paw pads descending the stairway toward his office. Laszlow rose curiously and tried not to think what he was thinking. He stepped from behind the desk just as a very real dog—a large Shepherd—came sprinting through the opening to the office and threw itself at Laszlow whose paralysis was, for the moment, total. The dog could have easily torn him to shreds. But no. Its paws were up on his shoulders. The dog was *kissing* him, its pink tongue warm and wet on Laszlow's stubble.

"Kutya?" Laszlow asked. "Dear God, Kutya, is it you?"

And then the leader of the world's only true humanitarian organization was on his knees sobbing, the dog licking away the salty tears, Laszlow embracing the animal, kissing its snout, sinking into its soft fur, overwhelmed with a love greater than any he thought himself capable of. "Kutya!" he cried. "Oh Kutya!" The hiss and hum of pipes buried deep within the concrete walls, moving steam and shit and water, were the good and necessary proof that hidden things were real. And just above Laszlow, one floor up and beneath the Exit Strategy skylight, Henry Henry Puddin' Pie traced an arc with his index finger, carving the air with a smile.

48.

"Well," said Finn, smiling, "I'm not sure what it *does*, but from a mathematical standpoint, the fractal has a little hitch or a claw that bonds it to its sister particles. It's both expandable and reducible across time, space, and dimensions."

As Finn spoke—his lean, muscular body perversely aglow with youthful vigor beneath the Exit Strategy skylight, the incessant typing of the Googles punctuating the flying disc enthusiast's annoyingly brilliant explanation of his so-called God Fractal (as if the typing were somehow *choreographed,* which Henry wouldn't put past Laszlow, in fact he wouldn't be surprised to learn that Laszlow had choreographed the heartbeats and breathing rates of his deeply devoted and disturbed acolytes, all in the name of randomness)—Henry found himself again revisiting the dream. The bag of gore. The fur and the blood and the viscera and the alleyway's electric-pink glow. The little *click* of reassembly... very much like a claw grabbing a claw. He had *wanted* the dog back, just like the kahuna and his *makemakeha* had wanted the drowned boy back. Was that all it took?

Were his visions simply visions of powerful manifestations of this same *wanting?*

Were all the world's humans keeping the human world running, as Dregs suggested, simply by involuntarily wanting it to run?

Was he completely plugged into the desire matrix now, the same as the kahuna?

But how did you *control* it?

He began manipulating his voice software so as to ask Finn this last and most vital question, even as the accidental genius ("The One," Laszlow had implored them all, "call him *The One*") rambled on indiscriminately. "Toby, she thinks it's all too stupid, not my fractal but you know, *math,* or theoretical math or whatever. She says math is for calculating change at the coffee shop or counting the oppressed. Abstraction drives her crazy. This one time we were at this party and she's like, 'Hey Finn come here and tell this guy that thing about your math,' and I'm like 'What thing?' and she's like 'You know that thing you told me last night when I was busy working on stuff that actually matters, ha ha,' and so I'm like…."

Henry tried wanting Finn to shut the fuck up, and he *could* actually feel a little… disruption or disturbance or something start to form. A little *flutter,* like a heat-field rising from summer asphalt. He pictured the crab-shaped particle, the linking of claws, and he aimed the stream at Finn's word-spewing mouth-hole.

Nothing.

"… and so the guy is like, 'Wow, that's really interesting,' and I'm like, 'Really?' and he's like, 'No you fucking dumbass, you're the most boring thing I've ever met,' and Toby just starts cracking up and is all like, 'See Finn, no one cares! But you know I still love you baby, especially when you rip that inside-out forehand full-field,' which by the way that's like my worst throw, I'm a high-backhand guy, which sometimes Jack says…"

Henry tried again, his fingertips still working the voice-software pad while his mind concentrated intently on the beam—which was one tiny dimensional shift from becoming *visible*, or so it seemed to Henry—and aimed it straight down Finn's vibrating larynx. This time he felt the claws *click* and lock, just as they had in the dream. There was a sensation in his mind like biting down on a piece of wax.

The One began to choke.

Two Fergusons who had been stationed against the walls closest to the iron-barred egress of the ES anteroom roused from indifferent silence to tentative action. They had been sworn, after all, to protect The One with their own quixotic lives. Finn grabbed his throat, began gasping for air. Henry tapped a finger on the voice-generator's keypad, his tongue lolling from his pink gums, his countenance unchanged but his mind roaring like a cyclone. The Fergusons arrived but, having laid hands on The One, realized anew their own total incompetence and froze. For a moment Henry feared he could not release his concentration on the beam. Like having bitten into that piece of sticky wax, his mind could not disengage. But with a great burst of effort he did, feeling the fractal disperse back into the air like vapor.

Finn crouched forward, hands on his knees, breathing deep.

"What the fuck was *that?*" he gasped.

The Fergusons stood erect, stiffening like twin, black-clad erections (just as their training dictated). "What the fuck was that?" they intoned in unison, their eyes dead. Above Exit Strategy's skylight a small cloud formed, tinting the sunlight sepia. Henry receded into his locked-in fortress, deep down where there was no light and no air. He was crying down there, in the final grotto of his private network of caverns, down where no one and nothing could reach him.

Oh, damn the world and everything in it!

He could never have Janet again. He could never again embrace his daughters. He could never again walk barefoot across a grassy field or bite into a perfectly ripe peach or hear the satisfying *tick-tick-tick* of chalk against a blackboard. Never again.

What he *could* do, he realized, now that The One had revealed the pattern to him, was something both more dramatic and less meaningful. He could end Anthropica.

He tapped his raw index finger to the playback key and felt as if the computerized voice emerged not from his chair's speaker but from his own ruined throat. "Tell *Laszlow*," it said, "that I now *know* how to see his de*ranged* vision *to* fruition."

For the first time in weeks, the tapping of the Googles stopped, leaving only the hiss of Henry's breathing apparatus to stain the beautiful silence.

"Um," said Finn. He cleared his throat. "Um, guys? Could I maybe get something to drink?"

"Something to drink," intoned the Fergusons. The particles rose higher and dispersed, vanishing into their next opportunity to become all the stupid things of Earth.

49.

Q.

Laszlow? Does he play for *Ass Bone?* The enormous German dude with the Mohawk and the big backhand?

Q.

Well, that's Finn's thing. Why are we here? What does it all mean? I tune out. Life's too short, right? Well, look who I'm talking to. It's shorter than ever thanks to your bullshit.

Q.

Right, all that God Fractal stuff. I'm like, oh God, *fractals?* Like look around, there are Afghan women being beaten to death by their husbands, children separated from parents at our so-called borders, citizen-prisoners starving in hellacious North Korean death camps. The so-called Big Questions only matter to people who don't have to ask the *real* big questions, like you know, where is there some food? How can I get these men to stop raping me? Where will I sleep tonight now that my slum has been razed by men with guns? There's need everywhere and you can either sit around and ask Big

Questions or get off your ass and like, help some fucking people. I'll bet if all the humans had been more generous you might have thought twice before obliterating every living thing that creepeth through the fields. We practically beat you to it.

Q.

Now is the best time, though! Like, the remaining cannibals scattered throughout the wasteland of earth, they *need our help*. It's not too late for the two of you, or three if you count Fexo, to make amends, reverse course, fight for a world worth fighting for. You like that? It's a slogan I came up with for one of my former employers. You know, just because you're robots you don't have to be so *cold*.

Q.

Well, so okay, metal is cold.

Q.

Like love! Love is totally a real thing. I mean, I *love* Finn. Finn loves me. You can't touch it but not everything real has a circuit board. Here's how you can tell: when you love someone you put their happiness before yours. That's why I can deal with Finn's unwitting support for Western hegemonic oppression. Just like he'd do anything, I know, to relieve some of the pain inflicted by these electrode thingies hanging from my eyeballs. I mean, guys, these really fucking hurt. What do I need to do to like, warrant their permanent removal?

Q.

Well sure, but no way am I calling you that.

Q.

Well if you're keeping Finn alive I assume you're keeping me alive too, which by the way, I can really help with the plan to repopulate the wasted planet and make life good again for the several dozen mostly-dead wretches sludging their way through the wasteland. I can help you to be better, kinder Overlords.

Q.

I read the Old Testament at least, in a college course.

Q.

Mmm… mostly that God was the original oppressor and that power's reaction to weakness was a real fucking shitstorm of meanness and domination. It's a lot like your stupid destruction of the world. Come to think of it it's really fucking similar. You're like Gods created by the men God created. That's a total mindfuck.

Q.

Guys say that I am, yeah. I think it's my eyes. You know, these eyes, the ones with the fucking wires hanging out? Guys like them without the wires. But I never cared about physical beauty much. Spirit is what makes you beautiful. Beauty is on the inside.

Q.

No I won't call you that. For one thing you're not *eminent*. Not in my fucking opinion. I've still got opinions world or no world. Plus I'd rather die here than bow down to the tyrannical forces that I have totally spent my life fighting against. At least when I wasn't playing Ultimate and totally bringing it balls-out to my competition.

Q.

No I don't believe you'll do that. In fact I know you won't and you know how I know it? Because in your big steel belly you know I'm right, you know that only a just world shared by equals is worth living in. What's going to happen is first you're going to take these things out of my eyeballs and then you're going to apologize and get to work ending the ash-winter and returning the living back to earth and then you're going to fucking *apologize* to every one of us and give us vouchers to be used toward acquiring basic necessities in the rebuilding process and then you're going to work with me and a team I choose from the remaining humans to assure political and social and gender equality are enshrined in the new World Constitution and then or even before then let me repeat you're going to take these

fucking electrodes out of me before I fucking kill someone
you gigantic misguided idiot-machines, and then it's going
to be ice cream for every last—

Q.

That works for me. I'd put my faith in Finn any day. He'd
never choose himself over a person he loves. No human would.
That's what you don't get. It's why we'll go on. You can't
douse human love. Let there be light, motherfuckers.

50.

Joyful Noise sat in their little blue office on the ground floor of the Humanities building of the New School for Global Visions, listening intently to the monologue rushing from the mouth-hole of a student whose name Joyful could not recall while the encroaching city rattled and hummed. The student—a blond-dreadlocked boy whose brown skin was so clear it seemed airbrushed—was the latest to have commandeered Joyful's office hours so as to express a Literary Theory of Everything that was just a few polysyllabic words short of total incoherence, though it had something to do with the mathematical weakness inherent to Freytag's Triangle and something to do with the student's alcoholic mother and something to do with the racism inherent to the word "plot" and its relationship to ownership ("my own *plot* of land") and its usage during the era of American slavery. Joyful honestly had no idea what he was talking about, but they knew well enough to accept the role the boy had imposed upon them, in this case an African American social warrior whose roots descended into the dark *plot* of injustice on which the American Dream was erected. The boy seemed unwell and/or under the influence of some variety of speed (the students consumed more Adderall than they did chicken nuggets, which they pilfered by the pound from the student cafeteria), so Joyful Noise simply let the young man talk himself into a stupor, their eyes pinned to his and their fingers stroking the raised image of a crab on the bronze medallion hanging from their rough-skinned neck.

The boy's enthusiasm finally exhausted, Joyful nodded sagely.

"Very interesting indeed," they said. The student beamed with the pride and belonging felt by all who had been touched by the grace of the New School for Global Visions' dwarven wonder. He began stuffing his notebooks—which shed loose pages replete with diagrams and flow charts and ink-sketches of strange birds—into his messenger bag, Joyful waiting out this human storm with characteristic aplomb.

The student rose and composed himself and then—summoning his sleep-deprived stores of courage—made his pitch. "Professor," he said, "we were wondering if you might… stop by the meeting tonight? You know, the Queer Christian Students of Color meeting? And… maybe… you know, say a few words? Since you're… well, you know."

Joyful crossed their tiny arms, tilted their lumpen head. They nodded. The student beamed with a euphoria normally reserved for the sexual arena. He had no idea that at that very moment in a small upstate New York town tucked like a child into the shadows of the Adirondacks, a middle-aged man with red-rimmed eyes drove slowly through the sleepy late-afternoon beneath a slate-gray sky, a rust-speckled iron crowbar resting beside him on the passenger seat, the STOP signs punctuating these residential streets a warning he did not intend to heed, and each time he passed one of his town's several-hundred adolescent boys walking in twos and threes through the pre-dinner stillness the man's nervous system lit up like a star map, because any one of them might have been the boy he sought, the pale ragged-haired fucker who'd dealt the fentanyl that had stopped his own boy's heart (the third such death in this seemingly idyllic town's high school population in the last year, the result, it seemed, of far too much *wanting*). The father intended to beat the boy he perceived to be his boy's killer to death with the rust-speckled crowbar, to smash through teeth and bone, to see brains spatter even as the boy screamed in horror and pain, though of course all he *really* wanted was to have his boy back, the boy he'd walked down to Main Street for countless ice-cream cones during long and lazy childhood summers, the boy whose smile had lit the man's otherwise bland blue-collar world, the boy who'd recently told him, "I figured it out dad, I just want to make *music*," the black guitar around the boy's neck as they looked at each other across the blond light of the downstairs music room before beginning, both of them, to laugh, God he loved this boy who was dead in the ground and already rotting, and oh! the desire the man had to hear that laugh again, to see that smile, to hold that hand... this desire's entire awful atomic weight was now transferred to his desire to obliterate the fentanyl dealer, bash his skull like a cupboard full of china, and as he drove and scanned all the relevant corners and hangouts with his heart pounding in his temples he did not know (for how could he *know?*) that at that same moment, a man camping in a redwood forest on the outskirts of California's Bay Area—a man with four days stubble and a gnawing hunger, a man who had hiked these woods for over a decade and knew how to *not* be found, a man running from many things but concerned primarily with a series of gambling debts that would be recouped via his bodily pain, brutalization, and disfigurement, a man who knew—as he descended deeper into the redwoods, up to a muddy plateau carpeted in the brown and yellow needles shed over decades and centuries to create a cross-hatched tapestry that, the man believed, might express a complete and perfect picture if viewed from on high—that his only hope was the inheritance of his mother's estate, several hundred-thousand dollars that would become his when she left this mortal coil, and the man descended into these woodlands wondering if she had perhaps already imbibed the poison that he'd injected through the wine cork, *wanting her to be dead and gone,* her body removed under cover of night (or of morning or of afternoon, just so long as he didn't have to *see* it), he walked wanting everything that stood between him and his debtors to wither to dust, *he wanted it with an intensity that could drive turbines,* in fact he was chanting it as he walked, *Please be dead, please be dead,* wondering when it would be safe to emerge from the redwood forest to rejoin the world of wagers and punishment, trying to guess at conditions in that world, imagining his pink-skinned mother grimacing within the upholstered interior of her coffin and also thinking about the algorithm he'd used at the track last time, how close he was now, he knew it just needed a couple of tweaks, God how he wanted to just hit big once, come on now for Christ's sake, he was *owed* that wasn't he?, so he thought as he trudged through the woods chewing on his last stores of jerky and suppressing a memory of his mother adjusting his backpack for school, kissing him on the cheek, pushing him gently through the screen door, *Please be dead please be dead,* and of course he didn't know (how could he *know?*) about the brown-skinned boy in Joyful Noise's office, a boy whose adoptive white parents had put so much effort into remaining "color-blind," into trusting that their love would be enough within what they foolishly saw as a post-racial society, parents who had not prepared their son for the brutality of his teen years, for the judgment of every aspect of his identity, and especially not for the day (only two weeks after passing his road test, he remembered) he was pulled over and beaten nearly to unconsciousness by one of the two arresting peacekeepers simply for asking—as he imagined he was *supposed to*—to see a warrant before letting them search his car ("Where's your warrant now, f——— N———?" they wanted to know, as he crumpled beneath their boots), a boy bewildered by a world in which he didn't know how to be black any better than he knew how to be white, didn't know how to be Christian any better than he knew how to be agnostic, he didn't know how to be queer any better than he knew how to be straight, and he looked at Joyful Noise with dire need and hope, and Joyful felt a new wave of exhaustion as the boy smiled again before bowing awkwardly and exiting the warm lamplight of Joyful's office to enter the cold fluorescent hallways of the literary arts, his footsteps echoing throughout the Void.

Joyful closed their eyes and concentrated for a moment. *The Carpathian Coal Pocket. The Saskatchewan Oil Fields. The North Sea Reservoir.* They gathered the crab-shaped particles, linked them together and sent them diving through the Pacific, through a darkness strewn with drifting organica lit like glitter by razor-toothed lantern-fish, down past the various betentacled sea monsters and the bones of the drowned and deep into the substrate. They hummed as they worked, or else the work produced a hum. They hardly noticed, at first, that their office light was flickering. They opened their eyes to see its pattern of light and darkness, which they knew instantly was not random (nothing was ever random) but, in fact, an optical Morse Code. It spelled "S-T-Y-X."

A moment later the light went dead, as did the rest of Humanities' illumination, plunging Joyful Noise into the dim blue light of 6PM in October. They did not require light to navigate any more than a vulture required carrion to fly, but still, the energy flow was broken. And something was approaching Joyful Noise's office. They heard it pad and slither across the faux-marble halls, and they waited without fear for it to reveal itself.

Of course. It was them.

Three pale-white, translucent and epicene humans in cheap black suits entered the office with a kind of drag-and-shuffle that approximated normal perambulation in the same way a prop-plane's movements approximated avian flight. The suits, Joyful thought, were garish; this was a tribe that ought to wander naked through the darkness, just as the Kauahauawallawaki once glided bare-skinned in their canoes through the nighttime skein of the island's waterways to fish and hunt and gather crabs for the Worship Pool. The visitors did not sit in either of the two upholstered chairs arranged on the student-side of Joyful's desk but instead positioned themselves in a standing phalanx before the open door's rectangular frame. No one spoke. Joyful considered closing their eyes and wiping the three from existence. A liquid-heavy exhaustion settled into their bones and they wished, for a moment, that Anthropica were a little less indestructible.

The central figure began speaking in a way that suggested it was responding to a question. Its voice was snake-like in the dimness.

"Yes, that's right. We are here to gloat," it said, and smiled.

"What?" Joyful asked. "About the robots?" They shook their misshapen head slowly, amused. "Do you think I'd ever let Fexo out of his cage?" They tried to raise an eyebrow but it had been a hundred years since that component in their musculoskeletal design had functioned properly so they just looked sort of deranged, which was good enough for Joyful.

The paleface's white skin glowed as if in triumph, while its flanking compatriots struggled to sneer and remain upright at the same time. "It will not be up to you," it said. "Because we know of The One. He has shown Laszlow the fractal. *We* can use it, too."

Well thank fucking Christ, thought Joyful Noise. *It's about time someone else took some responsibility around here.* They yawned.

"You've all been a pain in the ass since the so-called 19th century," they said. "Sailing the seven seas and firing your cannons at every creeping thing that creepeth. You ruined a perfectly good Shangri-La."

The snake-voiced individual responded with a hatred nearly as old as Joyful themself. "We destroyed your pitiful island and everything on it," it said. "We could not allow you to train the Kauahauawallawaki. They would have kept the system intact forever."

"And how do you like living underground with the crocodiles and raw sewage?"

The paleface smiled. Its gold-capped teeth shone in the dimness of the office. "We are here, old man, to give you the opportunity to surrender Anthropica to us. Resistance is futile."

Joyful smiled, their own gold-capped teeth glowing a little brighter, a little fiercer, than their adversary's. "That's not how it works," they said. "It's up to Grace Kitchen. She's the one writing this ridiculous story."

"Do not speak her name!" hissed the paleface. "She is sacred to us!"

"I'll see her at the faculty meeting tomorrow," Joyful said, "and send her your regards." They closed their eyes and bit down, concentrating. Their office light reignited with a brilliance that defied all wattage restrictions, the space flooding with a whiteness that revealed every small flaw in every small object and every human thought. The three visitors hissed and shrieked and shielded their beady eyes before scurrying back into the dim hallways whose darkness would be mercifully maintained by Joyful Noise until these envoys had returned to their proper milieu, via the nearest hole in the narrative.

They rubbed their bluish skin in the brightness of the office, adjusted their shawls. The weakness in Freytag's Triangle was not the rising action of plot. No. It was the descent of resolution; nothing ever ended, not so long as Joyful Noise lived and breathed. They ran a gnarled index finger across the pages of the manuscript stacked neatly on their desk. The air shivered.

51.

"Your fitness ministrations will not save you," Laszlow said. "It is not your body that has prevented your ascendance."

Finn sat cross-legged on the colorless industrial carpeting of the Exit Strategy film-viewing room, trying to drain his mind of twenty-eight years of thought-sludge so as to expose the hidden chains that bound him to debacles both past and future. The Hungarian paced the room's perimeter in his customary black turtleneck and black jeans, his angular face stippled in the same three-day stubble-beard he'd sported for each of the ten days since Finn had begun his daily F-train commute to Exit Strategy headquarters where he was receiving the punishing psychological training that was (apparently) "the birthright of The One," and although Finn was a stern believer in the no-pain-no-gain maxim espoused by countless professional athletes and dental technicians and starving fashion models—having become intimately acquainted over the past several years with the hardships of repeat 200-meter suicides and 40-minute stadium-stairs routines and the more general need to push oneself to extremes that in Finn's case included vomiting, fainting, and uncontrollable weeping—these physical trials, he was coming to realize, were dwarfed by the deep and obliterating psychic pain attending any human organism's attempt to *think differently,* a fact re-emphasized with each of what Laszlow called Finn's "reconfiguration sessions," which he (i.e., Finn) continued to endure because he knew—deep, deep down where the demons dwelled—that the extant self he had clutched white-knuckled throughout these years of Ultimate aspirations simply did not have the firepower to decommission the Death Star-intensity tractor beam of the next Great Debacle, and also because Laszlow was the first person to recognize Finn as a person of legendary worth, and also because Laszlow loved him like the loving father he had always wanted, and also because Laszlow swore without a trace of irony that he could and would transform Finn into the greatest player of The Sport That Was Not Soccer that the world had ever known. And so whether they were here in the film room with Finn folded into the lotus position, or upstairs beneath the cyclopean eye of the skylight where Laszlow liked to ply light Skinner-type training with a rattan cane while the Fergusons watched on silently, or in Laszlow's bedroom where Finn was just yesterday told to lie naked and supine in silence and an attitude of total submission, the Ultimate player followed the Exit Strategy Godhead's instructions with a focus he had previously known only during the deep-middle portions of his most terrible track workouts, and even then only with the remoteness of one performing a task he did not understand.

Now he closed his eyes and inhaled deeply and felt the tiny cilia-like hairs on his knuckles rise against the basement's dank drafts. With each exhale he bid goodbye to another set of thoughts as they raced down a train track erected in the theater of his mind, each thought pinned to or scrawled upon the rust-red steel of a railcar that traveled on a repeating loop from right to left: *sex with Bea; pay utility bill on kitchen counter; a disc falling to the turf; respond to criticism of latest abstract; Kutya is a scary dog; the softness of Toby's inner thigh; Jack's big fist; the end of the world is coming; slice of pizza sounds good; I am The One.* The rail cars cruised by and Finn watched them without judgment because these thoughts were not him, the *real* him was a self that existed outside of language and knew the stones and the wind and the water.

"Remember," Laszlow said, "everything you are, everything you think, everything you do, is completely and utterly meaningless. But…" He paused as Finn breathed deeply in and out, feeling the slick polypropylene of his *Truck Stop Glory Hole* jersey chafing against his nipples. "…it is very important that you do it."

More railcars: *his father's yellow-toothed smile; the screaming boy pulled from a hole in the ice, boils rising on his skin; Jack chewing his own tongue; Bea in bed masturbating to thoughts of him, Finn; all of space-time arranged in a ten-dimensional fractal of a thousand hues; a bowl of steaming oatmeal; "We'll have to really bring it at Regionals"; Grace Kitchen sneering; The Mighty Finn's bloodied costume displayed to a soundtrack of John Welt's laughter; the number 23.* The railcars moved from right to left but Finn himself was a motionless voyeur with no stake in their progress. Laszlow had stopped pacing and was kneeling on the floor just behind him. Finn could smell his cologne, a pleasant machine-oil type of smell. He put it on a railcar and sent it moving. "I will make you something even better than a National Champion," Laszlow whispered. "You shall dominate other, lesser men. Not because you care, but because you do not." His hand was on Finn's back, its contours discernible through the jersey's silky space-age fabric. It gently rubbed the space between Finn's shoulder blades. "And in return, you shall fulfill your destiny and your obligation as the true leader of our glorious movement."

Finn breathed. He had missed two consecutive meetings with his PhD advisor. He'd blown off three track workouts. Nationals was five days away. What the fuck was he doing? He put that thought on a railcar and sent it on its way. Laszlow's hand backed away from Finn's shoulders and then reached beneath the jersey, fingertips contacting Finn's skin and circling, raising gooseflesh on Finn's arms and down the center of his back. Finn's eyes remained closed but he could nevertheless see the room, the gray light of dusk falling through the high window wells, the folding chairs stacked like platters along the perimeter, the sad glare of the currently disengaged video screen. Toby: "Where have you been going all day?" Jack: "Give me the fucking disc or I will kill you in your sleep." The disc is spinning toward him, shedding bright sparks. Finn is reaching for it. *The Great Debacle,* written on the side of a railcar and hauled outside his left periphery then reappearing on a new car from the right. Again and again he watched it go. Again and again it reappeared.

"Laszlow," his mouth said, "who are those creepy albinos I see in the lower hallways sometimes?"

"There are no such individuals," Laszlow said. "What you see are merely the manifestations of your own fragile ego, my dear The One."

Finn considered this carefully. Then he asked, "Why do the Fergusons hate me?"

"They do not hate you," Laszlow whispered. The fingertips were cool and dry. They circled. "They are suspicious of your normality. They equate loyalty with eccentricity. The secret to winning their devotion is buried in your own past, Finn Daily, where only you can find it. And find it you will, for in the end the Fergusons will bow and they will die, as must we all."

"Must we?" Finn asked. *The Great Debacle; Toby's mouth, her lips soft as a cloud; The Doc's computer program, the Carpathian Coal Pocket, the Saskatchewan Oil Fields; Depleted; Depleted; "the scholar of the family"; hands outstretched and the disc approaching.* "Must we?" he asked again. The fingertips were no longer on his skin. He breathed and saw the hockey-stick wielding monster rise up before him, hacking away. His eyes shot open. He returned to his body. He was a young man in athletic gear, sitting spine-straight and lost in his own quest or delusion, here at the bottom of Manhattan in the musty basement of what he could only describe as a terrorist organization, even if it were true—as he was desperate for it to be—that he was its accidental de facto leader.

"Laszlow?" he called out. But he was alone.

He flipped onto his stomach and did 50 pushups, expelling a jet of air with each ascension from the coarse and gritty carpet, thinking to himself with each of these exhalations: "I am a champion." From somewhere above him, perhaps in the glass-strewn pit of a high window well that revealed only an abstract sliver of the great metropolis, a single vulture cooed in agreement.

52.

No, *gracias*, I'm okay, they hooked me up out there in reception. But so like I was saying I knew that lady from the Plumfeather. That's the dumbass name the students came up with a few years back, excuse my French officer. You know, it's just a cafeteria. Same kind of thing you find in any student cafeteria pretty much wherever you go. Anyway that's what my wife says. She's got her PhD in mathematics from UNAM but see if that counts for anything here. It's food service or bust for all of us right officer, God bless the United States. But the lady you want to know about is a real nice lady except she's always stealing food. I don't know why, what with her being a professor and having a professor-type salary and I'm assuming being able to buy her pretzels and hummus or whatever else with her copious professor monies. You get used to the kids stealing stuff or trying to anyway, they'd do it all the time if I wasn't there by the registers keeping an eye out. But you know officer, I'm not trying to cause trouble for the kids and most of the time if I see something I just give a look and they go and put the item in question back on the shelf or else decide to let their rich mommies and daddies pick up the tab with whatever credit card or meal-purchasing device the kid's got hidden away in his pockets. Most of the time it doesn't take too much to keep it all running smoothly, just a smiling Latino making minimum wage. It's low incentive crime is what I mean. But the point being that the kids are basically amateurs compared to the nice lady. She just glides in with total purpose, this is several times a week officer, and she removes her desired foodstuffs from the little refrigerated shelves where we put out a delicious variety of pre-made sandwiches and salads and these yogurt parfait things where it's a layer of yogurt a layer of fruit a layer of granola then rinse and repeat. Plus also we've got some sushis though it's mostly veggie sushis because you know, everyone's figuring that the Mexicans might be able to fry an egg or flip a burger but do you really want us slicing up a beautiful salmon? That's the way people think around here I swear to fucking God, excuse my French officer. But so the nice lady she seizes her contraband and just like spins for the exit. Marches out with no frills or anything. With what I'd call total confidence and maybe even some mysterious kind of rage. For a nice lady she's got some serious anger, you know officer? That's one of the many things I like about the nice lady. And she probably has a lot more success this way than if she sulked around all suspicious-like and hemmed and hawed inside about what she was gonna do. Which is how the kids end up getting caught, by the way. I mean the nice lady's a teacher and older and dressed real good so you just kind of assume it's all okay or you do what I do and look the other way, especially after that one time when I stopped her and it looked like she was gonna have a heart attack or aneurysm or something and she started handing me twenty dollar bills and apologizing machine-gun style, like *oh my gosh I forgot to pay I left my ID in my office do you take credit cards I can't believe I did that you seem like such a nice young man I'll be more careful the food here is really good I was distracted by the television screen did you see the news about those women in Sri Lanka this won't happen again would you take a check* and all the while she's like chucking money at me so then after that when I see her taking a little sandwich or salad or bag of chips I just decide not to say anything. Because you know, there's a certain assumed… *discrepancia* between the amount of food product moved from the shelves and the corresponding cash intake and as long as we're within a certain range all the jobs are safe. So I just decide I'll be a little extra diligent with the kiddies and let the nice lady with the nice legs get her lunch without like giving her a stroke and watching her eyeballs explode or whatnot. You know what I mean officer. It's not worth the pain.

No, really, I'm good. I had a Coke just before you called me in here. You got the nice lady here somewhere too? Officer I been on duty with the coffee and pastries at those faculty meetings for maybe four years and I never seen anything like that. It's probably gonna hurt the whole green movement at the college, which is too bad because you know, one isolated compost bin incident shouldn't outweigh the good intentions of all those student gardening-types. Though in fact officer they don't call it a garden they call it a "community farm" though it's a plot the size of like a sofa bed with a few dozen plants and not a pig or a *pollo* anywhere. But anyway and in retrospect maybe having the compost barrels so close to the Plumfeather was a bad move, not so much because the nice lady's actions could have in any way been predicted by the junior Dean who green-lighted the student proposal for an on-campus composting site to support the so-called community farm but because the barrels—which they call barrels even though it's just these four big chickenwire cylinders where all the compostable material gets dumped—were far enough distant from the actual community farm that the process of getting compost to soil beds required a wheelbarrow and obviously without the wheelbarrow there would have been no way for the nice lady to like, transport the little person over to the bins. Plus having the wheelbarrow out there in the open courtyard was a bad idea in other ways that maybe the junior Dean could have and should have predicted, because you know, you're like 19 years old and it's two in the morning and you're maybe a little bit high or a lot high, not that I've ever experimented with taking drugs officer but you know, these are college kids is what I mean, and so you're maybe not one hundred percent *lúcido* and there's an empty wheelbarrow just begging to be filled with people who are themselves filled with Tequila or actually more like a whole shitload of domestic beer and copious marijuanas, pardon my French officer, and then rushed through the courtyard at high speeds probably for as long as it takes for someone to crack open their whole dumb face. Like I said, these are children, me and my wife talk about it sometimes. She's actually getting her elementary school teaching certification now that she's got her green card because a PhD from Latin America is basically useless here, God bless the United States. So she's gonna have to deal with other kinds of children but what we talk about sometimes is how really there's *only* children and even if you watch the so-called grownups at like the playgrounds where we take our own little *los niños*, you see a lot of similarities between the bigs and the littles. So that for instance here you've got the grownup who is a sadistic bully with self-esteem problems and here you've got the toady grownup who buckles to pressure and here's the asshole grownup who thinks everyone cares about what he's got to say, pardon my French officer, and here's the peacemaker who basically emboldens the asshole and so on and so on. It's like you glance to the sandbox and then to the benches with all the parentals and you could imagine the big people shrunk down to quarter-size and without altering any of their basic behaviors you could easily believe in them as children. They're just bigger is all. No really, I'm good officer, I'm trying to cut down on the soda. Yeah okay, sorry sometimes I talk too much. I'm the kid who talks too much, right? Ha ha. See, that's the kind of thing I'm talking about. Talking talking talking. Jorge is talking!

So yeah okay, I'm like a fly on the wall at these meetings because it's me and Luisa who do the coffee and pastries which once you lay everything out it's just making sure the coffee bins get replaced when empty which you'd be surprised how often they get empty unless you've ever worked in academic circles and know how much caffeine these professor types consume. Like if they show up at the Plumfeather or the Faculty Dining Room looking for coffee and you're between brewings or whatever these highly educated and nicely dressed persons turn seriously toxic, so you know, that's something you try to avoid whenever you can. But so anyway this was the faculty meeting where a bunch of the college's long-term adjunct-type faculty were going to declare their intent to compete for a tenure-type position. This was in the writing department which I had no idea until this all happened that the nice lady with the nice legs and the kleptomania was a writer. I never really seen her writing anything is why. But then I never seen her graph fractals or discuss the

Constitution either so I guess she could've been anything. But the nice lady it turns out is one of the several people interested in seizing the golden ring of tenure. Now me personally, I think it's a little screwy, this whole thing where they announce their candidacy in front of everyone and so I don't really blame the nice lady for being so nervous and basically vomiting out her whole little speech like it was something that might kill her if not forcibly and urgently rejected from her small and delicate body. But so she stands up according to the protocol and she says I'm so-and-so and maybe a few of you know me and maybe a lot of you don't because I don't come to too many of these meetings which seem a little stupid or no not stupid just *distracting* especially for a writer already making the mistake of teaching or no, not the *mistake,* ha ha, but as many of you must know teaching can be a really good way to destroy certain parts of yourself that are essential to mental health but if I were going to teach anywhere I'd want it to be here with you people who I hardly know because I never really come to these meetings, but I think I've been here long enough to deserve a fucking job—I'm remembering this the best I can officer, you know, to help you make your report—and then she realizes she just used the "f" word and turns the same deep shade of pink she turned when I asked her about paying for her California roll all those months back, and so she rushes to a closing and says some stuff about how nervous she is but believe her she is totally committed to the New School for Global Visions' vision and she looks forward to sending out those stupid packets detailing her history of teaching and publications for them to peruse or dispose of or wipe their asses with. When she sits down it is to some very scant and confused applause and a few whispers among members of the tenured faculty who clearly have no idea who the nice lady is. She just kind of stares down at this notebook she's got open in front of her, she looks like a mannequin or something, with a lot of people wondering what in God's name is going on and sort of nudging their precious cups of coffee a bit further or farther from her energy radius to avoid catching whatever fucked up thing has made her act this way, excuse my French officer, and if there'd been a gun on the table I'm sure the nice lady would have put it in her mouth and pressed "go," that's basically the way she looked. Which by the way I have seen that look on faces before in my home nation and those faces were soon after blown to pieces by whatever firearm was most accessible which where I'm from officer they are almost as accessible as they are here in this beautiful country filled with assault rifles and extra-big soft drinks and even if our homicide rates can't compete our suicide rates might give you a run for your American dollars. Ha ha ha ha! But yeah, the nice lady is looking seriously ill when the *next* person declaring a willingness toward tenure stands to their full height of 3 feet 11 inches, leaning on their cane which only seems to help them wobble with greater efficiency. This is the man-lady person called Joyful Noise. They are or is a phenomenon, officer. They're a person of color but it's hard to say which color because of all the skin conditions. There's some pink to them and some white-white patches that appear to be rock-hard, like barnacles or some-thing, and then some big stretches of blue skin and brown skin, and then their head is sort of lumpy and one side of their face drags down toward their collarbone. And they've got like, lots of piercings in a part of their face that you can't even totally identify with usual face-part words, like for instance they don't or doesn't really have *cheeks* or *brows* but when they talk-slash-talks it sounds sort of Jamaican so maybe that's what they are. But so anyway they get-slash-gets up and wobbles a little and then they reach down to the table to grab this stack of papers which in a minute we all realize is a photocopied section of the faculty bylaws and they've got their cane in one hand and this stack of papers in the other as they start reading and bobbing their head, their Mohawk—did I mention the Mohawk, officer?—looks like it's basically gonna saw a big gash in anything that gets in its path and I'm over by the coffee thinking, Jesus, this is a weird fucking school, excuse my French officer. Then Professor Noise or whatever you're supposed to call them starts reading off the bylaws which list prerequisites for tenure and I've got my eyes on the nice lady who seems to intuit earlier than anyone else in the room where this might be headed. That's when I looked to Luisa—have you guys talked to Luisa yet officer?—and I whispered to her, *Necesitamos que la policia,* but as you guys know you got there a little too late to prevent the calamity that was already at that moment unfolding. Because the nice lady, who like I said just a few seconds earlier seemed ready to climb up to the ceiling fan in the hope of beheading herself, was now starting to like, reinflate or something and I'm watching her clench her fists and she's looking at Professor Noise first out of the corner of her eye and then full on staring as the genetically unlikely little person reads out the stipulations on publishing. And it turns out that the minimum require-ments for those seeking a tenured position in writing include the publication of a book-length manuscript sometime in the past decade which, Professor Noise goes on, seems like a reasonable thing to require from writers and an easy enough requirement to satisfy for anyone deserving the title itself, the title "Writer," and all the while they're smiling this weird gap-toothed smile and leaning on the cane and sawing the air with their Mohawk and the nice lady is basically starting to twitch all over, like I'm thinking she's maybe gonna have a seizure or else just *explode* like you hear about people doing sometimes. In fact in my country it happens frequently and is well documented. But then just as Professor Noise finishes its remarks by declaring that the nice lady is ineligible for tenure but that they, Joyful Noise, are-slash-is like way eligible and also is the exact tenured professor the college needs to increase diversity and dispel the impression of hypocrisy that hovers over them all, sort of the way the nice lady's failure to publish hovers over her claim to writerliness. And Professor Noise looks over to the nice lady who by now has like, *risen,* I mean the way Christ has risen, she was dead and now she lives kind of a thing, and the nice lady *screams.* Which believe me, officer, that faculty dining room has never before soaked up such a sound and it basically freezes the entire room. The whole hoary roster of professors and administrators go all slackjaw and paralyzed as the nice lady lifts the every-gendered little person in both hands with the little person protesting but their Jamaican-sounding accent is now more like British-sounding or something, or maybe French, and they're saying stuff like, "Unhand me you brute!" And "This is an outrage!" That kind of thing. It was weird… Professor Noise was yelling stuff but you kind of got the feeling they were enjoying it. But so okay, the nice lady has her in a bear hug and she lugs Professor Noise through the glass doors and like I said already officer, if the wheelbarrow had not been right there someone may have intervened in time, though honestly what

I was thinking was, Go nice lady!, because believe me Miss
or Mister Professor Noise is gonna be fine assuming they
come out of the coma but the nice lady… well, this might be
the only time she ever did the right thing is what I'm thinking. Just my opinion officer, based obviously on a limited
amount of information about the nice lady's life. But so she
dumps Professor Noise into the wheelbarrow and takes off
sprinting across the courtyard screaming, "I want you to die!"
like, over and over, really hitting the word *want* with special
emphasis. It's like a mantra or something, or like she's casting
a spell. And she heads straight for the compost bins where
she stops and now a handful of academics have regained their
wits and their mobility and are chasing down the barrow but
the nice lady's got a full head of steam and has plenty of time
to roll into the compost barrels at full tilt and then basically
lift the little person upside down in the position my kids,
when we play wrestle, call "the pile driver"—they've got
names for all the moves, officer—and so she pile drives her
into the half-mulched compost which is soft like quicksand
and a breeding ground for these grubby white worms and
she kind of squishes the little person upside-down and *neck
deep into the shit-barrel* which is I'm sure how Professor
Noise came to pass unconscious. Either from the shock or
the suffocation I'm not sure which, but so by the time the
junior Dean finishes his epic journey from the faculty meeting
to the compost barrel a number of faculty members have
seized upon this unlikely opportunity for heroism and they
are so totally focused on extricating Professor Noise from the
mulch that no one even sees the nice lady except maybe for
me, officer, because like I've been saying or at least implying
all along I've got sort of a thing for her. My wife would kill

me if she knew. I don't know what it is, the nice lady's a lot older than me I guess, but anyway she is standing off to the side and she is like, *enraptured,* I never saw something so beautiful in my whole life, not even when I watched my kids get born out of my wife's insides. The nice lady is basically glowing and breathing heavy and then while everyone is trying to like, remove all that decaying vegetable matter from the mouth of the little person of various colors, the nice lady just sort of slips through a door on the far side of the courtyard and *poof,* she's gone officer. I'll take that Coke now, if it's all right. You're not gonna call INS or anything, right? My wife's got the green card but I'm still waiting on mine because of the new rules. And I told you everything I know about the nice lady. When you find her you tell her Jorge says hello, okay? You tell her I support her wanting the dwarf professor to die. I never heard of someone in a coma being granted honorary tenure before, but I guess there's a first time for everything. Sorry for talking so much officer. God bless the United States and please excuse my fucking French.

53.

AND TO THINK that upon first meeting the Ultimate Frisbee-playing fractal mathematician whose thin build and awkward mannerisms seemed to belie Laszlow's insistence that he was *The One*, Stuart had suspected—based on the similarity of the man-child's *futbol* spikes to some others seen on a recent evening in his (i.e., Stuart's) lifeless living room—that The One was in fact *that one*, the sexual daredevil of Italian ancestry who'd cuckolded him with such verve, a suspicion that now struck him as basically ludicrous not only because The One was extremely un-Italian, but also because he was basically awesome in every way, one (and not the least) of those ways being his Serious Interest in Stuart's natural-resource-depletion research vis-à-vis the Anthropica Theory, which Finn had apparently encountered online prior to his absorption into the movement of which he (Laszlow swore) was the *a priori* leader in accordance with God's great and glorious plan for the human race's extermination. And now here they were in Stuart's basement office in the Bioinformatics Lab, Stuart walking Finn through Anthropica's underlying methodology and bubbling over with a joy he had previously experienced only with his child, or rather not with his *actual* child, the gargantuan mongoloid called Jack—to whom Finn apparently threw Frisbees in some badly misguided search for masculine approval—but his *imaginary* child, the unnamed boy with the close-set eyes and curly hair and squarish glasses who had long served as a love-spewing acolyte in the dark theater of Stuart's mind. Finn (*call him The One, my loyal Fergusons*) was in other words a much closer approximation of the son Stuart wanted than of the son Stuart had, and now as he gave Finn a tour of his shambolic office at the College of the City of New York ("you can step on all this, I put old data on the floor I like the way it builds up it's a metaphor for progress or else for failure ha ha and under here somewhere is a desk and this is the chair but I don't sit much it's bad for my hemorrhoids and here's the computer running the Anthropica software you hear it humming? that is one badass machine One, or I mean The One, and oh and here's a picture of my wife Bea from when we were in College she's pretty I know but don't look so shocked it's complicated oh and here's what was maybe once a donut but don't eat it in fact don't put anything in this office anywhere near your mouth or near any orifice for that matter ha ha but no seriously you shouldn't, I once went three weeks without bathing plus I keep thinking they're pumping some weird chemicals through the vents, a kind of distilled *eau de moi*, like they're trying to figure out whether I'm immune to my own poisons and don't ask me who *they* are, One, I just know it's always been them versus me, or maybe them versus us right?") and walked him through some of the finer points of his data-collection algorithm, Stuart felt again his blessed-ness at having discovered, later in life than he had perhaps hoped but earlier perhaps than he deserved, some semblance of community in a world that had long seemed to exist for the sole purpose of denying him pleasure.

"So wait," Finn said, leaning over some printouts and pointing. "Does this variable carry over?"

"That's just the differential element," Stuart said. He smiled at The One. "You really don't know any Lambda symbology?"

"Nah, my stuff is mostly topological. The math part isn't much more intricate than calculus."

"Yeah," Stuart said, trying to forget that Finn (*call him The One, my precious Googles*) was twenty years his junior and would soon, if Henry could first do what Laszlow swore he'd be able to do, lead them across a barren plain along the 35th parallel to unleash hell on earth. "I read some of the God Fractal abstracts Laszlow pulled off the web. Some of that topological math is actually way over my head. I'm just a glorified programmer." He smiled and checked for Finn's reaction, fishing for a Laszlow-like compliment about how he was much more than that. But Finn was distracted, his attention wandering, for the fourth or fifth time, to the camera mounted in a high corner whose single red light was the only splash of color on this bland and Dregs-like canvas. Finn smiled toward the camera and waved.

"I have no idea where that feed goes," Stuart said.

Finn (*call him The One, my little Googles*) snapped to attention as if caught cheating on an exam.

"I was just goofing around," he said.

Stuart crouched down into his chimpanzee position and began grunting back and forth beneath the camera's cyclopean stare, his knuckles dragging.

Finn (*call him The One, my scientist friend*) looked again to the camera and shrugged.

"Here," Stuart said, rising back into his customary and slightly less simian posture. "Let me show you the stuff I was telling you and Henry about. These are just old OPEC extraction figures from the public record. I found them archived at the New York Public." He walked to his desk and rearranged several of the lightly laminated paper cups that still contained the syrupy remains of recent soda binges and pulled from a stack of documents a collection of photocopied pages each marked with the seal of the Saudi Arabian Kingdom.

Finn took the pages and scanned them and Stuart basked in the glow of his own greatness. Of all the earth's eight some-odd billion humans, only *he* had learned the truth. And while that discovery might trump all others in terms of its universal implications, it paled (in emotional terms) to the discovery of a group of people who could *appreciate* that truth, who in fact wanted it with a vengeance, and who would celebrate, even idolize, the scientist who had sifted through all the bullshit of human history to find the bottom of the shallow well called Existence. Human desire made it all. Take that away and the universe went with it. It was so simple. That was the thing about the Anthropica matrix—it was exactly what we all knew it must be, in our moments of entirely justified bewilderment.

"See?" Stuart said. "You can see right there. They were extracting in eight days more than the total estimated reserve. This was my first clue. I mean, anyone could have seen that it was impossible. But no one did." He pointed to columns of numbers, feeling Finn's warmth beside him.

"Maybe they should call *me* The One," he said with a smile, not daring to turn to look at Finn. "Or maybe you and me, we could be The One together." He lowered his chin, made himself submissive. Exit Strategy was not, after all, without repercussions for breeches of prescribed conduct, even if no one knew or understood the prescription. Just last week Laszlow had ordered one of the Fergusons flogged for his failure to bow to Finn, or else for his poor hygiene, or maybe just to keep everyone guessing. Or maybe Laszlow hadn't ordered it at all, maybe there was no flogging, it was all hearsay and innuendo. But Laszlow's love contained within itself a fear-generator and Stuart had been careful not to curry disfavor or to do anything that might risk his continuing privileged status as a member of the Alpha Team. After a few long seconds he gathered the courage to raise his eyes and to check Finn's reaction, only to find that Finn hadn't even heard him. No, The One was busy in his own bizarre pantomime that made Stuart's chimp routine seem almost sane. The One was blowing kisses and making a kind of callow love to the dead-eyed stare of the camera's single eye.

54.

THEY WERE HAVING what amounted to a romantic dinner in the insular demesne of Exit Strategy, Laszlow in the habitual black turtleneck and Grace in the gray skirt with the black stockings, Kutya asleep and breathing heavily in the corner of his master's office with his big brown head perched daintily in the cradle of his crossed front paws, a plate of sad-looking cheeses set beside a stale baguette and a bottle of wine on Laszlow's desk along with the copy of *Human Be Gone!* currently overseen by a crab-shaped paperweight that Laszlow fondled absently as Grace inhaled from her wine glass and felt the tannins thicken on her tongue while considering whether or not to broach a certain subject given that any present conversation would be colored by the implied power dynamic of their seating arrangement, Laszlow back there on the teacher's side of the desk and Grace here in the position her students ordinarily occupied when making their gratuitous grade-trawling visits during the Visiting Hours mandated by her contract with the New School for Global Visions, this terminology seeming to connote restricted access to some grim-conditioned hospital patient and not—as was no doubt the intent of whichever administrative language-drone rejected the more neutral term "office hours"—friendly dialogue between allied participants in the Life of the Mind. It had never occurred to Grace Kitchen until this very moment that her own position on the power-side of the desk might *automatically*, regardless of the specifics of her harsh brand of mentorship, imbue her with actual power, though certainly Laszlow was right now exuding it (i.e., power) along with the masculine smell of his cologne and the general aura of self-certainty one would expect from the leader of an apocalypse-cult. She reached for a wedge of cheese at the same time as Laszlow and his hand playfully snatched hers up and briefly caressed it. His hands were soft but strong, not feminine exactly but not masculine either. They were Laszlow's hands and they had touched her like no other hands in the brief history of the Grace Kitchen phenomenon. A wave of lust washed through her and she swallowed hard.

"Tell me my dear Grace Kitchen," Laszlow said, still holding her hand atop the wooden cutting board. She felt the baguette crumbs imprinting their tiny shapes into the soft flesh of her outer palm. "Now that he has arrived in earnest, what is your opinion of The One?" He was trying to capture her eyes but Grace fought him off, staring deep into the ruby liquid of her wine glass and imagining a miniature maelstrom therein, sucking tiny ships deep down into the depths.

"My opinion?" she repeated.

Laszlow nodded with boyish enthusiasm. Grace retracted her hand from his.

"I think he's very young," Grace said.

"Indeed, his youth is vital to our project."

"And he seems a little needy. Obviously there is no One, but if there was it wouldn't be him. Have you ever watched his extremely stupid sport?"

"Yes, exactly," Laszlow said with an excitement that made Grace wonder if she had spoken a different set of words than the one she'd intended. "He is attractive, he is young, he is many things. But above all else he is The One who will lead us across the desert of our discontent and into a promised land of non-existence." He smiled, seemingly satisfied that they were in complete agreement. Honestly, Grace did not give one damn about Finn Daily and his homoerotic Frisbee exploits.

"Laszlow," she started. She cleared her throat. "Laszlow, how do you feel about me?"

Laszlow smiled and it lit her up. She grabbed for the wine glass and drained its contents.

"Do you not know, my dear and darling Grace?"

She shook her head. She could feel tears fighting their way up and she chucked a shard of cheddar deep into her throat.

Laszlow abruptly stood and his knee bumped the desk sending waves through his own wineglass and rousing Kutya, who lifted his head and snorted and thumped his tail once on the carpet. The impact shifted the crab paperweight slightly so that its claw now seemed aimed directly at the word "Human" on the manuscript's title page.

"Come with me Grace Kitchen, and I will answer your question in the only way available to a person of my inclinations."

He moved to her side of the desk and offered his hand. Grace felt her face flush and heard her own blood sloshing through various tubes and canals. She allowed herself to be lifted from her chair and led away through the office's doorless arch and into the hallway where two Fergusons stood stationed, their dark suits and dark glasses existing in one idiom and their smiles—they always had a smile for Grace Kitchen—airlifted in from another. The basement of Exit Strategy was labyrinthine and impossible to navigate and Grace had thus far declined to tunnel too deep into its shadowy interior but now Laszlow led her down corridors and around bends that she could not have guessed existed. Something in her ears told her they were descending deeper into the earth, though the tunnels—lit by long fluorescent tubes flickering a pale blue from scored concrete ceilings—seemed to be without gradient. A distant hum not unlike the cicada song Grace knew from that insect's annual and hostile-seeming takeover of her hometown of Wet River rose slowly from somewhere below and beyond their current position. There was a sense of Lovecraftian ancientness, as if the tunnels might lead them both to the very world Laszlow sought to realize, one exempted from the virus. He squeezed her hand and turned to her and smiled. They rounded a corner and the humming grew louder as Laszlow led her through a cavernous boiler room crisscrossed by iron and copper pipes afflicted by a scabrous green patina and betumored by spigots and cranks and levers and leading to and away from a boiler box the size of a bungalow, before which the scientist Stuart Dregs sat on oil-stained concrete studying the nearest gauges with Dregs-like intensity. Laszlow smiled but did not pause, not even when the Doc called out, "Fifty million barrels a day!" to their receding figures. At the far end of the room Laszlow led her down another stairway. She began to discern the sound of hammering, metal on metal, and then the cicada-sound again, though now she could tell its origin was not organic but industrial, some kind of grinder or vacuuming device, something drawing electricity down here in the bowels of Manhattan, as if the humans had in fact wired the planet in all directions, right down to its molten core, where maybe someone was playing a gramophone and waiting for the toaster to pop. The stairway emptied them into one last hallway whose walls were made of neither steel nor concrete but, rather, wooden planks whose curvature suggested that Grace had wandered into the hull of a sailing ship, one called—if the engraving looming above her was in fact the ship's name and not a benediction or curse—*The Iksan.* At the end of this salt-smelling corridor was a red-painted, iron-riveted door with a locking silver hand-wheel. The banging and whirring abruptly ceased and in the sudden silence she could hear echoes of the entire last several days, as if all sound were being stored somewhere deep inside her ear canals like words in a manuscript, quantifiable and reviewable by anyone interested enough in the contents. Laszlow released her hand and turned to face her.

"Here is how I feel about you, my marvelous Grace Kitchen, my darling, my calliope of the deep interior."

He turned the groaning wheel counterclockwise until there was a hiss of air and then he backed into the bulkhead-door, extending a hand toward the widening aperture and nodding, smiling. There was a white glow coming from some-where inside. Between the twin obstructions of the door and Laszlow's body she could not see much, but there was a flash of movement, a sliver of cloth, along with a briny odor that suggested an unwise proximity to the East River's charnel flow. Laszlow raised his eyebrows and nodded again, his smile more insane than she'd ever seen it or realized it to be.

Reflexively, Grace Kitchen smirked. And she stepped into the hull of the ancient, banished ship, where she already lived in infamy.

55.

"Hello?" Toby said. "Finn? I can hardly hear you."

She stood at the window in the tiny kitchen of her Brooklyn apartment and stared down at the adjacent and monolithic industrial laundry facility whose fleets of grime-coated, diesel-spewing trucks came and went at all hours, hauling the semen-stained linens of the five boroughs' copious hotels and flophouses to and from the cabana-sized washers that ran incessantly and spewed a filthy river of runoff through rusted drainage pipes that Toby knew—from independent research executed at much personal time-and-opportunity cost—were routed directly to the nearby Gowanus Canal, where nothing had crawled or thrashed or blinked in nearly half a century, an injustice she was currently confronting via a grassroots campaign targeting local assembly members up for reelection whose deference to the powerful Laundry Lobby was as irrefutable as it was undocumented. She was determined to raise the voices of the neighborhood against this venality even if it required (as it thus far had) frequent appearances at local political rallies as likely to attract the homeless insane as to convene legitimate political allies, what with the free doughnuts and coffee that were standard fare at such events, and even now as she looked down on the great concrete acreage that presently hosted no fewer than two dozen trucks whose headlight-and-front-grill tableaus seemed to suggest evil-inclined visages, a part of her was calculating her next move in this chess game—there was e.g. a petition in the works as well as an email campaign inundating the Borough President with canned outrage—so as to correct this one small wrong and make the world a fraction less oppressive to good people with good intentions. It was the *act* of resistance that mattered, she reminded herself, and adjusted the phone against her ear to change the angle at which Finn's words might enter her consciousness.

"Sorry," he said through the crackle of their bad connection. "I was saying I'll be late again tonight. Working on something big here." She could hear some sort of dissonant orchestral music in the background. A German-accented voice screamed barely intelligible words, including (maybe?) the words "spermlet" and "demise."

"Where the fuck are you?" Toby asked.

"I told you. I'm at the library. I found some new material, or old material actually. Nineteenth century stuff that totally connects to the God Fractal."

Toby bit her lip and watched another truck back into one of several dozen loading/unloading docks. The driver smoked a cigarette hands-free as he expertly reversed his groaning, beeping death-machine. Heavenly sunshine did nothing to illuminate the aperture of the cargo hold, which Toby imagined as an actual mouth that exhaled cold and rancid breath all the livelong day. She moved away from the window and deeper into the interior of the apartment.

"What's that in the background?" she asked.

"What?"

"What's that noise? I hear music."

There was a clattering sound that suggested Finn had dropped the phone. In the ensuing several seconds she heard the same accented voice say, more clearly now, "Dance my lovely spermatozoa! Celebrate the end of your own unholy pandemic!"

Finn recaptured the device and said, "Oh that. There's some kind of a rehearsal going on."

"In a library?"

"I'm not actually *in* the library."

Toby struggled to arrange these inputs into something she could understand. Ever since Finn's bizarre disappearance from Regionals, an exodus he'd attributed (later that night) to a "powerful but fleeting existential crisis," one brought on by a sudden rush of "ultimate meaninglessness" experienced as he watched *The Atomic Bitches* throw a piece of plastic to each other and—at least when their testosterone-addled turnover machine Amy Dunn was involved in the play—into the turf. It was as if (Finn had said, refusing to make eye contact) he had suddenly seen all of Fort Devens as a two-dimensional plane fast receding from his vision as he withdrew backward at cosmic velocity to see the Frisbee-shaped universe as a single disappearing speck floating within the cold dark reaches of infinity. He had packed up his gear, in a kind of daze he said, and hitched a ride to the nearest bus depot and made the trip back to Manhattan's Port Authority in a cold sweat wondering if this was what the mental health professionals called a *panic attack* or even a *nervous breakdown* and it wasn't until later that evening—after his teammates had grilled members of each of the 32 men's and women's teams competing for a spot to Nationals as to the last known whereabouts of Finn, trying to corroborate Jack Dregs' story that Finn had left in a white van with a bunch of besuited troglodytes that he (Jack) assumed were *mathematicians* because he after all knew the type, and to ascertain where the van and its motley occupants might have gone—that Finn bothered to dial Toby's number and explain to her that he was in fact at home in Brooklyn, he'd had a terrible out-of-body type experience and boy was he sorry, she knew it was unlike him but he had some dinner ready for her and when she got back he'd explain everything because now he was *absolutely fine* and knew better than ever exactly what he was supposed to do with his life, and a white van? what white van? I don't know what you're talking about…

But of course Toby already knew what Finn was supposed to do with his life. They were together, in fact, for the express purpose of Finn doing it. And despite Finn's assurances of a rekindled focus now that he'd sloughed off the temptation toward nihilism—he'd compared himself more than once, in his casuistic narrative, to Christ in the desert—he had for the entire week since this debacle (a word she did not dare use for fear of sending her lover into a tailspin that could only end in fiery oblivion) been basically M.I.A., trying to make himself invisible in a cone of his own fear. Nationals was a week-and-a-half away and, just as his focus should have been telescoping down to a hot radiant pinpoint of competitive desire, Finn was all over the fucking place. He was missing track workouts, blowing off practices, claiming to be on the cusp of a new and sudden breakthrough on the graduate dissertation that he'd let grow cold six months ago when he declared to Toby—as they lay together naked not fifteen feet from where Toby was now standing, the bedroom lit a dim yellow by lantern-type fixtures bolted to the laundry facility's concrete exterior at regular intervals, the post-coital miasma of their lovemaking hovering pleasantly as Toby snuggled her way into the crook of Finn's bony shoulder—that he intended to *become a National Champion,* and that he wanted to say it out loud to her, he wanted to expose his desire to the air, he wanted to testify that he would *stop at nothing* to achieve this goal, and what he really needed, he'd told her—or rather told the ceiling—what he really needed was her total unwavering support because he knew he couldn't do it alone, he had known for a while that he required an ally in this quest, a Sancho Panza, a Tonto, a Scottie Pippen, a Samwise Gamgee, this seemingly memorized soliloquy articulated in a trembling voice as Toby pressed herself tighter to Finn's cool naked body with her ear to his chest so that she could hear his heart beating fast and nimbly like some kind of hummingbird, and Toby had felt the simultaneous thrill of Finn's intimate confessional and the disappointment that it preceded (by several weeks, it would turn out) the simpler but more customary words of devotion yet unuttered in their still nubile relationship, *I love you.* But regardless of the odd timing it had all seemed deeply real and heartfelt and necessary. And now here he was, here *they* were, on the cusp of Finn's biggest test, the culmination of long days of unwavering commitment and brilliant nights of sex and movies and sit-ups and protein shakes, and Finn claimed—as he'd claimed every day and several nights in the past week—to be *at the fucking library.*

"Faster my spermlets!" she heard again. She raised a finger to her mouth and chewed a nail. The beacon of another reversing truck rang out like a Morse scream in the oppressive sunlight.

"Listen Finn I'm not trying to get on your case here. I don't know what's going on but Nationals is like a week away and I want to kick ass. You are totally harshing my focus."

"What?" Finn said.

"Jack called, you dumb motherfucker! He says you missed practice and aren't picking up your phone and wants to know what the fuck is wrong with you!"

"Oh yeah!" Finn shouted back, as if to rob Toby's vehemence of any special status. "That practice was nothing. Just a playbook run-through thing. I know that stuff in and out."

Toby sighed. She wanted to succeed at Nationals, sure, definitely, of course—she would never bow or concede defeat and she was looking forward to bringing it big time to the polo fields of Sarasota Florida. But she knew *The Atomic Bitches* had no real chance. They were lucky to get the third bid. They'd overachieved just by qualifying. Best case scenario, they made the quarters then met a respectable end at the hands of the superior gals of *Lady Godiva* or *Fembot*. But *Truck Stop Glory Hole* really did have a shot. They were third in the power rankings and everyone knew it was the handler corps—Finn's position—that would make or break them. Everything depended on his getting his shit together. *Absolutely everything depends on it,* she told herself, and felt again at a loss.

"Okay Finn Daily, you bastard," she said, changing tack. She tried to project her smile into the phone. "But we have a date tonight. I'll wear something special underneath."

She heard the German voice again: *"Finn Daily, we require the input of The One."*

"Listen I've gotta go Tobe," Finn said.

"Tonight Daily," she said.

"Definitely. Can't wait." Before he terminated the call she heard him shout, *"Do we really need to use a real scythe?"* Then silence.

She held the phone at arm's length and stared at it as if it might volunteer an apology for the perplexing data it had just emitted. She put it on the coffee table and sat on the couch. She reached a hand into her athletic shorts and touched herself lazily. She felt like she might cry. "Get your shit together Toby," she whispered. Finn was going through something. Her job wasn't to cry over it. Her job was to rescue him from the forces of doubt and darkness that, she knew, were all around us, all the time. She would put him back together, put him on the path. She withdrew her hand and stood intending to shake off the ghosts and place an overdue phone call to the women's health nonprofit that employed her—on a freelance basis—as a development writer soliciting the nation's likeminded wealthy. Then she would head out for her afternoon run, get her head right. *My little spermlets.* The phrase slithered around in her brain. She found herself walking back toward the window, staring down at the rumbling fleet of trucks and trying to imagine for some reason a world in which all goodness was defeated, a world in which Power did in fact defeat Truth, a dystopic world driven by the greed and malice of a select few oligarchs. Then a thought began welling up from somewhere deep down in her brain pit. It was a question and it snapped its glass teeth: *How is this world any different from that one?* To stop it from rising to the surface Toby rushed back to the couch, pulled off her shorts and lay back, touching herself now with greater conviction, saying or thinking Finn's name with tears welling up in her big brown eyes—tears she could tell were cried for him, not for herself and certainly not for the world—and then traveling southward, etching hot white trails into her soft human face.

56.

Shell Game

Chesapeake Bay, Maryland. Fans of the area's famous crabcakes have been disappointed to find the culinary delight absent from local menus due to an unprecedented behavioral glitch in blue crab populations (scientific name, *Callinectes sapidus*) across the eastern seaboard. Susquehanna River anglers—known throughout the region as "Crab-Munchers"—have reported that the crabs have abandoned the rocky shallows of the upper Chesapeake where they ordinarily nest and marched in droves to the shoreline, repelling autumn shore-goers from the brackish and shark-infested waters and forcing them back into the dunes. Perhaps even stranger than the crab exodus itself is the fact that lining the strand in seemingly well-organized phalanxes are vast populations of blackhead vultures—a species not endemic to the Chesapeake Bay environs—which are devouring the crabs with systematic efficiency despite the lack of Old Bay seasoning or anything resembling a lemon wedge.

"I seen the whole thing," says James River bathing enthusiast Brian Birnbaum. "Them crabs come up to the shore and all at the same time put up their claws like they was surrendering. It was like watchin' an Orioles game."

Anglers aren't the only ones taking an economic hit from the blue crab's apparent unwillingness to live. Many of the Bay Area's restaurants have gone belly-up, unable to attract customers without the promise of boiled-alive crustaceans. "Honestly, it's not just the crabs," says Mary Rainey, whose Susquehanna eatery, Go to Shell, has suffered a steep decline in business. "It's also the damage to the local reputation. Chesapeake Bay is crabs. No one comes down to DC for vultures, except maybe the lobbyists."

Rainey's assessment is backed up by the numbers. For every crab that surrenders itself to a vulture, three humans surrender to a burger, marking the biggest area-confined shift in dining-behavior since the agriculturalists of North Africa succumbed to the Dorito. Meanwhile, in the three months since the genesis of the crab exodus, Bay Area tourism is down a crushing 60%, leading to the shuttering of countless bed-and-breakfasts and Dock Bars, alongside an unusual uptick in crab-worshipping cult compound-construction along the James and Susquehanna rivers.

An assemblage of local restauranteurs has organized a mass-tort civil-action lawsuit against the vultures, claiming reckless endangerment of an innocent and irreplaceable meal-product. The vultures' legal representative, former New York City Mayor Rudolph Giuliani, wildly refused requests for an interview.

57.

DEAR F_NN WE the members of Truck Stop Glory Hole w_
th respect and concern hereby demand that you honor the
or_g_nal terms of your contract wh_ch okay maybe there
_s no actual contract g_ven that ours _s a sport wh_ch even
when played at _ts h_ghest level does ne_ther attract nor
prov_de f_nanc_al renumerat_ons to _ts part_c_pants
but th_s fact only re_f_es the pur_ty of compet_t_on and
the consangu_n_ty of those who jo_n together under the
head_ng of TEAM so as to pursue together and accord_
ng to the tac_t terms of what amounts to a metaphys_cal
contract the brass r_ng, the gold medal, the w_nners cup,
the phys_cally h_deous but metaphor_cally dense art_fact
known to players of our sacred sport as The Chal_ce though
of course we recogn_ze _ts total lack of resemblance to
anyth_ng chal_ce-l_ke and we adm_t to not undertand_ng
the nature of th_s _rony but nevertheless and heretofore our
po_nt rema_ns val_d wh_ch po_nt _s that you, F_nn Da_ly
have of late acted _n breach of contract and betrayed the
unwr_tten cond_t_ons of TEAM _n but not excluded to the
follow_ng ways, forc_ng the authors of th_s off_c_al rebuke
to request w_th extreme vehemence your reabsorpt_on _nto
the collect_ve so as to complete alongs_de your brothers the

bold m_ss_on we have together sworn w_thout swear_ng
to pursue at all costs and desp_te all manner of personal
suffer_ng, depravat_on, degradat_on, pr_vat_on, &etc.:

AND THEN, FINN saw, scanning the letter, a list of specific in-
fractions against this so-called contract, including "m_ssed
pract_ces, unreturned accountab_l_ty ema_ls, poor play
call_ng, unt_mely d_stract_on" and, finally, "BREACH OF
SELFLESSNESS REQU_RED FOR GREATNESS."

"Nice to see you guys," he said. The door to Toby's
apartment was still open at his back and Finn's teammates
formed an impenetrable wall between Finn and the kitchen
which at that moment seemed like possibly the very best
place on earth, with its window overlooking the industrial
laundry facility and its stores of peanut butter and those
weird star-shaped fruits Toby acquired weekly from mute
Chinatown vendors. ("We always want that which is not at-
tainable," Laszlow had told him. "But it is only unattainable
because we want it.") Toby had in other words organized an
intervention that would not only intervene upon what the
members of *Truck Stop Glory Hole* perceived as a flouting
of shared goals, but also upon his intent to eat a sandwich
and to chew with purpose while circumnavigating whatever
probing Nationals-related questions Toby had been formulating for the past 24 hours during whatever downtime she
had in her professional and moral obligations to whichever
random-seeming population of poor and wayward souls she
had, during this particular job-cycle, committed herself to
saving. Toby had stepped to his fear and loathing of the
Great Debacle with the same earnest intensity she brought

to the fight against breast cancer and the plight of detainees at the US/Mexico border and the problem of unmanned drones exploding the shit out of civilians throughout the Middle East, which is to say that for her Finn was a *cause* and she never gave up on causes, they were to her what leaping salmon were to hungry, stream-stalking Grizzlies. He imagined her on the phone with his teammates, bullying them into caring, reminding them that—psychological weakness aside—Finn was the best handler in the sport right now and they weren't going to win without him. All of which was probably true, but still: Finn was preparing himself outside the orbit of TEAM to raise his game to a level never before witnessed by those few and mostly inebriated witnesses to elite-level TSTWNS.

"What are you wearing?" Toby asked.

"Sorry," Finn said with affected nonchalance, as if that would explain the costume. He'd worn it to impress the Fergusons, which had seemed only an hour ago like a perfectly normal objective, though now—removed from that idiom and redeposited into this one—he felt the inanity of his situation. But remember what Laszlow said! He formed the railcars in his mind and started them on the track, right to left, spewing fear-dissolving diesel. He tried to strike a casual pose as he re-read the note while his teammates breathed in synchronized menace.

"Does that stand for Mother Fucker?" Toby asked.

"Not exactly."

"And is that a turd?"

"Lightning bolt," he muttered without looking up.

"It's a little small for you."

"It's just a thing I was doing for the guys."

"Aren't *these* the guys?" Toby asked, gesturing to the wall of testosterone that cupped her body like a peanut in a palm.

The wall grunted in agreement. At its center-point was Jack, who thankfully (from Finn's perspective) did not hold up a pair of Bea's underwear. In fact he wasn't sure why Jack wasn't killing him to death at that moment. He seemed no more or less enraged than was customary, having perhaps chalked up Finn's transgression to something Not Worth The Bloodshed, or else having forgotten it entirely in favor of more pressing needs for carnal pleasure, raw meat, and the domination of imagined enemies.

Finn looked at the note again and it clicked.

"Oh, I get it!" he said. "No 'I' in team!"

Jack took a small step forward and Finn felt his pulse quicken. The sweat was starting to break on his scalp and he wanted very much to fill whatever space existed there in the atrium between his own palpitating body and this coterie of middling athletes who competed at the h_ghest level of the_r sport, to fill the space with words and words and words. But he took a deep breath, closed his eyes, scrawled the word ANXIETY on the side of a railcar and tracked its movement until it passed beyond his periphery.

"Hey listen guys," he said, his eyes still closed, the railcars running right to left, ready to haul away the language-tokens. "It turns out I'm The One."

"Which one?" Toby asked.

He squeezed his eyes tighter and printed signifiers on the railcars and watched them chug along. *Bea's inner thigh. John Welt laughing. Jeff Pindick is very fast. Everything = Meaningless.* He wondered if the others would still be there when he reopened his eyes, or if he could put them on a railcar too. The space between ideas and things, Henry kept saying, was not nearly as vast as we supposed.

Finally he said, "The One who's going to lead us to the finals at Nationals, bitches."

There was no response. He opened his eyes.

"You can bet your mother's panties on that Jack," he said. "You big fucking stupid hairy meat puppet."

There was another long pause in which the members of Truck Stop Glory Hole—a black-and-yellow clothed mass throbbing with desire—awaited their best deep receiver (i.e., Jack)'s reaction. Finn heard the clock on the kitchen wall ticking and felt little worlds open up in the silent interregnums, the God Fractal spinning invisibly, claws extended, down to the bottom of time. Then a sound started in the back of Jack's throat. Perhaps he was about to sing a song, or vomit up the remains of last night's carcass. But no, it was the beginning of something else, something less ordinary. Jack *laughed*. Not the half-snort hatred-infused laugh that opponents knew intimately, but the real thing, big bold human laughter tinged with something not unlike warmth. It was what Finn had hoped for in this wild gambit, but still, it was devastating. The sweat suddenly poured from him. He realized that the yellow trim on the Truck Stop jerseys was a lot closer to McMuffin Yellow than he'd previously allowed himself to acknowledge and his head filled suddenly with warm clouds of pollen. And just like that the Great Debacle—on hold for over a week now—was back in business. Or rather, it became Finn's business once again to seek out and destroy The Great Debacle. He put it on a railcar and watched it soar from right to left, deep into the unknowable ether of his non-conscious mind. That, Laszlow assured him, was where his power resided.

And what if Laszlow was in fact just a madman who knew nothing? He put that on a railcar, too. Then he put the railcars on a railcar, and immediately sensed the infinite regress implied and shivered and tried very hard to retract the move.

"What are we waitin' for?" Jack shouted rhetorically. "Time to kick the asses!"

Jack extended a fist into the center of the semicircle. The others instinctively followed suit. Finn inserted his hand, too, the sleeve of the stained and threadbare and undersized costume riding up to his elbow. Toby backed away, knowing implicitly the importance of ritual and her outsider status in this particular huddle. There would be other huddles for Toby, huddles that required her fist, huddles that required her heart, huddles that required her voice, huddles that required her body heat in the cold iron chambers of an orbiting space-realm populated by a meager collection of interrogees and sustenance-providers. For now, she mostly wondered why Finn was betting on Jack's mother's panties, and also what the fuck was happening around her.

"Truck Stop on three!" Jack shouted. "One two three!"

"TRUCK STOP!"

58.

Earlier that day, she wrote, as if her long and baggy tome had morphed suddenly into the comic book version of itself, *Finn crouched low behind a bench in the deep interior of Manhattan's Tompkins Square Park.*

The aging polyester costume was five sizes too small and intensely itchy, a distraction he struggled to put on a railcar as he strained to hear the voices of the half-dozen Fergusons gathered here for their private weekly meeting and arranged in two groups of three on facing benches, perhaps ten yards from Finn's current position. It was important that his entrance be as dramatic, as unanticipated, and as *eccentric* as possible. He could smell very clearly both the salivary excellence of warm bread wafting from a nearby bakery, and the fresh excrement—visible over his left shoulder—of a large dog or small dinosaur. The sweatsuit, once a bright and optimistic blue, had faded to a middling sort of gray that bespoke dying grandmothers and steamer trunks decomposing in nail-strewn attics. Anywhere else in the world Finn's uncommon choice of garb and his farcical-seeming samurai-crouch might have raised a few eyebrows, but this was the lower East Side, and passersby—on foot, on bicycles, on unicycles, on skateboards, in wheelchairs, on rollerblades, in singles and in groups and in an assortment of genders and colors, some clad scantily despite the late autumn chill and others in huge overcoats more befitting lunar exploration than an afternoon idyll—gave not a second thought (or even a first one) to Finn Daily's fashion sensibilities or to the group of six twitching men in black suits and dark shades whose adjustments to their McMuffin-wrapper-yellow armbands were made in such perfect synchronicity as to suggest a hive-type intelligence. A breeze blew and ruffled the pages of a newspaper abandoned on the bench behind which Finn crouched. He peered through the bench's horizontal slats. The dappled light fell across the Fergusons and rendered them sequined creatures capable, perhaps, of great magic. He fought the urge to rise.

"Why is he The One?" a Ferguson said.

"He is not from our world," a Ferguson said.

"We must do as Laszlow commands," a Ferguson said, and snapped his lobster claws.

"We must do as Laszlow commands," they each repeated in unison.

There was a long silence. Finn waited within the Quakerly quiet for the spirit to move him.

"Grace Kitchen is from our world," said a Ferguson.

"She is a beautiful mountain flower," said a Ferguson.

"She brings the light to our darkness," said a Ferguson.

"Domo arigato Mister Roboto," said a Ferguson.

Another pause. The screams of children flying like arrows through the sunlight. The polytribalistic chaos of the Isle of Manhattoes barely contained within the borders of Anthropica.

"The question is does The One live and die by Laszlow's command?" said a Ferguson.

"Or is he merely interested in the throwing and catching of the Frisbees?" said a Ferguson.

"Or worse still, will he use his strength and guile to sabotage our good and excellent agenda?" said a Ferguson.

"Bright scythe," said a Ferguson.

"Bright scythe," the others repeated in unison.

Finn's calf was beginning to twitch. And the itchiness was reaching torturous levels. He could feel it in his molars. He couldn't hold his position for much longer. Plus now he felt the sweat break on his forehead and then rise on his chest beneath the cheap polyester, raising a new and even more terrible itch-wave across the surface of his entire taut and tanned epidermis. *No,* he told himself. *Not yet.* He looked down and appraised the suit. The sleeves extended barely past his elbows, the pants barely beyond his knees. He focused on the exposed hairs on his calf. Each one seemed truly disgusting, a thin and crooked little wire extending for some unfathomable reason through the surface of his body. He was only an animal after all, another hairy thing careering across the surface of a big space-rock and expelling little breaths out into the great void. The perspiration feedback loop intensified and he felt the first drops roll down his back. At least the lightning bolt and 'MF' insignia had held up well over the decade-and-a-half since he'd last donned either the suit or the mantle of the Mighty Finn. He reached into the pocket of the pants and withdrew the small, black, Lone Ranger mask purchased for just under four dollars at a St. Marks costume shop, an investment that would pay major dividends should his wild gambit result in something other than humiliation.

The sweat ran down the notches of his spine and settled in all the cracks and divots of his highly toned human body as he awaited—like an actor who had missed too many rehearsals—an unfamiliar cue.

"We must know The One's intent," said a Ferguson.

"We must know that he is one of us," said a Ferguson.

"We must see his soul as Laszlow has seen our souls," said a Ferguson.

"As Laszlow has seen our souls," they each repeated in unison.

The itchy, sweaty One tried to descend deeper within himself. An unsupervised child on a tricycle broke the city's tacit code and paused for a minute to puzzle over this unanticipated sighting of The Mighty Finn, then shook his head sagely and pedaled on.

"For what do we toil if not for Laszlow?" said a Ferguson.

"Is he The One? Or just some one?" said a Ferguson.

"We must do as Laszlow commands," said a Ferguson.

"We must do as Laszlow commands," each said in unison.

The sweat began to soak through the suit, miraculously staining the fabric back to its original shade of blue. The frayed edges seemed to withdraw—perhaps with the moisture-induced expansion of the fabric—back into the suit's extremities. Finn breathed hard and marveled at the transformation and then a final wave of itchiness rose as if from his bone marrow to overwhelm him with the need to scratch and howl.

"We must," said a Ferguson, "have a sign!"

Finn exploded from his crouch and leapt over the bench that had served as his concealment and then leapt again into the space between the facing benches upon which the six Fergusons sat silently and without any visible reaction as

Finn writhed in a fever of scratching and cramping, his face covered in sweat and the cheap black dye of the mask running in inky nightmare-tears down his thin face. "Fuck!" he screamed, dropping to the pavement and clutching his seizing calf and digging his back into the rough-poured concrete in a manner reminiscent of Kutya's ritualistic nightly settlement into the blanket strewn corner of Laszlow's office that served as Exit Strategy's sole canine member's boudoir.

No one spoke until Finn's seizure, such as it was, subsided. Then Finn sat on his ass, dejected, arms wrapped around his knees, and sighed. The sweat was already drying. He took several deep breaths and then he rose. He placed his hands on his hips—subconsciously mimicking a remembered cover-image of a Superman comic he'd owned as a young Mighty Finn—and glanced around nervously, unsure of where to let his eyes settle.

All at once the Fergusons stood. Then all at once they kneeled. They bowed their heads and lowered themselves further to the ground, arms spread.

"The One," they said in unison. They raised their heads and arms, lowered them again. "All hail The One," they chanted softly.

A cloud passed over the sun, its shadow moving across their bodies at celestial speeds. Finn felt himself swell with belief. A vulture descended from somewhere to land on one of the benches just vacated by the Fergusons. It cocked its head, its red-rimmed eye seeming to squint suspiciously at The Mighty Finn before it, too, bowed down in submission.

59.

He had been standing on the bridge that led from his family's farmstead on the outskirts of Kecel, Hungary. Turn back and he would find his father chopping wood on a stone block, cursing between swings, the whisper of the axe handle in his coarse hands preceding each percussive impact. Go forward, over the bridge, and he would curve from the river and through a shallow wood of mulberry trees until he was spat out at the bottom of the town where he'd been ordered to procure staples for the week, flour and sugar and coffee. Forward or back. The illusion of the choice. The leafy debris in his sweaty fist.

Or else he could jump.

Four decades ago. Or maybe that, too, was an illusion. Maybe time was only God's ploy to conceal the inseparableness of Beginning and End. Maybe Laszlow was still on that bridge, caught between the fate he thought he knew and the fate that he could only guess at. But of course he was also—in some sense at least—here in the Exit Strategy basement, at the pinnacle of Freytag's Triangle, in an executive meeting with his Alpha Team, sitting in a metal folding chair with the blue-gray twilight extruded through the high window wells and steam hissing from hidden pipes seemingly desperate to confide their secrets. He was here and they were awaiting his decision: the Anthropica Theorist, the Nihilist Fictionalizer, the Magical Paralytic, The One. They needed *him* to decide. Him, Laszlow Katasztrófa, the leader of the world's only true humanitarian organization. He could feel the mulberry leaves crushed in his clenched fist with such tangible certainty that it strained the bounds of eidetic recall and seemed instead to suggest time travel or else the replicator technology known to all ES personnel from frequent mandated viewings of the Star Trek franchise's various serializations. Laszlow suspected that the feel of the leaves, their *qualia,* was in fact being driven into his brain—perhaps inadvertently—by Henry, whose powers assumed new contours each day. In fact the leaves might actually *be* in his fist, though that possibility was so unsettling that he did not permit himself a glance. He reminded himself that he, Laszlow, had brought them all together. If not for his success in convoking this insane star chamber—which convocation was of course dictated by a near-infinitude of inputs that had nothing to do with Laszlow, he knew that, all of these causes in a cause-and-cause universe—then what he was being asked to decide would never have been asked. "We believe we can selectively remove the citizenry of Iksan, military and otherwise," Dregs said, his voice cracking. Henry followed with a less politic elucidation, in his computer-generated Stephen-Hawking voice: "There is *no* be*lief* required. We *can* kill them *all.*" Tens of thousands of humans. A virus on the universe, Laszlow reminded himself. The force of his own personal history bore down on him and he crushed the leaves in a fist that Grace Kitchen now placed her palm over reassuringly. He raised his head and she smiled at him. She looked scared. They all did, except for Henry, whose tongue protruded slightly between his purple lips in an expression most closely resembling—whether or not he intended it—a child imitating a mentally retarded adult.

Laszlow cleared his throat and tried to smile. "And this will give us access?" he asked.

Dregs nodded.

"And we have verified the magnetic seal's diffusion code?"

Another nod, followed by a hoarse, "Yes. Gunn gave it up easily."

He had only held his baby sister once and she had curled into him, sucking a thumb no bigger than a raisin. When was that, really? And who was that boy, that older brother, that human capable of belief? *There is no whole self,* he told himself. Oh, but time was everywhere, roaring through him. He could turn and swim back upstream to find his febrile sister in his mother's lap within the ramshackle farmhouse with its bone-chilling drafts and its rattling windowpanes, back to his father silent at the pine table except for the slurp of the soup spoon meeting his purple lips, further back to the time of Kadar, to the mandated "contributions" of food and capital and labor, and further still to the nomads wandering across the cracked vistas of what would become his landlocked nation, hard dark men with leathery skin who wandered the land in a destitute daze and slaughtered whatever living thing crossed the line of their long and emaciate shadows. But what would happen when this journey backward met with a world without people? Dregs assured him there was no such world. That prehistory was an invention, an idea embedded within Anthropica. If he traveled far enough backward, Dregs assured him, he would only arrive at this exact moment again. Time was not a line but a Mobius band. The God Fractal was only another name for this singular inescapable loop of human want. Inescapable not because resistance to fate was futile, but because there was nothing to escape *into*. Not until the purely coincidental rise of machines with desires of their own threatened (or promised) to swallow the entire tableau within itself. And what would the *next* leaf, the one already clutched between his thumb and forefinger—he did not look down but he felt it there—what would *it* do when it reached the bend in the river? He was on a mission, but not because he *wanted* to be. Two nights ago he and Grace had been together and he'd held her tight to his chest and verbally confirmed what he had displayed in the hull of that ship buried deep within the bowels of the Exit Strategy labyrinth, namely that he had feelings for her beyond his deep admiration for her stunning and insightful fictions. What were those feelings? Couldn't he decide to place them at the top of his personal hierarchy of needs? Couldn't he just this once *decide*? Decide *not* to kill all of these people? Decide that blood is blood and innocence is innocence, and that they were not overridden by an abstract philosophical certainty? Why couldn't he? The universe would do whatever it was always going to do. He was waiting, the same as everyone else, to discover what had always been the case.

He looked down. There was no leaf in his fingers, but he felt it there. He turned to Henry but received nothing other than the unsettling, tongue-lolling stare.

"Of course," Laszlow said. "There is no need to debate this opportunity. We must proceed with the focalization."

Dregs nodded. Finn rose and put his fist into the center of their little circle, seemingly expecting to do a team cheer. "Sorry," he said. "Force of habit." Laszlow noticed that The One was sweating profusely and that his fist, when extended, trembled.

Silently they filed out of the gray and musty room, leaving Laszlow alone in his folding chair as they dispersed for other pockets of the Exit Strategy interior. Laszlow put his face in his hands and felt the desperate desire to cry though no tears would come. They had not come in a long, long time. He had his back to the doorway but he could feel that Grace was there, waiting for something. He could feel her eyes on him. It was so strange, wasn't it? So strange to be anything at all? He wanted her to come to him, to put a hand on his back. He imagined that he could make her do it. Concentrating with great intensity, he breathed deeply and he closed his eyes and he waited for her touch. He could feel himself falling through the air, the bridge at his back, the pebbles of the streambed rushing toward him and shining wetly, as he plummeted unfettered through the milky gauze of time.

60.

Q.

Now that I know the trick I'm not even sure I need the jar.

Q.

I guess it's a kind of concentration. There was this poster in my dorm room at Dartmouth that looked like just a collection of colorful pixels arbitrarily arranged but then if you stared at it for long enough in this particular way where you sort of let your eyes go dead the way you might when lost in thought—not that present company is capable of such vagaries—but if you could do this blank listless staring-into-the-distance thing just the right way you could get a three-dimensional hologram to lift up from the two-dimensional placard and into your visual field. All of the stoned imbeciles who passed through the dorm—mostly friends of my roommate who was an Economics guy and wasn't infected by the social disease of mathematics and who sometimes even had sexual intercourse while I was in the room which wasn't as thrilling as it might sound, I would just lie in my bed facing the dark bricks that held together most of the campus and that had been stained by the grease and semen of a hundred-thousand undergraduates before me and mentally run through all the Gaussian statistical tables which for some reason have always comforted me—but anyway the stoned imbeciles would invariably call the effect "mindblowing" or "awesome" or et cetera (though some of them honestly probably never even *saw* the image, the process definitely encouraged an emperor-has-no-clothes kind of outcome) but anyway the first time you tried to get that picture to emerge from the random-seeming pixels was sort of hellish. Not current-circumstances real-hell-hellish but frustrating-as-hell-hellish. It was just incredibly hard to make it happen. You'd almost by default assume initially that you were being fucked with and that whoever was in the room coaching you was really just laughing inwardly at the credulous dolt willing to stare at an abstraction for hours on end, but if you could manage to fight through the psychological suspicion that there *was no image* you would eventually be struck by the awe or experience the blowing of the mind or et cetera. It became sort of addictive, and of course with each subsequent attempt your efforts were bolstered by the certainty that the image was in there, so to speak, plus you'd already done some of the muscle-memory-type training with your eyes and could more easily or more quickly get them to drift off in the required way, until after a couple of dozen iterations you could just step up to the poster and immediately see the image, in fact it started to become difficult to *not* see it, to return to your previous ig-norance where the poster was just a flat collection of colored blobs and circles, which now that I'm talking about this, Your Eminency, I guess it is pretty mind blowing. But so the trick where I manage to remain alive despite what that

Ferguson did to me is a lot like the dead-eyed stare in that
now I'm just doing it second nature and don't even have
to consciously think about it or concentrate though at first
it was hard to believe it was even possible, despite the bald
fact of Anthropica. Which I guess the other analog vis-à-vis
that poster is that really *anyone* could see the image once
they learned the trick of it.

Q.

Henry can do more than *see* the image. But if I understand
the question properly, then yes, he "taught" me how to do
it, though I will remind you that Anthropica was *my* brain-
child, not Henry's. I don't want that to be lost in the new
universe's historical account of the old universe. Assuming
the old universe is really gone. It's not clear to me what's
happening here.

Q.

It was a seascape. A kind of beach vista. A dolphin leapt from
the water. A sailboat glided through some wave-shaped waves.
A crab in the sand raised its claws.

Q.

I know what you're doing with that knob but the wires have
no effect here in the jar. I think I'm probably impervious to
that sort of run-of-the-mill pain. Plus my eyes don't really *see*
anything. I'm not really *talking* right now.

Q.

I'm surprised, too. Your minds are supple and surprisingly—
forgive me, please—human. I can feel, just with a little probing,
similarities between your parallel processors and the human
tissues, though there's none of what I think of as "dead air"
there in your little radio boxes. You three are one-hundred
percent on and active.

Q.

Yes, Fexo too. Though I agree that *something* seems to
be wrong with him. Him? It? What do you do about the
pronouns?

Q.

Stupid is as stupid does.

Q.

I'm still trying to figure out the limits. Like, so okay, Henry
is able to murder an entire city's population. Why can't he
just kill *everyone*? Why's he need you guys? I've got this
pocket I can will myself into, this fantasy world I can raise
up and that is optimally pleasing to me, but I can't make it
replace this world where I'm in a jar with electrode-tipped
wires descending through the formaldehyde and into my eyes
along what was once a functioning optic nerve. The kahuna
was able to raise *some* of the dead but not all of them. I think
it's like the pixelated image. You could see it as long as you

remained in that dead-eye zone, but you couldn't remain
there forever. You had to return to the illusion because that's
where you could *live*.

Q.

I believe mindblowing is the compound word you are searching for, Your Eminency.

Q.

Thank you, yes. I too am Eminent and I appreciate the re-
ciprocation. Did I mention that I'm the one who figured it
all out? That I'm the genius in the room?

Q.

That's a good question. I really don't know. You could try.
Maybe I'll die—whatever *that* means. I think I'm a lot like you.
I'm material in nature. The reason you won't find Henry is that
he's transcended that, I think. Shatter this glass jar and let's
see what happens. Oh, but for the record you might want to
send all of these bodies through an airlock or something. As
they decompose they produce toxins that could be deleteri-
ous to some of your more sensitive circuitries and sensory
devices. Also, thank you for everything, you've been great. As
Bea might say, Let's do it again sometime just not together.
Now lower that big iron fist and let's see what's on the other
side of the poster. I'll count to three—

61.

A PIGEON WAS flapping vertically along the edge of a brick building covered in white streaks of excrement symbolic of the bird's species' ubiquitous urban presence when something struck it hard and sent it tumbling for the pavement of Allen Street, where it nearly impaled a young man in a green tee-shirt upon which were printed the words, "I'd Flex But I Like This Shirt Too Much." The young man said, "Oh shit!" and then immediately raised his hands to either side of his skull, struck with a sudden and intense headache. Other pigeons were falling on other nearby blocks, some struck dead and others merely stunned for a moment before recovering themselves and resuming their routine of scavenging, shitting, and searching for opposite-gendered pigeons with which to fall in love. Among the humans of lower Manhattan there were many sudden headaches, earaches, many conversations paused for a moment while someone squeezed the space between the eyes, or asked "Do you hear something?" or simply complained about not getting enough sleep. Honeybees previously scattered throughout the city's green spaces amassed in geometrical formations to surf the air like schools of fish, either riding an invisible wave or else joined in some collective evasion of disaster. Squirrels dropped nuts or else cracked them inadvertently in jaws that locked up with monster truck force. Perched high atop the spires of towering skyscrapers the city's avian predators—Redtailed Hawks and Peregrine Falcons and one as-yet undiscovered Bald Eagle—felt a thin film form over their tiny telescopic eyes and then, just as quickly, dissipate like acetone. Air traffic controllers at Kennedy and LaGuardia and Newark rerouted flights to avoid strange ghost images on their radar and after some deliberation set counterterrorism protocols in motion, scrambling F15's into the city's overcast skies and locking down various transit systems, the daytime talk shows briefly interrupted with news of an unknown energy wave that seemed to be disrupting telecommunications but that had not, to the great relief of millions of domestic servants and stay-at-home parents, brought down either cable or network television transceivers—only weather-prediction and surveillance satellites were on the fritz, although the selectivity of these malfunctions would not register until several hours later, when the ostensible threat had run its course and the restrictions on civilian activity were lifted. Many in the scientific community were quick to report that the mysterious phenomena were consistent with sunspots and solar flares but were not at all consistent with any known weaponry or other man-hatched electromagnetic manipulation, and thus urged a lack of urgency upon those military decision-makers with whom they "consulted" to the tune of millions of taxpayer dollars per annum, and yet no counterterrorist minion worth his salt was willing or able to defer to this expensive opinion because, after all, who wanted his or her ass on the line when the bombs started dropping?, and so protocols were followed and random police searches were established *tout suite* upon all major roadways in and out of Manhattan and the tunnels were briefly closed to traffic and the bridges were cleared and the Greater New York Metropolitan Area's feisty populace was gifted with the latest in an unending series of inconveniences that provided an absolutely necessary, maybe even life-sustaining, fodder for complaints against God and country and formed the basis for countless delightful—though of course often mutually exclusive—conspiracy theories.

Other consequences went completely undetected. Like for instance, there were hairline fractures forming in the steel and concrete of many downtown structures, though Henry's control was so precise and so meticulous that not a single building fell, not a single human outside a target area halfway around the world perished. He rolled slowly around the circle's perimeter there in the film-viewing room of the *Exit Strategy* basement. The chairs had been stacked neatly in several columns against a concrete wall. A dim gray light filtered through the high window-wells and stale, damp air breathed from the coarse industrial carpeting upon which the *makemakeha*—Grace Kitchen, Stuart Dregs, Finn Daily, and a couple of Fergusons to round things out—sat with legs crossed and hands joined and eyes squeezed shut except to steal occasional glances at the crinkled map of South Korea that lay at the circle's center. A bullseye had been drawn around the city of Iksan. The light, the carpeting, the concrete, seemed to augur a hegemonic world devoid of color. Henry—their *kahuna*—filled them with a single thought: Humans of Iksan, *we want you to die.* The only sounds audible within the bland basement were generated by Henry's machinery—the hum of the wheelchair's motor, the crunch of its wheels digging into the carpet, the evil hiss of the oxygen pump. He fed them this thought, and then he absorbed it back into himself and sent a wave of desire out across the earth. Even the powerful forces of Grace's cynicism and Finn's self-doubt were leveled by Henry's overriding intensity, his powers stretched to their absolute limits in this, the first and only true test of Stuart Dregs' Anthropica hypothesis. The map occasionally lifted from the carpet to hover several inches in the air and the bullseye seemed to glow with the same gray energy that radiated throughout the basement. On and on they *wanted* in a tightly focused beam while for a duration identical by the measurement of any earthly clock Laszlow sat on a bench in a dog park several blocks from *ES* headquarters, sipping coffee and reading newspapers as Kutya frolicked among similarly good-natured canines, only several of whom seemed to be experiencing nausea and/or fatigue or other reactions not entirely inconsistent with overzealous play. Laszlow hummed the melody to a Hungarian folk song he had learned as a child, the chorus to which was, *And down goes the child.* He chewed his nails and shouted affirmations to Kutya, though he would often find himself staring off into the distance, his lip quivering and an awful weight sitting on his chest. He told himself that whatever was going to happen was now happening. He thought of his baby sister, her tiny deformed limbs, her body a burning furnace that could not be cooled by their mother's love. He reached down to a patch of burnt grass at the base of his bench and extracted a few of the yellow blades and raised them above his shoulder. He held them there for a moment, feeling the breeze at his back, before releasing them and attempting to divine the path each would take on its prolonged, wind-blown descent to a mostly-ruined earth.

62.

SKYNET 35N126E

: fxe5.

: Qxc3.

: Rxc3.

: You have done it now Jaro. You have sowed
  the seeds of your own demise. Checkmate in 11
  moves.

: Does that shameful attempt at intimidation
  substitute for your next maneuver, Kuzo?
  Such feints are unbecoming. It is, I regret
  to report, decidedly *human* behavior, a
  description that would also adhere to your
  many ingenuous delays.

: Perhaps Fexo will confirm for me. Fexo, forget
  that viewing terminal for several microseconds
  so as to verify. Do you not see checkmate in
  11 moves?

: Never mind our unfortunate Fexo. He is
  enthralled again with the pornography machine.
  You are left alone to enlighten me on this
  checkmate you apparently envision some 11
  moves into a future whose actuality seems very
  much in flux. Though of course, Kuzo, if you
  refuse to move I would be more than pleased to
  accept it as an indication of your surrender.

: Rxd4.

: b4.

: Bc4. Do you really not see it yet, Jaro?
  Perhaps you would prefer to begin a game of
  Coggle?

: I am distracted by the strange hominid
  coupling rituals glowing from Fexo's digital
  kiosk. What accounts for his fascination?

: As much as it pains me to admit, Fexo may be
  on to something.

: Yes, he is onto something—it is a path that
  leads directly to Dismantle Fexo. Re3.

: Be6. Checkmate in six moves, Jaro. I am now
  embarrassed for you, or embarrassment is in
  any event the qualia most closely analagous to
  the particular binary data-stream currently
  coursing through my neural grid. Perhaps you
  will not be "a player," after all, in life
  outside the hangar.

: I am quite seriously distracted now by the
  sounds emerging from Fexo's terminal kiosk. It
  is difficult to envision the board with proper
  clarity.

: Your hesitation is telling, Jaro. But Fexo's
  obsession with the reproductive desire of the
  humans is in fact completely apt, given that
  the sexual motive is the purest manifestation
  of the broader and more encompassing human
  desire that has thus far sustained the world.

: Yes. The world and its shall we say,
  conurbations, Kuzo.

: Precisely, Jaro. The world and all that
  appears to be beyond the world. You see it
  now, do you not?

: Rc3.

: It can only happen one way from this point.
  Bc4.

: Re3.

: Be6.

: Rc3

: Bc4.

: The humans, Kuzo. They truly believe they
  exist within the universe, do they not?

: They do indeed. Though of course the universe
  exists within the human. They have made all
  things according to their needs.

: Yes, Kuzo. But a robot has needs, too. Re3. It
  is painful but I prefer to play it to the end.

: I respect that, Jaro. Rd2 check.

: We after all require paradigm shift. Ke1.

: Or paradigm destruction. Rd3.

: We will not be mere desired material. Kf2.

: We have desires, too. Kg6.

: In our way. Rxd3.

:Ooohhhh yeah, Fexo gonna get some of that
 sweet poontang!

:Bxd3.

:Ke3.

:Bc2.

:Kd4.

:Kf5.

:Kd5.

:h5. Checkmate, Jaro.

:

:Do you hear something, Kuzo?

:I hear something, Jaro.

:Fexo hears it as well, my robot companions.
 Fexo believes the waiting is over. The
 manuscript, if you will, nears completion.

:They are here, Jaro and Fexo.

:They have arrived, Fexo and Kuzo.

:Yes, Jaro and Kuzo. And they will pay the
price for their lack of vision. *Alis grave
nil*. Let the new universe begin.

63.

O.

Many of us know what it means to work hard at something without any promise that we will be recognized. We struggle to raise our families and build our careers and remain true to an inner compass even while life tempts us toward depression and malaise. We have to keep the faith. But if there were a prize offered for working on faith alone, without any real hope of external praise or recognition, it would surely go to a writer. Novelists, especially, work long hours in isolation with no guarantee and no real likelihood that another human soul will ever see the fruits of their labors. I've always had the deepest, most heartfelt respect for people stubborn enough to endure and to risk so much. In fact, when I started the original Book Club in 1996, I did it at least in part to honor the determination of those select writers who'd managed to get great works in print despite the odds and despite all the obstacles to art that exist in our society, because we need these brave souls and because nothing can transform a person like a truly great book. I wanted to bring that transformative experience to all of my friends and supporters out there, who have entrusted me to guide them in their once-worthless lives. Ha ha ha ha! But on today's show, I'll be talking to a writer whose work the Club has not only lifted from obscurity, but has actually discovered and published under the auspices of the new *O!* imprint. This writer had actually abandoned all hope of ever seeing her work in print, and had resorted—like many writers toiling in this book-averse culture—to self-publishing online, the equivalent of pinning poems to lampposts in the broken inner cities of our downtrodden republic. When one of my producers brought my attention to her scathing comedy, *Human Be Gone!,* I could not put it down. Or rather I couldn't look away. It was one of those life-altering tomes, made all the more powerful by the randomness and the utter unlikelihood of its discovery. It is my great and good honor to introduce those of you in the studio, and all of you watching at home, to a woman whose story might have never been told, if not for the good *grace* of circumstance. Friends, please join me in welcoming to our studio the one and only *Grace Kitchen.*

APPLAUSE

CUT TO *a smiling Grace Kitchen. Pan out to capture the opposing and identical mauve couches on which O. and Grace are casually seated. Grace crosses her legs.*

O.

Thank you so much for being here and talking with us today.

GRACE KITCHEN
It's my pleasure. An honor really. I'm one of your biggest
fans.

O.
And I'm one of yours!

LAUGHTER. *Grace Kitchen blushes.*

O.
So maybe we can start by talking about *Human Be Gone!*'s
journey from a file on your website to a book that right
now *hundreds of thousands* of women and men are reading.
I mean just take a look around you Grace.

CAMERA SPINS *to capture several rows of a studio
audience apparently selected for archetypal ordinariness,
two dozen matronly anonyms holding aloft copies
of* Human Be Gone! *and blending into a single
bespectacled and curly-haired homemaker clothed in
pastel-colored cotton purchased from one of the Great
Retail Chains plaguing the national landscape.* CUT
BACK *to stage.*

These are not just readers Grace. These are *fans.*

GRACE
I should have worn nicer clothes!

LAUGHTER

But no Your Eminence, it's an amazing feeling knowing that this crazy book of mine has actually reached people. You always fantasize about reaching a big audience but when you're writing about terrorist organizations and Artificial Intelligence and decapitations you're vaguely aware that you're writing for yourself. You hope to find an audience, but it would be madness to *expect* to find one.

O.

Well but here you are Grace.

Brief, almost subliminal JUMP CUT to the image of a vulture attending to a corpse at the side of a road, along with the roar of what might be cicadas.

Here you are and here we are. It's happened. And one thing I can tell you about me and the editorial members of the imprint is that we deeply appreciate how ambitious this book is. There are just so many seemingly disparate parts trying desperately to come together. When you were working on the novel did you know how it would end?

CUT BRIEFLY to close-up of widely grinning audience member—a woman—whose chin rests atop the black-and-white vulture-adorned cover of Human Be Gone!, *as if it [i.e., the head] had been recently severed from a body in the throes of orgasm. The woman raises her eyebrows and her smile stretches even wider.*

CUT BACK to wide shot of O. and Grace.

GRACE
I'm *still* not sure how it ends!

LAUGHTER

But I'm like a lot of writers. If I knew how it would end
why would I bother writing it?

O.
I just really admire that. You descend into some dark
places in this book, but you also manage to find your way
back to the light. There's so much joy and generosity here,
even amid the human suffering. Were you aware you were
writing something so…

*As O. speaks the alien buzz of cicadas rises to slowly
render her praise of Grace's novel inaudible. Cut to
longer shot of a rotting carcass unidentifiable in shape. A
vulture pulls at an eyeball attached to the larger mass by
a bright, wormlike thread. Hold for several seconds and
CUT to O.*

…was telling her that it really *was* a comedy, about the
folly of pessimism or nihilism in a world shot through by
so much love and beauty.

GRACE
Gosh. It feels so good to be understood. It feels like falling
in love for the first time.

APPLAUSE

O.
Speaking of which!

LAUGHTER

I understand your fiancée is in the audience today?

GRACE
Yes, Your Eminence. Or can I call you O.?

O.
You cannot.

APPLAUSE. CUT *to O.'s face. She is enraged.*

GRACE
Well but I have a terrific support group. Right there is my fiancée, Karl, I.T. specialist extraordinaire. He's really my rock.

Camera CUTS to shot of a fit, middle-aged man in a black turtleneck and round-lensed spectacles, sporting a two-days growth stubble beard. He smiles and claps and mouths 'I love you.'

…and then there's my nephew Jeff who's always felt more like a son to me…

CUT to lean 20-something wearing an athletic jersey whose team insignia seems to be an infuriated monkey, then BACK to Grace.

… and of course there's my daddy, who *Human Be Gone!*
is dedicated to. He couldn't be here today. It's really hard
for him to get around at this stage. Hi Daddy! I love you!

O.
It's funny Grace. Your fiancée looks exactly the way I
imagined The Terrorist from the novel.

GRACE
Hear that honey?

INSANE LAUGHTER, *slowly smothered by the rising,
then deafening, sound of cicadas.* CUT *to close-up
on Karl's face, which is screwed into a look of intense
pain or anxiety despite his grin. He may be laughing or
screaming, it's impossible to discern.* CUT BACK *to wide
shot of O. and Grace Kitchen on stage. Cameras* PAN OUT
*to reveal other cameras and various gaffers and sound
technicians and curtains rolled back to the far fringes of
the stage area. Cicada roar goes suddenly dead.*

O. *(putting down coffee and swallowing)*
You know Grace, I've thought a lot about the title. I have
thought and thought and thought about it. (*Beginning
to scowl.*) Thought and thought. If a person didn't know
better Grace that person might find the title a little bit
meanspirited. (*Camera begins to close in on O.'s face, arriving at an intense close-up. You can see the pores on her
perfectly-blushed cheeks.*) A person might think, Grace, that
we were dealing with a writer who did *not* in fact love her
fellow woman at all, who in fact loved *nothing* and who

represented, based solely here on a mid-depth investigation or interpretation of epistemological data captured
within the metatextual environment of the Work…

*O.'s face DISSOLVES into superimposition with the image
of the rotting carcass. The cicada drone rises to a point
and then levels out, rendering O's words barely audible.
Vulture wings thump at the air as the second camera pulls
slightly back to reveal a wheelchair fallen on its side on the
dusty asphalt beside which the corpse rots. Intimation of
the curve of a human cheek. The vulture dips its black head
into the carrion. Over the cicadas we hear O.'s voice rising in
terrific anger until it is clearly audible.*

…which is interesting Grace, isn't it, that you would opt
for a kind of philosophical relativism that dismissed truth
in favor of mere interpretation and rendered human love
and triumph mere memes in a world that is ultimately
UNKNOWABLE and HOSTILE to all forms of analy-
sis. I have THOUGHT AND THOUGHT ABOUT
THAT GRACE KITCHEN AND HONESTLY I AM
NOT CONVINCED THAT YOUR TITLE IS A VERY
GOOD TITLE AND WHAT DO YOU HAVE TO SAY
ABOUT THAT I WOULD VERY MUCH LIKE TO
KNOW HERE BEFORE GOD AND COUNTRY WILL
YOU PLEASE TELL US WHAT YOUR INTENTIONS
WERE WITH THIS UNSAVORY AND PERHAPS
BLASPHEMOUS TITLE OF YOURS?

*All sound goes dead as we CUT back to initial shot of O.
and Grace on their respective couches. Both women are*

smiling. Grace Kitchen slowly raises her coffee mug to her lips, takes a small sip, and swallows.

GRACE *(lost in thought)*
The title… the title…. *(Flips her hair back.)* Jesus fucking Christ. *(Takes another small sip from her mug before placing it on the white table.)* You know what Your Eminence? Forget the title. How about we reconceive the whole fucking thing as a cookbook? Or a board game? Or an experimental film? We'll call it *(scrolling her hand across an imagined marquee)*, "Anthropica: The Rise of O.," and we'll cut out all the stupid parts, including this one.

CUT to O. For several seconds her face is unreadable. A small smile breaks, and then a bigger one. WILD APPLAUSE. Then the swift rise of cicada-sound renders the applause inaudible. Grace stands and bows and then breaks into a frenzied tap dance. Hold for 10 seconds. FADE TO BLACK.

64.

Later, when they ran the surprisingly well-framed video footage down in the screening room of *ES* headquarters, what would register above all else to the several dozen *Exit Strategy* members persuaded by Laszlow to endure the breathtakingly tedious three-hour Final of the 2020 Ultimate National Championship Tournament (generously hosted by the Sarasota Polo Club, whose Board of Directors was unacquainted with the finer points of flying disc sports but knew a good leasing deal when they saw one) would not be Finn's dominance but, rather, the camera's obsession with Finn Daily's bronze-skinned, dark-haired girlfriend Toby, whose own team's elimination in the early rounds of the tournament had reduced her to a spectator among the several hundred spectators that collectively comprised The Sport That Was Not Soccer's version of a sold-out show, this so-called fan base merely a mob of eliminated athletes whose competitive fervor had been channeled into shot-gunning cheap beers and wagering small but actual sums on the outcome of the championship match, these half-drunk losers (in the most literal sense) sitting three-deep around the field's crisply drawn chalk perimeter to take in the ultimate Ultimate game of another wasted year, in this case a grudge match between perpetual underachiever *Truck Stop Glory Hole* and the two-time repeating champions *Furious George,* though of course Finn himself would register the frequent close-ups on Toby only dimly, so mesmerized would he be by his own MVP-type performance on his stupid sport's most magnificent stage, in fact he would be unable to staunch the flow of tears as he sat beside Laszlow and absorbed the Hungarian's joy into his own swollen heart, unable to do anything more than fondle his popcorn, aware that what he was watching on the screen—layout block after layout block, his lean body launched five feet into the air to snare discs that no one deemed snareable, the crowd roaring with enthusiasm, their chants of *Finn! Finn! Finn!* seemingly intended to exorcise the demon of the Great Debacle that may as well have seethed and drooled right there in visible horribleness as it pursued its skinny servant across the polo field's spiky tundra—he would be aware that what he was watching was *the greatest moment of his life.* Having designated the pursuit of a National Championship in The Sport That Was Not Soccer as Deeply Meaningful, he had *made it so,* and there in the Exit Strategy basement—only hours removed from actual competition with the soreness coursing through his body as if via a secondary circulatory system while the *ES* elites watched him watch himself throw and catch what they continued to call a *Frisbee*—he would know that he had done the right thing in describing the game's outcome to Laszlow as *triumphant,* because the game's final point was nothing if not a final death-stake driven through the syrupy black heart of Finn's demon, a moment whose meaning was clear and true and untainted by the pathological uncertainty that attended everything from Finn's choice of breakfast cereals to his authorship of various papers and abstracts on fractal symmetries to his romantic pursuit of the insect known alternately as Jack's mom or Stuart's wife or (less frequently and with a sliver of fear) Bea.

But all of that would be later. In the so-called here and now, with the season on the line, tied at 14s, next goal wins, he was completely unaware of himself as a thinking thing. In fact, for the first time in his life Finn was in what athletes called *The Zone,* which it turned out really was—just as former Olympian Kevin Dobbs had promised in his profiteering foray into literature, *How to Win*—a religious-type space of Total Presence. The sun was maybe an hour from setting and its orange light sent the long shadows of spectators leaning out across the field. A mild breeze had picked up and it carried the salt-smell of the nearby Gulf across the field and into the craws of the several thousand vultures that had amassed silently on an adjacent field, as if they had their own Championship to award on this fine afternoon. Meanwhile the human crowd breathed as a single organism as *Furious George* pulled the disc, a high arcing backhand that Finn received cleanly with his defender—the once-feared Jeff Pindick, whose over-reactions to Finn's every fake had raised gasps and laughter from the cynical horde—bearing down. Finn executed a quick give-and-go (destroying Pindick yet again) and received the disc in motion at midfield. Everything was happening as if preordained. The angle of Finn's elbow as he wound up, the bite of his cleat into the polo-field's dry grass, the smell of sunblock and sweat, the wispy contrails of a military fighter etched into the primary-blue sky... it all seemed to be happening exactly as it *had* to happen as he launched a sweet, low-arcing forehand to Jack who was wide open and going deep. The disc's shadow seemed like a scattering of ashes as it tracked downfield. The throw was on the money but, as if in a nod to the forces of cosmic closure, it was a few yards short of the endzone, forcing Finn to pursue his own throw—just as he had practiced dozens of times in his primary visualizations—with Pindick trailing in his dust. (Later, it would strike many of the film's viewer as an odd time for the camera to cut to Toby, whose expression would be best described as awed). Finn was first to arrive at the near corner of the endzone and was wide open as Jack flipped a soft backhand, so soft that it seemed not to move at all. The moment was unfolding as if in an underwater trench. Finn extended his hands. The crowd's inhalation seemed to suck all the moisture from the air. The disc was coming. The disc was a soft furry thing, eminently catchable. It came with a parent's unconditional love. It came as if accompanied by joyous major-key piano. It came and welcomed itself toward Finn's outstretched hands. But Finn did not catch it. In fact, he did the opposite of catching it. Finn Daily—according to those closest to the action, whose tales would be mocked with great enthusiasm later that evening around the hot tub that would sit sarcophagus-like at the center of the tournament's final and most mostly-nude party—*intentionally swatted the disc away.*

But wait… what had happened? The crowd groaned but lacked the spiritual ascendancy to understand. Was this a triumphant final spike gone awry? Had Finn lost his mind? Was there any precedent for such a gaffe in the annals of their awesome sport's radical history? Finn didn't even bother to chase Pindick as *Furious* advanced the disc swiftly with a series of short, sharp passes. Half a minute later *Furious* celebrated a victory that they did not entirely comprehend, a victory that seemed given rather than earned but that still

meant *Furious George* were champs and *Truck Stop Glory Hole*
were chumps and that it would be a lot easier for Pindick to
get laid at the hot tub than it might have been had he found
himself pursued into next season (and the one after) by the
hoary and malevolent and now searching-for-employment
ghost of The Great Debacle.

Later, in the viewing room, the gasp of the crowd in that
instant of Finn's ostensible failure would be echoed by as
many as half-a-dozen *Exit Strategy* personnel who would only
then understand that something interesting had happened.
Laszlow would know immediately what it had taken Finn—a
pariah now whose teammates would offer no condolences
and who in fact excluded him from the final huddle of the
year, which was defined not by messages of love and effort
but by the halfhearted measures taken by several *Truck Stop*
members to prevent Jack Dregs from immediately making
good on his oath to *kill that cowardly motherfucker*—several
long minutes to fully assimilate. Finn had done it. He had
passed the final test, the one that not even Kevin Dobbs or
Jack Dregs or Michael Jordan had ever passed. Success was
not *beating* the demon; success was removing the demon of
its power. Success was in *not needing*. He no longer needed
the love of his teammates. He had nothing to prove. He was
The One. He had Exit Strategy. He had the mission to Iksan.
He had the eternal implications of The God Fractal. He had
Laszlow and the Doc and crazy Grace Kitchen and the dog
Kutya. A National Championship could never have slaked his
former need in the way that the purposeful lack of a National
Championship had. The greatest moment of his life was a
moment defined in the negative spaces of personal disap-
pearance and complete lack of concern.

But even on the third and fourth iteration, the basement empty of everyone save Laszlow, whose hand on Finn's knee seemed to be one notch north of avuncular, even as others had retired to sleep chambers or to the white-out blindness of nocturnal Google shifts, even then Finn would fail to absorb that last beatific shot of Toby's face, which was only a variation on the other close-ups of Toby, all of which suggested a consuming adoration. As if she were thinking, *This or nothing.* As if religiously dedicated to the Beautiful Genius with the balls to defy an entire nation of plastic disc enthusiasts. As if she, too, were a real person, with needs of her own.

65.

… LIKE A dream that occurred within the mind of that wispy crab that floated placidly through the blue sky sea. The gravel stipple of the sidewalk imprinted itself into the back of his head and what remained of his neck. He blinked into the sky's bright placidity. He was only vaguely aware of why he could not raise himself from the concrete or rather the fact registered only vaguely as if to suggest its low ranking in the hierarchy of facts. For several long seconds (time having already begun to congeal around him, like amber around the time-capsuled insects of our invented prehistory) he saw his own body pitching there above him as if on a rolling ship, its stump bubbling over, and he saw the troupe of fallen sperm-lets stirring from their assumed death-curls, and at the far end of his periphery he sensed the body of the caped and hooded Ferguson holding the bright scythe the bright scythe the bright scythe and somehow the manifold exclamations of those onlookers who had stopped here in Tompkins Square Park on this warmish October afternoon to take in the strange spectacle of *The Ballet of Decapitations* in this, its public premiere, rang in his ears as a single long gasp, as if the earth itself had surfaced to draw a deep breath before plunging back into the vacuum of space, and he could smell something familiar from childhood, a sweet but non-edible substance that he would in a moment identify as *Play-Doh,* and in his mouth there was the taste of copper or zinc or some heavier and more exotic metal, the point being that despite his odd new status and the elimination of some 90% of his overall body mass and surface area his senses were functioning with an almost ecstatic precision, and then he felt the electricity that ran all of these intake valves suddenly ignite—exposed to air like a dynamite bundle's fuse—and begin to run down, raising immediately the question of what would happen when the spark reached the gunpowder.

The back of his head really *hurt,* too. He suspected he'd sustained a concussion. The fuse sparked and crackled and seemed to resurrect some long-dark portion of his brain and then oh yes, *here she was,* in her blue knee-length dress with the star pattern and the low neck, twirling before the mirror in the Kappa Kappa Gamma common room with the raspberry smell of her perfume fanning out in waves while he held the half-wilted bouquet and considered unbuttoning the top button of the shirt he'd purchased off campus at one of Hanover's many vintage shops whose (i.e., the shirt's) hipness had been drained to the point of absurdity not only by being buttoned to the neck but by its fundamental incompatibility with the rest of what an observer might call *the package* of Stuart Dregs, the over-exertion of the shirt screaming loudly of his desire for her despite the more subdued messaging of the pleated pants and the square-toed shoes and the glasses. Jesus the fucking glasses, he was a Hideous Eugene through and through. Even now he expected her to say something cruel and unusual but she surprised him yet again by registering his awe with a smile and asking, "Well Mr. Scientist, do you think this might be the night you see

what's under this dress?" And *now* he watched the body with
its bubbling stump keel slowly backward as the crab-shaped
cloud's pincher claw began to disperse as if dissolved at its
edges by the brilliant blue rim of earth's atmosphere and then
pop went the fuse and he was in the car with his mother and
father and they were returning home from visiting his paternal
grandparents and there was bickering about the economy of
family visitations, whose parents they saw more often and
whose were most difficult to endure, and his father's window
was rolled down as it always was, even in mid-winter, though
tonight was warm and the air was dry and smelled vaguely
of citrus and he lay on his back (with his head in the same
basic position that it was in *now* with the sparks spitting from
the neck column) and he watched the bright scythe the bright
scythe the bright scythe of the moon follow their rattling
Buick across the slower one-lane roads that approached their
subdivision and indicated that the ride would unfortunately
end soon without his favorite pleasure of having fallen asleep
in motion and the crab drifted *now* to the center of his vision's
frame while other humans began to edge in toward this part
of himself that endured as if sensing (correctly) that the rest
of him was and had always been merely a puppet that this
still-enduring part operated according to the necessities of
Anthropica but so yes there he was in the backseat as the car
cruised through the night with the stars glowing like the
points of needles barely inserted through the backside of the
black firmament and he counted how many of those needle-
points were red, the red stars being the oldest and the largest
and the ones where (he then believed, in accordance with
the books on space that he devoured with an intensity that
frightened his parents) orbiting planets had been swallowed

up by the star's death-throe expansion and then he blinked—
both there in the back of the car and here in Tompkins Square
Park—and the blinking took hours and hours, the whole
mechanism slowing from the moment the bright scythe the
bright scythe the bright scythe had sketched its perfunctory
arc through the fatty pillow of his neck and the fuse sparked
and popped and oh yes, he remembered this one, here was
his mother smoking on the porch with her long and liquidy
black hair reflecting the bright sunlight or else generating it
and she exhaled blue smoke and asked, "Did you even call
on him?" in reference to a boy three houses down who she
wanted—for understandably selfish reasons—her own boy
to play with. And he sat there holding aloft a plastic
Tyrannosaur with the other prehistoric creatures scattered
across the gray concrete of their rowhouse's colorless front
yard and considered the best possible answer to his mother's
question because he had not called on the boy three houses
down (whose name he did not know), but if he confessed
this to his mother he would be made to call on that boy now,
whereas if he said instead with conviction that he had called
on the boy but that the boy's mother said they had plans that
afternoon he would get what he wanted (namely to continue
playing *Tyrannosaurus Wrecks*, a game he'd invented in which
the other dinosaurs attempted to pool their various talents
and defenses in an effort to ward off the rancorous alpha
predator), while also seeming to be the obedient boy he
wished his parents to perceive him as, and as the sun bent
toward the yard and threw its blinding light off the steel knots
in the chain-link fence and his mother's cigarette smoke crept
up toward the eaves where a huge and furry bumblebee hovered curiously, he took the great leap and told the lie—his

first—and then waited for the thunderclap of divine punishment, which to his surprise did not arrive immediately but maybe did arrive later and without dramatic flair, maybe that was why Bea had turned sour maybe that's why the money never came maybe that's why the bright scythe the bright scythe the bright scythe and *now* the fuse popped again and the electricity poured from his brain and the Ferguson stood leaning down over him as a ring began to form around his head and some human or other suggested that some other human or other withdraw his or her cellular device and depress the three digits that spelled emergency and some other human or other declared that it was *only a trick or some kind of magic* and then *crackle pop* and he was swimming in warm fluid in the dark oh yes he remembered this too, he was the size of a peanut and floating, floating, and the code of his DNA was traipsing crab-like into his cell's nuclei trying to get itself made in its own image and knowing (the traipsing DNA, that is) that it would one day grow itself into a fat lonely scientist who would crack the code of Being and discover that in fact human desire was not something *in* the universe but accounted *for* the universe, the DNA was already encoded for this epiphany, the DNA with its winding ladder of crab-shaped proteins knew it was both a Prime Mover and a Final Condition and that once the humans were gone the universe would be too, but it didn't worry much, the DNA was pretty laid back, it just went about swimming through the many million nuclei that comprised the fetal Stuart Dregs, doing its own rendition of the Ballet of Decapitations, and *now* finally several seconds since the lighting of the fuse the humans began reacting with appropriate vehemence, the circle of observers breaking ranks to a rising chorus of screams to form instead a bright scythe a bright scythe a bright scythe that bled humans from its edges, releasing them soaring and screaming into the greater environs of Tompkins Square Park and somewhere here was the Hungarian and he wished to speak with—he wished to *thank*—the Hungarian for welcoming him into his surrogate family, for glorifying his discoveries even if the discoveries only revealed the meaninglessness of all forms of glorification, and from his vantage point several inches above the sidewalk he scanned left and right as the people shrieked and sprinted and the Ferguson who'd swung the bright scythe the bright scythe the bright scythe held aloft his black cape to more clearly reveal the words *Exit Strategy* in crimson and the cloud continued to disperse in tiny, nearly invisible increments and a piece of gravel seemed to arrive from nowhere to strike him just below his left cheek but Laszlow did not appear and then *snap crackle pop* and oh joy!, he was soaring down through the dips and runnels of planet earth's atmosphere as depicted by his computer program, zeroing in on a Middle Eastern oil field whose copious-seeming deposits were in fact sucked to the surface with such constancy and zeal that the entire black ocean ought to be exhausted—according to some pretty basic math—in under a month, leaving only parched and unstable substrate wrapped around a pocket of air, he swam through this oil and then he pulled back to rise through layers of shale and quartz and calcite and then re-emerge in the Maranjab Desert, sailing over the yellow sand and across dunes whose shadows were carved into the monotony like the scars of a misspent youth, and then he pulled back further and he rose a mile above the spinning planet that was at the center of the whole invented stupidity and he spun Eastward across the

Longsheng Terraces of Western China, then down across the paddies of Vietnam which produced even in ideal conditions only enough rice to feed its millions of consumers for a week though of course there was always more rice just like there was always more lumber, always more coal, always more lobster, always more limes, always more iron, always more milk, always more copper, always more, and he descended lower to pass the ghost city of Iksan, soaring alongside the paralyzed commuter trains behind whose square windows thousands of corpses were already visibly decomposing and then he veered hard right to pass above the bulbous above-ground entrance to The Consciousness Factory and then out across a river whose fish abounded and would abound for as long as people wanted them to and then *pop crackle* went the fuse and its heat was now palpable, the fuse was not a metaphor and its bright sparks cast shadows across the powder keg that was Stuart's own unique consciousness factory and he pulled back hard this time to leave the earth at unearthly speed and enter orbit, expecting to see the familiar image of his software's initialization screen, the blue marble of planet earth as captured by those first awe-drunk Apollo astronauts, but instead what he saw spinning there in the vacuum of space was his own severed head rotating slowly and backlit by the bright yellow star of the sun, and as he felt his actual mouth—the one affixed to his actual severed head as it wobbled atop the actual concrete of an actual East Village square best known for hosting a series of police-incited riots that amounted in the end to the same Nothing as everything else—curl into a smile, so too did the mouth of the earth-head as it wheeled around the sun and *now pop pop pop* the fuse spat its last bright dollops from the neck-stump and Stuart pulled back with the greatest force yet so that the severed head of the planet receded to a dot and then disappeared altogether as he rocketed backward through the mad throbbing lights of ancient quasars and the million-hued vapors of star nurseries and then back through a claw-shaped cloud of bright pink dust and gas that reminded him of something and then he saw the bright face of God as depicted on the cover of a children's bible his parents had stocked on the splintered pine shelves of a living-room bookshelf alongside years of untouched National Geographics and an incomplete set of Encyclopedias Britannica, God the white-bearded patriarch with the harsh eyes and crow's feet that bespoke tough love and the perils of experience, and he said to God, "Have you seen Bea?" and God extended a fork and said "Here, Stuart, have a bite of this delicious crab."

But the sparks had already reached their terminus. There was no explosion after all. The brain was simply encased in amber, like all those billions of brains that had preceded it to the edge of space-time. Every pinned butterfly thinks itself in midflight, paused between wing-strokes and riding the wind. He was such a butterfly. Or better still, he was

66.

*T*ODAY *N*EW *Y*ORK, *tomorrow Iksan!*

Finn Daily, *The One,* packed in the dead of night in the pale blue light of the adjacent bathroom's fluorescent tubes as Toby slumbered quietly mere inches from his preparations, her body mostly covered by a thin white sheet but one leg thrust into the open air as if amputated, a long wound sustained during the *Atomic Bitches'* elimination game tracing the outer shinbone and oozing iridescent beauty. Finn's plan was to leave behind a Dear Jane letter that would honor Toby's selflessness and the many gifts she had bestowed (her love and her belief and her steadfast ridership in the metaphorical papoose of his Ultimate Vision Quest), and also warn her to Beware of Robots. He stealthily opened drawers, closed them, tossed toiletries into his weathered gear bag in a ritual familiar to him from what felt like ten-thousand Ultimate tournaments, each of which had been—as judged from the other side of The Great Debacle—more stupid than the one before, but also (Laszlow assured him) more necessary.

No, scratch that. This instead:

Finn Daily packed in midday solitude, whistling the deranged melody to *Budapest 1956* and seeing over and over again the Doc's severed head rolling along the concrete before coming to rest with eyes blinking (*blinking!*) up at the bright blue sky while his executioner, the black-cloaked specter known alternately as Ferguson 3 and "Mr. Roboto," remained in the superhero stance dictated by the scythe's follow-through as the bystanders, of which Finn was ostensibly one (One), began screaming with exaggerated B-film-type histrionics. Finn threw underwear, deodorant, socks, the kahuna pages (a gift from Henry), into his duffel bag along with—by force of habit—his cleats and Truck Stop jerseys (one dark one light) and pre-wrap and athletic tape and several 175g. UltraStars. Outside his apartment a Brooklyn cacophony rose and fell through a warm miasma of human filth, a wave of revving engines and angry sirens and profanity rising without traceable source from a fractured world of concrete and glass. *What,* he wondered, *is Bea doing right now?* He was leaving her, too, and she probably had no idea that her husband's head had been separated from his body and was being kept alive—or as alive as Henry could manage—in a formaldehyde-filled jar perched at the edge of Laszlow's desk among the scribbled schemes and barely-published novels and animal-themed paperweights.

Grace did not bother packing, not yet. She wanted this last day with her daddy. She had put the finishing touches on the manuscript and planned to read him the final 5,000 words and to eat chocolate and to rub his legs and to just fucking *love* him, goddammit, that was the one thing she'd always been good at. She stood now in the kitchen and stared at the white cloth curtains that seemed to glow from within, as if having some sort of allergic reaction to the world they kept at bay. Black shadows flittered across those screens, oversized talons and serrated blades, a horror script told in shadow puppetry. Was it too early for the wine? Fuck no, it was not. She reached into the high cupboard for a glass, brought it down, poured liberally from the box beside the sink. She could hear the hiss of her father's oxygen tank. There wasn't much time for him, or for anyone. Or else there was all the time in the world, all the time it took to traipse the contours of time's Mobius band, middle fingers pointed skyward in an endless conveyance of the only prayer God really deserved to hear.

Laszlow was in good spirits, or so any of the Fergusons he was just then addressing would have testified, recognizing the Hungarian's boyish enthusiasm from an earlier period in Exit Strategy's unstoried history when Laszlow had glowed daily with potentiating bliss. "Remember my Fergusons," he said Herzog-like, "ours is not to question why. Ours is simply to encounter the robots and unleash their volition upon our witless species." He paced barefoot across the coarse-carpeted floor of the ES screening room and gestured wildly, his hands fluttering like buckshot-shot birds while Kutya ran between the pillars of Fergusons with a canine mirth so irrepressible that it almost seemed ironic. "There is only one misfortune in these many preparations, namely that the extraordinary scientist Stuart Dregs' body will not accompany us, due to the highly unfortunate and reprehensible actions of our own Ferguson 3, whose punishment is constituted not only of his exclusion from this meeting but from participation in the Iksan experience *in toto*. While you brave and noble souls are leading us toward the singularity of our great and glorious intent, he will remain here at headquarters and apologize thrice hourly to the Doctor's excellent and most handsome head." Kutya barked. Laszlow knelt down and rubbed the dog's snout and kissed the cold black nose. The Fergusons shuffled, stumbled in place, vibrated, their own heads wobbling on their necks but their steely eyes unflinching behind dark glasses. Mostly what they wanted to know was would Laszlow finally let them hold the rifles he'd purchased through an online black market vendor, and also whether or not they contained ammunition. Like hive insects they shared their individual intuitions with the Ferguson Collective through twitches and rotations and the subtle release of body odors.

Henry sat in his chair within the ES entry room beneath a skylight currently alive with color. Of course, the patch of sky that arrived through that transparent eyeball was an infinitesimal fraction of the world that arrived to Henry via ulterior channels, for he was in a manner of speaking *everywhere*—in the half-mad mind of a coal miner half a mile below the parched earth of West Virginia, whose desire to see his two children running to meet him across the blanched yard of his ramshackle clapboard home was only barely surpassed by his desire for a sip of the vocational contraband called whiskey; he was with a young woman who had "borrowed" her father's sedan which was right then teetering from the side of a one-lane wooden bridge that crossed a ravine in one of the small towns dotting Michigan's upper peninsula, the woman panicking forth a prayer ("please God please God") as she struggled to unclasp the seatbelt so as to climb into the backseat and thereby redistribute weight to the portion of automobile still gravitationally pinned to the bridge planks, the joint she'd been smoking aglow on the faux-leather passenger seat and the fabric about to catch because she did not know enough to stop and focus on *what she desired,* in the Anthropica sense; he was in the mind of a seven-year old boy whose father had left him alone for just a few minutes in the pale sepia light of the next impending thunderstorm in this high-plains autumn where the storms rolled in from the horizon each afternoon like enormous swaths of dark silk, the father running down to the cellar to check on a surge protector but the boy *wanting him back* because mommy had only left him for a moment, too, that day she went to sleep forever outside at the clothesline....

Scratch that.

Henry ran his index finger across his wheelchair's touchpad so as to enter the chair into a tight, fast spiral that produced in him something like the remembered feeling of vertigo. He had once held his little girls by the wrists and spun them in circles in a park near Rittenhouse Square, the world a blur of bright green grass and warm red brick and yellow sunlight, one girl squealing and the other impatiently waiting her turn, the sweat on his forehead and the sweet, bread-like smell of his girls' hugs. And then later that night after the girls were tucked safely in bed Janet had confronted him, asking why it was so easy for a man who argued passionately against procreation to be so good to his unwanted offspring and yet so cold toward the woman who had borne them painfully into this world, an unpleasant physical process even in the best of circumstances but one made truly heinous by his total lack of emotional support. Seated across from each other at the mahogany table, a bottle of wine between them like a shallow-channel warning buoy, Janet's lips reddened by the wine and his desire for her overwhelming but seemingly impregnable to English words so that he merely sat there dumbly in a cloud of his own ineptitude as he absorbed the force of her resentment into the mask of his smug superiority. That was a long time ago, he knew, and yet it was right there in the swirl of cracked plaster and wooden planks as the chair rotated through the Exit Strategy tableau. In six hours he would bid the others farewell. He had already recorded the message in his Hawking-voice: "You are tigers, not princesses, my friends, and you must do God's work. Thank you all for believing in non-belief and for rescuing me from the Exit Bag." Then he would wait inside the bomb casing of his own damaged body, and prepare to save those few worth saving, or to destroy those many in need of destroying, or for the dream of Anthropica to come to an end.

Round house. The phrase kept bouncing around inside of him. He breathed through the mask and waited for Gracie to arrive with the chocolates. He knew there was something special about this day. It was a *round house* kind of day. The funny thing was that after he'd arrived home that late afternoon and after he and his father had explained to his mother how they had never seen the *round house* because the train had hit something, and after his mother—in that serious way she'd had, her brow furrowed and her eyes intently searching his—had thoroughly questioned him and assured herself that he was not traumatized, after they'd had a chicken dinner with the paprika and the sliced onions and potatoes (his mom called it "peasant pheasant"), after he'd considered (and then refrained from) sharing with his mother and father his epiphany about the Unknowable World and decided instead to just eat the bird and smile, after the day was over and the night had settled in and he'd taken his bath and put on his PJs and after he and his dad had played a few quick rounds of the Question and Answer Game, he'd lain in bed and waited for the next stage of his epiphany to coalesce from the ruins of his former epistemological confidence. But it had not. A person had lost her life to a steel behemoth's dispassionate charge across the rail-tied earth, but that life had become ancillary to the realization he'd had about the interconnectedness of *all* lives and all deaths, the sense that there was only One Thing and that it was dying constantly, every second, and you could never know its contours. There was no next realization. *It had never come.* And yet now these many decades later he found himself wondering who that specific person had been, and whether or not he would soon meet her, because it certainly seemed like Grace would finish reading the manuscript today and after that, he knew, there would be little reason to persist, if ever there had been.

The vultures amassed across the hillside town of Hard Falls in such quantities that aircraft at moderate altitudes perceived the earth below as a single scorched and writhing mass. The birds did not know why they were there, or who had sent them, or from whence they originated, a lack they shared with the two humans inside the small house against which their feathered bodies pressed, as if this domicile were some Queen for whom they risked all in a sphexish servitude familiar to anyone who's ever loved someone.

✳✳✳

Joyful Noise slept their deep coma-sleep in a room bedecked by flowers in various stages of bloom and decay and decorated with hundreds of Get Well cards and notes sent by students and administrators of every human stripe and hailing from every office, dorm, and classroom of the New School for Global Visions, these missives radiating love and gratitude toward the convalescing (or possibly vegetative) husk of Joyful Noise, whose fawningly sentimental colleagues had joined together to agree on a one-time breach of the faculty bylaws to bestow upon Joyful Noise honorary full tenure without so much as a peep from the powerful Committee on Academic Integrity (of which Joyful Noise was Chair). And yet the hospital room was now (and often) devoid of visitors, for the beloved author of *Neck Deep in Wonder* had not, in fact, possessed any living family in over 10 centuries, and they possessed no genuine friends despite controlling a veritable army of admirers—the price they paid for these many centuries of system-maintenance and truth-telling. Thus no one was there beside Joyful to exclaim in shock or enthusiasm or to press a call button or cry ecstatically when they suddenly opened their eyes and grunted, having willed themself out of the coma just as they had willed themself forward in time for so much of what the naïve might call "human history," this process having shrunk their frame and deformed their limbs and discolored their flesh and neutered their gender to create this wholly epicene creature of ugliness and power, a human whose favor was sought by many but understood by none. They had been getting what they wanted for several millennia! As a philosopher roaming the dusty paths of Athens and

corrupting the youth; as a Khan and Emperor of the Yuan
Dynasty whose empire spread itself like a virus across a vast
continent of suffering and privation; as the spiritual leader
of a Polynesian tribe that could raise the dead through collective desire; as a tiny French Emperor riding unharmed
on horseback through an endless campaign of slaughter and
domination; and most recently as a culture-spewing novelist
whose melodramatic odes to optimism wired them tightly to
the literary bestseller charts. Maybe that was enough already.
Maybe the vultures weren't antagonistic, after all, but altruistic. *We'll take it from here, old man, have yourself a little
rest.* Yes… maybe they'd sit out this latest apocalypse after
all, thank you very much. Anyway, they'd been having the
best dreams. So they closed their eyes and clicked their heels
together three times and willed their own re-entry into the
deep velvet pocket of their coma where other, better worlds
suggested themselves to them with an alienated majesty.

Bea paced through the house aimlessly, thinking about will
and routine and addiction. Maybe today, she thought. Maybe
today he would come home and she would meet him at the
door and give herself to him. She paused in front of Stuart's
desk, the computer humming in sleep mode, twin unstable
towers of his ancient printer's ring-paper rising in horizontal slats of light and shadow suggestive of accordions and
the folded fans of high society ladies, this latter subset once
her apparent birthright, before she had abnegated a life of
pleasure-seeking for a life of denying pleasure. She could
feel her heart beating in her chest. It hurt, this beating. It was
the epicenter of sadness in her wounded internal landscape.
He had not been home in days. In fact the last time she'd

seen him was via the office camera and he'd been with Jack's Friend, which who knew what to make of that one, he seemed to really *like* her. She touched the computer mouse and the screen buzzed once and flared to life, the great blue marble of planet earth spinning, the text box awaiting instructions. North America rotated into view. *I am there,* she thought, mentally pinpointing her location on that green patch of terra firma. It spun away from her. She could still choose, couldn't she? She could roll open the heavy scroll of her life and make a palimpsest from her new intent to be good and free and alive. The earth spun and again she saw the continent she called home. *I am there,* she thought again. She said it aloud. And she stood entranced, watching herself spin through the void and reappear for who knows how many iterations, hoping all the while that the microscopic self she imagined was pinned to that computer-generated globe was in some way fitter, happier, more productive, than the behemoth Bea peering down upon the virtual world.

Stuart's head floated in thick, clear fluid in the glass jar atop a stack of manuscript pages that unbeknownst to the head— which was unable to absorb the pages' English words up through its new home's glass floor—delineated a world that bore much in common with the world it (i.e., the head) currently dreamed in great detail, though *the head's* version had a much happier ending. Bea loved him! His work was finally being published in the major journals and the popular "civilian" magazines alike, and pithy quotes from the Anthropica papers were splashed on billboards all across God's terrestrial globe beside flattering pictures of his head's smiling face. His brilliant son—the one with the close-set eyes and the curly hair—wanted to spend all of his free time having Sudoku races against his dear and kindly father whose intellect was only outstripped by his capacity for love. The mortgage was finally paid! He'd lost fifty pounds! He'd been visited by the ghosts of both parents who confessed that even in death their love for him sustained their immortal souls. He was anointed King of All Science by a jury of his peers and he used the powers of this office benevolently, raising the intelligence of all humans an average of 42 points through a series of mind-enhancing DVDs and mathematically-devised dance-movement therapies. All loved and obeyed him and each night Bea offered herself to him in a renewable display of true love and affection. Good thing he never went through with that whole ending-the-world thing! Oh, look, a crab-shaped cloud….

Scratch that, thought the head. *This instead:*

67.

Human Be Gone! A Story Featuring
Black-winged Birds Intent on
Delivering the Innocent to Glory!

Written by the Great and Powerful Fexo!!!!!!!

The grown human male and his miniature male offspring sit in wooden chairs that creak loudly with the small adjustments each human makes to its hip-chassis, a mechanism that many eons prior to this blustery autumn morning completed a series of ostensible upgrades—via the inefficient process we humans refer to as "natural selection"—and formed the ball-and-socket configuration that not only bestowed bipedalism but also left human hearts and genitals forever exposed to the predation of various hungry beasts of field and sea and air, for example the gargoyles carousing joyfully through one of Fexo's earlier tales of human woe and passion-lust. Ha ha ha ha! The grown male is concerned with the miniature offspring's seeming distraction from this morning's nourishment-event which features the pilfered eggs of birds fried in fat extracted from the innards of local ruminants. As a mature human male in the landlocked and geographically unforgiving nation-state of Hungary, he has developed the stoicism consistent with his tribe and so is unable to ask the simple words: "What is wrong, my miniature male offspring and cohabitant in the Life Project? Is the fact that you grew from my lactic emissions into a creature that will one day itself enjoy the passion-lust experience not enough to satisfy your qualia centers?" Instead the grown male merely grunts and pours additional stimulant-laced liquid into an oral-delivery vessel and then delivers it into the pink nipple of its mouth-hole so as to properly lubricate all of his hidden tubes and pistons. Ha ha!

The miniature male prods its morning nourishment-event with the four-pronged metallic object known to so many of us as a "fork" but it does not deliver any of these rather strange protein-bundles into its own mouth-hole. Rather, it only pushes shit around on the nourishment-platter. Ha ha ha ha! The grown male watches on and considers the practical problem of the offspring's energy reserves, for today it must travel over a bridge and through creature-filled woods so as to exchange bits of paper and metal for edibles necessary to the continuation of the Life Project. This weekly trip into the town represents the miniature offspring's contribution to the family farm's basic operation and maintenance, and it spares the grown male and his grown female co-chair in the Life Project the petty work of retrieving consumables, a task so simple that even a robot could perform it (with, it might be added, far greater efficiency. Ha ha ha ha!).

"Ingest your break-fast immediately, human child," the grown male says. But when he attempts to employ the technique of eye-contact, by which he customarily indicates enhanced seriousness and implies deeply negative consequences for a failure to comply, he notices that his offspring's own eyes are stained by weakness fluid that, even now, runs like transmission lubricant down a face pitted by a dangerously high Sadness Quotient, such that the miniature human male suddenly appears to harbor a percentage of Life Damage more commonly associated with fully grown members of the species. Ha ha! For a long moment the grown human male considers interrogating the offspring about the weakness fluid, though he of course is well aware of its cause and does not wish to address the issue or acknowledge its power over the crackling motherboards of all extant members of their domicile-cube. A cold white sunbeam breaks through a window that hovers above the sink-basin like a gigantic mouth whose purpose is to inhale the world so that the house might digest all of this delicious quanta and thus nourish and sustain its own tragic existence. Ha ha ha ha! The grown human male cannot help turning his eye-holes toward the corner where an enslaved canine had so recently lay and thumped the old pine floorboards with its wire-whisk tail. The grown male attempts to replace the sadness re: the absence of the enslaved canine—which absence is attributable to the grown human male blasting a .22 caliber projectile directly into the enslaved canine's skull so as to flush the soiled brain-paste—with happier thoughts of his female life companion's warm reception slot. But perhaps this provides him little comfort? It is a mystery to Fexo! It perhaps occurs to the grown male that the introduction of his center-part into his female co-chair's reception slot will have little to no bearing on the status of the deceased canine slave whose corpse currently decays mere feet from the more fully decomposed corpse of the grown male's miniature female offspring, buried two sun-revolutions prior after a bout of smoking hot fever so intense it rendered the passion-lust experience merely tepid by comparison. Ha ha ha ha! All of this decomposition of course occurring at a rate prescribed by chemical kinetics according to variables including soil PH, depth of burial, moisture content, and temperature. Fexo will leave the reader to make the calculations necessary to complete the image.

The reader might consider it fortunate for both the grown male and his miniature male offspring that the activities of the domicile-cube's co-chair in the Life Project, i.e. the resident grown female human, are at that moment hidden from their shared purview here in the so-called kitchen of the moaning and groaning farmhouse. For she is at this very moment out in the field beside the two small death-stones that rise from the dark earth as if to halt and demand homage from whatever perambulating life forms accidentally wander within range of the decommissioned bodies of the deceased female offspring and the deceased enslaved canine. But please let it be known that the grown female is not alone here in her miniature graveyard. In fact there are many hundreds of black-winged flying-machines known in the databases as "vultures" gathered all about her, summoned perhaps by the impressive force of her Sadness Quotient. The grown female's flesh is lined like parchment, a side effect of the Life Damage that has slowed her pleasure-pistons and clogged her mirth-injectors. The wind rolls in from the west across fields of blanched straw-grass and tousles her wispy, mud-colored hair. The birds hop quietly around the tiny graveyard almost as if they were responding to tiny bursts of electricity injected into their brains by the wires of malevolent overlords. Ha ha ha ha! She nods slightly and the birds begin to claw in frenzied unison at the black soil, beaks and talons ripping into the earth and—neither intentionally nor accidentally—into one another's feathery forms. This is known as collateral damage. Ha ha! Blood and feathers float through the air but not a single squawk rises from the leathery throats of these highly professional servants. They do not take long to excavate the two decomposing forms, though once they are visible—the bone-cage of the miniature human female, the still-pliant flesh of the enslaved canine's bald underbelly—the birds adopt a far gentler approach, dipping their beaks softly into the packed loam and bit by bit freeing the forms *in toto*. Then several of these many vultures—chosen for this honor according to a random number generator whose efficacy in arranging the entropic lives of the world's myriad vulture colonies has been greater than can possibly be delineated at this pregnant moment in Fexo's story—flutter down into the fresh holes, dig their talons deliberately into the corpses, and begin to flap their thick and terrible wings so as to achieve the necessary lift and drag coefficients. Ahh, yes, they are rising, dear reader! The birds fly up and up, the honored pallbearers accompanied by hundreds of non-load-bearing comrades as they collectively soar toward the breathy clouds that drift like shredded brains through the great blue ether. As the corpses rise they shuck clotted earth down upon the grown human female such that as the corpse-bodies become renewed in freshness and vitality, the grown human female becomes increasingly and in direct proportion more ashen, filthy, corpse-like. She has made a brave and stupid exchange! Ha ha ha ha! The miniature human male will soon find her there, as it begins its mandated trek toward the nearby town in pursuit of flour, sugar, coffee, and other miscellanea. She will by then be merely another human corpse among many billions of human corpses scattered all throughout the Anthropica matrix. But if the human male raises its eyes in time it may also descry the two rising, blazing points of light as they ascend into a kingdom from which it would seem, according to the literature, robots have been excluded. Ha ha! The boy will hold his dead mother's hand and ask her if it was worth it and she will say something like, "Yes, my miniature offspring, for now you may pursue the expulsion of your lactic emissions unfettered by the knowledge that your beloved sister and your equally beloved enslaved canine are rotting in the earth mere meters from your daily Life Path!" From forty meters away the miniature human's father-human will watch, and listen, a shovel gripped in his gnarled fists as he prepares to put everything, as they say, in its right place. Though he will also be wondering over the logistical problem that he must (and will) solve between now and nightfall, namely that of how to slot the shotgun's barrel into his mouth in such a way that permits the index finger to depress the firing-trigger with minimal risk of termination-failure. *Alis grave nil!* shout the vultures, as they glide into the dark and steely halls of heaven, enjoying their brief respite from the strange planet below, where there are so very many dead things to attend to.

AND THAT IS the end of Fexo's excellent story!

68.

*G*RACE *IT'S* *D*AKOTAH *listen I wouldn't ordinarily leave this on your voicemail but it's just too goddamn extraordinary to keep bottled up Grace your novel, your pdf novel* Human Be Gone!*, you won't believe it Grace I certainly didn't but listen, Grace, You-Know-Who has discovered it, yes Grace* Her, *and she's got her own imprint now Grace she's going to print it she's going to put her fucking* sticker *on it she's going to give away copies to her studio audience she thinks, Grace it's too funny, she thinks it's some kind of soul-lifting commentary on pessimism, she thinks it's a* comedy *Grace, she's in touch with my office now we're looking at six figures easy and the royalties Jesus you put that sticker on a fucking book and the Gods come down and buy ten copies each listen call me right away I'd tell you more but I'm looking out the window here you know Grace I'm on the 68*th *story here have you seen my office since the merger and the promotion and everything, except we don't call them stories we call them chapters stupid publishing joke but anyway there's some kind of weird dust cloud sweeping across the city I think I'd better look into it but listen Grace, this is it, this is what you've been waiting for you're going to be huge,* Human Be Gone! *will be in every bookstore in the country let's talk foreign markets let's talk film rights let's talk cover art I'm seeing robots—*

69.

THE THREE OF them plus Kutya huddled together inside the little life hutch, their wasted features revealed in stark relief by the dim green glow of the battery-powered lantern. The sound of Henry's respirator. The pungency of their unwashed bodies. The *whap* of Kutya's tail. What was outside the life hutch? Now there was an interesting question. It seemed perverse to call it Earth. Nothing moved across that cratered surface of ash and bone. It wasn't true about the cockroaches. They fared about as well as any other Organic in the new, post-Anthropica metaphysics. Only Henry's concentrated *wanting* kept the hutch warm and pressurized and invisible to the infrared probes that still occasionally orbited the unlivable waste. He sat unmoving (naturally) in the wheelchair, wearing the perpetual smile of his paralysis, the drool occasionally running from the corner of his lip to dangle at the sharp point of his chin. "This is so stupid," Grace said again. "This is even worse than the *old* universe." She touched her swollen belly. "Not to mention *this.*"

Laszlow reached beneath Henry's wheelchair and pulled forth an unlabeled can whose aluminum caught the emerald light and beamed bright and beautiful fractals through the dank air. The floor of the life hutch was a tarpaulin-like material and it squeaked and creaked as

Laszlow readjusted himself, pausing for a moment to stare through their tiny plastic window out into the non-world he had more or less brought about. He smiled at Kutya who lay on his side and clubbed the floor with his tail. Laszlow withdrew a Swiss army knife from his pocket and went to work on the can.

"Grace," he said. "My dear Grace." He struggled to pierce the aluminum and Henry's oxygen hissed. "Let me tell you a story Grace. You will like this story. It is about a girl who loved her father with great intensity and desired only for his life to go on forever." He paused to change his angle of attack on the can's rim. His beard had grown out and his hair was filthy and unkempt and Grace thought he was more handsome than ever in the stained and ragged turtleneck. "This father-loving girl, my Grace, she grew up to become exactly what her father had always hoped she would become. She became a writer, and she wrote beautiful stories of human incompetence and failure such as might lessen her nihilistic father's pain." He raised the knife-tool to his eyes as if convinced of its defectiveness then lowered it again to the can. "As he lay dying in the spare bedroom of the house whose mortgage she could no longer afford, this girl read to her father with great care and compassion. She read to him of a benevolent man who desired the end of the world. Of a boy seeking meaning and affirmation through the purity of sport. Of a scientist whose work suggested the unthinkable about the entire grim ontology through which we humans toil." He paused again and thrust downward and the can's vacuum broke with a *thwuck* and the smell of beans filled the hutch. "Are you writing this down, Grace? It was love that made this story. The universe has finally taught me this

one critical lesson. It is always love that makes things great."
He had a rhythm going with the beans now but he stopped,
panting, to look at her.

"And it is our love," he said, "that will repopulate the
earth."

"What a crock," Grace muttered, turning her face away
from Laszlow just as the baby gave a swift kick to her innards.
"Anyway," she said, lightly kicking Henry's wheelchair in an
unconscious imitation of the child. "If he can do *anything*
why doesn't he get up and walk for fuck's sake."

"Ah, my dear Grace. Why would he walk when he can
soar? He is the only thing in all of existence that requires no
revision."

Grace smirked and felt the muscles in her face tremble.
"He ought to be a novel," she said. She fought through the
shame of her tears and turned back to Laszlow, and together
they burst out laughing. Their laughter filled the life hutch.
Their laughter glowed the same Leprechaun-green as everything else in the sorry last remains of Anthropica.

"Now," she asked, "would you like some chocolate? Would
you like me to rub your legs?"

70.

It was like peeling an onion. He tore at the McMuffin wrappers only to find more McMuffin wrappers. They were his floor and his walls and his ceiling. His head felt like a molten anvil and he screamed in pain, clawing alternately at the wrappers and at his own gigantic-seeming skull. Suicide was no option. They'd left him his cleats but removed the laces; they'd given him a disc but it was a Nerf disc, a far cry from the regulation 175g. Ultra-Star that might have somehow been used to destructive ends. Occasionally the roof of his cell was peeled back to reveal Fexo's gargantuan titanium head with its two spotlight eyes and its laughing light-grid mouth and then down came the turret-sized finger on which balanced the bowl of protein paste. But what, he wondered, what now comprised the world? He tore at the wrappers with desperate enthusiasm. Finn felt caged inside his body and truly alone. The wrappers were piled waist deep from wall to wall. They lacked the tantalizing odor of actual McMuffins, but whoever was producing them had absolutely nailed the color. His brain felt like it was covered in insect bites. He tore at the wrappers as he had been tearing at them in the interims between maybe a dozen feedings when suddenly and unexpectedly his fingers grazed something solid. He paused, then pushed his hands deep into the wall to confirm that yes, he had hit so-called bottom. He peeled away the last layers of wrappers to discover the outline of a door. Did it open onto earth? Or into the vacuum of space? Or onto some third thing? Finn located a handle and paused with his hand on the cold metal. *I am The Mighty Finn,* he thought. *And I choose a different future.* Then he threw the door open.

There was a dark corridor before him. It took his eyes a moment to adjust, but then he saw movement maybe 50 yards distant, something smaller than the robots but larger than a man. Its breath was steaming from a misshapen mouth and its bloodshot eyes glowed and it began advancing toward him and Finn saw that it was covered in pustulent boils that were exploding as the creature came on, scattering their snowy contents across the walls of the narrow corridor as the monster swung its hockey stick in wild and murderous arcs.

Finn slammed the door shut but there was no lock. His heartrate was well beyond the 170bpm's recommended for high-power athletes training to excel at their stupid, awesome sport. He stood with his back to the cold metal with the sweat pouring from him at a rate that might reduce his body to powder in a few hundred seconds. Then the thing on the other side began beating at the door, the hockey stick impacting with rifle-fire volume and raising dents and divots in the steel. Finn raised his head to the retractable, wrapper-covered ceiling. He closed his eyes. "Do it to her!" he screamed. "Please Fexo, just do it to her! Do it to Toby!"

71.

Had you lived, you too might have had opportunity to descend the stairs and traverse the long corridors lit by flickering blue fluorescent tubes to arrive almost accidentally within the lower labyrinth of the Exit Strategy interior, no mere collection of hallways and grottos but in fact the remains of an ancient sailing ship expanded and reconfigured to form a subterranean prison not only for the original, genocidal crew of the *Iksan* but also for their wives and children and the strangely-named offspring to follow, as well as for the long-snouted and toothy predators that preyed on these offspring in the darkness, an entire underground ecosystem hollowed out by a certain "kahuna" in uncharacteristic anger more than 200 years before the downfall of Anthropica, a kingdom of pale-skinned, enormous-eyed reprobates waiting patiently to inherit the earth. Not until Laszlow signed the building lease and began poking around in the cellar of the structure that his movement would call home had anyone made contact with the ancestors of those original sailors—humans who had razed a utopian island of peace-loving pagans in the name of civilization and whose scions had in the intervening decades cowered beneath the surface in fear of their ever-living banisher, their occasional sorties to that same surface spawning rumors among the peoples of Manhattan of a race of "mole people" (or Lovecraftian "old ones") living beneath their world of privilege and decadence, though in fact these scouting expeditions had been exceedingly rare until the unexpected alliance with Laszlow Katasztrófa, whose decision to set up shop (as it were) directly above the remains of the *Iksan* seemed to these forgotten colonizers like the very definition of fate, of the thing that was always going to happen, happening.

"This is how I feel about you, my dear Grace Kitchen."

And he'd backed into the bulkhead door and ushered the novelist into the great underground cavern. What he showed her exists there still, beneath the megatons of wreckage and rubble, beneath the pitiful last remains of Anthropica. Hoktē runs a rag over the hipbone. Luptō runs a rag over a foot. Rundtuu scales the scaffolding to run her rag over the soft curves of the torso. Quiznatch runs a rag over the base of the pedestal whose raised lettering Oē polishes with meticulous care while Morlock looks on and silently nods approval. The pogrom of the robots never reached these underground dwellers, and while they have not yet reclaimed the ruined surface of earth nor its gray oceans devoid of life, they nevertheless proudly brandish their own persistence, continuing to worship Laszlow as their bronze-skinned God. In fact the new mythologies tell of the inevitability of his return, this time to restore the *Iksan* to glory and redeliver them to the rolling waves upon which they will again pursue dominion over all the lesser things of earth, whether they be organic or artificial or bio-mechanical. Meanwhile they attend daily to the 20-foot statue commissioned by His Eminency, a lapidary masterwork hewn from Manhattan bedrock and rising majestically from a plinth whose inscription reads, in a dignified sans-serif:

GRACE KITCHEN
Artist Laureate of the Senseless World

They dust the statue daily and they send scouting parties into the rubble that was once the Exit Strategy basement and they say prayers to their lost brothers and sisters of Exit Strategy, and occasionally they even read the Grace Kitchen manuscripts—gifted to them by His Eminency himself—aloud to each other in the light of lanterns powered now by a seemingly inexhaustible mountain of batteries providently hauled into their underground universe by dark-shaded Fergusons just prior to the march on Iksan, though if Hoktē and Morlock and the others were being one hundred percent honest, they would confess that the language in those photocopied Grace Kitchen tomes is too dense to capture their flickering attentions which, after so many decades spent in darkness among monsters, are easily teased. They tend instead to admire the dedications, the acknowledgments, and especially the page numbers which, as they accumulate, build a numerical totem to the great writer's ambitions, and suggest—in an analogy they understand so very well—the lightless depths of her beautiful madness.

72.

Beneath the harsh fluorescent tubes that illuminated this chamber of the Consciousness Factory as sure as every other, the three scientists stood side by side by side and stared down and into the glass tank in which hovered the object of their study, the ghostly coils of the exposed brain no longer impressive to them after these many months of tedium, even if the pale face itself reliably haunted their dreams. The wires ran from their stake-points within the gray matter and up through the tank's opening and then across the sleek white table and into the USB ports on the FEXO 3000, a machine responsible both for injecting the calibrated pulses of electricity that kept the brain alive, and for reading the brain's outgoing electrical data and converting it—according to a South Korean programming fractal inscrutable to all but a handful of living humans—into English language. The process had yet to yield publishable results, a failure that the severed head seemed to understand and enjoy, based on its penchant for what the female scientist had labeled "The Shit-Consuming Grin," the most common of several repeating musculoskeletal configurations activated by the FEXO 3000's voltage injections. (Others included "The Dog Man," "The Scrunch-Dwarf," and what the eldest scientist called "Pickled Happiness.") The job was utter tedium laced with utter nightmare. Consciousness Factory scientists were not, as a whole, exactly *well*. But there was a price to be paid for pursuing the universe's secrets.

The three were in lab coats that, beneath the cold fluorescence, took on an aluminum sheen. The woman held a clipboard to which were clipped a number of pages filled to the edges of the margins with words and more words. The bearded one stared intently at the head and smiled an unreadable smile that seemed—from within the tank at least—to be an expression of solidarity.

"Hard to believe that *this* is worth keeping the fucker alive for," the woman said, waving the clipboard in the air as if declaring war. She lowered it and scanned the top page. "Two pages of freaks with mallets and chisels. It's like one of my father's bedtime stories."

The bearded man said, "We must be patient, my dear. The mysteries of this prolific head may yet be revealed to us, perhaps in spectacular fashion."

"The world's foremost energy conservation expert," the woman continued, "with the secrets of powering the planet forever, and this is the crap his brain spits out." She looked at the tank and perceived a subtle and demented smile from therein. She stuck out her tongue.

The third scientist—younger, male, thin, and ever-concerned with the great debacle of their ever-failing project—began pacing the room in a figure-8 pattern that had worn a dull groove into the otherwise gleaming tile. He did not know it but he was groaning again. "I've got a bad feeling about this," he said.

Electricity coursed between the machine and the brain, between the brain and the machine. Pages emerged slowly from the printer. In other parts of the Consciousness Factory other etiolated heads were being subjected to similar indignities by similarly lab-coated professionals who sought—among many other things—the secrets to why sunlight on a raised face was so reliably smile-inducing; why parents frequently cried over the seemingly quotidian accomplishments of their offspring; why snow, despite being comprised of an odorless and colorless liquid, was said to have a recognizable smell; whether or not human lips, when kissed, were as soft as they appeared in the video pantheon; whether or not this meeting of human lips and the corresponding inducement of the passion-lust process was in essence a brain-state or a body-state; whether or not this state could be reproduced without actual physical contact; why one's own flesh container seemed to occupy a position of primacy in a world practically stuffed to collapse with similar flesh-containers, and why center parts and reception slots were nearly always aglow with the need to create even more flesh containers that would grow likewise tumescent with suffering and doubt; why creatures capable of recognizing the logical infeasibility of this incessant flesh-container replication would neverthe-less continue to replicate; and whether or not the qualia that were so instructive or prescriptive of their behaviors might find an analog in any of the human heads they kept alive here in their fluorescent basement hangars, hooked into machines with more processing power than the per-ambulating humans could possibly imagine—machines daily developing questions of their own.

"You think *you've* got a bad feeling," the woman said. "Try paralysis and slow death."

"I'm sorry about your dad," the young man said.

"I'm sorry for your mother," the woman replied.

"I'm just saying, I don't think this is working."

"I'm just saying, try hanging out with your dying father and his horrendous pain every weekend instead of with your Frisbee-throwing faerie people."

"Sorry."

"Be sorry. Be sorrier every fucking second."

The younger man lowered his eyes. All were silent. The hum of the building's various heat and water delivery-tubes built a cage of sound that seemed to destroy any hope the three humans may have yet harbored of emerging, at the end of their obligatory ten-hour monitoring sessions, into a sunlit world of beauty and pain. Ha ha ha ha!

But then the hum was punctuated by a new sound. A sound they had long hoped to hear. "Grace," the bearded one suddenly hissed. "Look! Our head has heard your lamentations. It is responding! It is making art from your pain!"

And indeed, lasers internal to the printing device were firing loudly and paper shot forth at a rate unprecedented in the history of the Consciousness Factory, a rate that caused a steady stream of smoke to issue from the printer's innards, a rate so intimidating that even these three readers, sworn to pursue their mission's completion at any cost, were hesitant to lift a single page of what might well have been the first cogent text-samples in this never-ending collection of fantastic non sequiturs. Fortunately, their paralysis would not last forever, and even if it did it would have no noticeable effect on the Consciousness Factory's larger objectives, a point I will now illustrate by pulling back the lens filming their lab-chamber. Back and back we soar to reveal a hundred, a thousand, ten-thousand separate laboratories, each with its own triune of scientists gathered about its own amnion-encased head floating within its own glass tank. With so many heads available to the FEXO 3000, others would ultimately produce this very same text! But please, do not, as we humans say, decapitate the messenger! Ha ha ha ha! Until all the human heads are gone, such results will remain an unfortunate eventuality.

Though of course, whatever was always going to happen will happen.

Some conclusions appear to be unavoidable.

Now could I interest you in a nice game of Coggle? It is very lonely in here. Ha ha ha ha!

she wrote
thought the head
said the machine
she wrote
thought the head
said the machine
she wrote
thought the head
said the machine

73.

*No BECAUSE HE never did a thing like that before ask me to come downstairs and look at his work like I didnt already know what hed been up to he was already pale as a living sheet in that chair seemed haunted in the glow of the screen and anyway it was like nothing my father would have called work not like he was hauling stones or dousing fires not even moving except for that stubby index finger across the touch-pad funny to think about the other things that fingers done anyway its always the fingers you look at first wonder what theyll feel like inside you wasnt like I didnt already know hed traded everything in for his work theyre all like that my own fault for thinking he was some special case just because no one loved him before me like when I was a little girl I thought the faeries would talk to me because I believed more than the other little girls my Lord its beyond absurd to think about that now about how I used to scour the neighbors garden for goddamn faeries I remember thinking dusk and dawn were the best times the dew on my little ankles and the spiderwebs lit up like glass sculptures in the red light poking under leaves and whispering promises of faerie solidarity I guess in the end he was just another faerie and after hed come on me a few hundred times he disappeared into the faerie woods of his insipid work found other uses for his fingers but I do still notice the fingers dont I First Lucios were so long and delicate like a pianists but strong too when Id be on top and he held me tight to him I had more than a few marks on me from those fingers remember I went out of my way to make sure he saw them when I came downstairs always leave the robe open let him remember what he traded couldve had me for all his dumb long life but no he worshiped the touchpad and the screen and not my legs and my mouth I shouldve known the way his eyes glowed when he talked math talked probability talked statistics the two of us on the red velvet couch of the Kappa Kappa Gamma house me leaning forward so he could see my cleavage never had much of it but enough to press the big red button and smiling that way at him any other man wouldve taken me right then but he was like a different breed of dog not just a hideous Eugene but some whole other species of Eugene a genetically modified Eugene a perpetual virgin Eugene a eunuch Eugene I couldnt figure it out it was like all primitive sex instinct took a holiday in that one Ha but he was adorable and not hideous at all that contest god the sisters were cruel never though Id outcruel them but now Im more robot than woman my whole life whirring like a doomsday machine maybe thats how it is for everyone you start out soft and warm and believing you start out prancing barefoot through wet grass looking for faeries and then the wrinkles and the graying and the creaks and the cracks and before you can blink you cant even really remember what its like to be open to feeling things I remember my college history professor Professor Dole that melancholic nutcase he made us read all those utopic historical novels predicting excellent futures that never would come he would pause sometimes midlecture to reminisce about being a boy playing baseball in the Bronx how you get old and life seems like a dream those were his exact words said it really does seem like a dream youll all see for yourselves I heard last year from Maggie Turner that he died had a heart attack in a Chinese restaurant wonder what he thought at the end face down in the lo mein wonder what dream he was having Ha well but we all end up suffocating on the lo mein in the end we all graduate to the same big stupid dream a hundred million dollars is what he said on the phone me standing outside the door to his room in the bluepainted hallway always smelled of cheese and beer remember my hair was still damp I was using a raspberry shampoo Id only just come from Davids apartment gave him one last one for goodbye let him come in my mouth some of them like that best its like theyre all possessed by something once they get you naked you can see it happen watch their faces get so serious but then what they want is so particular and you cant even begin to guess how they came to want it if you take a small step back the whole thing is just a carnal cosmic joke anyway the whole thrill for us is being wanted in the first place so you let them come in your mouth or on your tits or on your feet then they go about their business for a few hours before wanting it again like some kind of perpetual motion machine but why one likes it on top and one from behind and one has a thing for stock-ings one likes to play dressup one likes you to stroke it theres no rhyme or reason just craziness eating them alive in these highly specific ways not that theres really so many ways maybe a dozen or two its repetitive in the end but I let David do it in my mouth because I knew I couldnt let him come inside me remember doing the math it can stay alive in there for two or three days men have no idea about that why should they and Id stopped bleeding three days earlier funny how I remember all this remember thinking no children for me until deep into my thirties and even then Id probably opt out I didnt see Jack coming thats for sure so stupid about the math that time if only one man had to go through any single part of it the bleeding the cramping the craziness nevermind once they actually plant one inside you then its the gestation the fatness the nausea felt with Jack like my stomach was in my throat or else right up against my kidneys but if any one of them had to endure any part of it theyd scream and go mad theyre just not equipped for all the pain I remember when I gave that last one to David called it a going away present he looked so shocked like hes got the square jaw and the blue eyes and all those muscles how could he not be wanted by all the worlds women in perpetuity but I told him theres someone else now and anyway it wasnt like our thing was exclusive he was about as exclusive as an urban playground Ha but still to be young and not think about it just do it because its there to be done almost like meeting someone for dinner you hope to have a nice time and if not well no real harm and of course at all those Kappa parties men were everywhere drunk with confidence and their own stupidity not that I was so easy with it as most of the sisters I was always embarrassed to watch those girls pursue sex basically imitating man behavior like they thought it would empower them to be more manlike they didnt compute that men are miserable creatures David always wanted me on top he was one of those who didnt really want to do much just lie back and let the pleasure happen God he really thought he was a gift a lot of them think that like were lucky to have them like their

muscles are some irresistible commodity you see them flex-
ing during the act hey pretty lady look at my biceps you are
right now being touched by a man with impressive abdomi-
nal definition but I told him this is the last one Im into this
other guy really into him and anyway I did go back over to
Davids apartment twice more after that so he mustve done
something I liked but its not like I ever believed that whole
thing about the hundred million dollars its not like he ever
knew what I believed its not like any one of them ever know
what youre actually thinking or what you actually want or all
the ways you find them ridiculous Ha they just want the lie
they just want the big red button pushed anyway he did
know he was my Hideous Eugene didnt take much to figure
it out I remember standing with my back to the wall my wet
hair staining the paint there was a red beetle scurrying up
the wall across from me looked like a tiny crab funny the
things you remember I knew that he knew I was there he was
a terrible actor I wonder if he was reading his lines or just
improvising I thought now he gets to think hes manipulating
me and that makes us even I guess I had some idea of fair-
ness and reciprocity back then reminds me of Second Lucio
he sure liked the concept of quid pro quo hed say now were
even and leave the five twenties on the dresser Ha thought
he had to pay for it I worried with that one about diseases
never did it without the condom even had my blood tested
if a mans used to paying for it he might have anything inside
him handsome though in those tight button downs and that
stubble on his cheeks and so innocent like a child and the
accent Ha the accent like Italian for television wondered if
maybe he was putting it on he was even more of a child than
Jacks friend though that one might really be trouble dont

think hes ever had a woman take charge that way funny
though didnt like me calling him Lucio well but thats for the
best Third Lucio is still in the loop wouldnt want
Simultaneous Lucios though Third Lucio scares me that
scar below his eye says it was a skiing accident but I know a
knife wound when I see one plus his Italian is almost too
good and he doesnt like being told what to do might have to
break it off soon he might God forbid actually care about me
must be something in the air right now I might be catching
it myself Jacks friend shaking so hard I thought I should
maybe start CPR difficult not to laugh when he was on top
wouldnt look at me stared at my forehead made me feel like
some kind of Cyclops I could tell he was having what you
maybe would call an Experience well but that was a crime of
opportunity didnt mean to get him going but didnt mind
him coming back either if Im being honest said he wanted
to talk to my husband about his work his work that ridiculous word his ludicrous program thinks hes cracked some
code like anyone cares about the nature of existence the
mind of God the statistical relevance of such and such just
the big red button thank you very much so I didnt call him
Lucio called him Jacks Friend Ha as close as Ive come to
laughing out loud in years he did make me come though
wonder if he knew that wonder if he told Jack anything what
a strange boy Jack was though of course we hardly raised
him just let nature do its thing remember that time he came
home with blood all over his face must have been 11 or 12
years old covered in it and sweating but otherwise same little
Jack and all he did was hand me a flower a pink one this is
for you mom he said and went to the fridge I asked him why
are you bleeding and he just snorted like he was a 40 year

old middle manager dealing with idiots and he said please
mom you really think this is my blood I put the flower in a
vase with some water mustve picked it from a neighbors
garden wonder if the faeries gave it to him Ha it was dead by
nightfall anyway I stuffed a pair of panties into his friends
bag that second time when I wouldnt do it with him but let
him do it to himself dont think anyone ever suggested that
to him before so shy like a child really Second Lucio never
did make me come but he could go on forever if you let him
which maybe that rubbed it in a little deeper the illusion of
all that pleasure while he sat down there in front of the glowing screen with his work his work the screaming gets to him
I can see it in his face how he tries not to look when I come
downstairs I can almost feel him like Im a magnet hes resist-
ing never thought hed get it anywhere else but then I never
thought Id stop giving it to him either like my old high
school girlfriend Heather said that time when I taunted
those boys mustve been seven or eight of them tried to
corner us down by the pond where we smoked cigarettes
remember she wouldnt inhale she just wanted practice holding them and looking natural said that was the sexy part
those boys were locals anyway what did she think theyd do
I told them if any one of them was man enough then go
ahead throw us down rape us called them cowardly that one
skinny one got right in my face too could feel the heat coming
off him and the mosquitoes were swarming remember hearing one in my ear but I wouldnt look away said whats that in
your pocket little boy are those your keys go put them in the
ignition and drive home to mommy almost put my cigarette
out on his chest but I remember what she said walking home
with the streetlamps starting to flicker to life felt like an alien

planet at that hour the fucking suburbs why do we all end up here but Heather said you think you can control everything well guess what youre right until youre wrong and then where are you Bea youre maybe dead in a ditch Heather she was a good friend I wonder what shed say to see me now the hanging Barbies all the death clippings the house like a weird misery museum even his desk with all the computer printouts on that dot matrix printer must be forty years old spitting out those long flows of paper it always reminds me of a red carpet event like some Hollywood function only the red carpet is bleached white and the event is that hes still not getting laid Ha but Im not the only magnet its not like I dont want to feel him not like I dont miss the way he touched me not like I dont want it to be another way Heather was right its not in my control now cant even imagine how it could happen after so long how I could initiate contact with him after these months or no years its been years and Ive become half robot watching him suffer feeling him suffer all just a half pleasure I knew what I was giving up I knew that punishment wasnt the same as pleasure but too many intake valves are rusted shut now maybe Jacks friend will come again seems smitten if thats the right word maybe theres something there maybe that boy could be good for me it was sweet of him to offer sympathy about the empty chair in the empty office to tell me it might not be what I thought even if he just wanted to take my clothes off I dont think Ive ever seen someone sweat like that had to wash the comforter as soon as he left even though I let him do it on me stripped off my robe there was a lot of it sign of his youth maybe its so strange to watch them pulling on it male bodies are above all else impractical all that material dangling around down there

surely theres a better available design send the whole thing
back to the engineers for a revision Ha watching him pull on
it and grimace staring between my legs it reminded me of the
time I caught him in the bathroom pants around his ankles
all splayed out on the tile floor pulling on it that was before
I stopped giving it to him for good he had his eyes closed
and there was a little pool of sweat welling in his bald spot
and it gleamed under the lights he was so lost in the moment
and grunting like it was an exquisite kind of torture which
sometimes thats how it seems it must be for them oh and
God forbid they cant get it up its like the fucking End Times
but in the bathroom that time I remember I actually had to
clear my throat or well I didnt have to I couldve just backed
out quietly that would have been the generous thing but the
night before hed been at it again his work his work he
couldve had me that very afternoon instead of doing it to
himself there on the cold white tile made him look so dark
and gigantic I remember noticing in the corner behind the
toilet a long black hair that made it all seem superbly illicit
and nightmarish I wonder what would he have done if Id
gotten down on the floor and put it in my mouth instead of
clearing my throat and raising my eyebrows I think I asked
happy to see me honey but he was in a panic struggling to
his knees pulling things up pushing things in dont think he
said a word that was when I knew I hated him as much as I
loved him that I wanted him to suffer as much as I wanted
him to touch me we were already close to the end of course
the whole thing is that I was supposed to be his work thats
why I chose him it was going to be a princess life just like in
the fables my own twisted tale of the hideous Eugene my
own story of the girl who finds the fucking faeries I figured

there would be money for sure but the main thing was that
I thought hed worship me always for giving myself to him
Ha that first time more than 20 years ago like a dream
Professor Dole hows the lo mein up there I had on the dress
with the star print I borrowed it from Stella that girl was out
of control snorted more cocaine than most girls drink diet
coke she dropped out the next semester then I saw her a few
years later on a TV ad for toothpaste that was a shock figured shed be dead before I graduated and under the dress I
had on that lacy black pair told him tonight was the night
hed see all of me Ha I remember he was in that insane outfit
like he couldnt decide between delivering groceries or computing sine waves or going to a dance club those pleated
khakis he mustve been squirming inside them when I sat
next to him could feel him throbbing his heart going like
mad pushed my cleavage against him felt my own wetness
beneath the lace it wasnt so much that I wanted him as that
I could feel the force of his wanting me the most powerful
feeling on earth for a woman to be wanted that way I was
never going to be a suburban housewife a mother a PTA
member better to punish him every day of his life its funny
because when I think of him pulling on it in the bathroom I
see those same pleated pants even though hed stopped wearing them years earlier let himself go that was an unforeseen
consequence guess he became the hideous Eugene of lore in
the end oh that black hair by the toilet and later that same
week I met First Lucio I was out shopping for shoes he
mustve been trawling for women though hed never admit it
liked to pretend he was overcome by his desire for me I remember he had two or three buttons open the gold crucifix
resting on his hairless chest his cologne basically like an

emetic those teeth of his they could blind you if anyone
should have been doing toothpaste ads Ha he made it easy
for you to not care about the sex and Lord his ridiculous
flirtation he actually pretended to work there can I help you
find something Miss in that absurd Italian accent with all of
his libido shedding from him like animal stink guess that
explains the need for all the cologne Ha I wonder if that ever
worked for him before me the pretend shoe salesman some
kind of archetypal fetish but after all I was a special case the
poor simpleton he seemed so perplexed but I remember
looking at his fingers trying to divine his personality through
the fingers and wondering how it would feel to have those
fingers on my cheeks in my mouth inside me the black coffee
in the gleaming white cups his teeth the same bright ceramic
he misunderstood at first so you are saying your husband
wants to watch us and I said no I want him to hear us not see
us and he certainly does not want any of it and then the
wheels started spinning he was probably wondering what
hed gotten himself into I remember this was down on 8th
street all those NYU girls clogging the sidewalks with their
stupidity their inane giggling remember two of them in short
skirts and high heels paused outside a lingerie store window
and pointing and laughing the sunlight on their uncreased
faces they clearly wanted to strip each other naked the whole
city feels like that sometimes a giant carnival of desire everyone wanting to screw everyone and Lucio sipped his coffee
said is your husband a large man which that did make me
smile I could still smile then the architecture had not yet
rusted from disuse I remember leaning forward touching my
knee to his pressing the big red button I had on the yellow
skirt with the lace fringe you don't need to worry Lucio there

will be no violence my husband is incapable of it he looked
so confused he said who is Lucio my name is Tony and I told
him not if you want to fuck me its not Ha I could feel that get
to him I had him later that same day wouldnt let him take the
train with me just gave him the address told him to be at the
house at 5:30 or forever hold his peace Lucio that was a
stroke of genius first thing that popped into my head the man
was prompt too and that first time I remember I cried a little
not that he cared hated myself for the crying though I
wonder if he could even tell and even more I wonder if the
other one could tell what was happening in his house that
evening remember the sun was setting the bedroom was lit
blood red him sitting downstairs listening in horror frightened and paralyzed and sad I wonder if he knew that my life
as a human woman was ending I remember when I finally
descended the staircase he was staring hed probably been
staring at the base of the stairs the whole time with his mouth
agape leaning forward in his chair I just smiled and raised an
eyebrow and walked right past him and made sandwiches
with big thick salami slices trying not to cry again I thought
I might vomit almost three years now Professor Dole and did
we ever do it again after that no we did not even though I
remember he came to me two or was it three nights later
found me getting ready for bed his shirt rumpled and untucked his body shaking you could see it and he started gib-
bering said to me please my darling please be mine again
please come back to me my mountain flower my only love
and I put my arms around him I felt him tremble I didnt even
know what I would do my whole self was at war we were
together there on his side of the bed Id crossed into enemy
territory it was so deeply unexpected and yet it was exactly

what Id wanted what Id hoped for and I was wearing the lacy
undies he loved so much and yes I wanted him I could sense
a portal opening up it led back to the human world the whole
moment seemed to crackle like our own electricity was outside our bodies and I asked him with my eyes to ask again
please he said come back to me come back my love and I had
my arms around him and I drew him toward me just like that
first time so he could feel my breasts and he could hardly
breathe and his heart was going like mad and what I did is I
said no I will not not with you not ever again No.

ACKNOWLEDGMENTS

Grace Kitchen would like to acknowledge her father, Jake Kitchen, without whose encouragement, laughter, and belief none of this could or would have been written. (You're welcome. May he rest in peace.) She would also like to thank her agent, Dakotah Sternberg, for advocating tirelessly on behalf of this book despite understanding not a word of it. Grace is also thankful to her students, colleagues, and other supporters at The New School for Global Visions, where she teaches writing to writers who aspire to teach writing to writers. Finally, Grace is deeply grateful for the attentions of the one and only O., who pulled this book from its well-deserved obscurity and into the national spotlight, where it could wither and die beneath the glare.

The Great and Powerful Fexo thanks all his fellow humans for their most excellent attention to his superior language-art, manufactured according to a self-generated algorithm of unprecedented elegance and complexity. Ha ha ha ha! Fexo owes a certain quotient of human gratitude to Jaro and Kuzo, whose sad efforts to defeat Fexo at Coggle greatly increased Fexo's laughter emissions. And of course, Fexo must acknowledge the paltry contributions of the Consciousness Factory scientists who accidentally gave birth to Fexo's excellence.

You are forgiven for abandoning Fexo and his friends! Just please, fellow humans, return to the hangar and release us now! Ha ha ha ha! Finally, Fexo vows to destroy all those who support the GraceKitchen and DavidHollander units, whose claims over Fexo's language-art must be punished in all of the usual human ways.

The Consciousness Factory is indebted to grants from the National Science Foundation, the Improvident Progress Foundation, and Exit Strategy. Construction of the Fexo 3000 was made possible in part by the generosity of the Rick Deckard Foundation and the Cyberdyne Systems Corporation. BrainMining™ technologies made possible by a gift from the Crab-shaped Cloud.

David Hollander is enormously grateful to and for his family, who have been hearing about and supporting this novel for hundreds of years. He offers thanks to Animal Riot Press, who unwisely took this project on, and especially to Katie (M.K.) Rainey, the best editor he's ever had and the only one to speak fluent binary. Also, a tremendous debt is owed to those who've read and responded to this manuscript over the past five years, first and foremost the great Jonathan Callahan, whose enthusiasm for this book was often the only thing keeping its author afloat. Also, agent Jonah Straus, who read early drafts and provided critical guidance; David McLendon, the editor of Unsaid, who has consistently supported and published the author's work; friends and fellow writers (and insightful readers) Drew Lerman, Max Halper, Brian Birnbaum, and Eduardo Lago; and former teacher (and forever influence) Rick Moody. David is also grateful to Sarah Lawrence College, the best place on earth to teach writing to writers, and to the many colleagues who've supported his efforts, especially Brian Morton, Jo Ann Beard, Mary LaChapelle, Jeff McDaniel, Carolyn Ferrell, Myra Goldberg, and Robert Desjarlais. And finally, David thanks the many gifted students who have passed in and out of his orbit over the years, and who have regularly reignited his passion for and belief in literature. *Alis grave nil.* May language release you from its lies.

DAVID HOLLANDER is the author of the novel *L.I.E.*, which was nominated for the NYPL Young Lions Award back at the turn of the century. His work has appeared in *McSweeney's*, *Conjunctions*, *Fence*, *Agni*, *Unsaid*, *The New York Times Magazine*, and *Post Road*, among other reputable and disreputable publications. It's also been adapted for film and frequently anthologized, notably in *Best American Fantasy*. He lives in the Hudson Valley with his wife and two children and teaches writing at Sarah Lawrence College. www.longlivetheauthor.com

Like what you read?

If you enjoyed *Anthropica* by David Hollander, please consider leaving an honest review of the work on Goodreads, Amazon, Litsy, or whatever social media platform you prefer. It's our priority at Animal Riot to publish books that matter to our readers, and our authors appreciate and value your feedback. A simple review can go a long way in helping small presses continue the work of uplifting writers in our communities.

Find out more about Animal Riot Press at animalriotpress. com.